A LESSON IN PASSION

Jared put down his brandy glass and got to his feet. "As you have pointed out to me, Miss Wingfield, one does not have to travel widely in order to gain experience of the world."

"True enough." She watched him as he walked deliberately toward her. "Is there something the matter, Mr. Chillhurst?"

"Yes." He walked around the desk, reached down, and lifted Olympia straight out of her chair. "There is something I wish to learn tonight, Miss Wingfield, and only you know the answer."

"*Mr. Chillhurst.*" Olympia could hardly breathe. Excitement flashed through her. "What is your question, sir?"

"Will you kiss me, Miss Wingfield?"

Olympia was so shaken she could not find the words to respond. She did the only thing she could. She put her arms around Jared's neck and lifted her mouth to his in silent invitation.

"*Siren.*" Jared's arms closed very tightly around her as he crushed her lips beneath his own. . . .

Deception

Amanda Quick

BANTAM BOOKS

2009 Bantam Books Mass Market Edition

Copyright © 1993 by Jayne A. Krentz

Published in the United States by Bantam Books, an imprint of The Random House Publishing Group, a division of Random House, Inc., New York.

BANTAM BOOKS and the rooster colophon are registered trademarks of Random House, Inc.

Originally published in hardcover in the United States by Bantam Books, an imprint of The Random House Publishing Group, a division of Random House, Inc., in 1993.

ISBN 978-0-553-59282-5

Cover art: copyright © 1994 by Eric Peterson

Printed in the United States of America

www.bantamdell.com

2 4 6 8 9 7 5 3 1

Deception

Prologue

"Tell her to beware the Guardian." Artemis Wingfield leaned across the tavern table. His faded blue eyes were intent beneath his bushy gray brows. "Have you got that, Chillhurst? She is to *beware the Guardian.*"

Jared Ryder, Viscount Chillhurst, braced his elbows on the table, placed his fingertips together, and regarded his companion with his one-eyed gaze. Wingfield had grown comfortable with him during the past two days, he thought, so comfortable that he no longer stared at the black velvet patch that covered Jared's sightless eye.

It was obvious that Wingfield had accepted Jared for what he purported to be—another adventurous Englishman like himself bent on travel now that the war with Napoleon had finally ended.

The two men had wound up spending the past two nights at the same inn in this grimy little French port awaiting the ships that would take them to their respective destinations.

Perspiration dripped down Wingfield's brow and into his whiskers. It was a warm evening in late spring and the smoke-filled tavern was crowded. Jared privately considered that Wingfield was suffering unnecessarily from the heat. The older man's chin-high collar, elegantly knotted cravat, snug-fitting waistcoat, and well-tailored jacket were definitely contributing to his obvious discomfort.

The fashionable attire was not well suited to the balmy night or to the environs of a port tavern. Wingfield, however, was the sort of Englishman who valued appearances far above personal comfort. Jared suspected that his new acquaintance dressed for dinner every night during his travels even if the meal happened to be served in a tent.

"I comprehend your words, sir." Jared tapped his fingertips together. "But I don't take your meaning. Who, or what, is this Guardian?"

Wingfield's whiskers twitched. "Lot of nonsense, to be perfectly frank. Just part of an old legend surrounding a diary that I'm shipping back to my niece in England. The old count who sold the volume to me told me about the warning."

"I see," Jared said politely. "*Beware the Guardian,* eh? Interesting."

"As I said, merely the remnants of an old legend connected to the diary. Nevertheless, a rather odd incident occurred last night and one cannot be too careful."

"Odd incident?"

Wingfield narrowed his eyes. "I believe my room here at the inn was searched while I was dining."

Jared frowned. "You said nothing about it at breakfast this morning."

"Wasn't certain. Nothing taken, you see. But all day long I've had the most peculiar sensation that I'm being watched."

"Unpleasant."

"Indeed. And no doubt entirely unrelated to the diary. Still I've become a bit concerned. Wouldn't want to put her in any danger."

Jared unsteepled his hands and took a swallow of his weak ale. "What is this diary you say you are sending to your niece?"

"It's a lady's journal actually," Wingfield explained. "Belonged to a woman named Claire Lightbourne. That's all I know about it. The entries are completely unintelligible for the most part."

"Why is that?"

"It appears to be written in a hodgepodge of Greek and Latin and English. Rather like a private code. My niece believes that the Lightbourne diary holds clues to a fabulous treasure." Wingfield snorted.

"You do not believe the tale?"

"Not bloody likely, if you ask me. But Olympia will have fun attempting to decipher the diary. She enjoys that sort of thing."

"She sounds like a rather unusual female."

Wingfield chuckled. "She is that. Not her fault, I suppose. She was raised by a rather eccentric aunt and the aunt's companion. I was never well acquainted with that side of the family but word had it that both the aunt and her friend undertook to educate Olympia themselves. Filled her head with a lot of strange notions."

"What sort of notions?"

"Olympia don't give a fig for propriety, thanks to her schooling. Don't mistake me, she's a fine young woman. Her reputation is spotless. But she ain't interested in the sort of things young females are supposed to be interested in, if you see what I mean."

"Such as?"

"Fashion, for one thing. Got no interest in clothes. And that aunt of hers never taught her the useful things a lady needs to know such as how to dance or flirt or make herself agreeable to a potential suitor." Wingfield shook his head. "Very odd upbringing, if you ask me. The chief reason she's never found herself a husband, I suspect."

"What does interest your niece?" Jared was growing genuinely curious in spite of himself.

"Anything that has to do with the customs and legends of foreign lands fascinates the chit. Very active in the Society for Travel and Exploration, you know, even though she's never been out of Dorset in her life."

Jared looked at him. "If she does not travel, herself, how is she able to be active in the society?"

"She tracks down old books and journals and letters that deal with travel and exploration. She studies what she finds and writes up her conclusions. Published several papers in the quarterly journal of the society during the last three years."

"She did?" Jared was becoming more intrigued by the moment.

"Yes, indeed." A fleeting expression of pride flickered in Wingfield's gaze. "Very popular pieces because they incorporate all sorts of instructive information on the customs and habits of foreigners."

"How did she discover the Lightbourne diary?" Jared asked carefully.

Wingfield shrugged. "Through a series of letters that

she turned up in her research. Took her nearly a year, but she finally located the diary in a small town here on the French coast. It was originally part of a much larger library that was destroyed during the war."

"You came here specifically to purchase the diary for your niece?"

"It was on my way," Wingfield said. "I'm en route to Italy. The diary apparently passed through a number of hands during the past few years. The old man who sold it to me was hard-pressed. He needed money and was more than happy to sell off some of his books. I picked up a number of other volumes for Olympia in the bargain."

"Where is the diary at the moment?"

"Oh, it's safe enough." Wingfield looked smug. "I packed it yesterday and saw it safely stowed in the hold of the *Sea Flame* along with the rest of the goods I'm sending to Olympia."

"You're not concerned about the goods while they're on board the ship?"

"Good lord, no. The *Sea Flame* is one of the Flame-crest ships. Excellent reputation. Reliable crews and experienced, trustworthy captains. Fully insured. No, no, my goods are in safe hands while they're at sea."

"But you're not so certain of the safety of English roads, is that it?"

Wingfield grimaced. "I feel much better about that part of the matter now that I know you'll be accompanying the goods to Upper Tudway in Dorset."

"I appreciate your confidence."

"Yes, sir, my niece is going to be as happy as a lark when she sees that diary."

Jared privately concluded that Olympia Wingfield was, indeed, a very odd creature. Not that he didn't know a thing or two about odd creatures, he reminded himself. He had, after all, been raised in a family of outrageous, flamboyant eccentrics.

Wingfield leaned back in the booth and surveyed the tavern. His gaze fell on a scarred, heavily built man who was sitting at the next table. The man wore a knife and a brutish expression that did not bode well for anyone who might want to share the table with him. He was typical of many of the tavern's patrons.

"Rough looking lot, ain't they?" Wingfield asked uneasily.

"Half of the men you see in here tonight are little better than pirates," Jared said. "Soldiers who had nowhere else to go when Napoleon was finally defeated. Sailors waiting for a ship. Men looking for a willing wench or a fight. The usual riffraff that hangs about in port towns."

"And the other half?"

Jared smiled briefly. "They probably are pirates."

"Not surprised. You said you've done a great deal of traveling, sir. You must have been in a number of places like this in your time. Expect you've learned to handle yourself."

"As you can see, I've managed to survive thus far."

Wingfield glanced meaningfully at the black velvet patch that covered Jared's ruined eye. "Not completely unscathed, I notice."

"No, not completely unscathed." Jared's mouth curved humorlessly.

He was well aware that people generally did not find his appearance reassuring. It was not merely the eye patch that made them wary. Even under the best of circumstances, when his hair had been properly trimmed and he was dressed in more fashionable clothes, members of his own family had frequently remarked that he looked like a pirate.

Their chief regret was that he did not act like a pirate.

When all was said and done, Jared knew, he was a man of business, not the flamboyant, exciting, hot-blooded son his father had hoped would carry on the family traditions.

Wingfield had been cautious of him at first. Jared knew it was his quiet manner and his educated speech, not his looks, that had convinced the older man to accept him as a fellow gentleman.

"How did you happen to lose the eye, if you don't mind my asking?"

"It's a long story," Jared said. "And a somewhat painful one. I'd rather not go into it at the moment."

"Of course, of course." Wingfield flushed a dull red. "Sorry for the impertinence."

"Do not concern yourself. I'm accustomed to having people stare."

"Yes, well, I must say I'll feel less concerned once the *Sea Flame* sails in the morning. Knowing that you're going to be on board and will be escorting my goods on to Upper Tudway is a great comfort. I thank you again for undertaking the task."

"As I'm on my way back to Dorset myself, I'm happy to be of assistance."

"I don't mind telling you, it'll save me a bit of blunt," Wingfield confided. "Won't have to hire the usual firm in Weymouth to handle the goods and see that they're sent on to Olympia. Just as well I won't have to pay for the service this time. Very expensive."

"Importing goods is never cheap."

"No, and unfortunately Olympia hasn't been able to get as much money as I had hoped for on the last two shipments. Thought we'd both come out a bit further ahead by now than we have."

"The market for imported items can be unpredictable," Jared said. "Is your niece an astute woman when it comes to matters of business?"

"Lord, no." Wingfield chuckled fondly. "Olympia has no head for business. Smart as a whip but she's got no interest at all in financial matters. Takes after my side of the family, I'm afraid. Longs to travel as I do, but of course that's impossible."

"A woman alone would have great difficulty traveling in most parts of the world," Jared conceded.

"That fact wouldn't have stopped my niece. I told you, she ain't your typical English miss. She's five-and-twenty now and she's got a mind of her own. No telling what she might have done if she'd had a decent income and if she hadn't gotten saddled with those three hellion nephews of hers."

"She's raising her nephews?"

Wingfield's whiskers twitched. "Calls 'em her nephews and they call her Aunt Olympia, but the truth is, the relationship is a bit more distant. The boys are the sons of a cousin and his wife who were killed in a carriage accident a couple of years ago."

"How did the children end up in the care of your niece?"

"You know how such things go, sir. After the death of their parents, the boys got passed around from one relative to another and finally landed on Olympia's doorstep six months ago. She took 'em in."

"Quite a handful for a young woman on her own."

"Especially one who's always got her mind on her investigations of other lands and old legends." Wingfield scowled thoughtfully. "Those boys are growing up wild. They've chewed three tutors that I know of into little pieces. Fine youngsters, but full of mischief. Whole household always seems to be in an uproar."

"I see." Jared had been raised in a household that

was forever in an uproar. He had not cared for the experience. He preferred a calm, orderly existence.

"I try to help Olympia out, of course. Do what I can when I'm in England."

But you do not stay in England long enough to take those three young boys in hand, do you? Jared thought. "What else are you shipping to your niece in addition to the Lightbourne diary?"

Wingfield swallowed the last of his ale. "Cloth, spices, and a few trinkets. And books, of course."

"And she'll see to it that they're sold in London?"

"All except the books. They're for her library. But the rest goes to London. She uses some of the money to run her own household and saves the remainder to help finance my travels. The system has worked rather well for both of us, although, as I said, I thought we'd do a bit better out of it than we have."

"It's difficult to do well in one's business affairs if one does not pay close attention to one's accounts," Jared observed dryly.

He thought about the problems he had been noting in his own business accounts during the past six months. He was going to have to press harder on his inquiries in that direction. There was no longer any doubt but that several thousand pounds had been embezzled from the extensive Flamecrest financial empire. Jared did not care for the notion that he had been deceived. He did not relish playing the fool.

One thing at a time, he reminded himself. At the moment he must deal with the matter of the diary.

"Quite right about the need to pay attention to one's accounts, sir, but the fact is, neither Olympia nor myself can be bothered with those sorts of dull details. Still, we get by." Wingfield peered closely at Jared. "I say, you're certain you don't mind undertaking this favor for me?"

"Not at all." Jared looked out through the window at the night-shrouded harbor. He could see the dark bulk of the *Sea Flame* where it rested at anchor, awaiting the morning tide.

"Appreciate it, sir. I say, great luck running into a gentleman such as yourself here in this part of France. Extremely fortunate for me you're bound for England on board the *Sea Flame*."

Jared smiled slightly. "Yes, quite fortunate." He wondered what Wingfield would say were he to learn that Jared controlled not only the *Sea Flame* but the entire Flamecrest fleet.

"Yes, well, I feel much better knowing you'll see that the shipment and the diary get safely to my niece. Now I can get on with the next leg of my journey."

"You are bound for Italy, I believe you said?"

"And then on to India." Wingfield's eyes filled with the anticipation of the inveterate traveler. "Always wanted to see India, you know."

"I wish you a good journey," Jared said.

"Same to you, sir. And, again, my thanks."

"My pleasure." Jared pulled his gold watch out of his pocket and consulted the time. "Now you must excuse me." He slipped the watch back into his pocket and got to his feet.

Wingfield looked up at him. "Turning in for the night, eh?"

"Not yet. I believe I'll take a walk along the quay to clear my head before I go upstairs to bed."

"Watch your back," Wingfield advised in a low tone. "Don't much care for the looks of this bunch in here. No telling what sort of villains are outside at this hour."

"Do not concern yourself on my behalf, sir." Jared inclined his head in a polite farewell. He turned and walked toward the door.

One or two of the men who sat hunched over their mugs eyed his expensive boots with a speculative glance. Then their eyes slid upward to the knife strapped to his leg and higher still to the black patch over his eye.

No one rose to follow Jared outside.

The breeze off the sea stirred Jared's long, untrimmed hair as he stepped out into the night. Unlike Wingfield, he was dressed for the warm climate. He wore no neckcloth. He detested neckcloths and cravats. The collar of his finely woven cotton shirt was open and the sleeves were rolled up on his forearms.

Jared started along the stone quay, his mind on the business at hand, his senses attuned to the night. A man who had lost one eye had good reason to take care of the other.

A lantern bobbed at the far end of the quay. As Jared drew closer he watched two men step out of the shadows. Both were big, nearly as tall as Jared, and almost as wide across the shoulders. Their rough-hewn faces were framed by silvered whiskers and manes of white hair. They walked with bold, swaggering strides even though each was past sixty. *Two aging buccaneers,* Jared thought, not without affection.

The first of the two men hailed Jared with a smile that gleamed in the shadows. The color of the older man's eyes was washed out by the moonlight, but Jared was quite familiar with the unusual shade of gray. He saw the same color in the mirror every morning when he shaved.

"Good evening, sir," Jared said politely to his father. Then he nodded to the other man. "Uncle Thaddeus. A fine night, is it not?"

"About time you showed up." Magnus, Earl of Flamecrest, beetled his brows. "I was beginning to think your new acquaintance was going to keep you talking for the better part of the night."

"Wingfield is very fond of conversation."

Thaddeus hoisted the lantern higher. "Well, lad? What did ye learn?"

Jared was thirty-four years old. He had not considered himself a lad for many years. In fact, he often felt aeons older than anyone else in the family. But there was no point correcting Thaddeus.

"Wingfield believes he has found Claire Lightbourne's diary," Jared said calmly.

"*Bloody hell.*" The satisfaction in Magnus's face was plain to read in the glow of the lantern. "So it's true, then. The diary has finally been found after all these years."

"Damme," Thaddeus exclaimed. "How the devil did Wingfield get to it first?"

"I believe it was his niece who actually located the volume," Jared said. "You will notice it was found here in France. My cousins were obviously wasting their efforts two months ago when they went chasing off into the hills of Spain to look for it."

"Now, Jared," Magnus said soothingly, "Young Charles and William had good reason to believe it had been taken there during the war. You're just a mite annoyed with your cousins because they got themselves captured by those damn bandits."

"The entire affair was something of a nuisance," Jared allowed grimly. "Furthermore, it cost me nearly two thousand pounds in ransom money, not to mention a great deal of time and effort spent away from my business affairs."

"Damnation, son," Magnus roared. "Is that all you can ever think about? Your business affairs? You've got the blood of buccaneers in your veins, by God, but you've got the heart and soul of a tradesman."

"I'm well aware that I'm something of a disappointment to you and the rest of the family, sir." Jared leaned on the stone wall that fronted the harbor. "But as we've discussed the matter on several previous occasions, I do not think we need go into it again tonight."

"He's right, Magnus," Thaddeus said quickly. "Got more important things to deal with at the moment. The diary is practically in our grasp. I say we have at it."

Jared arched one brow. "Which of you made an effort to have at it last night? Wingfield says his room was searched."

"It was worth a try," Thaddeus said, unabashed.

Magnus nodded. "Just took a look around, that's all."

Jared bit back an exasperated oath. "The diary has been stowed on board the *Sea Flame* since yesterday afternoon. We'd have to unload the whole damn ship to get at it."

"Pity," Thaddeus muttered, defeated.

"In any event," Jared continued, "the diary belongs to Miss Olympia Wingfield of Meadow Stream Cottage in Dorset. She has bought and paid for it."

"Bah, the diary is ours," Magnus said stoutly. "It's a family heirloom. I say she has no right to it."

"You appear to have forgotten that even if we get our hands on it, we shall very likely not be able to decipher it. However . . . " Jared paused just long enough to get his father's and uncle's full attention.

"Yes?" Magnus asked eagerly.

"Artemis Wingfield feels certain that his niece will be able to unravel the code in which the diary is written," Jared said. "Apparently Miss Wingfield excels at that sort of thing."

Thaddeus brightened immediately. "I say, lad, your course of action is clear, then, ain't it? You'll have to follow the diary to its destination and then proceed to

insinuate yourself into Miss Wingfield's good graces so
that she'll tell you all she learns."

"Brilliant notion." Magnus's whiskers jerked in excitement. "Charm her, son. Seduce her. When she melts
in your hands, get her to tell ye everything she learns
from the diary. Then we'll snaffle it away from her."

Jared sighed. It was difficult being the only sane,
sensible soul in a family filled with eccentrics and Originals.

The search for the Lightbourne diary had preoccupied all the Flamecrest males except Jared for three gen-
erations. Jared's father, uncle, and cousins had all
pursued it at one time or another. So had his grandfather and his great-uncles. The lure of treasure had a
truly mesmerizing effect on a clan descended from a
genuine buccaneer.

But enough was enough. A few weeks earlier his
cousins had very nearly gotten themselves killed because
of the diary. Jared had decided it was time to end the
nonsense once and for all. Unfortunately, the only way
to put a stop to the matter was to recover the diary and
see if it did indeed contain the secret of the missing
treasure.

No one had argued when Jared had announced that
it was his turn to pursue the mysterious fortune that
had vanished nearly a hundred years earlier. In truth
everyone, his father especially, was only too pleased to
see Jared show some interest in the matter.

Jared knew he was considered useful to the family
because of his talent for business. But that did not account for much in a family famed for its dashing, hot-
blooded men.

His relatives considered Jared depressingly dull.
They said he lacked the Flamecrest fire. He, in turn,
considered that they lacked self-restraint and common
sense. It had not escaped his notice that they were quick

enough to come to him when there was a problem or when they needed money.

Jared had been putting matters right and attending to the boring little details of life for the Flamecrest clan since he was nineteen. Everyone in the family agreed it was the one thing at which he excelled.

It seemed to Jared that he was forever rescuing one member of the family or another.

Sometimes, when he sat up late at night making notes in his appointment journal, he wondered fleetingly if someone would ever come along to rescue him.

"It's all very well for you two to talk about charm and seduction," Jared said, "but we all know that I did not inherit the Flamecrest talent for either."

"Bah." Magnus waved that aside with a sweeping motion of his hand. "The problem is that you've never applied yourself to the matter."

An expression of grave concern crossed Thaddeus's face. "Well, now, Magnus, I wouldn't go so far as to say he ain't tried his hand at that sort of thing. There was that unfortunate situation three years ago when the lad tried to woo himself a wife."

Jared looked at his uncle. "I think we can dispense with a discussion of that subject. I do not intend to seduce Miss Wingfield or anyone else into telling me the secret of the diary."

Thaddeus scowled. "How will ye go about worming it out o' her, then, lad?"

"I shall offer to purchase the information," Jared said.

"*Purchase it.*" Magnus looked shocked. "Ye think ye can buy a legendary secret like that with mere money?"

"It has been my experience that one can purchase almost anything," Jared said. "A straightforward, businesslike approach works wonders in virtually every conceivable situation."

"Lad, lad, what are we going to do with you?" Thaddeus moaned.

"You are going to let me handle this my way," Jared said. "Now then, let us understand each other. I will pursue the diary. In the meantime, I want your word that you will remember our agreement."

"What agreement?" Magnus asked blankly.

Jared's jaw tightened. "While I'm engaged in this undertaking you are not to interfere in any way in Flamecrest business matters."

"Bloody hell, son, Thaddeus and I were running the family business before you were even born."

"Yes, sir, I know. The two of you ran it straight into the ground."

Magnus's mustache jumped in outrage. "Not our fault we had a bit of a bad spell there. Business was poor during those years."

Jared wisely decided not to pursue the point. They all knew that the earl's lack of business sense coupled with the equally poor abilities of his brother, Thaddeus, had combined to destroy what little was left of the Flamecrest family fortune.

It was Jared who had taken over at the age of nineteen, barely in time to salvage the one decrepit ship that the family had still owned. He had pawned his mother's necklace to raise the money he had needed. No one in the family had ever really forgiven him for his shocking want of sentiment, including his mother. She had actually mentioned the matter for the last time on her deathbed two years ago. Jared had been too grief-stricken to remind her that she had enjoyed the fruits of the new Flamecrest fortune to the hilt, as had everyone else in the clan.

Jared had rebuilt the Flamecrest empire from that

one ship. He sincerely hoped he would not have to repeat the feat when he returned from this crazed venture.

"Hard to believe that at long last the missing Flamecrest fortune is nearly within our grasp." Thaddeus squeezed his hand into a triumphant fist.

"We already possess a fortune," Jared pointed out. "We do not need the stolen treasure Captain Jack and his partner Edward Yorke buried on that damn island nearly a hundred years ago."

"It was not stolen treasure," Magnus thundered.

"If you will recall, sir, Great-grandfather was a pirate while he lived in the West Indies." Jared's brow rose. "It's highly unlikely that he and Yorke came by that treasure in an honest fashion."

"Captain Jack was not a pirate," Thaddeus said fiercely. "He was a loyal Englishman who sailed under a commission. That treasure was lawful spoils taken off a Spanish vessel, by God."

"It would be interesting to hear the Spaniards' version of the story," Jared remarked.

"Bah." Magnus glowered at him. "They're to blame for this situation. If the blasted Spaniards hadn't given chase, Captain Jack and Yorke wouldn't have been obliged to bury the booty on that damned island and we wouldn't be standin' here tonight workin' out a way to get it back."

"Yes, sir," Jared said wearily. He had heard this many times before. It never failed to bore him.

"The only real *pirate* around was Edward Yorke," Magnus continued. "That lying, cheating, murderous knave who betrayed your great-grandfather to the Spanish. It was only by the grace of God that Captain Jack managed to escape the trap."

"It all happened nearly a hundred years ago. We do not know for certain that Yorke betrayed Captain

Jack," Jared said quietly. "In any event, it really does not matter much now."

"Of course it matters," Magnus snapped. "You follow in a proud tradition, my boy. It's your duty to find that missing treasure. It belongs to us and we have every right to claim it."

"After all," Thaddeus said gravely, "you are the new Guardian, lad."

"Bloody hell," Jared said under his breath. "That is a lot of nonsense and you know it."

"T'ain't nonsense," Thaddeus insisted. "You won the right to the title years ago, the night you used Captain Jack's own dagger to save your cousins from that smuggler. Have ye forgotten?"

"I'm hardly likely to forget the incident, as it cost me an eye, sir," Jared muttered. He did not, however, want to get into an argument over yet another idiotic family legend. He had his hands full dealing with the old tale of buried treasure.

"No gettin' around the fact that you're the new Guardian," Magnus said with a sage expression. "You blooded the dagger. Furthermore, you're the spittin' image of Captain Jack, himself, as a young man."

"Enough." Jared removed his watch from his pocket and held it close to the lantern so that he could read the face. "It's late and I must rise early tomorrow."

"You and that bloody watch of yours," Thaddeus grumbled. "I'll wager you've got your appointment journal with ye, too."

"Of course," Jared assured him coolly. "You know I depend upon it."

His watch and his appointment journal were the two things he valued most in his daily life, Jared thought. For years they had provided him with a means of establishing order and routine in a world often made chaotic and unstable by his wild, unpredictable family.

"I cannot believe it." Magnus shook his head in sorrow. "Here ye be about to sail off in search of the secret to a grand treasure and you're consulting your watch and checkin' your appointment journal like a dull man o' business."

"I am a dull man of business, sir," Jared said.

"It's enough to make a father weep," Magnus growled.

"Try to show some of the Flamecrest fire, lad," Thaddeus urged.

"We're on the brink of recovering our lost heritage, son." Magnus gripped the edge of the quay wall and gazed out at the night-darkened sea, the very image of a man who can see beyond the horizon. "I can feel it in me bones. After all these years the Flamecrest treasure is almost within our grasp. And you have the great honor of recovering it for the family."

"I assure you, sir," Jared said politely, "my excitement at the prospect knows no bounds."

Chapter 1

"I have another book which you might also find very interesting, Mr. Draycott." Olympia Wingfield balanced one slippered foot on the library ladder, wedged her other toe onto the edge of a shelf, and reached out to pluck a volume from the top of the bookcase. "This one also contains some fascinating information on the legend of the Island of Gold. And I think there is still another one you should examine."

"Have a care, I beg you, Miss Wingfield." Reginald Draycott gripped the sides of the ladder to steady it. He gazed up at Olympia as she leaned out to fetch another

book from a high shelf. "You will surely fall if you do not watch yourself."

"Nonsense. I promise you I am quite accustomed to this sort of thing. Now, then, I used this particular work when I wrote my last paper for the quarterly journal of the Society for Travel and Exploration. It's extremely useful because it contains notes on the unusual customs of the inhabitants of certain South Seas islands."

"Kind of you to loan it to me, Miss Wingfield, but I am really growing very concerned about your position on this ladder."

"Do not fret, sir." Olympia glanced down at Draycott with a reassuring smile and saw that he had an extremely odd expression on his face. His pale weak eyes had a glazed look and his mouth was hanging open.

"Are you feeling ill, Mr. Draycott?"

"No, no, not at all, my dear." Draycott licked his lips and continued to stare.

"You're quite certain? You look as though you might be nauseous. I shall be glad to fetch these books at another time."

"I wouldn't hear of waiting another day. I vow, I am quite well. In any event you have whetted my appetite for every scrap of information on the legend of the Island of Gold, my dear. I could not bring myself to leave here without more material to study."

"Well, then, if you're quite certain. Now, this volume relates some fascinating customs of the legendary Island of Gold. I, myself, have always been fascinated by the customs and habits of other lands."

"Have you, indeed?"

"Oh, yes. As a woman of the world, I find such matters quite stimulating. The wedding night rituals of the inhabitants of the Island of Gold are particularly interesting." Olympia flipped several pages in the old book and then chanced to glance down at Draycott's face again.

Something was definitely amiss, she thought. Draycott's expression was beginning to make her a trifle uneasy. His eyes were not meeting hers; rather they appeared to be fixed somewhat lower.

"Wedding night rituals, did you say, Miss Wingfield?"

"Yes. Very unusual customs." Olympia frowned in concentration. "Apparently the groom presents the bride with a large gold object shaped rather like a phallus."

"A phallus, did you say, Miss Wingfield?" Draycott sounded as if someone were throttling him.

It finally struck Olympia quite forcibly that in his present position at the foot of the ladder Draycott had an excellent view straight up under her skirts.

"Good heavens." Olympia lost her balance and grabbed the top rung of the ladder. One of the books that she had been holding fell to the carpet.

"Is something wrong, my dear?" Draycott asked quickly.

Mortified by the realization that she was exposing a great deal of her stocking-clad legs to his unimpeded gaze, Olympia turned very warm.

"Nothing's wrong, Mr. Draycott. I have found the volumes I wanted. I'm coming down now. You may step aside."

"Allow me to assist you." Draycott's soft, pudgy hands brushed against the calves of Olympia's legs beneath her muslin skirts.

"No, please. That's quite all right," Olympia gasped. She had never before experienced the feel of a man's hands on her legs. Draycott's touch sent a chill of alarm through her.

She tried to climb back up the ladder to escape

Draycott's hands. His fingers closed around her ankle before she could get out of reach.

Olympia tried and failed to jerk her leg free. Embarrassment turned to annoyance. "If you will just get out of my way, Mr. Draycott, I shall be able to climb down safely."

"I cannot let you risk a fall." Draycott's fingers slipped higher up her leg and squeezed.

"I do not need any assistance." Another of the books Olympia had been holding slipped out of her arms and fell to the carpet with a thud. "Kindly let go of my ankle, sir."

"I am only trying to help you, my dear."

Olympia was outraged now. She had known Reginald Draycott for years. She could not believe that he would not do as she asked. She kicked out wildly. Her foot struck Draycott on the shoulder.

"Umph." Draycott staggered backward a step. He gave Olympia an injured look.

Olympia paid no attention to the accusation in his eyes. She scrambled down the ladder in a flurry of muslin. She could feel her hair coming free of the knot in which she had secured it. Her white muslin cap was askew.

When the toe of her slipper touched the carpet, Draycott's hands closed around her waist from behind.

"My dearest Olympia, I cannot hold back my feelings any longer."

"That is quite enough, Mr. Draycott." Abandoning any further effort to deal with the situation in a ladylike manner, Olympia rammed her elbow into his midsection.

Draycott groaned but he did not release her. He was panting in her ear. She could smell onions on his breath. Her stomach churned.

"Olympia, my darling, you are a woman of mature

years, not a green girl fresh out of the schoolroom. You have been buried alive here in Upper Tudway all of your life. You have never had a chance to experience the joys of passion. It is time you *lived*."

"I believe I am going to be ill all over your boots, Mr. Draycott."

"Don't be ridiculous. You are no doubt a bit nervous because you are unfamiliar with the pleasures of physical desire. Have no fear, I shall teach you everything you need to know."

"Let me go, Mr. Draycott." Olympia dropped the last book and clawed at his hands.

"You are a lovely woman who has never known the taste of *l'amour*. Surely you do not wish to deny yourself the ultimate sensual experience."

"Mr. Draycott, if you do not let go of me at once, I shall scream."

"There is no one home, my dear." Draycott wrestled her over to the couch. "Your nephews are gone."

"I am certain that Mrs. Bird is somewhere about."

"Your housekeeper is out in the gardens." Draycott started to nuzzle her neck. "Have no fear, my sweet, we are quite alone."

"*Mr. Draycott.* You must get hold of yourself, sir. You do not know what you are doing."

"Call me Reggie, my dear."

Olympia made a wild grab for the silver statue of the Trojan horse that stood on her desk. She missed.

But to her amazement Draycott suddenly yelped in alarm and released her.

"Bloody hell," Draycott gasped.

Free at last, but off balance, Olympia stumbled and nearly fell. She caught hold of the desk to steady herself. Behind her she heard Draycott cry out once more.

"Who the devil are you?" he began in an outraged voice.

There was a sickening sound of flesh slamming into flesh and then there was a sudden thud.

Cap dangling over one ear, Olympia spun around. She pushed several tendrils of hair out of her eyes and stared, astounded, at Draycott. He was lying in a crumpled heap on the floor.

With a strange sense of inevitability, Olympia's gaze went to the pair of black boots that were planted on the carpet beside Draycott. Slowly she raised her eyes.

She found herself staring at the face of a man who could have walked straight out of a legend involving buried treasure and mysterious islands set in uncharted seas. From his long, wind-whipped black hair and velvet eye patch to the dagger he wore strapped to his thigh, he was an awe-inspiring sight.

He was one of the most powerful looking men Olympia had ever seen. Tall, broad-shouldered, and lean, he radiated a supple sense of strength and masculine grace. His features had been carved with a bold, fearless hand by a sculptor who scorned subtlety and refinement.

"Are you, by any chance, Miss Olympia Wingfield?" the man asked calmly, just as if having an unconscious person at his feet were an everyday occurrence.

"Yes." Olympia realized her voice was a mere squeak of sound. She cleared her throat and tried again. "Yes, I am. And your name, sir?"

"Chillhurst."

"Oh." She gazed at him blankly. She had never heard the name. "How do you do, Mr. Chillhurst."

His riding coat and breeches fitted him well enough but even she, who had lived in the country all her life, recognized them as being sadly out of style. A man of modest means, obviously. Apparently he could not even afford a neckcloth because he certainly was not wearing one. The collar of his shirt was open. There was something a little uncivilized, even primitive, about the sight of his bare throat. Olympia realized she could actually see a small portion of his chest. There appeared to be dark, curling hair on it.

The man looked dangerous standing here in her library, Olympia realized. Dangerous and utterly fascinating.

A small shiver went down her spine, a shiver that was not at all akin to the unpleasant sensation that had gripped her when Draycott had taken hold of her ankle. This shiver was one of excitement.

"I don't believe I know anyone named Chillhurst," Olympia managed to say smoothly.

"Your uncle, Artemis Wingfield, sent me."

"Uncle Artemis?" Relief rushed through her. "You met him somewhere on his travels? Is he well?"

"Quite well, Miss Wingfield. I encountered him on the coast of France."

"This is wonderful." Olympia gave him a delighted smile. "I cannot wait to hear all the news. Uncle Artemis always has such interesting adventures. How I envy him. You must dine with us this evening, Mr. Chillhurst, and tell us everything."

"Are you all right, Miss Wingfield?"

"I beg your pardon?" Olympia stared at him in confusion. "Of course I'm all right. Why shouldn't I be all right? My health is excellent. Always has been. Thank you for inquiring, Mr. Chillhurst."

The black brow over Chillhurst's good eye rose. "I was referring to your recent experience at the hands of this person on the floor."

"Oh, I see." Olympia abruptly recalled Draycott's presence. "Good heavens, I almost forgot about him." She saw Draycott's eyes flicker and wondered what to do next. She was not particularly skilled at handling difficult social situations. Aunt Sophy and Aunt Ida had never concerned themselves with teaching her such niceties.

"This is Mr. Draycott," Olympia said. "He's a neighbor of ours. Known him for years."

"Has he always made a habit of assaulting ladies in their own homes?" Chillhurst said dryly.

"What? Oh, no." Olympia flushed. "At least, I do not believe so. He appears to have fainted. Do you think I should call my housekeeper and have her fetch the vinaigrette?"

"Do not concern yourself. He'll awaken soon enough."

"Will he? I have not had much experience with the effects of pugilism. My nephews are great admirers of the sport, however." Olympia gave him an inquiring look. "You appear to be very well versed in it. Have you studied at one of the London academies?"

"No."

"I thought perhaps you had. Well, never mind." She looked down at Draycott again. "He was certainly making a nuisance of himself. I do hope he has learned his lesson. I must say, if he continues to act in such a manner in the future I will no longer allow him to make use of my library."

Chillhurst looked at her as if she were slightly mad. "Miss Wingfield, allow me to point out that he should not be permitted to enter your home again under any circumstances. Furthermore, a woman of your years ought to know better than to receive gentlemen callers alone in her library."

"Do not be ridiculous. I am five-and-twenty, sir. I have little to fear from gentlemen callers. In any event, I am a woman of the world and I am not easily overset by unusual or extraordinary circumstances."

"Is that a fact, Miss Wingfield?"

"Certainly. I expect poor Mr. Draycott was simply

overcome with the sort of intellectual passion that is frequently engendered by a keen interest in ancient legends. All that business about lost treasures and such has a very inflammatory effect on the senses in some people."

Chillhurst stared at her. "Does it have an inflammatory effect on your senses, Miss Wingfield?"

"Yes, indeed." Olympia broke off, aware that Draycott was stirring. "Look, he's opening his eyes. Do you suppose he'll have a headache because of that dreadful blow you gave him?"

"With any luck, yes," Chillhurst muttered.

"Bloody hell." Draycott mumbled. "What happened?" He gazed blearily up at Chillhurst for a moment. Then his eyes widened in astonishment. "Who the devil are you, sir?"

Chillhurst looked down at him. "A friend of the family."

"What the hell do you mean by attacking me?" Draycott demanded. He gingerly touched his jaw. "I'll have the magistrate on you for this, by God."

"You will do no such thing, Mr. Draycott," Olympia said crisply. "Your behavior was quite atrocious, as you are no doubt well aware. I'm sure you will want to take your leave immediately."

"He will apologize to you first, Miss Wingfield," Chillhurst said softly.

Olympia glanced at him in surprise. "Will he?"

"Yes."

"Damnation. I didn't do anything wrong," Draycott said in an aggrieved tone. "I was merely trying to assist Miss Wingfield down the ladder. And this is the thanks I get."

Chillhurst reached down, took hold of Draycott's neckcloth, and hauled the groggy man to his feet. "You will apologize now," he said deliberately. "And then you will leave."

Draycott blinked several times. His eyes met Chillhurst's unblinking gaze and slid uneasily away. "Yes, of course. All a mistake. Terribly sorry."

Chillhurst released him without warning. Draycott stumbled and stepped hurriedly back out of reach. He turned to Olympia with an expression of acute discomfort.

"I regret any misunderstanding that may have occurred between us, Miss Wingfield," Draycott said stiffly. "Didn't mean to give offense."

"Of course you didn't." Olympia could not help but notice that Draycott appeared very small and quite harmless standing next to Mr. Chillhurst. It was difficult to recall that for a few minutes there she had actually been somewhat alarmed by his behavior. "I believe it would be best if we both were to forget this matter entirely. Let us pretend it never happened."

Draycott cast a sidelong glance at Chillhurst. "As you wish." He straightened his coat and adjusted his neckcloth. "Now, if you will excuse me, I must be off. Don't bother summoning your housekeeper. I can see myself out."

Silence descended on the library as Draycott walked hurriedly out the door. When he was gone, Olympia looked at Chillhurst. He was studying her, in turn, with an unreadable expression. Neither said a word until they heard the outer door close in the hall behind Draycott.

Olympia smiled. "Thank you for coming to my rescue, Mr. Chillhurst. It was quite gallant of you. I've never been rescued before. A most unusual experience."

Chillhurst inclined his head with mocking civility. "It was nothing, Miss Wingfield. I'm glad I could be of service."

"You certainly were, although I doubt that Mr. Draycott would have done anything more than try to steal a kiss."

"You don't think so?"

Olympia frowned at the skepticism in Chillhurst's eyes. "He's really not a bad sort. I've known him since I came here to live in Upper Tudway. But I must admit that he's been acting rather oddly ever since his wife died six months ago." She paused. "He has recently developed a great interest in old legends, which happens to be my own field of interest."

"Somehow that does not surprise me."

"What? That I am interested in them?"

"No, that Draycott developed a sudden interest in them." Chillhurst's expression was grim. "He obviously did so in order to seduce you, Miss Wingfield."

Olympia was appalled. "Good heavens, surely you do not believe that what happened here this afternoon was intentional."

"I suspect it was very much a premeditated action, Miss Wingfield."

"I see." Olympia considered that briefly. "I had not thought of that possibility."

"Apparently not. You would be wise not to see him alone again."

Olympia brushed that aside. "Well, it's not really all that important. It's over. And I am completely forgetting my manners. I expect you'd like a cup of tea, wouldn't you? You've probably had a very long journey. I shall summon my housekeeper."

The sound of the outer door being flung open with a crash interrupted Olympia before she could ring for Mrs. Bird. A loud barking filled the hall. Dog claws scrabbled on the wooden floor outside the library. Boots pounded. Youthful voices rose in a booming chorus.

"Aunt Olympia? Aunt Olympia, where are you?"

"We're home, Aunt Olympia."

Olympia looked at Chillhurst. "I believe my nephews have returned from their fishing trip. They'll be anxious to meet you. They're very fond of Uncle Artemis and I'm sure they'll want to hear everything you have to tell us about your visit with him. You might also mention your skills in pugilism. My nephews will have a great many questions about the sport."

At that moment a massive furry dog of indeterminate breed burst into the library. He barked once, very loudly at Chillhurst and then galloped toward Olympia. He was soaking wet and his massive paws left muddy tracks on the library carpet.

"Oh, dear, Minotaur is off his leash again." Olympia braced herself. "Down, Minotaur. Down, I say. That's a good dog."

Minotaur bounded forward without pause, his tongue lolling out of the side of his grinning mouth.

Olympia hurriedly backed away from him. "Ethan? Hugh? Please call your dog."

"Here, Minotaur," Ethan yelled from the hall. "Here, boy."

"Come back here, Minotaur," Hugh yelled.

Minotaur paid no attention. He was bent on greeting Olympia and there was no stopping him. He was a friendly monster of a dog and Olympia had actually grown fond of him since her nephews had found him abandoned and brought him home. Unfortunately the beast had absolutely no manners.

The huge dog halted in front of her and leaped up on his hind legs. Olympia held out a hand to fend him off but she knew it was a useless effort.

"Stay, boy. Stay," Olympia said without much hope. "Please sit. *Please*."

Minotaur yelped, sensing victory. His dirty paws began their inevitable descent toward the front of Olympia's clean gown.

"That's quite enough," Chillhurst said. "I have never liked having unschooled dogs about the place."

Out of the corner of her eye, Olympia saw him move. He took a single, gliding stride toward Minotaur, grabbed the animal's leather collar, and tugged him firmly downward until all four wet paws were once more on the floor.

"Stay," Chillhurst said to the dog. "Sit."

Minotaur looked up at him with an expression of canine astonishment. For a moment dog and man eyed each other. Then, to Olympia's everlasting surprise, Minotaur obediently sat back on his haunches.

"That was quite amazing," Olympia said. "How on earth did you manage that, Mr. Chillhurst? Minotaur never obeys commands."

"He simply needs a firm hand."

"Aunt Olympia? Are you in the library?" Ethan came barrelling around the door, his eight-year-old face alight with excitement. His sandy brown hair was plastered to his head. His clothes were as wet and muddy as Minotaur's fur. "There's a strange carriage in the drive. It's ever so big and it looks like it's packed with trunks. Has Uncle Artemis come to visit again?"

"No." Olympia frowned at his dripping attire and started to ask why he had gone swimming in his clothes.

Before she could speak, Ethan's twin, Hugh, charged into the room. He was as covered in mud as his brother. In addition, his shirt was torn.

"I say, Aunt Olympia, have we got visitors?" Hugh asked eagerly. His blue eyes gleamed with enthusiasm.

Both boys skidded to a halt as they caught sight of Chillhurst. They stared at him while water and mud dripped onto the carpet at their feet.

"Who are you?" Hugh asked bluntly.

"Are you from London?" Ethan asked eagerly. "What have you got packed away in your carriage?"

"What happened to your eye?" Hugh demanded.

"Hugh, Ethan, have you both forgotten your manners?" Olympia gave each boy a gently admonishing look. "That is no way to greet a guest. Please run along upstairs and change your clothes. You both look as though you fell into the stream."

"Ethan pushed me in, so I pushed him in," Hugh explained briefly. "And then Minotaur jumped into the water after us."

Ethan was immediately outraged. "I did not push you into the water."

"Yes, you did," Hugh said.

"No, I did not."

"Yes, you did."

"It doesn't matter now," Olympia said quickly. "Go upstairs and make yourselves presentable. When you come back down I shall introduce you properly to Mr. Chillhurst."

"Ah, Aunt Olympia," Ethan said in the obnoxious whining tone he had recently perfected. "Don't be such a killjoy. First tell us who this cove is."

Olympia wondered where Ethan had picked up the cant. "I shall explain everything later. It is really quite exciting. But you are both very muddy and you really must go upstairs first. You know how annoyed Mrs. Bird gets when she finds mud on the carpet."

"The devil with Mrs. Bird," Hugh said.

"*Hugh*," Olympia gasped.

"Well, she's always complaining about something, Aunt Olympia. You know that." He looked at Chillhurst. "Are you a pirate?"

Chillhurst did not reply. Most likely because there was yet another crashing noise from the hall. Two spaniels bounded into the room. They barked joyously to

announce their arrival and dashed about wildly. Then
they rushed across the library to see what the matter
was with Minotaur, who was still sitting politely at
Chillhurst's feet.

"Aunt Olympia? What's going on? There's a strange
carriage in the drive. Who's here?" Robert, two years
older than the twins, appeared in the doorway. His hair
was darker than his brothers' but his eyes were the same
vivid shade of blue. He was not soaking wet but his
boots were caked in mud and there was a great deal of
dirt on his face and hands.

He had a large kite tucked under one arm. The long,
dirty tail dragged on the floor behind him. Three small
fish dangled from a line he was holding in his other
hand. He stopped short when he saw Chillhurst. His
eyes widened.

"Hello there," Robert said. "I say, who are you, sir?
Is that your carriage outside?"

Chillhurst ignored the bouncing spaniels and gazed
meditatively at the three expectant youngsters. "I'm
Chillhurst," he said finally. "Your uncle sent me."

"Really?" Hugh asked. "How do you come to know
Uncle Artemis?"

"We met recently." Chillhurst said. "He knew I was
traveling to England and he asked me to stop here in
Upper Tudway."

Robert beamed. "That means he probably sent presents to us. Are they in your carriage?"

"Uncle Artemis always sends presents," Hugh explained.

"That's right," Ethan chimed in. "Where are our
presents?"

"Ethan," Olympia said, "it is extremely impolite to
demand one's gifts from a guest before he has even had
a chance to freshen up from his journey."

"It's quite all right, Miss Wingfield," Chillhurst said

softly. He turned to Ethan. "Among other things, your uncle sent me."

"*You.*" Ethan was thunderstruck. "Why would he send you?"

"I am to be your new tutor," Chillhurst said.

A stunned silence gripped the library. Olympia watched as the expressions on the faces of her three young nephews changed from eager expectation to horror. They stared, aghast, at Chillhurst.

"Bloody hell," Hugh breathed.

"We don't want another tutor." Ethan wrinkled his nose. "The last one was a great bore. He was forever droning on in Latin and Greek."

"We don't need a tutor," Hugh assured Chillhurst. "Ain't that right, Robert?"

"Right," Robert agreed quickly. "Aunt Olympia can teach us whatever we need to know. Tell him we don't want a tutor, Aunt Olympia."

"I do not understand, Mr. Chillhurst." Olympia stared at the pirate standing in her library. "Surely my uncle would not have hired a tutor for my nephews without first consulting me."

Chillhurst turned to her with an odd glittering expression in his silvery gaze. "But that is just what he has done, Miss Wingfield. I hope that does not present a problem. I've come all this way on the promise of a position. I trust you will find me useful."

"I'm not at all certain I can afford another tutor," Olympia said slowly.

"You need not concern yourself with my fee," Chillhurst said gently. "It has been paid in advance."

"I see," Olympia said. She did not know what to say.

Chillhurst turned to the three boys who were watching him with acute dismay and apprehension. "Robert, you will go back out the way you came. You will take those fine-looking fish around to the kitchens and clean them."

"Mrs. Bird always cleans 'em," Robert said quickly.

"You caught them, you will clean them," Chillhurst replied calmly. "Ethan, Hugh, you two will remove all dogs from the premises immediately."

"But the dogs always come into the house," Ethan said. "Leastways Minotaur does. The spaniels belong to one of the neighbors."

"Henceforth no dogs except Minotaur will be allowed inside and Minotaur may only enter the house if he is clean and dry. See that the spaniels are sent home and then take care of your own dog."

"But, Mr. Chillhurst," Ethan began in his new high-pitched, grating tone of voice.

"There will be no whining," Chillhurst said. "Whining annoys me." He removed a gold watch from his pocket and checked the time. "Now, then, you have half an hour to get yourselves bathed and into clean clothes."

"I don't need a bath," Robert grumbled.

"You will take one and you will be quick about it." Chillhurst slipped his watch back into his pocket. "When you are all three finished we shall meet together and I will outline the course of studies that you will be following while in my charge. Is that understood?"

"Bloody hell," Robert whispered. "He's a raving madman, he is."

Ethan and Hugh continued to stare at Chillhurst with stricken expressions.

"I said, is that understood?" Chillhurst repeated in a dangerously soft tone.

Ethan's and Hugh's eyes went to the knife that was strapped to Chillhurst's thigh.

"Yes, sir," Ethan said quickly.

Hugh swallowed. "Yes, sir."

Robert gave Chillhurst a sullen look but he did not argue. "Yes, sir."

"You are dismissed," Chillhurst said.

All three boys turned and bolted for the door. The dogs followed in a concerted rush. There was a temporary crush in the doorway but it was soon cleared.

In a moment the library was quiet once more.

Olympia stared at the empty doorway, awed. "That was absolutely incredible, Mr. Chillhurst. You may consider yourself hired."

"Thank you, Miss Wingfield. I shall endeavor to earn my keep."

Chapter 2

"I must be completely honest with you, Mr. Chillhurst." Olympia folded her hands on top of her desk and peered at Jared. "I have hired three tutors in the past six months. None of them stayed longer than a fortnight."

"I assure you I shall stay as long as is necessary, Miss Wingfield." Jared sat back in his chair, propped his elbows on the upholstered arms, and regarded Olympia over his steepled fingers.

Bloody hell, he thought. He could not take his gaze off her. She had fascinated him from the moment he had walked into her library.

No, he realized, his fascination had

begun the other night in that grimy French port tavern when Artemis Wingfield had described his unusual niece. Jared had spent the entire trip across the channel speculating about the woman who had managed to locate the Lightbourne diary. Various members of his own family had spent years attempting to discover it and had failed. What sort of female had beaten them all to it, he wondered.

Even allowing for his curiosity, however, he still did not understand the strange shock of awareness that had gone through him when he had seen Draycott seize Olympia. The sensation that had washed through Jared in that moment had been deep and disturbing, almost savage in its intensity.

It was as if he had walked into the room and discovered his woman being mauled by another man. He had wanted to strangle Draycott. At the same time he had been outraged at Olympia's obvious lack of common sense. He had longed to shake her and then drag her down onto the carpet and make love to her.

Jared was dazed by the strength of his feelings. He recalled his emotions the day he had found his fiancée, Demetria Seaton, in the arms of her lover. His reaction on that occasion had not been nearly as violent as what he had experienced today.

It made no sense. There was no logic to it.

But even knowing that, it had taken Jared mere seconds to make his reckless decision. In a heartbeat he had tossed aside his coolly conceived, eminently logical plans. All thoughts of purchasing the diary and its secrets and then returning to his business affairs vanished in an instant.

With a breathtaking, completely uncharacteristic disregard for common sense he had consigned the Lightbourne diary to hell. A mundane business arrangement was the very last thing he wanted to enter into with Olympia. Indeed, he could not bear the thought.

He wanted her. *Wanted her.*

Once that blazing realization had struck him all that had seemed important was that he discover a way to stay here in the vicinity of his enchanting siren. He needed to explore this fierce, powerful, passionate attraction if it was the last thing he did on earth.

Nothing else mattered quite as much, not his sensible plan to secure the diary and thereby put an end to his family's pursuit of it, not his far-flung business affairs, not even tracking down the person who was systematically embezzling from him.

His family, his business affairs, and the damned embezzler could all take care of themselves for a while. For the first time in his life he was going to do something he wanted to do and the devil with his responsibilities.

With his customary ruthless intelligence he had grasped the obvious solution to his new dilemma and presented himself as the new tutor. It had been remarkably easy, almost as if fate itself had taken a hand.

It was only now that he had had a chance to reflect upon his stunning impulsiveness that Jared wondered if he had lost his wits.

Still, he could not bring himself to regret his rash action. He knew very well that the twist of desire in his gut and the sensation of heat in his veins were dangerous threats to his much-prized self-control. But for some reason he did not care a jot about the risk.

That very lack of concern amazed him more than anything else that had happened thus far. The one thing Jared had always valued above all was the calm, cool, logical approach he applied toward every aspect of his life.

In a family where everyone around him had always

appeared to be at the mercy of their passions and whims, self-control and cold restraint had offered Jared inner peace and a reassuring sense of order. He had mastered his own emotions so thoroughly that lately he had begun to question whether he even had any left.

Now Olympia Wingfield had proven to him that he did. She was definitely a siren, he thought. One who did not yet know her own power.

It was not her beauty that had sliced through the armor that had shielded him for so long. He recognized that Demetria had been far more elegantly beautiful.

But Olympia, with her wild, sunset-red hair, expressive features, and eyes the color of a hidden lagoon, was something other than beautiful, Jared thought. She was exciting. Intriguing. Vivid. There was an innocent charm about her that was more alluring than he could ever have imagined.

It seemed to him that her entire slender, gently curved body sang a silent, sensual song beneath the modest muslin gown she wore. The Reginald Draycotts of the world would have to go elsewhere for female companionship for a while, Jared decided. He wanted Olympia and he did not intend to allow any other man to come close while he, himself, was under her spell.

Even caught as he was in the gossamer web of curiosity and fascination, Jared could not help but notice that Olympia had a rather disorganized and disheveled air about her. From the muslin cap that sat askew on her fiery hair to the cotton stocking that had come free of its garter and slipped down to her ankle, there was a cheerfully distracted quality to her attire. She had the appearance of a woman caught between the everyday world and some fabulous landscape that only she could see.

She was an obvious bluestocking, clearly doomed to be left on the shelf, but she showed every sign of being content with her fate. Jared could well believe that she relished her spinsterhood. By now she had undoubtedly discovered that there were very few men who could understand, let alone share, her private inner world.

Olympia bit her lip. "It's very kind of you to promise to stay and I'm certain you have the best of intentions. The thing is, my nephews are somewhat difficult to manage. They have had some trouble settling in here, you see."

"Do not concern yourself, Miss Wingfield. I shall manage them." After years of dealing with wily men of business, belligerent ships' captains, the occasional pirate, and the unpredictable members of his own family, the prospect of dealing with three rowdy young boys did not alarm Jared.

For an instant a hopeful expression lit Olympia's magnificent blue-green eyes. Then she suddenly scowled. "I trust you do not mean to try to control my nephews with floggings, Mr. Chillhurst. I will not allow them to be beaten. They have suffered quite enough in the two years since they lost their parents."

"I do not believe that one should control either a boy or a horse with a whip, Miss Wingfield." Jared was mildly surprised to realize he was repeating something he had overheard his father say years ago. "Such methods serve only to break the spirit or create a vicious streak in the victim."

Olympia brightened. "Precisely my sentiments. I realize that many people believe in such old-fashioned techniques of discipline but I could never countenance them. My nephews are good boys."

"I understand."

"They have only been in my care for six months," Olympia continued. "They were handed off from one relative to another after their parents died. By the time they landed on my doorstep, they were quite anxious and very dispirited. Hugh still suffers from the occasional nightmare."

"I see."

"I realize they are somewhat undisciplined. But I am greatly relieved that in the past few months they have started to become more cheerful. They were much too quiet during those early weeks. I consider their present high spirits a good sign that they are happier now."

"They very likely are happier," Jared allowed.

Olympia's laced fingers tightened together. "I knew just how they felt that day when their aunt and uncle from Yorkshire left them with me. I had experienced the same dreadful loneliness and apprehension myself when I was deposited on Aunt Sophy's doorstep."

"How old were you at the time?"

"Ten. After my parents were lost at sea, I, too, was passed around from one relative to another, just as my nephews were. No one really wanted to be bothered with me, although some tried to do their duty."

"Duty is a poor substitute for affection."

"Very true, sir. And a child knows the difference. I eventually wound up here in Aunt Sophy's house. She and Aunt Ida were both past sixty at the time, but they took me in and gave me a real home. I am determined to do the same for my nephews."

"Very commendable, Miss Wingfield."

"Unfortunately I do not know much about raising young boys," Olympia admitted. "I have feared to discipline them because I have not wanted to make them feel unwanted or unwelcome."

"An orderly routine and reasonable discipline do not make a young boy feel unwanted or unwelcome," Jared said quietly. "Indeed, just the opposite is the case."

"Do you think so?"

Jared tapped his fingertips together. "It is my opinion as a tutor that a firmly established schedule of lessons and instructive activities will greatly benefit your nephews."

Olympia heaved a small sigh of relief. "I would certainly be very grateful to have this household restored to some semblance of order. I vow it is very difficult to work with all the noise and the dashing about that goes on these days. I have not been able to write a single paper in the past few months. It seems as though some crisis is always occurring."

"Crisis?"

"Last Sunday Ethan brought a frog to church. You would not believe the commotion it caused. A few days ago Robert tried to ride a neighbor's horse without a saddle and got thrown to the ground. The neighbor was furious because he had not given Robert permission to ride the beast. I was terrified that Robert had been seriously injured. Yesterday Hugh got into a fight with little Charles Bristow and the young man's mother created a dreadful fuss."

"What was the fight about?" Jared asked curiously.

"I have no notion. Hugh would not tell me. But he got his nose bloodied and I was very worried that it might be broken."

"I take it Hugh lost the fight?"

"Yes, but that is neither here nor there. The important thing is that he got into a fight in the first place. I was quite alarmed. Mrs. Bird said I should take a switch to him, but I certainly will not do that. In any event, that is a small sampling of what life has been like around here every day for the past few months."

"Hmm."

"And there always seems to be so much *noise*," Olympia continued unhappily. "It is always like Bedlam around here." She rubbed her brow. "I confess that it has been somewhat trying at times."

"Do not concern yourself, Miss Wingfield. You are in good hands. I shall establish an orderly household routine for the boys that will enable you to carry on with your work. Speaking of which, I must say I am very impressed by your library."

"Thank you." Momentarily distracted by the comment, Olympia glanced around the room with pride and affection. "I inherited the majority of my books from Aunt Sophy and Aunt Ida. In their younger days they traveled widely and they collected books and manuscripts everywhere they went. There are many, many treasures in this room."

Jared managed to drag his gaze away from Olympia long enough to examine her library more closely. The room was as unexpected and intriguing as the woman herself.

It was a scholar's retreat, crammed with volumes, maps, and globes. There was not a book of pressed flowers or a sewing basket in sight. Olympia's desk was a large and substantial item of furniture made of highly polished mahogany. It bore no resemblance to the delicate little writing tables most ladies used. In fact, Jared thought, it reminded him of his own library desk.

"About your position here, Mr. Chillhurst." Olympia frowned uncertainly. "I suppose I ought to ask for references. Mrs. Milton, a neighbor of mine, has informed me that one should never hire a tutor who does not provide excellent references from several sources."

Jared glanced back at her. "Your uncle sent me. I assumed that would be sufficient recommendation."

"Oh, yes." Olympia's expression cleared. "Yes, of course. What better reference could you possibly have?"

"I'm glad you feel that way."

"That's settled, then." Olympia was obviously relieved not to have to worry about such pesky details as a tutor's references. Her eyes grew wistful. "You say you met Uncle Artemis in France?"

"Yes. I was en route to England from Spain."

"You have been to Spain?" Olympia was obviously entranced. "I have always wanted to go to Spain. And to Italy and Greece."

"I have been to all of those places, as it happens." Jared paused to study her reaction. "And to the West Indies and America."

"How thrilling, sir. And how I do envy you. You are, indeed, a man of the world."

"Some would say so," Jared agreed. He was only a man, he thought with rueful amusement. He could not help but be warmed by the light of feminine admiration that he glimpsed in the siren's eyes.

"You are no doubt well versed in the customs of the inhabitants of other lands, I should imagine." Olympia looked at him expectantly.

"I have made a few such observations," Jared said.

"I consider myself a woman of the world because of the excellent education I received from my aunts," Olympia confided. "But I have never had the opportunity to actually travel abroad. My aunts were not well off in their later years. I get by on the small inheritance I received from them but it is certainly not enough to finance an interesting journey."

"I understand." Jared smiled slightly at the notion of Olympia as a woman of the world. "Now then, there are perhaps one or two small matters we should discuss about my position in this household, Miss Wingfield."

"There are?"

"I'm afraid so."

"I thought we'd settled everything." Olympia sank back into her chair. She heaved a sensual sounding sigh that in another woman might have been mistaken for passion. "I have never met anyone who has traveled as widely as yourself, sir. I should dearly love to ask you a great many questions and to verify certain facts that I have gleaned from my books."

Jared realized that she was gazing at him as though he were the most handsome, the most fascinating, the most desirable man on the face of the earth. No woman had ever looked at him with such unabashed longing. She did not even appear to mind his sightless eye.

He had never considered himself a skilled seducer of women. For one thing he had simply been too busy since the age of nineteen to devote much time to the matter. And, as his father had often pointed out, he seemed to lack the Flamecrest fire.

It was not that he did not experience the normal male appetites, Jared thought. He was only too well acquainted with them. He was very aware of what it was like to lie awake late at night and hunger for a warm, loving woman.

The problem was that it was not his nature to become involved in a series of shallow affairs. The few he had had over the years had left him feeling restless and dissatisfied. He suspected his partners had felt very much the same. As Demetria had taken pains to point out, once one got past his title and expectations, there was nothing very interesting left to discover.

But today some deep masculine instinct told Jared that it would be quite possible for him to seduce Olympia Wingfield. She would not require poems and bouquets and smoldering looks.

All he had to do was ply her with travelers' tales.

He considered just how he would proceed with the seduction. She would no doubt smile at him for the story of an adventure in Naples or Rome. She would likely melt for a tale of a voyage to America. There was no telling what she would do if he gave her a story of a journey to the West Indies. His body grew hard as he contemplated the possibilities.

Jared took a deep breath and clamped down on the hot, aching need that had seized his insides. He did what he always did when he felt his self-control slipping. He reached into his inside coat pocket for his appointment journal. He was aware that Olympia watched with interest as he opened it to the page that contained his list of notes for the day.

"First, we should discuss the shipment of goods your uncle entrusted to my care," Jared said.

"Yes, of course," she said briskly. "It was very kind of you to escort the shipment to me. Uncle Artemis and I have worked out a very profitable arrangement, as I expect he explained to you. He selects a variety of interesting items in the course of his travels and ships them back to me from various points along the way. I, in turn, sell them to some London merchants."

Jared tried and failed to envision Olympia as a shrewd merchant of imported luxuries. "Do you mind my asking how you go about finding a buyer for your goods, Miss Wingfield?"

She gave him a sunny smile. "It is really quite simple. One of my neighbors, Squire Pettigrew, has been kind enough to assist me in that regard. He says it is the least he can do out of respect for my dear aunts who were his neighbors for so many years."

"Just how does Pettigrew handle the goods?"

Olympia waved her hand in a vague gesture. "I believe his man of affairs in London sees to all the details."

"You are satisfied that Squire Pettigrew's man of affairs strikes a good bargain?" Jared persisted.

Olympia chuckled. She leaned forward with an air of imparting a deep confidence. "We realized a sum of nearly two hundred pounds off the last shipment."

"Is that right?"

"Of course, that was an exceptional shipment. Uncle Artemis sent several lengths of silk and a large variety of spices on that occasion. I doubt that we'll do as well this time."

Jared thought of the approximately three thousand pounds worth of goods that he had accompanied from France. He had been obliged to hire two burly men to act as guards after the ship had docked in Weymouth.

Jared withdrew a piece of folded foolscap from his journal. "This is a copy of the list of goods your uncle sent to you this time." He handed the paper to Olympia. "How does it compare with the last shipment?"

Olympia took the sheet of paper from him and perused it with a distracted frown. "I cannot recall all of the items on the previous list but there does not seem to be quite as much lace this time. And I do not see any of those Italian fans Uncle Artemis sent with the last lot."

"There are several bolts of silk and some velvet in this shipment," Jared pointed out softly.

Olympia lifted one shoulder in a tiny shrug. "Squire Pettigrew tells me that unfortunately the market for silk and velvet is not strong at the moment. All in all, I expect we shall probably not do quite as well as we did on the last shipment. Nevertheless, we'll see a nice bit of the ready out of it, as my nephews would say."

Jared wondered how long Squire Pettigrew had been systematically fleecing Olympia. "I have had some experience with the business of importing goods, Miss Wingfield."

"Have you, indeed?" She looked at him with polite surprise.

"Yes." Jared reflected briefly on the hundreds of thousands of pounds worth of goods that filled the holds of Flamecrest ships every year. "If you like, I can deal with this shipment for you."

"That's very generous of you." Olympia was clearly overwhelmed by his helpfulness. "But are you quite certain you wish to undertake such a task? Squire Pettigrew tells me it is a very time-consuming business. He says one must be constantly on the alert for swindlers."

"I expect he knows what he's talking about." Jared privately considered that Pettigrew certainly ought to recognize another swindler when he saw one. "But I believe that I can do at least as well for you as Squire Pettigrew has done in the past. Perhaps better."

"You must take a suitable commission out of the proceeds, of course."

"That will not be necessary." Jared's calculating brain skimmed over the problem, weighing and assessing the task. He would entrust the goods to his man of affairs, Felix Hartwell. When he sent instructions to Hartwell, he would utilize the opportunity to inquire about any progress that might have been made in the embezzlement situation. "I shall consider the task part of my normal duties as a tutor in this household."

"You will?" Olympia stared at him in amazement. "How very odd. None of the other tutors offered to extend their services outside the classroom."

"I trust you will find me useful about the place," Jared said softly.

The door of the library opened abruptly to admit a stout, sturdy female in an apron and cap. She held a tea tray in her work-reddened hands.

"Here, now, what's all this about a new tutor?" She glowered at Olympia. "Are ye going to blight the hopes and dreams of yet another poor soul who believes he can instruct those little monsters?"

"My nephews are not monsters." Olympia gave the older woman a disapproving frown. "Mrs. Bird, this is

Mr. Chillhurst. Uncle Artemis sent him to me and I believe he is going to prove extremely helpful. Mr. Chillhurst, this is Mrs. Bird, my housekeeper."

There was nothing about Mrs. Bird that put one in mind of a delicate, winged creature of the air, Jared thought. She was a robust woman with a heavy face and a large nose who looked as if she had spent her entire life with both feet flat on the ground. There was a look of wary suspicion in her faded eyes.

"Well, well, well." Mrs. Bird set the tray down on the desk with a clatter. She peered at Jared as she poured the tea. "So those three hellions upstairs were right. Ye look more like a bloodthirsty pirate than a tutor, Mr. Chillhurst."

"Do I, indeed?" Jared's brows rose at the housekeeper's familiar manner but he noticed that Olympia apparently considered nothing amiss. He accepted the cup and saucer with cool politeness.

"No matter." Mrs. Bird gave him a considering look. "It'll take someone who can handle a cutlass and a pistol to keep them rascals in line. Nigh broke the last three men o' learning that Miss Olympia hired, they did."

Olympia glanced quickly at Jared. Her eyes filled with anxious alarm. "Really, Mrs. Bird, you mustn't give Mr. Chillhurst a bad impression."

"Why not?" Mrs. Bird snorted. "He'll find out the truth soon enough. Be interestin' to see how long he lasts. Going to put him up in the old gamekeeper's cottage like ye did the others?"

Olympia smiled at Jared. "Mrs. Bird is speaking of the little cottage at the foot of the lane. Perhaps you noticed it when you arrived?"

"I did. It will do nicely."

"Excellent." Olympia looked relieved. "Let's see now. What else do we need to discuss? Oh, yes. You're welcome to join us for meals. There is a room on the floor above which functions very nicely as a schoolroom. And of course you're free to make use of my library." She paused, apparently trying to recall anything she might have overlooked. "You may begin your duties in the morning."

Mrs. Bird rolled her eyes. "What about his wages?" She cast a sidelong glance of warning at Jared. "Ye'll have to get used to the fact that Miss Olympia ain't much good at keepin' accounts. Ye'll probably have to remind her about yer wages and such. Don't be shy about it."

Olympia glared at her. "That is quite enough, Mrs. Bird. You make me sound like a featherbrained idiot. As it happens, Mr. Chillhurst's wages have been paid in advance by Uncle Artemis. Is that not correct, Mr. Chillhurst?"

"There is no need to concern yourself with my wages, Miss Wingfield," Jared said gently.

Olympia shot a triumphant look at her housekeeper. "There, you see, Mrs. Bird?"

Mrs. Bird snorted loudly. She did not look entirely convinced but she let the matter drop. "If ye'll be joinin' the family at dinner, ye might like to know there's some claret and sherry in the cellar."

"Thank you," Jared said.

"Miss Sophy and Miss Ida always had a sip or two of one or t'other before dinner and a swallow of brandy afore they went to bed. Good for the digestion, y'know. Miss Olympia has carried on the tradition."

"Especially since my nephews arrived," Olympia muttered.

"Thank you, Mrs. Bird." Jared smiled fleetingly at Olympia. "I could do with a glass or two of claret before dinner tonight. It's been a long trip."

"I reckon." Mrs. Bird walked heavily toward the door. "Wonder how long ye'll last?"

"Long enough," Jared said. "By the way, Mrs. Bird, what time is dinner served in this household?"

"How should I know? Depends on when Miss Olympia can get those three hellions to the table. They're never on time for meals. Always got an excuse."

"I see," Jared said. "In that case, Mrs. Bird, dinner will be at six tonight and every other night. Anyone who does not appear at the table on time will not eat. Is that clear?"

Mrs. Bird glanced back at him with a somewhat startled look. "Aye, it's clear enough."

"Excellent, Mrs. Bird. You may go now."

She glared at him. "And just who's givin' the orders around here now, I'd like to know?"

"Until further notice, I am," Jared said coolly. He saw Olympia's eyes start to widen. "On behalf of my employer, of course."

"Bah. I doubt ye'll be givin' orders long," Mrs. Bird declared as she stalked out of the room.

Olympia bit her lip. "Pay no attention to her, Mr. Chillhurst. She's a bit brusque, but she means well. Indeed, I don't know how I could have gotten along without her. She and her late husband were employed by Aunt Sophy and Aunt Ida for years, and she has stayed on with me. I am quite grateful to her. Not everyone wants to work for me, you see. I am considered rather odd here in Upper Tudway."

Jared saw the faint flicker of old loneliness that appeared in her eyes. "Upper Tudway is no doubt unaccustomed to having a woman of the world in its midst," he said.

Olympia smiled wryly. "Very true. That's what Aunt Sophy and Aunt Ida always used to say."

"Do not concern yourself. I'm sure Mrs. Bird and I will deal well enough with each other." Jared took a sip of his tea. "There is another matter I wish to speak to you about, Miss Wingfield."

Olympia's gaze narrowed in concern. "Have I forgotten something? I fear Mrs. Bird is correct. I am always overlooking some annoying detail that seems extremely trivial to me but which everyone else believes to be vital for one reason or another."

"You have overlooked nothing of importance," Jared assured her.

"Thank goodness." Olympia relaxed back in her chair.

"Your uncle asked me to inform you that in addition to the items that are to be sold, he has also sent along several volumes. One of them is an old diary."

Olympia's natural air of delightful distraction vanished in the blink of an eye. Her attention was riveted. "What did you say?"

"There is a volume known as the Lightbourne diary in the shipment of goods, Miss Wingfield." Jared did not have to wait long for the reaction.

"*He found it.*" Olympia sprang to her feet. Her face was flushed with excitement. Her eyes glowed with the brilliance of a turquoise flame. "Uncle Artemis found the Lightbourne diary."

"That is what he said."

"Where is it?" Olympia demanded eagerly.

"Packed in one of the trunks or crates I brought with me in the carriage. I'm not certain which one."

Not that he hadn't been tempted to look for it. But the truth was, there had been no opportunity to stop and search for the diary after the ship had made port. Jared had secured a carriage and the two guards, loaded the crates and trunks aboard, and traveled through the night from Weymouth. He had not stopped until he had arrived at Upper Tudway. The risk of highwaymen had seemed preferable to the risk of having the goods pilfered by thieves at an inn.

"We must unpack the carriage at once. I cannot wait to see the diary." Olympia was bubbling over with enthusiasm and excitement.

She rounded the desk, picked up her skirts, and flew toward the door.

Jared watched, bemused, as she dashed out of the library. If he was going to be obliged to live in this chaotic household for a time, he would have to establish his own rules and prepare to enforce them, he told himself. There was no substitute for an orderly routine.

He must start as he intended to go on.

Alone in the library, Jared calmly finished his tea. Then he put down his cup, pulled out his watch, and consulted the time. Ten more minutes before his young charges were due downstairs.

He got deliberately to his feet and walked toward the door.

Chapter 3

Several days later Mrs. Bird barged into the library with a tea tray.

"Strikes me that it's a mite too quiet around here lately." She plunked the tray down onto Olympia's desk. "Downright eerie and that's a fact."

Olympia reluctantly tore her attention away from the complicated language of Claire Lightbourne's diary. She scowled at Mrs. Bird. "Whatever do you mean? I thought the silence was rather pleasant. I vow this is the first real peace we've had since my nephews arrived."

The past few days had been nothing short of halcyon as far as Olympia was concerned. She could hardly believe the difference Jared Chillhurst had wrought in the household in such a short period of time.

There had been no muddy boots in the hall, no escaped frogs in her desk drawer, and no squabbling within hearing distance. All three boys had been on time for every meal and, even more impressive, each one had been neat and clean.

"T'ain't natural." Mrs. Bird poured tea into the single cup on the tray. "What's that pirate doin' up there in the schoolroom with those young hellions, I ask ye?"

"Mr. Chillhurst is not a pirate," Olympia said crisply. "I will thank you to cease referring to him as such. He is a tutor. An excellent one, judging by what we have seen thus far."

"Hah. He's up there torturin' them poor boys, that's what he's doin'. I'll wager he threatened to make 'em walk the plank if they don't behave."

Olympia smiled briefly. "We don't have a plank around here."

Mrs. Bird squinted. "Well, then, mayhap he's threatened to beat 'em with a cat o'nine tails if they don't do what he tells 'em."

"I'm certain Robert would have come to me immediately if Mr. Chillhurst had made dire threats," Olympia said.

"Not if that pirate threatened to slit poor Robert's throat for talkin'."

"Oh, for pity's sake, Mrs. Bird. You've been saying all along that my nephews needed a firm hand."

Mrs. Bird set the pot down on the tray and leaned over the desk. "Didn't say I wanted to see 'em terrified into obedience. When all is said and done, they're good boys."

Olympia tapped her quill pen on the desk. "Do you really believe Mr. Chillhurst has threatened them with violence in order to get them to behave properly?"

"Ain't nothin' else except a threat of violence would have gotten results like this in such a short period of time, if you ask me." Mrs. Bird looked meaningfully up at the ceiling.

Olympia followed her gaze. There were no thumps, bumps, or distant shouts to be heard from the floor above. The abnormal silence was a trifle unnerving, she thought.

"I suppose I had better see what is going on." Olympia rose reluctantly and closed the diary.

"Ye'll have to be crafty about it," Mrs. Bird warned. "Mr. Chillhurst appears to be bent on makin' a good impression on ye. Likely he cannot afford to lose the position. If he knows yer observin' him, he'll be on his best behavior."

"I'll be cautious." Olympia took a hasty sip of hot tea to fortify herself. When she was finished, she set the cup down and started determinedly for the door.

"One more thing afore I forget," Mrs. Bird called after her. "Squire Pettigrew sent a message around earlier sayin' he's back from London. He'll be callin' this afternoon. No doubt wants to help ye out with that last shipment of goods."

Olympia paused in the doorway. "Oh, dear. I forgot to notify him that I will no longer need his assistance in such matters."

Mrs. Bird frowned. "Why ever not?"

"Mr. Chillhurst has said he will handle those sorts of annoying little details for me."

Mrs. Bird's expression went from a disapproving frown to a look of genuine alarm. "Here now, what's that supposed to mean?"

"Just what it sounds like, Mrs. Bird. Mr. Chillhurst has kindly offered to take charge of disposing of Uncle Artemis's latest shipment."

"Ain't sure I like the sound of that offer. What if Chillhurst makes off with the goods?"

"Rubbish. If he had been going to do that, he would never have brought them to us in the first place. He would have absconded with them upon his arrival in Weymouth."

"Well, mayhap he intends to cheat ye, then," Mrs. Bird warned. "And how would ye know if he did? Ye'd only have his word that he got the best price he could for the lot. I told ye, the man looks like a pirate. Best have Squire Pettigrew handle things, just as he has in the past."

Olympia lost her patience. "I'm quite certain we can trust Mr. Chillhurst. Uncle Artemis did." She sailed through the door before Mrs. Bird could respond.

Out in the hall, Olympia picked up the skirts of her ankle-length printed muslin gown and went quickly up the stairs.

She paused on the landing and listened. It was quiet even up here.

She tiptoed down the hall to the schoolroom and put her ear to the door. The deep-sea rumble of Jared's voice filtered softly through the heavy wooden panels.

"It was an ill-conceived scheme from the start," Jared said. "But Captain Jack was prone to wild notions. The predilection later proved to be an unfortunate family trait."

"Does that mean there were other pirates in Captain Jack's family?" Ethan asked eagerly.

"Captain Jack preferred to be called a buccaneer," Jared said sternly. "And while I do not believe that there were any more in the clan, I fear there were several descendents suspected of engaging in the free-trade."

"What's the free-trade?" Hugh demanded.

"Smuggling," Jared explained dryly. "Captain Jack's family seat was on the Isle of Flame. It's an exceedingly beautiful place but very remote. Robert, show us where the Isle of Flame is located."

"Here," Robert said enthusiastically. "Off the Devon coast. See? There's a tiny dot right there."

"Very good, Robert." Jared said. "As you will see, the isle is an excellent site for smuggling. Convenient enough to the coasts of France and Spain, yet quite remote from the authorities. The preventive service is seldom seen in the vicinity and the local inhabitants may be counted upon not to talk to outsiders."

"Tell us about the smugglers," Ethan said.

"No, I want to hear about Captain Jack's plan to cross the Isthmus of Panama first," Robert said.

"Yes, tell us about the buccaneers' scheme to capture a Spanish galleon, Mr. Chillhurst," Hugh said eagerly. "You can tell us about the smugglers tomorrow."

"Very well," Jared agreed. "But first you should know not only how idiotic the notion was, but also how dangerous. The Isthmus of Panama is extremely treacherous terrain. It is densely forested and filled with many strange and deadly creatures. Many men have died trying to reach the sea on the other side."

"Why did Captain Jack and his crew want to cross the isthmus in the first place?" Ethan asked. "Why didn't they stay in the West Indies?"

"Gold," Jared said succinctly. "Captain Jack had a partner at the time. They had heard tales of the legendary treasure that Spain was routinely transporting from its colonies in America. The two buccaneers decided to see if they could slip across the Isthmus of Panama with a band of men, capture a Spanish ship or two, and get rich immediately."

"Bloody hell," Robert whispered in awe. "What an exciting venture. I wish I could have been with Captain Jack when he made the trip."

Olympia could stand it no longer. The words *leg-*

endary treasure and *buccaneers* dazzled her. She was as enthralled as her nephews by Jared's tale. She opened the door very quietly and slipped stealthily into the room.

Ethan, Hugh, and Robert were grouped around the large globe that stood near the window. They did not look up as Olympia crept into the schoolroom. Their entire attention was riveted on the globe.

Jared was with them. He had one hand on the globe. In his other hand he gripped his dagger. The point of the blade rested in the region of the West Indies.

Olympia frowned at the sight of the dagger. She had not noticed it during the past two days. Jared no longer wore it strapped to his thigh as he had when he arrived. She had presumed he had packed it away in one of his trunks. But this morning he had obviously brought it into the classroom and there was no doubt but that he held the old blade with a certain casual ease.

He looks altogether dangerous, as usual, Olympia thought as she studied his grim features in the morning light. If one did not know him better, one might be rather wary. But she was getting to know him very well indeed because he had taken to joining her in the library after dinner in the evenings.

Jared had immediately established a pleasant habit of sharing a glass of brandy with her before retiring to the old gamekeeper's cottage. Last night he had read for a while and then talked at some length about his travels. Olympia had hung on every word.

"Are all tutors as widely traveled as yourself, sir?" she had asked.

Jared had given her an unreadable look. "Ah, no. I have been rather fortunate in that regard. I have worked for some people whose business ventures frequently took them abroad. My employers chose to travel with their families."

Olympia nodded sagely. "Naturally they would wish their children's tutor to accompany them on an extended journey. What a wonderful career you selected for yourself."

"It it only lately that I have come to fully appreciate it." Jared rose from his chair, picked up the brandy decanter, and poured more of the amber liquid into her glass. "I see you have a rather nice chart depicting the South Seas on your wall."

"I have done a great deal of research on legends that originate in that part of the world." What with the combined effects of the fire and the brandy, Olympia was feeling pleasantly warm and quite relaxed. *A woman of the world conversing with a man of the world,* she thought with satisfaction.

Jared poured a bit more brandy into his own glass and replaced the decanter on the table. "One of my more interesting trips took me to a number of islands in that region," he said thoughtfully. He sank back into the depths of his chair.

"Really?" Olympia gazed at him in wonder. "That must have been thrilling."

"Oh, it was." Jared touched his fingertips together. "There are a variety of interesting legends from that part of the world, as you are no doubt well aware. One in particular rather intrigued me."

"I should love to hear about it," Olympia whispered. The library seemed to be filled with a dreamlike quality, as if the entire room, complete with Jared and herself inside, had been transported to another place and another time.

"It has to do with a pair of lovers who were not allowed to marry because the young woman's father was opposed to the match."

Olympia took another sip of brandy. "How very sad. What became of the lovers?"

"Their passion was such that they were determined to be together," Jared said. "So they arranged to meet secretly at night on the beach of a hidden cove."

"I suppose they talked until dawn." Olympia said wistfully. "No doubt they whispered words of poetry to each other. Confided their most intimate secrets. Dreamed of a future together."

Jared looked at her. "Actually, they spent the time making passionate love."

Olympia blinked. "On a beach?"

"Yes."

Olympia cleared her throat. "But wouldn't that have been somewhat uncomfortable? I mean what with the sand and all?"

Jared smiled slightly. "What is a little sand to a pair of lovers who are desperate for each other?"

"Yes, of course," Olympia said hastily. She hoped she had not sounded too terribly naive.

"And besides, this was a very special beach. It was sacred to a certain island deity who is said to have taken pity on the lovers."

Olympia was still not entirely convinced that making love in the sand was a particularly sound notion, but she certainly did not intend to argue the matter. "Do go on, sir. Tell me the rest of the legend."

"One night the lovers were discovered by the woman's irate father. He killed the young man."

"How terrible. What happened?"

"The young woman was grief-stricken, naturally. She waded out into the sea and disappeared. The deity in charge of the beach was outraged. He punished the young woman's father by turning all the sand on the beach into pearls."

"That was a punishment?" Olympia asked, startled.

"Yes." Jared smiled coolly. "The man was so excited about the discovery of the pearl beach that he went home to rouse the rest of his family. But the deity cast a magic spell over the cove, making it invisible to all those who searched for it."

"So this pearl beach was never found?"

Jared shook his head. "To this day the islanders still talk of it. Many have searched for it. But no one has ever seen it. It's said that it can only be discovered by a pair of lovers whose passion is as great as the two who used to meet there and make love in the moonlight."

Olympia sighed. "Just imagine risking all for love, Mr. Chillhurst."

"I have begun to believe that a great passion is like a great legend," Jared said quietly. "It is worth any risk."

A shiver coursed through Olympia. She felt first hot and then cold. "You are no doubt correct, sir. In any case, I thank you for the tale. I have never heard it and it is a lovely legend."

Jared looked deeply into her eyes. Something dark and disturbing moved in his own gaze. "Yes," he said softly. "Quite lovely."

In that moment Olympia could almost believe that he was speaking of her, not the legend. A sense of excitement stirred deep within her. It was similar to the thrill she got when she pursued a legend, but it was far more powerful. It left her feeling oddly shaken, a little giddy.

"Mr. Chillhurst . . . ?"

Jared removed his watch from his pocket. "I see it is very late," he said with obvious regret. "It is time I went back to my cottage. Perhaps tomorrow night I shall have an opportunity to describe a rather unusual custom that was practiced by the inhabitants of another South Seas island which I chanced to visit."

"I should like that very much," Olympia breathed.

"Good night, Miss Wingfield. I shall see you at breakfast."

"Good night, Mr. Chillhurst."

A shimmering sense of longing had welled up within Olympia as she accompanied Jared to the front door. She had stood watching as he walked off into the night and became one with it.

And then she had gone to bed and dreamed of being kissed by Jared on a beach scattered with pearls.

Now, in the bright light of day, she listened to him tell tales to her nephews and realized that Jared had very quickly become an important part of her small household. She was learning a great deal about this man who had the face of a pirate and she was finding that she liked him very much. *Too much perhaps*, she thought.

She must not forget that someday Jared would leave and she would again be alone with her library and no other adult companion with whom she could share the intellectual pleasures it contained.

At that moment Jared glanced up and saw her standing just inside the schoolroom. The corner of his mouth curved faintly.

"Good morning, Miss Wingfield. Was there something you wanted?"

"No, no," Olympia said quickly. "Please carry on. I merely wished to observe the lesson."

"By all means." Jared indicated the globe. "We are studying geography this morning."

"So I see." Olympia took a step closer.

Ethan grinned. "We are learning all about the West Indies, Aunt Olympia."

"And about a pirate named Captain Jack," Robert added.

Jared cleared his throat slightly. "It should be noted that Captain Jack was a buccaneer, not a pirate."

"What's the difference?" Hugh demanded.

"Very little, in point of fact," Jared said dryly. "But some people are quite insistent upon the distinction. Buccaneers sailed with a commission. In theory they were authorized by the crown or by local authorities in the West Indies to attack enemy ships. But it got rather complicated at times. Why was that, do you suppose, Robert?"

Robert straightened his shoulders. "Because so many different countries have colonies in the West Indies, I expect, sir."

"Precisely." Jared smiled approvingly. "Back in Captain Jack's time there were English, French, Dutch, and Spanish vessels in the region."

"And the buccaneers were not supposed to attack the ships and towns of their home countries, I'll wager," Ethan said. He frowned. "That would mean the English would have sailed against the French and the Spanish and the Dutch. The French would have attacked the English and the Spanish and the Dutch."

"It does sound rather complicated," Olympia said. She abandoned any pretense of being an interested observer of Jared's instructional methods. She hurried across the room to join her nephews. "What was this about a venture across the Isthmus of Panama in search of treasure?"

Jared's smile was slow and mysterious. "Would you care to join us while I tell the tale, Miss Wingfield?"

"Yes, indeed," Olympia said. She smiled gratefully at Jared. "I should like that very much. I am quite interested in such tales."

"I understand," Jared said softly. "Come a little closer, Miss Wingfield. I would not want you to miss a single thing."

Squire Pettigrew arrived at three o'clock that afternoon. Olympia was back in the library when she heard the clatter of the gig's wheels in the drive. She rose from the desk and went to the window to watch Pettigrew alight from his carriage.

Pettigrew was a heavily built man in his late forties. At one time he had been accounted a handsome fellow and he continued to act as if every female in the neighborhood still found him irresistible. Olympia did not understand what anyone had ever seen in the squire.

The truth was, Pettigrew could be a dreadful bore although Olympia was much too polite to say so. She knew that she was probably not a very good authority on the subject. After all, she found the majority of the males in Upper Tudway extremely dull and uninspiring. Their pursuits and interests rarely coincided with hers and men did tend to lecture so to females. Pettigrew was no exception. As far as Olympia could ascertain, his chief passions consisted of hounds, hunting, and farming.

Nevertheless, she knew very well that she was indebted to him for handling her uncle's periodic shipments and she was truly grateful for everything Pettigrew had done for her.

The library door opened just as Olympia sat down again. Pettigrew swaggered into the room. The strong scent of the eau de cologne he favored wafted ahead of him.

Pettigrew traveled quite frequently to London and took advantage of the opportunity to stay abreast of current fashion. This afternoon he was attired in a pair of trousers that were trimmed with an array of small pleats. His frock coat was extremely snug and cropped at the waist. The back of the coat fell in two long tails that reached his knees. Beneath it he wore an elaborately pleated shirt. His cravat was so high and rigid that Olympia suspected it was held in place with some sort of stiffener.

"Good afternoon, Miss Wingfield." Pettigrew gave her what was undoubtedly meant to be a charming smile as he walked toward the desk. "You're looking very fine today."

"Thank you, sir. Please sit down. I have some interesting news for you."

"Do you indeed?" Pettigrew swept the long tails of his coat aside with a practiced motion of his hand and sat down. "I suspect you are about to tell me of your uncle's latest shipment of goods. Never fear, my dear, I have already received word of it and stand ready to assist you, as always."

"That is very kind of you, sir, but the good news is that I will no longer require your services for such matters."

Pettigrew blinked rapidly several times as if he had a speck in his eye and then he went very still. "I beg your pardon?"

Olympia smiled warmly. "You have been extremely helpful, sir, and I am most grateful to you, but I cannot impose upon you any longer."

Pettigrew frowned. "Now see here, Miss Wingfield, I do not consider it an imposition to assist you in disposing of those shipments. Indeed, I feel it is my duty to aid you. I would be remiss in my obligations as a friend and neighbor were I to allow you to fall into the hands of the sort of unscrupulous scoundrels who would not hesitate to take advantage of an innocent such as yourself."

"You need not fear for Miss Wingfield," Jared said very quietly from the doorway. "She is in good hands."

"What the devil?" Pettigrew turned swiftly to face the door. He stared at Jared. "Who are you, sir? What are you talking about?"

"I'm Chillhurst."

Olympia sensed a sudden tension in the air between the two men. She hastened to diffuse it by making introductions. "Mr. Chillhurst is my nephews' new tutor. He has only been with us for a few days but already he has done wonders. The boys have been studying geography all morning and I'll wager they now know more about the West Indies than any other boy in Upper Tudway. Mr. Chillhurst, allow me to present Squire Pettigrew."

Jared closed the door behind himself and walked to the desk. "Mrs. Bird told me that he had arrived."

Pettigrew's gaze was fixed on the black velvet patch that covered Jared's eye. Then he scowled at Jared's bare throat and the open collar of his shirt. "Damme, man, you don't look like any tutor I ever saw. What is going on here?"

Olympia was irritated. "Mr. Chillhurst most certainly is a tutor. A very excellent one. Uncle Artemis sent him to me."

"Wingfield sent him?" Pettigrew shot her an annoyed look. "Are you quite certain?"

"Yes, of course, I'm certain." Olympia strove for patience. "And as it happens, Mr. Chillhurst is skilled in financial matters. He has offered to act as my man of affairs. That is why I shall no longer be requiring your assistance in disposing of my uncle's shipment, sir."

"*Your man of affairs.*" Pettigrew was dumbfounded. "Now see here, you don't need a man of affairs. You've got me to look after your finances and such."

Jared sat down. He rested his elbows on the arms of the chair and steepled his fingers. "You heard Miss Wingfield, Pettigrew. She will no longer be requiring your services."

Pettigrew shot him a scathing glance and turned back to Olympia. "Miss Wingfield, I have warned you often of the dangers of dealing with persons whose backgrounds you know nothing about."

"Mr. Chillhurst is a perfectly respectable person," Olympia said firmly. "My uncle would not have employed him to work in this household if he were not a man of excellent character."

Pettigrew gave Jared a disparaging look. "Have you reviewed his references, Miss Wingfield?"

"My uncle took care of that sort of thing," Olympia said.

Jared smiled coldly at Pettigrew. "I assure you, sir, there is no cause for concern. I shall see to it that Miss Wingfield realizes a fair profit off the goods her uncle sent to her."

"And who's to say what that fair profit is?" Pettigrew retorted. "Miss Wingfield will have no way of knowing if you take advantage of her, will she? She will have to depend upon your word in the matter."

"Just as she has been forced to rely upon your word in the past," Jared said softly.

Pettigrew drew himself up. "Are you implying anything, sir? Because if so, let me inform you that I will not tolerate it."

"Not at all." Jared tapped his fingertips together in a slow, silent drumroll. "Miss Wingfield tells me that she realized nearly two hundred pounds off the last shipment."

"That is quite correct," Pettigrew said stiffly. "And she was extremely lucky to get that much out of it. Why, if it had not been for my contacts in London, she would probably have received no more than a mere hundred or hundred and fifty pounds."

Jared inclined his head. "It will be interesting to see if I can do as well on her behalf as you have done, will it not? Perhaps I shall even be able to improve upon your efforts."

"I say," Pettigrew sputtered indignantly. "I don't care for your attitude, sir."

"Your opinion of me is neither here nor there, is it?" Jared observed mildly. "But I assure you that I will pay close attention to Miss Wingfield's financial affairs. After all, she needs the money, does she not? A single woman burdened with the responsibility of three young boys can certainly use all the income she can get."

Pettigrew's heavy face turned an unpleasant shade of red. "Now see here, sir, I cannot allow you to take possession of Miss Wingfield's goods without so much as a by-your-leave. You might very well up and disappear with them for all we know."

"The goods have already disappeared, so to speak," Olympia said. "Mr. Chillhurst had them sent off to London this very morning."

Pettigrew's eyes widened in astonished fury. "Miss Wingfield, surely you have not done anything so rash as to allow this man to whisk your goods out of Upper Tudway."

Jared continued to tap his fingertips together. "They are safe enough, Pettigrew. They were dispatched under guard. A trusted acquaintance of mine will receive them when they reach London and see to their disposal."

"Good God, man." Pettigrew rounded on him. "What have you done? This is outright thievery. I shall inform the magistrate at once."

Olympia jumped to her feet. "That is quite enough. Mr. Pettigrew, I am satisfied that Mr. Chillhurst has only my best interests at heart. I really do not wish to be rude, sir, but I must insist that you cease prattling on in such an insulting fashion. Mr. Chillhurst might take offense."

"Yes." Jared drummed his fingertips together and

looked as if he were contemplating the possibility. "I might."

Pettigrew's mouth worked for a moment but no words came out. Then he heaved himself up out of the chair and glowered at Olympia. "So be it, Miss Wingfield. If you choose to put your trust in a stranger rather than in a neighbor you have known for years, that is your affair. But I expect that you will regret this reckless piece of work. Your new tutor looks altogether too much like a bloody pirate to me and that's a fact."

Olympia was outraged. Jared was, after all, in her employ. It was up to her to defend him. "Really, Mr. Pettigrew, you go too far. I cannot allow you to speak in such a fashion to anyone on my staff. Good day to you, sir."

"Good day, Miss Wingfield." Pettigrew stalked to the door. "I only hope you have not lost a packet by trusting this . . . this person."

Olympia watched the door until it closed behind Pettigrew. Then she risked a quick, awkward glance at Jared. She was relieved to see that he had stopped tapping his fingers together. She suspected that the mannerism did not bode well.

"I apologize for that unfortunate little scene," Olympia said. "Pettigrew means well, but I believe he was somewhat insulted by the fact that I have turned my uncle's shipment over to you to handle."

"He called me a pirate."

Olympia cleared her throat delicately. "Yes, but please do not take offense. He is not entirely to blame for making such a remark. Indeed, Mrs. Bird commented upon the resemblance earlier. There is something about you, sir, that does tend to put one in mind of a pirate."

Jared's mouth curved. "I am glad that you are able to look beneath the surface, Miss Wingfield."

"Aunt Sophy and Aunt Ida taught me not to judge by appearances."

An enigmatic expression lit Jared's gaze. "I hope you will not be disappointed by the man you discover beneath the pirate's face."

"Oh, no," Olympia whispered. "I could not possibly be disappointed, sir."

The following evening Olympia sat at her desk and contemplated Jared's hair. The heavy, midnight black stuff was brushed back behind his ears and reached his collar. There was no question but that the style was unfashionable and that it contributed to Jared's rather savage appearance. But Olympia did not care. All she wanted to do was run her fingers through it.

Never in her life had she wanted to run her fingers through a man's hair.

Jared was sitting in an armchair in front of the fire, his booted feet stretched out in front of him. He was reading a book that he had selected from a nearby shelf.

The glow from the hearth etched his already stern features into even harsher lines. He had discarded his coat after dinner. Olympia had grown accustomed to the lack of a cravat but she found it almost overwhelming to be in the same room with Jared when he was in his shirtsleeves.

The disturbing sense of intimacy made her feel lightheaded. Whispering shivers of awareness coursed through her. She could not help but wonder if Jared was feeling anything at all other than tired after a long day.

It was nearly midnight but he still showed no signs of taking his leave. Mrs. Bird had retreated to her room after dinner. Ethan, Hugh, and Robert had gone to bed hours ago. Minotaur had been banished to the kitchen. Olympia was alone with Jared and she was consumed with a strange, unfamiliar restlessness. The feelings had been increasing in intensity every night since Jared's arrival. As far as she could tell, he was not uncomfortable at all with these intimate evenings together in the library.

Olympia had a sudden urge to talk to him. She hesitated and then closed the Lightbourne diary with a loud snap.

Jared looked up from his book and smiled quizzically. "Making progress, Miss Wingfield?"

"I believe so," Olympia said. "Most of the entries are quite prosaic. On the surface, it's merely a journal of daily events. It appears to cover the period of Miss Lightbourne's engagement and the first few months of her marriage to a man named Mr. Ryder."

Jared's gaze was enigmatic. "Mr. Ryder?"

"She seems very happy with him." Olympia smiled wistfully. "She calls him her 'beloved Mr. Ryder.' "

"I see."

"In fact, that's the only way in which she refers to him, even though he's her husband. Rather odd, but there you have it. She must have been a very proper sort of lady."

"So it would seem." There was an odd note in Jared's voice. He sounded almost relieved.

"As I said, for the most part the journal appears quite ordinary, except for the fact that it is written in a combination of English, Latin, and Greek. But every few pages I come across an odd series of numbers mixed in with a phrase that seems to make little sense. I believe those numbers and words are the clues for which I am searching."

"It sounds rather complicated but I suppose that is the way with codes."

"Yes." Olympia detected the lack of interest in his tone. She knew she should change the subject.

She was beginning to realize that, for some reason, the mystery of the Lightbourne diary held no intellectual appeal for Jared. In fact, he appeared to be positively bored by it. She was rather disappointed because she would have liked very much to discuss her discoveries with him.

Still, she could hardly complain if he wished to avoid that one topic, Olympia thought. Jared was, after all, more than happy to converse about virtually any other matter.

"You are at ease with Latin and Greek?" Jared asked casually.

"Oh, yes," Olympia assured him. "Aunt Sophy and Aunt Ida instructed me in both."

"You miss your aunts, do you not?"

"Very much. Aunt Ida died three years ago. Aunt Sophy followed her within six months. They were the only real family I had until my nephews arrived."

"You have been alone for some time."

"Yes." Olympia hesitated. "One of the things I miss most is the conversations we were all accustomed to share in the evenings. Do you know what it is like to have no one about with whom you can converse, Mr. Chillhurst?"

"Yes, Miss Wingfield," he said quietly. "I understand very well. I have felt the lack of such a close companion most of my life."

Olympia met his steady gaze and knew that he was giving her a small peek into his very soul. *Fair enough,* she thought. She had just given him a glimpse of her own. Her hand shook as she took a sip of her brandy.

"No one here in Upper Tudway is interested in the customs and legends of other lands," Olympia confided. "Not even Mr. Draycott it seems, although for a while I had hoped . . . " Her voice trailed off.

Jared's hand tightened around his glass. "Draycott

is not interested in such matters, Miss Wingfield, but I am."

"I sensed that you were, sir. You are truly a man of the world." Olympia gazed down into her brandy and then raised her head to look at him again. "Last night you mentioned that you had heard about some rather unusual customs practiced by peoples of a certain South Seas island."

"Ah, yes." Jared closed his book and gazed into the fire. "Very interesting courtship customs among the islanders."

"You promised to go into greater detail this evening, if you will recall," Olympia prompted.

"Certainly." Jared took a sip of his brandy and assumed a contemplative expression. "Apparently it is the habit among the islanders for the prospective suitor to take his lady to a place in the jungle that is considered to be magical. I'm told it's a lagoon where a large waterfall cascades down a wall of rock."

"I see. It sounds very lovely." Olympia took another sip of her brandy. "What happens next?"

"If the lady wishes to be courted she allows the man to kiss her beneath the waterfall." Jared turned the glass in his hands. "He gives her a token of his affections to signify his love. Legend has it that any union which begins in such a fashion will prove harmonious and fruitful."

"How interesting." Olympia wondered what it would be like to be kissed by Jared. He looked so lean and strong and powerful sitting here with her. He could doubtless pick her up with just one hand, she thought.

She wondered what it would feel like to have Jared lift her right up off her feet.

And hold her against his chest.

And cover her mouth with his own.

Appalled at the direction of her thoughts, Olympia

gave a start and fumbled with her glass. Brandy splashed on the desk.

"Are you all right, Miss Wingfield?"

"Yes, yes, of course." Olympia hurriedly righted the glass and set it down. Mortified by her own clumsiness, she dabbed at the spilled brandy with a handkerchief and cast about wildly for something intellectual to say.

"Speaking of interesting tokens of affection in the South Seas." Olympia concentrated on wiping up the last of the brandy. "I, myself, have recently read about a very unusual practice carried on in that part of the world."

"Have you, Miss Wingfield?"

"It seems that among the inhabitants of one of the islands it is the custom for the groom to present his bride with a large golden object in the shape of a phallus."

There was a deep silence from the other side of the room. Olympia glanced up, wondering if Jared had failed to hear her. A strange sensation went through her when she saw the disturbing expression on his face.

"A golden phallus?" Jared asked.

"Why, yes." Olympia dropped the brandy-soaked handkerchief onto the desk. "A very odd custom, wouldn't you say, sir? What do you suppose one does with a large golden phallus?"

"I cannot say offhand, but I suspect there is a very interesting answer to that question."

"No doubt." Olympia sighed. "But I shall probably never learn the answer because I shall likely never travel to the South Seas."

Jared put down his brandy glass and got to his feet. "As you have pointed out to me, Miss Wingfield, one does not have to travel widely in order to gain experience of the world."

"True enough." She watched him as he walked deliberately toward her. "Is there something the matter, Mr. Chillhurst?"

"Yes." He walked around her desk, reached down, and lifted Olympia straight up out of the chair. "There is something I wish to learn tonight, Miss Wingfield, and only you know the answer."

"Mr. Chillhurst." Olympia could hardly breathe. Excitement flashed through her. She felt as though she were about to melt. "What is your question, sir?"

"Will you kiss me, Miss Wingfield?"

Olympia was so shaken she could not find the words to respond. She did the only thing she could. She put her arms around Jared's neck and lifted her mouth to his in silent invitation.

She knew with sudden and absolute certainty that she had been waiting all of her life for this moment.

"Siren." Jared's arms closed very tightly around her as he crushed her lips beneath his own.

Chapter 4

Fire—a current of wild, scorching flame—cascaded through Olympia. She was at once stunned and exhilarated.

Jared's mouth was hot, persuasive, and demanding. He coaxed and conquered, cajoled and stole. Olympia trembled with reaction as his lips moved on hers.

She could feel the heat of his body and the strength of his hands. He was overwhelming her senses, but she felt no fear, only a boundless, thrilling delight. She wrapped her arms more tightly around his neck and held on for dear life as he plunged her into a sea of sensation.

Jared groaned when she opened her mouth under his in response to his gentle insistence.

"I cannot wait to hear your song, my sweet siren," he muttered against her lips and then he was inside.

The feel of his tongue touching hers startled Olympia. Instinctively she tried to retreat.

"Not yet," Jared whispered. "I want to taste you."

Olympia was captivated by the words. "Taste me?"

"Like this." Jared took her mouth again, savoring her with great thoroughness. "And this. My God, you are more intoxicating than the finest brandy."

Olympia's head fell back and her eyes closed. With joyous delight, she abandoned herself to the experience of being kissed by Jared.

She felt his arms shift, sliding under her knees and around her shoulders. She drew in a quick, startled breath when he lifted her and carried her across the room.

Olympia opened her eyes and looked up at Jared as he settled her onto the velvet cushions of the sofa. She saw the enthralling hunger in his stark expression and felt something deep inside her respond. She had never felt more gloriously alive.

"This is all very strange." She touched the side of his face with a sense of deep wonder. "I feel as if I have begun a mysterious voyage to an unknown land."

"It is the same for me." Jared's smile was slow and achingly sensual. He went down on one knee beside the sofa. "We shall make this journey together, my lovely siren."

Bereft of words, Olympia caught hold of his hand and drew it to her lips. She kissed his palm with a sense of blossoming joy.

"My God, you do not know what you are doing to me." Jared put his other hand on her throat and slowly, deliberately drew his fingers downward until his palm rested on her breast.

Olympia looked up at him from beneath her lashes. "This is passion, is it not, Jared?"

"Yes, Olympia. This is passion."

"I did not know it was so powerful a force," she whispered. "Now I understand why it lies at the heart of so many legends." She reached up to pull his mouth back down to hers.

Jared gently explored the shape of her breast with his cupped palm as he kissed her. Olympia's whole body throbbed with a strange eagerness. She stirred on the sofa, seeking even greater intimacy.

Jared sucked in his breath and began to undo the tapes of Olympia's gown. His powerful fingers trembled a little.

"Jared? Are you feeling as warm as I am?"

"I am not merely warm, my sweet siren. I burn."

"Oh, *Jared*. It is the same for me."

"I fear that the farther one travels on this voyage, the harder it is to turn back." Jared slipped her bodice down to her waist.

Olympia shivered from head to toe as he took her nipple into his mouth. "I do not ever want to turn back."

"Nor do I." Jared lifted his head to look very steadily down into her eyes. "But as much as I want you, I do not want to take you further than you would willingly go. If you would have me stop, tell me now while I am still able to do so."

"I'm five-and-twenty, Jared." Olympia caressed his cheek. "And I am a woman of the world, not a green girl fresh out of the schoolroom. I was taught to make my own decisions and not to be bound by ordinary notions of propriety."

He smiled slowly. "I was told that you were a most unusual female." He looked down at her bared breasts. "You are also a very beautiful one."

Olympia trembled in anticipation. She was torn between a desperate need to shield herself from his gaze and a fierce delight that he found her attractive. She had never thought of herself as beautiful but with Jared looking at her like this she felt glorious.

"Do you know how much I want you?" Jared stroked her nipple with his finger. "Can you even begin to guess?"

"I am glad, so very glad, that you want me, Jared." Olympia arched herself against his hand. She felt her breast swell and tighten. The peaks seemed unbearably sensitive to his touch.

"You are going to drive me to madness and I shall revel in the journey." Jared slid his hand down to her ankle and eased his palm up under the skirts of her gown.

Olympia felt his fingers on the inside of her leg and something deep within her start to throb. Liquid heat filled her. She suddenly needed to touch him and explore him just as he was touching and exploring her.

She fumbled with the fastenings of his shirt and finally got the garment parted. The sight of the dark, curling hair on his chest fascinated her. She flattened her hand against his skin and felt the taut, hard muscles beneath it.

"I knew that you would feel like this," she breathed in awed wonder. "So warm. So strong. So powerful."

"Olympia . . . My siren . . . "

Jared's hand tightened around her upper thigh just above her garter. He kissed the valley between her breasts.

A short, thin cry of fear and anguish pierced the shimmering cloud of passion that enveloped Olympia. She froze as if she had been dropped into a cold stream.

Jared's head came up swiftly. "What in God's name was that?"

"It's Hugh." Olympia struggled to sit up. Her fingers trembled as she attempted to refasten her gown. "I told you that he still occasionally suffers from bad dreams. I must go to him at once."

Jared got slowly to his feet. He stared down at her as she tried to set her gown to rights. "Allow me."

Grateful for the help, Olympia whirled about and stood impatiently as he adjusted the bodice of her muslin dress. "Please hurry. He gets so frightened."

" 'Tis done." Jared stepped back.

Olympia rushed toward the door, flung it open, and hurried across the hall to the staircase. She was aware that Jared was following her. When she glanced over her shoulder she saw that he was methodically refastening his shirt and stuffing it back into the waistband of his trousers.

When she reached the landing she ran down the hall toward Hugh's bedchamber. The door on the left opened as she went past. Robert appeared in his nightshirt.

"Aunt Olympia?" Robert rubbed the sleep from his eyes. "I thought I heard Hugh."

"You did," Olympia paused briefly to touch his shoulder. "Another nightmare, no doubt. Go back to bed, Robert. I'll tend to him."

Robert nodded and started to close the door. He stopped when he caught sight of Jared. "Mr. Chillhurst. What are you doing here, sir?"

"I was with your aunt when she heard Hugh cry out."

"Oh. Hugh gets scared, you know."

"Why?" Jared asked.

Robert shrugged. "He's afraid we'll be sent off any day to the next relation who will not want us. Ethan's just as frightened. I have told them that they must be brave about it, but they're still quite young, you see. It's hard for them to understand."

"No one is going to be packed off, Robert," Olympia said firmly. "I have told you that."

"Yes, Aunt Olympia," Robert said with a rare, ominous politeness.

Olympia sighed. She knew Robert did not entirely believe her yet, even though she had been reassuring him for the past six months. But there was no time to go over it all again tonight. She had Hugh to deal with first.

She went down the hall to Hugh's bedchamber. The boy's muffled sobs were audible through the door.

Olympia opened the door softly and walked into the shadowed room. In the pale moonlight that came through the window she could see the pathetic, huddled shape beneath the quilt.

"Hugh? Hugh, it's Aunt Olympia." She went over to the bed and sat down beside the little quivering mound. She pulled back the covers and put her hand on Hugh's shaking shoulders. "It's all right, my dear. Everything is all right. I'm here."

"*Aunt Olympia.*" Hugh sat up slowly and stared at her with wide, terrified eyes. Then he threw himself against her, sobbing. "I had the dream again."

"I know, dear. But that's all it was, just a dream." Olympia hugged him close and rocked him gently. "You're safe here with me. No one's going to send you away. This is your home now."

There was a soft scratching sound in the darkness. Light flared as Jared lit a candle. Hugh raised his head quickly from Olympia's shoulder.

"Mr. Chillhurst." Hugh blinked and ducked his head, clearly embarrassed to be caught with the evidence of tears on his face. "I didn't know you were still here."

"I was downstairs in the library when you had your dream," Jared said calmly. "Feeling better now?"

"Yes, sir." Hugh wiped his eyes with the back of his sleeve. "Ethan says I'm nothing but a bloody watering pot."

"Is that right?" Jared's brow rose. "I seem to recall Ethan watering a few daisies himself yesterday when he fell out of that tree."

Hugh brightened. "Yes, he did, didn't he?"

Olympia looked at Jared. "No one told me that Ethan fell out of a tree."

"There was no great harm done," Jared said easily. "A scraped knee was the extent of the damage."

"Mr. Chillhurst said there was no need to tell you about it," Hugh explained. "He said females are easily overset by the sight of blood."

"Did he, indeed?" Olympia shot Jared a reproving look. "Well, that only goes to show how much Mr. Chillhurst knows about females."

Jared's smile was dangerously amused. "Are you implying that my knowledge of the female of the species is deficient in some ways, Miss Wingfield?"

"That is precisely my implication, Mr. Chillhurst."

"Then perhaps I should endeavor to study the subject more closely. I am, after all, committed to the loftiest ideals of education and instruction. I will need a serviceable specimen for my studies, of course. Would you care to volunteer?"

Olympia was thrown into a strange confusion. She knew he was teasing her but she did not know what the teasing signified. Did he think less of her now that she had lain half-naked in his arms, she wondered.

Aunt Sophy and Aunt Ida had warned her that many men secretly disapproved of free-thinking women of the world even though those same men were quite content to become intimate with such females.

For a heart-stopping moment Olympia wondered if she had sadly misjudged Jared. Perhaps he was not the man she had believed him to be. Perhaps he was no different than Reginald Draycott or any of the other men of Upper Tudway. She felt herself turn hot and then cold and was grateful that only one candle illuminated the bedchamber.

"Are you all right, Aunt Olympia?" Hugh asked with a frown of concern.

Flustered, Olympia turned her attention back to him. "Of course. What about you?"

"Yes." He wiped his nose on the back of his sleeve. "I'm sorry I alarmed you."

"Everyone has nightmares now and again, Hugh," Jared said.

Hugh blinked. "Even you?"

"Even me."

"What kind of nightmares do you have?" Hugh demanded with keen interest.

Jared watched Olympia's averted profile. "I have one particular dream that has come back often during my life. In it I am on an uncharted island. I can see the distant sails of a ship in the harbor."

"What happens to you in the dream?" Hugh asked, wide-eyed.

"I know that the ship is about to sail and I know that I must be on it or I shall be left behind. But I cannot get to the ship. I keep looking at my watch but I know that no matter what I do, I will not be able to reach the vessel on my own. If someone does not rescue me, I will be left alone on my island."

Olympia looked up quickly. "I have had dreams like that," she whispered. "One knows one will be alone forever and one can hardly bear the knowledge."

"Yes. Very unpleasant." Jared stared down at her.

For an unguarded instant a remote loneliness as well as a deep, raging hunger gleamed in his shadowed gaze.

Olympia knew in that moment that she had not misjudged him after all. She and Jared shared a bond that could not yet be translated into words. She wondered if he understood that as clearly as she did.

"But it is only a dream, Aunt Olympia," Hugh assured her.

Olympia shook off the enthrallment that had descended on her and smiled at Hugh. "Quite right. Mere dreams. Now then, I believe that is quite enough discussion on the subject." She rose from the bed. "If you are certain that you will be able to go back to sleep, Hugh, we shall take our leave."

"I shall be fine, Aunt Olympia." Hugh snuggled down beneath the covers.

"Very well, then." Olympia bent down to kiss his forehead. Hugh grimaced as he always did, but he did not turn away. "We shall see you at breakfast."

Hugh waited until Olympia had put out the candle and started toward the door. "Aunt Olympia?"

"Yes, dear?" She turned to look at him.

"Robert says Ethan and I must be brave because you will likely grow tired of us eventually and decide to send us off to our relatives in Yorkshire. I was wondering how long you think it will be before you do grow tired of having us about the place."

Olympia's throat tightened. "I shall never grow tired of having you about the place. Indeed, I do not know how I got along before you came here to live with me."

"Is that true?" Hugh demanded eagerly.

"Oh, yes, Hugh," Olympia said with grave honesty. "It's true. Life was extremely dull around here before you and your brothers arrived. I can think of nothing that would dampen my spirits more than to have you three leave."

"Are you certain?" Hugh asked anxiously.

"I vow, if you and Ethan and Robert were to go away, I would quickly turn into a very odd bluestocking who would have to be content to find all her excitement in her books."

"That's not true," Hugh said with startling vehemence. "You are not odd. Charles Bristow said you were and I hit him because it's not true. It's *not*. You are very nice, Aunt Olympia."

Olympia was shocked. "Is that why you got into a fight with Charles Bristow? Because he said I was odd?"

Hugh's suddenly abashed glance slid to Jared. "I did not mean to tell you. Mr. Chillhurst said I was right not to discuss it with you when it happened."

"Quite right," Jared said. "A gentleman who engages in a duel to defend a lady's honor does not discuss the fight with her either before or after the occasion."

"Good grief." Olympia was outraged. "I will not tolerate anyone getting into a fight on my behalf. Is that quite clear?"

Hugh sighed. "It does not matter. I lost. But Mr. Chillhurst says he will teach me some tricks that will help me do a better job of it next time."

Olympia glared at Jared. "Did he, indeed?"

"Do not concern yourself, Miss Wingfield," Jared said.

"You keep saying that, but I am beginning to wonder if I had not better pay much closer attention to the lessons you are teaching to my nephews."

Jared arched a brow. "Perhaps it would be best if we discussed this alone, Miss Wingfield. Good night, Hugh."

"Good night, sir."

Olympia stepped stiffly out into the hall. Jared followed and quietly closed the door of the bedchamber.

"Really, Mr. Chillhurst," Olympia said in a low

voice, "I cannot allow you to encourage my nephews to get into brawls."

"I have no intention of doing any such thing. You must trust me, Miss Wingfield. It is my unshakable conviction that an intelligent man seeks nonviolent remedies for resolving confrontations whenever possible."

She peered at him. "Are you certain of that?"

"Quite certain. But the world is sometimes a less than peaceful place and a man must be able to defend himself."

"Hmm."

"And a woman's honor," Jared concluded gently.

"That is an old-fashioned notion of which I do not approve," Olympia said grimly. "Aunt Sophy and Aunt Ida taught me that a woman must take care of her own honor."

"Nevertheless, I hope you will continue to place your faith in my instructional methods." Jared caught hold of her hand and drew her to a halt. "And in me."

She studied his face in the light of the mirrored sconce. Her anger faded. "I do trust you, Mr. Chillhurst."

Jared's mouth curved slightly. "Excellent. Then I shall bid you good night, Miss Wingfield." He bent his head and kissed her, very hard, full on her mouth.

Before Olympia could even begin to respond to the kiss, it was over. Jared let her go. He went down the stairs without another word and let himself out the front door.

Olympia moved down the stairs slowly. She tried to identify the array of emotions that swirled about inside her but it was a wasted effort. There was too much that was new and strange and wondrous. It was dazzling and disquieting and, perhaps, a little dangerous.

She felt as though she had walked into the heart of a legend that had been written just for her.

With a dreamy, thoughtful smile, she slid the front door's big iron bolt home. Then she went into the library and picked up the Lightbourne diary. She stood in the center of the room for a few minutes savoring the memory of Jared's embrace. It was entirely appropriate that he had kissed her for the first time here in this very special place.

Olympia remembered her first glimpse of the library. It had been on that dark, rainy day when she had been left with Aunt Sophy and Aunt Ida. She had been cold and terrified and desperately determined not to reveal her fears as she was deposited on the doorstep of yet another anonymous relative.

The two years of being shuffled from one branch of the family to the other had left their marks. At the age of ten, Olympia had been too thin, too quiet, overly anxious, and prone to nightmares.

Some of the nightmares had taken human guise. There had been Uncle Dunstan, for example, who had watched her with a strange, glittering look in his eyes. One day he had followed her into a room and closed the door. He had started talking to her, telling her how pretty she was and then he had reached for her with his great, sweaty hands.

Olympia had screamed. Uncle Dunstan had released her at once and pleaded with her to stop screaming, but Olympia could not stop. She had screamed until Aunt Lilian had opened the door. Aunt Lilian had taken in the situation in a glance. She had said nothing, but the next morning, Olympia had found herself on her way to the next relative on the list.

And then there had been her cousin Elmer, a malicious boy three years older than Olympia. He had taken great delight in terrifying Olympia at every opportunity. He had leaped, screaming, out of dark nooks in the hall whenever she went past. He had set fire to the only doll she owned. He had threatened to lock her in the cellar. Within weeks Olympia had become fearful of every small movement. She had started at every shadow. The doctor had diagnosed her as having a nervous disease and she had promptly been dispatched to yet another relative.

The next relative in line had been Aunt Sophy. She and Aunt Ida had taken Olympia into the library that first day. They had given her hot chocolate and told her that she had a permanent home. Olympia had not believed them at first, of course, but she had tried to be polite about it.

Aunt Sophy had exchanged a knowing glance with Aunt Ida and then she had taken Olympia by the hand and led her over to the huge globe.

"You may come into the library any time you wish, Olympia," Aunt Sophy had said gently. "In this room you are free. Free to explore strange lands. Free to dream any dream that you care to dream. There is a whole world in this room, Olympia, and it is yours."

It had taken time, months, in fact, before Olympia had begun to blossom beneath the gentle nurturing she had received from Aunt Sophy and Aunt Ida. But blossom she had. And as she had grown more cheerful and more secure in her new home, she had spent endless hours in the library.

The library had quickly become her favorite place. It was her own, private world, a place where anything could happen. A place where even a legend might become real. It was a place where being alone did not matter quite so much.

It had been the perfect place to experience a pirate's kiss.

With the diary tucked under her arm, Olympia walked slowly back through the house. She checked the latches on the windows and put out the candles and then she went up the stairs to her bedchamber.

———

It was a fine evening. Jared could not recall a more pleasant night. The temperature was balmy, the moon was full, and the scents of late spring filled the air. It seemed to him that if he listened very carefully he might even hear faerie music in the meadow.

It was the sort of night that caused a man to be fully aware of his manhood, a night made for soft murmurs and the sweet sighs of desire. It was a night on which anything could happen.

A night when a man could seduce a siren.

Indeed, if young Hugh had not shattered the magic a short while earlier, Jared thought wryly, Olympia would have been his by now.

The vision of Olympia in the throes of passionate surrender caused his whole body to tighten once more. She had been so lovely lying there in the firelight, he thought. He ached with the memory.

Her hair had been a river of flame as it spilled across the sofa cushions. Her breasts had been firm and high, beautifully curved and tipped with plump nipples the color of pink coral. Her warm skin had been as soft as silk. Her mouth had been all honey and spice. The scent of her still filled Jared's head.

And she had wanted him, responded to him, abandoned herself to him.

A rush of hot satisfaction poured through Jared. It was the first time in his life that he had known for certain that a woman desired him simply because of himself. As far as Miss Olympia Wingfield was aware, after all, she had been seduced by her nephews' tutor.

Jared smiled. She found him exciting. She melted at his touch. Her gaze had reflected her sweet, honest passion.

There had been no coldness in her as there had been

in Demetria. And Jared was almost certain that there was no other lover in Olympia's life, at least not at the moment.

He could not be certain of the past because Olympia claimed to be a woman of the world. The implication was that she was not a virgin. But Jared did not think that she had ever known the depth of passion she had experienced tonight, even if she had lain with another man.

He had seen the surprise and wonder in her eyes, felt it in her touch. And he had known that he was the first man to arouse her to such a pitch of emotion. Even if there had been another man before him, Jared thought with sudden, soaring confidence, he could make her forget him.

Unlike Demetria.

Beware the Guardian's deadly kiss when you peer into its heart to find the key.

Olympia frowned over the phrase she had painstakingly pieced together. She did not understand it, but she was confident that she had just discovered the first clue in the diary.

She yawned as she scratched the words onto a sheet of foolscap. It was very late, nearly two in the morning. The candle had burned low beside the bed. She had been unable to sleep after Jared had left so she had attacked the diary with renewed vigor.

Beware the Guardian's deadly kiss when you peer into its heart to find the key.

Olympia had no notion of what the words meant but she sensed that they were important. She started to turn the page. A muffled bark from the vicinity of the kitchen made her pause.

Something had awakened Minotaur.

Alarmed, Olympia put down the diary and flung back the covers. She got out of the high bed, crossed the bedchamber to the fireplace, and grabbed an iron poker. Then she put on her wrapper.

She went to the door and opened it cautiously.

Silence flowed up from the first floor in a great wave. Minotaur had stopped barking. Whatever had disturbed him was gone, Olympia realized. Perhaps he had been awakened by a cat or a small animal that had come nosing around the kitchen door in search of scraps.

Nevertheless, she could not shake off the feeling that something was very wrong.

Clutching the poker, Olympia lifted the hem of her wrapper and went slowly down the stairs. Cool, night-scented air greeted her at the foot of the staircase. It seemed to be coming from the library.

Olympia went toward the library door which was still partially ajar, just as she had left it earlier. She used the poker to edge it fully open.

The strong smell of brandy made her wrinkle her nose. Frowning, she walked slowly into the room.

There was just enough light to see the drapes rippling slightly on the soft, evening breeze. Olympia shivered. She was very certain she had not left the window open. She was always careful to lock the ground floor doors and windows at night.

Of course, she reminded herself, tonight had not been a normal sort of night. Her mind had been whirling with thoughts of Jared when she had gone upstairs earlier. She could easily have forgotten to check the library windows.

The smell of brandy grew stronger as she walked toward the window. It was not until her bare feet touched the wet spot on the carpet that Olympia realized the truth.

Fear lanced through her. She fought it back and hurried over to the desk. She fumbled with the oil lamp and finally got it lit. The reassuring glow revealed that the room was empty.

It also showed very clearly that the damp spot on the carpet had been caused by the brandy that had spilled from the overturned decanter.

Olympia caught her breath. Someone had been prowling about in her library only a few minutes earlier.

Chapter 5

"What are we going to study this morning, Mr. Chillhurst?" Ethan asked as he spread jam on his toast.

Jared opened his appointment journal which lay beside his plate. He glanced at the entry he had made under *morning lessons*. "Geometry."

"Geometry." Ethan gave a heartfelt groan.

Jared ignored the reaction as he closed the journal. He glanced again at Olympia's tense, abstracted expression. Something was wrong but thus far he had no notion of what the problem was. A cold sensation went through him at the

thought that she might be having regrets about last night.

He had rushed her, he thought. He must give her more time to adjust to the passion that had sprung up like wildfire between them. He must not ruin everything by pushing too hard, too fast.

"I do not care for mathematics," Hugh announced.

"Especially geometry," Robert added. "We shall be stuck indoors all morning."

"No, we will not be indoors today." Jared looked at Mrs. Bird. "A bit more coffee, if you please, Mrs. Bird."

"Aye, sir." Mrs. Bird lumbered over to the table with the pot. She scowled at Ethan as she filled Jared's cup. "And just what do ye think yer doin' with that bit o' sausage?"

"Nothing," Ethan replied, his expression angelic.

"Yer feedin' it to that dog under the table, ain't ye?"

"No, I'm not."

"Yes, you are," Hugh said cheerfully. "I saw you."

"You cannot prove it," Ethan retorted.

"Don't have to prove it," Hugh said. "We all know it's true."

Olympia looked up, momentarily distracted from her quiet contemplation of the eggs on her plate. "Are you two arguing again?"

"The argument is finished," Jared said calmly. He gave the twins a quelling glance and they immediately subsided. "Mrs. Bird, perhaps it would be best if you removed Minotaur from the room."

"Right ye are, sir. I never did approve of having dogs in the house." Mrs. Bird went to the kitchen door and snapped her fingers at Minotaur.

The big dog reluctantly inched out from under the table and, with a last hopeful glance at Ethan, slunk into the kitchen.

"How are we going to study geometry outdoors, Mr. Chillhurst?" Robert asked.

"We will begin by measuring the distance across the stream without actually crossing it," Jared said. He watched as Olympia went back to concentrating on her eggs.

"How can you do that?" Ethan asked, his curiosity apparently piqued.

"I will show you," Jared said, his eyes still on Olympia's face. "And when you have the knack of it, I shall tell you the tale of how Captain Jack used the technique to find his way out of a jungle."

"A jungle in the Isthmus of Panama?" Hugh asked.

"No, this was a jungle on an island in the West Indies," Jared explained. He smiled to himself when Olympia glanced up, her attention caught at last. *Good old Captain Jack,* he thought ruefully.

"What was Captain Jack doing in the middle of an island jungle?" Ethan asked.

"Concealing a treasure chest, of course," Jared murmured.

Olympia's eyes widened with interest. "Did he ever go back to the island to dig up his chest?"

"I believe he did go back for that one," Jared said.

"Did Captain Jack really use geometry to find his way off the island?" Robert asked.

"Yes, he did." Jared took a sip of coffee and studied Olympia's expression over the rim of the cup. The unfocused look had returned to her eyes. She was lost in her thoughts again. Even the bit about Captain Jack had not held her for long this morning. Something was definitely wrong.

"Did Captain Jack slit a man's throat and leave his bones on the treasure chest as a warning to anyone who dug it up?" Hugh demanded.

Jared nearly choked on his coffee. "Where the devil did you get a notion like that?"

"I've heard that pirates always did that," Hugh said.

"I have told you, Captain Jack was a buccaneer, not a pirate." Jared drew his watch from his pocket and checked the time. "If you are finished, you may leave the table. I want to speak privately with your aunt. Run upstairs and gather some pencils and paper. I'll join you in a few minutes."

"Yes, sir," Robert said eagerly.

Chairs scraped loudly as the three youngsters scrambled to leave the room.

"One moment, if you please," Jared said quietly.

All three turned back obediently.

"Did you forget something, Mr. Chillhurst?" Robert asked.

"No, you did. All three of you forgot to excuse yourselves properly to your aunt."

"Sorry, sir." Robert sketched a little bow. "Please excuse me, Aunt Olympia."

"Beg pardon, Aunt Olympia," Hugh said. "Have to leave now."

"Excuse me, Aunt Olympia," Ethan sang out. "Got to prepare for our studies, you know."

Olympia blinked and smiled vaguely at all three. "Yes, of course. Have a pleasant morning."

There was another concerted rush to the door. Jared waited patiently until the room had been cleared. Then he gazed down the length of the table at Olympia.

She looked so very pretty sitting there in a shaft of warm sunlight, he thought. There was an astonishing sense of intimacy to be found in this business of sharing the morning meal with her. A now-familiar stab of desire went through him.

Today Olympia's striking, intelligent face was framed by the neatly pleated frill of a modest white lawn chemisette. The bright yellow shade of her high-waisted gown accented her red hair, which was loosely pinned beneath a dainty white lace cap.

Jared wondered fleetingly what she would do if he got up and went down the length of the table to kiss her. That thought led to a vision of Olympia lying atop the table amid the clutter of dishes and teacups. He could see her now with her lovely legs dangling over the edge of the table, her skirts pushed up to her waist and her hair in wild disarray.

He could also see himself in the mental image. He was standing between Olympia's soft, white thighs, his body violently aroused, honey on his hands.

Jared stifled a groan of frustration and made a grab for his self-control. "Something appears to be troubling you this morning, Miss Wingfield. May I inquire what the problem is?"

Olympia glanced quickly toward the kitchen door and then cast another hurried look at the door that had closed behind her nephews. She leaned forward and lowered her voice.

"As it happens, I have been very anxious to talk to you all morning, Mr. Chillhurst."

Jared wondered fleetingly if she would continue to call him Mr. Chillhurst after she had reached her first climax in his arms. "I believe we have some privacy now. Pray, tell me what is on your mind."

Olympia's brows drew together in a look of intense concentration. "Something very strange happened in the library last night."

Jared's stomach knotted. He strove to keep his voice calm and reassuring. "Unfamiliar, perhaps, Miss Wingfield, but I would not term it strange. Men and women have, after all, been enjoying such pleasant interludes since the days of Adam and Eve."

Olympia stared at him blankly. "What on earth are you talking about, sir?"

Just his luck, Jared thought gloomily. At long last he had found his own personal siren only to discover that she was cursed with the sort of brain that tended to concentrate on one thing at a time.

Nevertheless, it was an enormous relief to know that she was not, apparently, having second thoughts about the passion that had flared between them.

"Do not concern yourself, Miss Wingfield." Jared rested his elbows on the table and planted his fingertips together. "I was referring to something quite inconsequential."

"I see." Olympia shot another cautious glance toward both doors. "About last night . . . "

"Yes?"

"Minotaur barked sometime around two. I went downstairs to see what had alarmed him." She pitched her voice even lower. "Mr. Chillhurst, I found the brandy decanter overturned."

Jared stared at her. "Are you talking about the one in your library?"

"Yes, of course I am. It is the only brandy decanter I own. It was Aunt Sophy's, you see. She and Aunt Ida always kept it in the library."

"Miss Wingfield, perhaps it would be best if you continued with your tale," Jared said.

She gave him an impatient look. "That is precisely what I am attempting to do, sir, but you keep interrupting me."

"My apologies." Jared drummed his fingertips together.

"In addition to the overturned decanter, I also discovered that a window in the library was open."

Jared frowned. "Are you certain? I do not recall a window being open in there earlier."

"Precisely. There were no windows open."

"Perhaps the breeze from the window knocked the decanter over," Jared said slowly.

"Not likely. That decanter is extremely heavy. Mr. Chillhurst, I believe someone entered my library last night."

"Miss Wingfield, I must tell you that I am not pleased."

Olympia's eyes widened. "Neither am I, sir. Nothing like this has ever happened before around here. It is rather alarming."

Jared studied her over his steepled fingers. "Are you telling me that you went downstairs all by yourself to investigate strange sounds in your library? You did not wake Mrs. Bird or loose the dog first?"

Olympia brushed the matter aside. "There is no cause for concern, sir. I was armed with a poker. In any event the library was quite empty by the time I got there. I suspect Minotaur's barking frightened off the intruder."

"A poker? Good God." Jared was suddenly furious at her lack of common sense. He got to his feet and started toward the door. "I believe I shall have a look at the library, myself."

Olympia jumped up quickly. "I'll come with you."

He opened the door of the breakfast room and gave her a hard, disapproving look as she went past him into the hall. Olympia took no notice of his expression.

She hurried on down the hall ahead of him and rushed into the library. Jared forced himself to follow at a more deliberate pace.

When he entered the room a moment later he found Olympia examining one of the windows.

"See here?" She pointed to the latch. "It has been broken. Someone forced this window last night, Mr. Chillhurst."

Jared took a closer look at the window latch. The old metal hardware had, indeed, been bent. "The latch was not in this condition earlier?"

"No, I would have noticed. I have checked the latches on these windows every night for years."

Jared swept the room with a glance. "Is anything missing?"

"No." Olympia went to her desk and tested the locked drawers. "But it was a near thing. Whoever broke the window latch would have had no trouble getting into my desk."

Jared gave her a sharp glance. "You believe someone was after something in your desk?"

"Of course. There is only one thing anyone could want to steal from me, Mr. Chillhurst, and that is the Lightbourne diary."

Jared stared at her, dumbfounded by her conclusion. "No one knows you have it." *Except me,* he thought.

"We cannot be certain of that. I gave Uncle Artemis strict instructions not to tell anyone about the diary, but there is no way of knowing who might have discovered that he sent it to me."

"It is highly unlikely that your uncle mentioned the fact to anyone," Jared said carefully.

"He told you about it, did he not?"

Jared tensed. "Yes, he did."

"Of course he did so because he knew that he could trust you. But I believe there are others who knew that my uncle had purchased the diary."

"Who are you referring to, Miss Wingfield?"

"Well, there is the old Frenchman who sold the diary to Uncle Artemis in the first place." Olympia tapped the toe of her slipper-clad foot. "He may have learned that the diary was being sent on to me. He could have told any number of people."

She was right. And if she knew the whole truth, Jared thought, she would likely consider her nephews' new tutor the most logical suspect. But he had spent the night in his own bed contemplating the pleasures of seducing a siren, not rifling through a library.

Jared tried to suppress his growing unease. Over the years others had chased the secret of the Lightbourne diary but to Jared's knowledge the only people who knew about it these days were the members of his own family. Everyone else involved in the hundred-year-old legend had long since died.

He had given orders to the members of his family to stay out of the matter while he pursued the treasure. But now Jared wondered if one of the unpredictable, hotheaded Ryders had decided to defy his edict.

Jared's jaw tightened. If any member of his clan had resorted to the burglary of Olympia's home in an effort to retrieve the diary, there would be hell to pay.

But there were other, more logical explanations for the intrusion into the library, he reminded himself.

"Miss Wingfield, I think it far more likely that if someone did, indeed, enter your home last night, it was to search for something more valuable than an old diary. That brandy decanter, for example. It would bring a nice bit of blunt to any cracksman who managed to filch it."

Olympia frowned. "I doubt that whoever invaded my library last night was after the brandy decanter or the candlesticks or anything else. We have never had that sort of trouble in this neighborhood. No, I have given this a great deal of thought and I have concluded that the warning I discovered in the diary is clear."

"Bloody hell." A terrible premonition came over Jared. "What warning?"

Olympia's eyes sparkled with excitement. "Last night I unraveled the first of the concealed clues in the diary. It was 'Beware the Guardian's deadly kiss when you peer into its heart to find the key.'"

"Are you certain?"

"Absolutely certain. The Guardian, whoever he is, may be extremely dangerous. We cannot be too careful."

Good God, Jared thought. He had to distract her from that line of speculation immediately.

"Now see here, Miss Wingfield, I do not believe that we need concern ourselves with an old legend. If there ever was a Guardian, he would be dead by now."

"It has been my experience that behind every old legend there is usually a kernel of truth. It is obvious I must continue with my study of the diary. Perhaps I will find some further reference to this Guardian or an explanation of who he is."

"I doubt it," Jared muttered.

"In the meantime, I must protect the diary. It is only merest chance that I had it upstairs in my bedchamber last night when the intruder came looking for it." Olympia examined her library with a thoughtful look.

The thundering sound of footsteps and the scrabble of dog claws on the hall floor interrupted Jared before he could respond. He glanced at the open doorway as Ethan, Hugh, Robert, and Minotaur bounded into the room.

"We're ready for our geometry lesson, Mr. Chillhurst," Robert announced.

Jared hesitated and then nodded. "Very well." He turned briefly back to Olympia. "We shall finish this conversation later, Miss Wingfield."

"Yes, of course." But it was obvious that Olympia's attention was no longer on the discussion. She was too busy surveying the library for potential hiding places.

Jared followed the boys outdoors. Matters were get-

ting complicated, he thought. Olympia was preparing
to defend herself and the diary from an ancient legend.

Meanwhile, the legend in question wanted nothing
more than to make wild, passionate love to Olympia.

Jared pushed the problem of seduction aside in favor
of more mundane matters. He was at his best when it
came to such things, he reflected dourly.

He prepared to make a note in his appointment
journal of matters that needed to be attended to as soon
as possible. For starters he would check all the locks
and latches in the house and see to it that the broken
hardware was repaired.

The odds were that whoever had entered the library
last night had simply been after a few valuables that
could be easily sold. The culprit had no doubt been
scared off by Minotaur's barking and was highly unlikely to risk returning.

But Jared did not intend to take any chances.

Shortly after three o'clock that afternoon, the clatter
of carriage wheels in the drive interrupted Olympia's
work on the diary. She listened for a moment, hoping
that whoever had come to call would go away again
when Mrs. Bird announced that she was busy.

"Miss Wingfield is not receiving visitors this afternoon," Mrs. Bird announced loudly to whoever was at
the door.

"Nonsense. She will see us."

Olympia groaned in dismay at the sound of the familiar female voice. She closed the diary as Mrs. Bird
opened the library door.

"What is it, Mrs. Bird?" Olympia asked in what she
hoped was an authoritative tone. "I gave instructions
that I was not to be disturbed this afternoon. I am very
busy."

"Mrs. Pettigrew and Mrs. Norbury to see you, Miss Wingfield," Mrs. Bird said sullenly. "Real insistent about it, I might add."

Olympia knew there was little point in trying to evade the visit. She and Mrs. Bird could have handled Mrs. Norbury, the vicar's wife. The poor woman was easily intimidated having had a great deal of practice being browbeaten by her overbearing husband. But there was no stopping Mrs. Pettigrew who was just as forceful in her own right as the squire.

"Good afternoon." Olympia managed a weak smile for her visitors as they were shown into the library. "What a pleasant surprise. Will you have a cup of tea?"

"Of course." Mrs. Pettigrew, a large, substantial woman who favored large, substantial hats, took a chair.

Olympia had always privately considered Adelaide Pettigrew a good match for her husband. As the wife of the most important landholder in the neighborhood, she was very conscious of her position in local society. She was also, in Olympia's opinion, much too concerned with the proper positions of everyone else in the vicinity. Ethan, Hugh, and Robert called her a nosy old busybody.

Years ago Aunt Sophy and Aunt Ida had formed the same opinion.

Mrs. Norbury gave Olympia an uncertain nod as she seated herself in the small chair. She placed her small reticule primly on her lap and clutched it nervously with both hands. She was a pale little mouse of a woman whose gaze was always sliding off into the corner as if seeking her rightful hole in the wall.

Olympia did not like the fact that Mrs. Pettigrew had brought the vicar's wife along for the visit. It did not bode well.

"I'll fetch the tea tray," Mrs. Bird grumbled.

"Thank you, Mrs. Bird." Olympia faced her visitors,

took a deep breath, and prepared herself. "Lovely day is it not?"

Mrs. Pettigrew ignored the remark. "We are here on a matter of grave concern." She shot her companion a commanding look. "Is that not correct, Mrs. Norbury?"

Mrs. Norbury flinched. "Quite correct, Mrs. Pettigrew."

"What is this grave concern?" Olympia asked.

"An issue of propriety has arisen," Mrs. Pettigrew announced in ominous accents. "To be frank, I confess I was surprised to see that your household was involved, Miss Wingfield. Heretofore, your behavior, while admittedly eccentric and occasionally downright odd, has rarely been lacking in appropriate decorum."

Olympia gazed at her, mystified. "Has something about my behavior changed recently?"

"It most certainly has, Miss Wingfield." Mrs. Pettigrew paused for effect. "We understand that you have hired a most unsuitable tutor for your three nephews."

Olympia went utterly still. "Unsuitable? *Unsuitable?* What in heaven's name are you talking about, Mrs. Pettigrew? The tutor I have employed is an excellent instructor of youth. Mr. Chillhurst is doing a fine job."

"We are told that your Mr. Chillhurst has an extremely menacing appearance and that he likely cannot be trusted." Mrs. Pettigrew glanced at Mrs. Norbury for support. "Is that not so, Mrs. Norbury?"

Mrs. Norbury clutched her reticule more tightly. "Yes, Mrs. Pettigrew. Extremely menacing appearance. Looks like a pirate, we're told."

Mrs. Pettigrew turned back to Olympia. "We are given to understand that he not only looks exceedingly rough and dangerous, but that he has a violent temperament."

"Violent?" Olympia glowered at Mrs. Pettigrew. "That is ridiculous."

"He is said to have struck Mr. Draycott a most ferocious blow," Mrs. Norbury vouchsafed. "Indeed, they say both Mr. Draycott's eyes are still black from the experience."

"Oh, you are referring to that little incident the other afternoon here in my library." Olympia smiled with quick reassurance. "It was nothing. An unfortunate misunderstanding."

"Hardly a misunderstanding," Mrs. Norbury said grimly. "Your Mr. Chillhurst is obviously a threat to the entire neighborhood."

"Nonsense." Olympia stopped smiling. "You exaggerate, Mrs. Pettigrew."

"Not only is he a danger to us all," Mrs. Pettigrew retorted, "but my husband has reason to believe that he may well have taken advantage of your naive nature, Miss Wingfield."

Olympia glared at her. "I assure you, Mr. Chillhurst has not taken advantage of me."

"He apparently absconded with a shipment of goods that your uncle sent to you," Mrs. Pettigrew said.

"Quite untrue." Olympia got to her feet. "Mrs. Pettigrew, I regret that I must ask you to leave. I have a great deal of work to do this afternoon and I cannot afford to waste my time like this."

"Have you seen any sign of the proceeds that you ought to have realized from your uncle's last shipment?" Mrs. Pettigrew asked coldly.

"Not yet. But there has hardly been time for the goods to have been sold in London, let alone for us to have received the funds."

"My husband informs me that you are highly unlikely to see any money from that shipment," Mrs. Pettigrew said. "But, to be sure, your financial situation is not my major concern."

Olympia flattened both of her hands on top of the desk and set her teeth. "Just what is your major concern, Mrs. Pettigrew?"

"Your reputation, Miss Wingfield."

Olympia stared at her in disbelief. "My reputation? How is my reputation in danger?"

Mrs. Norbury apparently felt it was time for her to do her part. She coughed slightly to clear her throat. "It is not proper for a single woman such as yourself to have, shall we say, a close association with a person of Mr. Chillhurst's sort."

"Quite right," Mrs. Pettigrew said. She gave the vicar's wife an approving look and then rounded on Olympia once more. "Your Mr. Chillhurst must be dismissed at once."

Olympia narrowed her eyes at both women. "Now see here, Mr. Chillhurst is a tutor in this household. As it happens, he is a very good tutor and I have absolutely no intention of dismissing him. Furthermore, neither of you has any right to spread lies and rumors about him."

"What about your reputation?" Mrs. Norbury piped up anxiously.

A movement at the corner of Olympia's eye caught her attention. She turned her head and saw that Jared was leaning very casually in the doorway. He smiled slightly at her.

"My reputation is my concern, Mrs. Norbury," Olympia said bluntly. "Do not bother yourself about it. No one else has bothered about it for the past several years and I have gotten along just fine."

Mrs. Pettigrew lifted her chin. "I regret to say this, but if you will not listen to reason, we may be obliged to take action."

Olympia eyed her in disgust. "And just what sort of action would that be, Mrs. Pettigrew?"

"We have a duty to see to the welfare of those three innocent young boys who are in your care," Mrs. Pettigrew said coldly. "If you will not provide them with a proper home then my husband will have to take steps to see that they are removed from your household."

Panic and rage ignited like dry tinder inside Olympia. "You cannot take my nephews away from this house. You have no right to do so."

Mrs. Pettigrew gave her a thin, superior smile. "I'm certain that if my husband were to contact a few of the boys' other relatives and inform them about the situation in this household he would find one or two who would be willing to take charge of your nephews."

"Not bloody likely," Olympia shot back. "They're here in the first place because no one else wanted them."

"That situation might alter when they learn that the boys are being raised by a young woman of dubious morals. I'm sure Mr. Pettigrew will find someone in your family who can be persuaded to do his duty by the boys." Mrs. Pettigrew's smile grew more threatening. "Especially if Mr. Pettigrew offers a small stipend to provide for your nephews to be sent away to school."

Olympia was literally shaking with the force of her anger. "You would pay someone to take my nephews away from me and put them into a school?"

Mrs. Pettigrew gave a brisk nod of her head. "If necessary, yes. For their own good, of course. The young are so very impressionable."

Olympia could not stand it any longer. "Please leave at once, Mrs. Pettigrew." She glanced at the vicar's wife who was cowering in her chair. "You, too, Mrs. Norbury. And do not bother to return. I will not tolerate either one of you in this household again. Is that quite clear?"

"Now, see here, young woman," Mrs. Pettigrew began sharply.

Whatever she was going to say was forestalled by a startled shriek from Mrs. Norbury who had risen from her chair and turned toward the door.

"May the lord have mercy, that must be him." Her hand went to her throat in a fluttery little gesture of fascinated horror. "It is just as you said, Mrs. Pettigrew. The man looks very much like a murderous, bloodthirsty pirate."

Mrs. Pettigrew swung around and regarded Jared with grave disapproval. "A pirate, indeed. Allow me to tell you, sir, that you have no business in a decent household."

"Good afternoon, ladies." Jared inclined his head in a graceful, mocking bow. "I do not believe we have been properly introduced. I am Chillhurst."

Mrs. Pettigrew marched toward the door. "I do not hold conversations with your sort. If you have any claim to civility, you will leave this household at once. You are causing great damage to Miss Wingfield's reputation and there is no knowing how much damage you have already done to the minds of her young nephews. To say nothing of the harm you have done to her financial affairs."

"Leaving so soon?" Jared straightened and got out of Mrs. Pettigrew's path.

"My husband will deal with the likes of you." Mrs. Pettigrew sailed out into the hall. "Come along, Cecily. We are leaving."

Mrs. Norbury nervously eyed Jared's black velvet patch.

"I beg your pardon, sir," she mumbled. "I hope we have not offended you."

"Ah, but I am offended, madam," Jared said very softly. "Deeply offended."

Mrs. Norbury looked as if the devil himself had spoken. "Oh, dear."

Jared gave her a chilling smile. Then he went to the front door and opened it wide.

"Do hurry, Cecily," Mrs. Pettigrew snapped.

"Yes, yes, I'm coming." Mrs. Norbury collected herself and darted toward the door.

"Here now, what's going on?" Mrs. Bird appeared from the kitchen, tea tray in hand. "I've just got the bloody tea ready."

Olympia went to stand in the hall beside Jared. "Our guests will not require tea this afternoon, Mrs. Bird."

"Typical," Mrs. Bird complained sourly. "Go to a lot of trouble and no one drinks it. Some people have no consideration for common folk."

Olympia stood beside Jared and watched as Mrs. Pettigrew's coachman clambered down from his perch to usher the two women into an elegant new landau. The twin folding hoods of the carriage had been raised, even though the weather was very fine that afternoon.

Mrs. Pettigrew stepped into the vehicle, followed closely by Mrs. Norbury. The coachman closed the door.

A scream echoed across the garden.

"*God save us*," yelped Mrs. Norbury. "There's something in here. Open the door. *Open the door*."

"Get us out of here, you dolt," Mrs. Pettigrew shouted to her coachman.

The coachman hurried to open the carriage door. Mrs. Pettigrew leaped from the landau. Mrs. Norbury was not far behind.

Olympia heard the unmistakable *rivit-rivit* of several frogs. Through the open carriage door she could see what appeared to be at least half a dozen of the creatures hopping about inside the landau.

"Remove those horrible creatures at once," Mrs. Pettigrew ordered. "Get them out or you will be dismissed immediately, George."

"Yes, ma'am." George took off his hat and frantically began scooping frogs off the cushions.

Olympia watched the confusion in the drive with a sense of growing trepidation. Between the croaking frogs, the swearing of the coachman, Mrs. Norbury's cries of dismay, and Mrs. Pettigrew's venomous glances, she sensed impending disaster.

Jared watched it all with a small, quiet smile.

When the last of the frogs had been evicted from the landau and Mrs. Pettigrew and the vicar's wife installed instead, Olympia turned at last to look at Jared.

"What became of the geometry lesson?"

"It was temporarily put aside in favor of a lesson in natural history," Jared said.

"When was that decision made?"

"When Robert, Hugh, and Ethan saw the Pettigrew carriage pull into the drive a short while ago."

"I was afraid of that," Olympia said.

"There is no great harm done," Jared said. "I believe all of the frogs have survived. They shall find their way back to the pond."

"Mr. Chillhurst, you have no notion of the harm that has been done. Matters could not be worse." Olympia turned away in despair and walked back into the library.

Chapter 6

Surprised by Olympia's grim expression, Jared followed her into the library and closed the door.

"What's the matter, Miss Wingfield? Surely you are not overly concerned about the frogs in the Pettigrew carriage?"

Olympia gave him a dismayed look. "That business with the frogs could not have come at a worse moment."

"Why?" Jared watched her intently. "Do you regret your defense of me already?"

"Of course not. You are a member of my staff and as such you are under my protection." Olympia went to the win-

dow and stood looking out at the garden. "Mrs. Pettigrew is an extremely unpleasant woman who has a habit of interfering in everyone else's affairs. I do not regret defending your presence in this household for one moment."

"Thank you." Jared studied the proud line of her graceful spine. "I do not believe anyone has ever done that before."

"Done what?"

"Leaped to my defense."

"Oh. It was nothing." Olympia lifted one shoulder in a small shrug.

Jared smiled slightly. "Not in my view, Miss Wingfield."

"Mrs. Pettigrew had no right to attack you in that manner. And neither did Mrs. Norbury, although I suppose one must find some excuse for her. She is not a very strong female."

"Unlike yourself," Jared said. "But even the strongest of females must have a care for her reputation. I collect from what I overheard a few minutes ago that Mrs. Pettigrew is deeply concerned about yours."

"Apparently." Olympia did not turn around.

"What about you, Miss Wingfield?" Jared took a step closer and stopped. He was not certain what to do or say next. No woman's reputation had ever before been in jeopardy because of his actions. Dull, unexciting men of business such as himself rarely got into situations in which they succeeded in being a threat to any female.

"I do not give a fig for my reputation." Olympia clasped her hands very tightly in front of her. "Aunt Sophy always said that a reputation was nothing more than the world's opinion and the world was frequently wrong. The important thing was one's honor and she made it clear that was a private matter between oneself and one's conscience. I am not the least concerned about what Mrs. Pettigrew thinks of me."

"I see." Jared supposed he should be relieved to hear that Olympia was not going to hold him responsible for damaging her reputation. He wondered why he felt no great weight being lifted from his shoulders. "If you are not dispirited because of Mrs. Pettigrew's opinion, then what is the problem, Miss Wingfield?"

"Did you not hear her, sir? She threatened to send my nephews away," Olympia whispered. "She said that they should not be exposed to the immoral influences in this household and that her husband would be willing to pay some distant relative to take them."

"Bastard," Jared said under his breath.

"I beg your pardon?"

"It was nothing, Miss Wingfield. It just occurred to me that Pettigrew is more desperate than I had realized."

"Yes. I was not aware that Squire Pettigrew and his wife were quite so concerned about my reputation." Olympia swung around to face him. Her eyes gleamed with determination. "It might be best if we took the boys out of Upper Tudway for a while. Do you think we shall realize enough money from the sale of my uncle's goods to provide for a trip to the seaside?"

Jared elevated one brow. "Yes, I am quite certain you will have enough money to go to the seaside."

"Excellent." Olympia brightened. "When do you think we shall hear from your friend in London?"

"Any time, Miss Wingfield. Perhaps tomorrow or the next day." It would not take Felix Hartwell long to dispose of Olympia's goods, Jared thought. He only hoped that Hartwell was making some progress on his investigations into the embezzlement matter. Perhaps there would be news on that front when word came of the sale of the Wingfield shipment.

"I am very glad to hear that," Olympia said. "If we remove ourselves from Upper Tudway for a fortnight or so, perhaps Mrs. Pettigrew will calm down. I am also hopeful that Squire Pettigrew will not be overly enthusiastic about the notion of paying someone to take my nephews. He is rather careful with his money."

Jared contemplated the situation for a brief moment. "Miss Wingfield, your plan to take the boys and decamp to the seaside is not a bad one, but I believe it will be unnecessary."

Olympia's eyes widened in surprise. "Why is that?"

"I had intended to pay a call on Pettigrew in the near future. Now that Mrs. Pettigrew has begun making threats, I believe I shall not put the conversation off any longer. I shall call on him tomorrow."

Olympia eyed him with a quizzical gaze. "I do not understand, Mr. Chillhurst. Why do you wish to speak with Squire Pettigrew? What will you say to him?"

"I shall endeavor to explain to him that neither he nor his wife will be allowed to make any more threats or to overset you in any way. In short, I shall tell him to stay out of your affairs."

"*Jared.* I mean, Mr. Chillhurst, you must not do anything that will cause yourself more trouble." Olympia hurried across the room and put her hand on Jared's arm. "You must consider your own reputation."

Jared smiled briefly. "My reputation?"

"But of course. A tutor must be extremely careful. I shall be most happy to give you an excellent reference when you leave us, of course, but if Squire Pettigrew puts it about that you are a wicked influence on youth, well, there is no telling how difficult it might be for you to obtain another position."

Jared covered her hand with one of his own. "You need not concern yourself with my reputation, Miss

Wingfield. I assure you, I will never have any trouble obtaining a living."

She searched his face with troubled eyes. "You're quite certain of that?"

"Absolutely positive, Miss Wingfield."

"Nevertheless, I still think it would be best if we left Upper Tudway for a while."

"As you wish, Miss Wingfield." Jared hesitated. "I assume I shall be going with you?"

Olympia gazed at him in surprise. "Of course. You're part of my household staff. I do not know what I would do without you."

"Thank you, Miss Wingfield." Jared inclined his head in a small bow. "I make every effort to give satisfaction."

"Rest assured that you do, Mr. Chillhurst."

The message from Felix arrived in the morning post. Mrs. Bird brought it to the breakfast table and handed it to Jared.

"Thank you," Jared said.

"Don't get much mail here at Meadow Stream Cottage," Mrs. Bird informed him. She stood waiting, coffeepot in hand.

Jared realized that she was hoping to hear the contents of the letter. He glanced down the table at the row of other eager faces. Olympia and her nephews were watching him expectantly. Even Minotaur appeared interested. Communications from the world beyond the vicinity of Upper Tudway were clearly something of a treat.

"Is the letter from your friend in London?" Olympia asked.

"Yes it is, as a matter of fact." Jared broke the seal and opened the single sheet of foolscap.

"Did Mr. Hartwell sell everything for us, Mr. Chillhurst?" Ethan asked.

"I'll wager your friend got every bit as much as Squire Pettigrew did on the last shipment," Robert said.

"I'll wager he got even more," Hugh declared.

Jared looked up briefly. "You are correct, Hugh."

"Really?" Olympia glowed with anticipation. "Enough to enable us to go to the seaside for a fortnight?"

"More than enough." Jared glanced down at the note and read it aloud.

Chillhurst:

I have followed your instructions and sold the contents of the rather mixed assortment of goods you had conveyed to me. Not quite your usual style of business, if I may say so. Nevertheless, the deed is done. I have deposited a draft in the sum of three thousand pounds to the account of Miss Olympia Wingfield. Please let me know if I can be of further assistance. . . .

Robert nearly exploded out of his chair. *"Three thousand pounds."*

"Three thousand pounds," Hugh echoed in awe.

Olympia just stared in open-mouthed amazement.

Jared gave up trying to read the letter aloud as chaos broke out in the breakfast room. He quickly scanned the rest of the letter in silence as everyone exclaimed in excitement.

As to the other matter you have instructed me to look into, I regret to say that I have made very little progress. I believe the embezzled monies were pocketed by one of your ship's captains but we shall never be able to prove it. My advice would be to dismiss the captain in question. Let me know your wishes in the matter and I shall act accordingly.

Yrs,
Felix

Jared frowned thoughtfully as he refolded the letter. He made a mental note to tell Felix to take no action against the captain yet.

He placed the letter beside his plate and glanced up to see that everyone at the table was still in shock from the news of the profit that had been realized on the shipment of goods.

Hugh and Ethan were bouncing up and down in their seats. Robert was giving Olympia a string of suggestions about what could be done with the money. Minotaur had somehow gotten hold of a sausage.

"A bloody fortune, it is," Mrs. Bird said in a dazed fashion. She repeated the phrase over and over again. "A bloody fortune, it is."

Olympia looked torn between delight and dread. "Mr. Chillhurst, are you quite certain there has been no mistake?"

"There is no mistake." Jared picked up his fork and began to eat his eggs. "I assure you, Hartwell does not make mistakes when it comes to money." Which meant that Felix was no doubt correct in his conclusion that one of the Flamecrest captains was responsible for the large sums of money that had disappeared during the past year. But Jared was not satisfied with that answer. He wanted more proof.

"But there must be a mistake," Olympia insisted. "Perhaps he meant three hundred pounds, although even that would be a great sum compared to what we got from the last lot of goods."

"Obviously the market for imported items has improved considerably in the past few months," Jared said dryly. "Now, if you will excuse me, I am going to delay the start of today's lessons for an hour or so."

"Why?" Hugh demanded. "We're supposed to study the properties of clouds and wind this morning."

"Yes," Ethan said quickly. "You said you would tell us how Captain Jack once managed to elude a Spanish vessel because he knew more about meteorology than the Spanish captain did."

"We will get to that eventually." Jared rose from the table and checked the time on his watch. "This other matter must be attended to first." He slipped the watch back into his pocket.

Olympia got up to follow him out into the hall. When they were beyond the hearing of the boys, she put an anxious hand on Jared's arm.

"Mr. Chillhurst, are you quite certain that you are not taking any undue risk by calling upon Squire Pettigrew?"

"Quite certain." Jared plucked his coat from a brass hook. He could feel the weight of the dagger lodged firmly in its hidden sheath. The blade settled comfortably against his ribs as he shrugged into the garment.

Olympia frowned. "Perhaps I should come with you."

"That will not be necessary." Jared was touched. It really was very odd and not at all unpleasant to have someone else take such a keen interest in his welfare. "I assure you I have been looking after myself for some time now."

"Yes, I know, but you are employed in my household and I feel I have a responsibility toward you. I would not want you to come to any harm."

"Thank you, Miss Wingfield." Jared caught her chin

on the heel of his hand and brushed his mouth against hers. "But I assure you I am not in any danger from Pettigrew." He smiled wickedly down at her. "There is only one genuine threat that I am aware of at the moment."

Olympia's eyes widened in alarm. "What is that?"

"The possibility that I might burst into flames at any second due to the smoldering effects of unsatisfied desire."

"*Mr. Chillhurst.*" Olympia turned a vivid shade of pink, but her eyes lit with a deep, answering glow of feminine excitement.

"Until later, my sweet siren."

Whistling softly, Jared left Olympia standing in the hall and walked out into the warm spring morning.

"Mr. Chillhurst, wait." Olympia hurried out onto the front steps.

Jared turned around and smiled. "Yes, Miss Wingfield?"

"You will be careful, will you not?"

"Yes, Miss Wingfield. I will be very careful."

Minotaur came bounding around the corner of the house. Tongue lolling, he wagged his tail and looked hopefully up at Jared.

"I'm afraid you cannot come with me this morning," Jared said. "Stay here and keep an eye on things for me. I shall return soon."

Minotaur sat down on the steps and leaned heavily against Olympia. The dog was clearly disappointed, but philosophical.

It was a relatively short stroll to the Pettigrew farm if one cut through the meadow and the patch of trees that bordered the stream. Jared spent the time contemplating the strange turn his life had taken of late.

The scene he had come upon yesterday afternoon in Olympia's library had given him pause. Mrs. Pettigrew's remarks about Olympia's reputation had been annoying, but he was forced to concede that they were not without merit. Jared knew, even if Olympia did not, that they were playing fast and loose with her reputation.

Passion was an amazing emotion, he thought. Now that he had experienced it firsthand, he had the greatest respect for its power. Nevertheless, he was a gentleman and he had no intention of ruining Olympia. Even if she did not seem to mind being ruined.

The yelps of a kennel full of hunting hounds greeted Jared as he walked up the lane to the Pettigrew house. He examined the property with great interest. The farm was obviously a prosperous one. Jared wondered idly how many of the improvements had been paid for with funds that had been stolen from Olympia and her uncle.

Jared went up the steps and knocked loudly on the front door. It was opened a moment later by a middle-aged housekeeper in a gray dress, a white cap, and an apron. She stared first at Jared's eye patch.

"Ye be the new Wingfield tutor they're all talkin' about, ain't ye?" she demanded.

"I'm Chillhurst. Kindly tell Pettigrew that I wish to speak with him."

"He ain't here," the housekeeper said quickly. "I mean, he ain't in the house at the moment."

"Where is he?"

"Around at the stables." The housekeeper continued to gaze at him in rapt fascination. "I'll fetch him for ye, if ye like."

"Thank you. I'll find him, myself."

Jared turned and went down the steps. He walked around the corner of the house and saw the freshly painted stables.

High-pitched, excited voices caught his attention as he passed the open kitchen door.

"It's him, I tell ye," the housekeeper said to someone else in the house. "The new tutor. They say he's a pirate what's been ravishin' Miss Wingfield every night since he arrived there at Meadow Stream Cottage."

"I heard he was living in the old gamekeeper's cottage at the foot of the lane, same as the others she hired," came the tart reply.

"Well, who's to know just where he spends his nights, I ask ye?" the housekeeper retorted. "Strikes me anything could be goin' on there and no one the wiser. Poor Miss Wingfield."

"I ain't so sure she's to be pitied."

"How can ye say such a thing? She's a proper young lady, she is," the housekeeper insisted. "Even if she is a bit odd. Not her fault. She was raised odd by them two aunts o' hers."

"I never said she weren't a proper young lady. But she's five-and-twenty and ain't got a prayer of ever gettin' herself married. Leastways she don't as long as she's got those three young hellions to look after. I'll wager she's havin' a grand time bein' ravished every night by a pirate. I can think of worse fates."

"Not for Miss Wingfield." There was genuine shock in the housekeeper's voice. "Ain't never been a word o' scandal about her and well ye know it. No, that bloody pirate is takin' advantage of her, he is. Lord only knows what he's doin' to her at night."

"Something interestin' I hope, for Miss Wingfield's sake."

Jared set his back teeth and stalked on toward his destination.

The scent of hay and manure greeted him a few minutes later as he walked into the shadowed stables. A sleek, well-muscled bay gelding whickered inquiringly and stuck his head over a stall door. Jared ran a critical eye over the expensive looking horse.

The sound of Pettigrew's voice came from a stall at the far end of the dimly lit stables.

"I've arranged to have the mare covered by Henninger's new stallion. He's a prime bit of blood and that's a fact. It'll cost me a packet, but it'll be worth it."

"Aye, sir."

"Did you get a new shoe on the bay's left fore?" Pettigrew emerged from the stall, a riding crop in his hand. He was followed by a short, wiry groom.

"Took 'em down to the blacksmith's yesterday," the groom said. "He's right as rain now, Mr. Pettigrew."

"Excellent. I mean to ride him in the local hunt next week." Pettigrew slapped his leg absently with the riding crop. "Let's have a look at the hounds." He squinted against the sunlight that poured through the stable door behind Jared. "What's this? Who's there?"

"Chillhurst."

"Chillhurst?" Pettigrew eyed him warily. "What the bloody hell are you doing in my stables?"

"I came to have a few words with you, Pettigrew."

"Now see here, I've got nothing to say to you. Get off my land."

"I'll leave soon enough but first there are a few things you ought to know." Jared flicked a glance at the sullen looking groom. "I suggest we have this conversation in private."

"Damned bloody arrogant *tutor*." Pettigrew scowled ferociously but he sent the groom from the stables with a flick of the small whip.

Jared waited until the groom had vanished through the door.

"I won't take up much of your time, Pettigrew. There are just two points I want to make. The first is that there are to be no more threats made to Miss Wingfield."

"Threats? How dare you, sir?" Pettigrew sputtered furiously. "I have never threatened Miss Wingfield."

"No, I believe you had your wife do the job for

you," Jared said. "It does not signify. The only thing you need to remember is that the threats are not to be repeated, let alone carried out."

"Damnation. You're gettin' a bit above yourself, you bloody upstart bastard. What the devil are you talking about?"

"You know very well what I am talking about, Pettigrew. Miss Wingfield was told that unless she got rid of me, her nephews would be sent away."

"Miss Wingfield should get rid of you immediately," Pettigrew blustered. "You can hardly claim that you're a good influence on impressionable young boys. Or on an impressionable young woman, for that matter."

"Be that as it may, I shall be remaining in my position in the Wingfield household. And if you so much as even attempt to have the boys removed from Miss Wingfield's care, you will regret it."

Pettigrew narrowed his eyes. "I have known Miss Wingfield for years, sir. Indeed, I counted myself a friend of her aunts. I feel a responsibility to do what I believe is best for Miss Olympia. Furthermore, I do not intend to let you intimidate me, Chillhurst."

"But I am going to intimidate you." Jared smiled slightly. "If you make one move to take the boys away from Miss Wingfield, I shall see to it that the manner in which you have been systematically cheating her becomes public knowledge."

Pettigrew stared at him in slack-mouthed shock. A dark red flush suffused his heavy face. "How dare you accuse me of cheating her!"

"Easily enough, I assure you."

"It's a damnable lie."

"No," Jared said. "It's the truth. I am well aware of the contents of the previous shipments of goods which you handled for Miss Wingfield. They were similar to the contents of the one I disposed of for her. They should have fetched a similar amount, somewhere in the neighborhood of three thousand pounds and I'll wager they did."

"That is not true," Pettigrew hissed.

"You stole that money, Pettigrew."

"You cannot prove a thing, you bastard."

"Ah, but I can. I have an acquaintance in London who could quickly discover all the facts. And I will instruct him to do so if you do not make good on what you owe Miss Wingfield."

Pettigrew's face contorted with fury. "I'll teach you to threaten me, you bloody bastard." He raised the riding crop and brought it downward in a swift, slashing movement aimed at Jared's good eye.

Jared blocked the blow with one arm. He jerked the whip from Pettigrew's hand and tossed it aside in disgust. Then he reached inside his coat and slipped the dagger from its sheath.

He shoved the stunned Pettigrew back against a stall door and held the tip of the blade to his throat. "You have offended me, Pettigrew."

Pettigrew could not take his eyes off the dagger. He licked his lips. "You cannot do this. I'll have you taken up by the magistrate. You'll hang, Chillhurst."

"I doubt that. But you are certainly free to speak to the magistrate if you wish. First, however, you will make out a draft to Miss Wingfield for the money that you owe her from those last two shipments."

Pettigrew shuddered. Desperation appeared in his eyes. "I haven't got it. Already spent it."

"On what?"

"See here," Pettigrew whispered. "You do not understand. I needed the money from the first shipment to pay off some debts of honor."

"You lost Miss Wingfield's money in a card game?"

"No, no, I lost my farm in the damned card game."

Sweat beaded Pettigrew's brow. "I thought I was finished. Ruined. And then Olympia came to me for advice on how to dispose of a shipment of goods her uncle had recently sent to her. It was like the answer to a prayer."

"Your prayers, not Miss Wingfield's," Jared said.

"I meant to pay her back as soon as everything came right." Pettigrew gave Jared a beseeching look. "Then the next shipment arrived and I realized I could make a variety of improvements to my farm."

"So you could not resist stealing the second shipment." Jared smiled thinly. "And you have the gall to call me a pirate."

"With the new improvements the farm will be much more productive," Pettigrew said earnestly. "I shall be able to reimburse Miss Wingfield very quickly."

Jared nodded toward the expensive gelding. "Was the bay one of the necessary improvements you felt obliged to make around here?"

Pettigrew was incensed. "A man's got to have a proper horse for the hunt."

"And what about that new landau your wife arrived in yesterday?"

"She has her position in the village to maintain. Look here, Chillhurst, I shall be able to pay Miss Wingfield back within a year or two. I swear it."

"You will begin paying her back immediately."

"Damnation, man, I haven't got the blunt."

"You can start raising the necessary by selling that bay gelding. He'll bring four or five hundred guineas at least."

"Sell the bay? Are you mad? I just bought him."

"You will find a buyer for him," Jared said. "And when you have sold the gelding, you had best find someone to purchase the landau. I calculate that you owe Miss Wingfield nearly six thousand pounds."

"Six thousand pounds?" Pettigrew looked dazed.

"You have two months to come up with the money."

Jared released Pettigrew. He sheathed the dagger, turned, and walked back out of the stables. Outside he noticed Pettigrew's sullen-eyed groom watching him from the kennels.

Jared hesitated as a thought struck him. He walked over to stand directly in front of the groom.

"You left muddy footprints on Miss Wingfield's carpet night before last," Jared said casually. "And you knocked over her brandy decanter. I should probably make you pay for the window latch that you ruined just as I am making your employer pay for the monies he stole."

Shock lit the groom's eyes. He gaped at Jared and then began to stammer wildly. "Now, see here, I don't know what yer talkin' about. I wasn't in Miss Wingfield's library last night or any other night. I swear I wasn't. I don't care what the squire says."

"Did I say the footprints and the decanter and the broken latch were in her library?" Jared asked politely.

The groom's eyes widened in horror as he realized he had fallen into the small trap. "It weren't my fault. I was only doin' what the squire ordered me to do. I didn't hurt anyone. I would never have hurt anyone. I was just lookin' for somethin' the squire wanted, that's all. He said he'd dismiss me if I didn't look for it."

"What were you searching for? A letter, perhaps?"

"Papers," the groom said. "He told me to bring back any notes or letters and such pertaining to financial matters that I found in her desk. But I never had a chance to get into the bloody thing. The damned dog barked and then I heard sounds upstairs and I got out of there."

"Stay out of there," Jared advised. "The next time you try anything of that nature you will very likely trip over me instead of the brandy decanter."

"Yes, sir. I won't go near the cottage again."

There were certain advantages to having the face of a pirate, Jared thought as he walked back toward Meadow Stream Cottage. People tended to take one seriously.

Jared went up the steps of the cottage, opened the door, and was greeted with a scene of chaos and confusion. He had only been away an hour and already the household had fallen into an uproar. Jared smiled wryly. A tutor's work was never done.

Minotaur yelped excitedly as Jared walked into the hall. Ethan and Hugh called loudly to each other as they hauled a large, dusty trunk down the stairs. Robert shouted instructions from the landing. He grinned widely when he spotted Jared.

"Mr. Chillhurst, you're back. Aunt Olympia says we won't be having our lessons today. We're to pack for the journey."

"I see your aunt has determined to set out for the seaside without delay." Jared was amused by Olympia's decisiveness. She was certainly determined to whisk her little household to safety.

"No, no, Mr. Chillhurst." Ethan struggled with his end of the huge trunk. "We're not going to the seaside after all. We're going to London."

"London?" Jared was startled.

"Yes. Isn't it exciting, sir?" Hugh grinned. "Aunt Olympia says that since we now have a packet of money, we are going to use it to go to London. We've never been there, you see."

"Aunt Olympia says the trip will be very educational," Robert explained. "She says we shall visit museums and see Vauxhall Gardens and do all sorts of things."

"Aunt Olympia says there will no doubt be a fair

underway in one of the parks and we may see fireworks and eat ices and see a balloon ascension," Ethan added.

"She says we shall probably go to a theater called Astley's where they have acrobats and magicians and trained ponies," Hugh offered. "She read about them in advertisements in the London papers."

"I see." Jared's brows rose as Mrs. Bird appeared with a stack of folded shirts. "Where is Miss Wingfield?"

"In the library." Mrs. Bird looked glum. "Lot of nonsense, this is. Don't see why we cannot stay put like normal folk. No need to go chasing off to London."

Jared ignored her. He walked into the library and closed the door. Olympia was seated at her desk, her head bent over a copy of one of the London papers. She glanced up quickly when she heard him enter the room.

"Jared. I mean, Mr. Chillhurst, you're back." She studied him anxiously. "Did all go well?"

"Squire Pettigrew will not be bothering you or the boys again. I will explain it all to you later. What is this about a trip to London?"

"A famous notion, is it not?" Olympia smiled brilliantly. "It occurred to me that with the three thousand pounds we received from my uncle's shipment of goods, we can afford to go all the way to London. It will be a wonderful experience for the boys and I shall be able to use the time to do some research on the diary."

"Research?"

"Yes. I would like to consult some maps of the West Indies that belong to the Society for Travel and Exploration. The diary makes reference to an island which I cannot seem to locate on any of my own maps of that region."

Jared hesitated as he swiftly calculated the potential problems involved in a journey to London. "Where do you plan to stay?"

"Why, we shall take a house for a month. It should be a simple matter."

"No."

Olympia blinked, astonished. "I beg your pardon?"

Jared realized he had momentarily forgotten his position in the household. He was supposed to take orders from Olympia, not give them to her. Unfortunately giving orders was an old habit.

"A trip to London at this particular juncture strikes me as a very unsound notion, Miss Wingfield," he said carefully.

"Why is that?"

"For one thing, I would be obliged to find lodgings, too. They would most likely be located at a considerable distance from the house you obtain. I do not care for the thought of you and the boys being alone at night in London." He paused delicately. "Not after what happened here two nights ago."

"You mean that business of someone creeping about my library?" Olympia frowned in thoughtful consideration.

"Precisely," Jared said smoothly. "We cannot take any chances, Miss Wingfield. Here in the country I am only a short distance away down the lane. I can hear you if you call for help."

It was only one more small deception, he assured himself. He would tell her soon enough that he was certain last night's intruder had been Pettigrew's groom. In the meantime he needed an excuse to avoid this harebrained trip to London.

Olympia hesitated and then a look of satisfaction appeared in her eyes. "The solution is obvious. You shall stay with us in town."

"With you? You mean in the same house?" Jared was staggered at the thought.

"Of course. There is absolutely no need to go to the

extra expense of paying for separate lodgings for you. It's a waste of money. Furthermore, if we must take steps to defend ourselves against this Guardian person, whoever he is, then you should be near at hand at all times."

"Near at hand," Jared repeated blankly.

"Under the same roof," Olympia said helpfully.

"I see." *The same roof.*

The notion of spending his nights under the same roof as his lovely siren was enough to take away his very breath. He would no doubt sleep in a bedchamber next to Olympia's. He would hear her when she got dressed in the morning and listen to her get undressed at night.

Jared's mind churned out a myriad fascinating visions. He would see Olympia in the hall when she was on her way to have her bath. He would join her on the stairs when she went down to breakfast or a late night cup of tea. He would be near her morning, noon, and night.

He would go mad, he thought. His passions would consume him. He would have every opportunity to abandon himself to the siren's call.

It would be heaven living under the same roof as Olympia.

Or hell.

"Is there some problem with my plan, Mr. Chillhurst?"

"I believe so." For the first time in his entire life Jared found it extraordinarily difficult to think clearly and decisively. "Yes. There is a problem."

Olympia tilted her head inquiringly. "What is it?"

Jared drew a deep, steadying breath. "Miss Wingfield, need I remind you that your reputation in this district is already hanging by a thread? If I go to London with you and reside under the same roof, you will soon have no reputation left at all."

"My reputation is of no concern to me, sir, but I

am aware that we must take care to protect yours. After all, as I pointed out earlier, you cannot afford to have gossip follow you to your next position."

Jared seized on that argument. It was the only one she seemed willing to concede. "An excellent point, Miss Wingfield. Gossip can be quite harmful to a tutor, as you so wisely noted."

"Have no fear, sir. I would not dream of jeopardizing your reputation." Olympia smiled reassuringly. "But I do not see that there is any difficulty here. After all, no one in Upper Tudway will know we are staying in the same house in London."

"Ah . . . well . . . yes, there is that, however—"

"And no one in London knows you, either, except your friend who disposed of Uncle Artemis's goods. Surely he will not gossip about you."

"Ah . . . well . . . "

"It is not as though we shall be going about in social circles. Indeed, we shall be quite anonymous in the crowds that throng a large city such as London." Olympia chuckled. "Who would even notice us, let alone gossip about us?"

Jared struggled to inject some common sense into the situation. "The landlord of the house you propose to rent, perhaps? The members of the Society for Travel and Exploration whom you plan to contact? Any number of people might talk about us, Miss Wingfield."

"Hmmm." Olympia tapped her quill gently against the desktop.

Jared did not care for the expression on her face. "Miss Wingfield, allow me to tell you that a young woman in your position simply cannot—"

"I have it," she declared suddenly.

"Have what?"

"The perfect answer. If we are discovered and your

reputation appears to be in danger, we shall pretend to be a married couple."

Jared stared at her, stunned into speechlessness.

"Well, sir? What do you think?" Olympia waited expectantly. When Jared failed to respond, she prompted him gently. "Do you not think it an extremely clever scheme?"

"Ah . . . well—"

"Come now, Mr. Chillhurst. It is the logical thing to do, not only for the sake of economy but for the sake of efficiency and safety. There really is no other intelligent solution to the problem."

Jared wanted to inform her that intelligence was a commodity that was singularly lacking in this matter but he could not seem to find the words. The thought of not only living in the same house as Olympia but of pretending to be married to her was dazzling him to the point of lunacy.

The siren's song had rendered him mad.

"What will you tell your nephews?" he finally got out.

Olympia scowled briefly as she mulled that over for a few seconds. Then her glorious smile returned in full force.

"They need know nothing about it, of course," she said. "It is highly unlikely that they would come into contact with any adults who might think to question them in depth on our connection. You are their tutor, nothing more nor less. No one will pry further. Is that not correct?"

"I suppose so," Jared agreed reluctantly. Adults rarely came into contact with young children.

"And we will not be entertaining visitors so there will be no problem from that quarter," Olympia continued with enthusiasm.

"We are headed for disaster," Jared muttered under his breath.

"What was that, Mr. Chillhurst?"

"Nothing, Miss Wingfield. Nothing at all."

And there, in the blink of an eye, Jared thought, went the benefits of a lifetime's cultivation of common sense, practicality, and sober consideration.

He was no longer the man he had been some days ago; no longer the levelheaded, unimaginative man of business who had innocently set out to buy a stupid diary with the pragmatic intention of keeping the rest of his family out of trouble. He had become, instead, a man in the grip of an all-consuming desire; a man soaring on the wings of passion. He was a poet, a dreamer, a romantic.

He was an idiot.

Matters would have been so much simpler if he had not abandoned his quest for the diary in favor of answering the siren's call.

Jared looked at Olympia's lovely, hopeful face and heard the crash of waves against the rocks. He mentally consigned himself to his fate.

"I see no reason why your plan should not work, Miss Wingfield. It sounds like a logical solution to the problem and at the same time it will give your nephews the benefit of an educational experience."

"I knew you would see the cleverness of my scheme."

"Quite right. And you need not trouble yourself with finding a house to let. As your man of affairs, I shall arrange for a suitable residence."

"Thank you, Mr. Chillhurst. I do not know what I would do without you."

Chapter 7

The lecture rooms of the Musgrave Institution were only sparsely filled for Mr. Blanchard's talk on travels in the West Indies.

"Not at all as large as the crowd that turned out for Mr. Elkins's wonderful discourse on his trip to the South Seas," a plump woman seated next to Olympia confided. "But then I fear Mr. Blanchard's manner of speaking is not nearly so entertaining as Mr. Elkins's."

Olympia could not argue with that. Mr. Blanchard was obviously a well-traveled man gifted with a highly observant eye but he lacked the first qualification for

speaking in public. He failed to entertain his audience.

Olympia had attended the lecture with high hopes of gaining new information about the geography of the West Indies. It had become obvious from her reading of the Lightbourne diary that one of the keys to solving the puzzle was to locate the island Claire Lightbourne referenced, a small bit of land to the north of Jamaica.

She had attempted to explain that to Jared last night while they were sharing their evening brandies but, as usual, he had changed the subject.

Olympia, Jared, and the rest of the household, including Minotaur, had been settled in London for three days now. This was her first foray to an event sponsored by the Society for Travel and Exploration and she had been quite looking forward to it.

Unfortunately, Mr. Blanchard's dull talk was not holding her attention. She glanced down at the small watch pinned to her bodice and saw that it would be another half hour before Jared and the boys arrived to fetch her.

Jared. In the privacy of her thoughts she called him by his Christian name. The degree of intimacy that she felt growing between them made it impossible to think of him as Mr. Chillhurst. She was careful to address him properly by his last name whenever she spoke to him aloud, however.

It took considerable willpower to stay on formal terms when she was around him, though. Every time she encountered him in the hall or on the stairs, she was nearly overcome with a desire to throw herself into his arms. Their evenings together in her little study were becoming almost intolerable. Olympia did not know how much longer she could restrain herself.

Adding to the thrilling tension was the knowledge that Jared was forced to exert an equal amount of self-discipline whenever he was near her.

That very morning there had been another heart-stopping encounter in front of his bedchamber door. Olympia had been hurrying downstairs for breakfast, her vision obscured by a stack of journals and a globe that she was carrying. Jared had just stepped out into the hall.

The collision that had ensued had been an act of fate as far as Olympia was concerned. She even wondered if some small part of her had actually planned it. After all, she had known precisely when Jared would leave his bedchamber. He was a man who valued habit and routine. After three mornings of listening to his movements on the other side of the wall that separated them, Olympia knew that Jared went downstairs at the stroke of seven.

"Good heavens. I beg your pardon." Olympia had staggered and clutched at the globe as Jared had turned away from the door and walked straight into her path.

Even though she had come up on his blind side, his reaction had been swift and unhesitating. He had deftly caught the globe as it tumbled from her hands.

"Your pardon, Miss Wingfield. Did you sleep well?"

Olympia had been so riveted by the sight of him standing so close at such an early hour that she had had a difficult time answering the simple question. For a few seconds all she could do was gaze at him and wonder desperately if he would take the opportunity to kiss her.

"Yes, I slept very well, Mr. Chillhurst," she said, disappointed when he made no move to crush her mouth beneath his own. "And yourself?" How was she going to stand this every morning for an entire month? she wondered frantically.

"I do not have much time for sleep lately," Jared said. His gaze went to her lips. "At night my thoughts are filled with you, siren."

"Oh, Jared," Olympia breathed. "I mean, Mr. Chillhurst." An aching longing deep inside her made her feel curiously weak. "I think about you for the better portion of most nights, too."

Jared smiled his faint, slightly amused smile. "One of these nights we shall have to do something about our mutual problem or we shall never get any sleep."

Olympia's eyes widened in dismayed understanding. "Yes, of course, I am no doubt creating havoc with your schedule. I am sorry to interrupt your routine, sir. I know how important it is to you. I realize that it is crucial for reasons of health to get a proper night's sleep."

"I believe I shall survive, Miss Wingfield."

And then he *had* kissed her, right there in the hall. It had been a swift, stolen kiss taken after Jared had glanced about to make certain there were no young boys peeking out of their bedchambers.

When it was over, he had calmly carried the globe downstairs for her.

It seemed to Olympia that her lips were still tingling from the kiss. She straightened in her chair and tried to refocus her thoughts on the lecture.

Hunched over his notes on the lectern, Mr. Blanchard droned on in a monotone that had already put several members of the audience to sleep. "In addition to sugar, the islands in the West Indies export a variety of goods including tobacco, coffee, shells, and timber. They must, of course, import nearly every item deemed necessary to civilized living."

Olympia's mind began to wander again. She was here to learn about lost islands and legends, not imports and exports. To break the boredom she covertly examined the small group of people seated around her. Most were members of the Society for Travel and Exploration, which was sponsoring Mr. Blanchard's lecture. No doubt she had corresponded with some of them. She wondered how to go about introducing herself after the talk.

"Have you attended the other lectures in this series?" the plump woman whispered behind her gloved hand.

"No," Olympia admitted in a low voice. "I am a member of the society but I have only recently arrived in London. I have not had an opportunity to attend any of the public lectures until now."

"Pity you had to begin with this one. Mr. Duncan's talk on the Ottoman Empire was quite fascinating."

"I was looking forward to this lecture because I am especially interested in the geography of the West Indies."

The woman leaned closer. "Are you, indeed? So are Mr. Torbert and Lord Aldridge. You must meet them."

Olympia was delighted. "I should love to meet them. I have read their papers on the West Indies in the quarterly journal."

"They are both here today. Sitting on opposite sides of the room of course." The woman chuckled. "Expect you know that they are bitter rivals. Been feuding for years."

"Is that so?"

"I shall be happy to introduce you to them. But first allow me to introduce myself. I am Mrs. Dalton."

"I am Miss Wingfield of Upper Tudway in Dorset," Olympia said quickly. "So nice to meet you Mrs. Dalton."

Mrs. Dalton's eyes widened in pleased surprise. "Not the Miss Wingfield who writes those wonderfully interesting papers on legendary treasures and unusual customs of other lands?"

Olympia blushed. It was the first time anyone had actually complimented her on her work. No one in Upper Tudway even bothered to read the society's quarterly journal.

"I have written one or two articles of that nature, yes," Olympia said in what she hoped was a modest manner.

"My dear, this is quite exciting, not only for me, but for several other members of the society. As soon as Mr. Blanchard has finished his lecture, I must introduce you to everyone."

"That is very kind of you."

"Not at all, you are practically a legend yourself my dear Miss Wingfield. Why, Torbert and Aldridge were saying just the other day that they would not think of leaving England without taking along one or two of your papers to guide them in their travels."

"Posing as a tutor? Outrageous. What devilish game are you playing, Chillhurst?" Felix Hartwell slanted a glance that was half-amused and half-respectfully wary at Jared.

"I'm not at all certain I know the answer to that, Felix." Jared's mouth curved wryly. He kept his gaze on Ethan, Hugh, and Robert who were some distance away, struggling to get a new kite into the air.

The kite had been purchased shortly after they had all escorted Olympia to the Musgrave Institution. After seeing her safely inside the lecture rooms, Jared had taken the boys to a nearby park and sent a message around to Felix.

Felix had appeared within minutes. That was one of the many things Jared appreciated about his trusted man of affairs. Felix had the same respect for punctuality as Jared. They had worked well together over the years and Jared had come to consider Felix a friend, virtually the only one in whom he could confide.

Indeed, the two men were much alike in many ways, Jared acknowledged. They both had calm, unemotional—some said dull—natures. They shared a logical, pragmatic approach to both personal affairs and matters of business. Two men with the souls of tradesmen, as his father would say, Jared thought.

But things had changed recently. Jared wondered how Felix would react when he learned that his employer had become a helpless victim of passion.

Felix snorted. "I know you too well to believe that you do not know what you are doing and why, Chillhurst. You never do anything without forethought and planning. It is not in your nature to act on whim or fancy, sir."

"You see before you a changed man." Jared glanced at Felix and grinned briefly.

Felix stared back, amazed. Jared was not surprised. After all, he himself was still coming to grips with this new aspect of his personality. It was no wonder that Felix should be stunned and somewhat confused by the transformation.

Although he corresponded with him frequently, it had been several months since Jared had last seen his man of affairs in person. The last occasion had been when Felix had journeyed to Jared's home on the Isle of Flame off the coast of Devon in order to spend a fortnight reviewing Flamecrest business plans.

Jared rarely traveled to London. He much preferred the spectacularly rugged landscape of his island home to the shallow glitter of the city.

Although he saw him infrequently, it seemed to Jared that Felix changed little over the years. Felix was a man of the town and it showed in the softness of his hands and the fashionable cut of his coat. His friendly, open features concealed a shrewd intelligence that Jared valued highly.

"Changed? You?" Felix chuckled. "Not likely. I have never known a more deliberate strategist in my life. Working for you is like working for a consummate chess player. I cannot always envision how the moves will play out, but I have learned that you are always in command of the game."

"I am not playing chess this time." Jared watched, pleased, as the colorful kite took to the air. Ethan and Hugh cheered and started to run after Robert who was dashing off, string in hand. "Indeed, fate has made a helpless toy of me. I am rather like that kite at the moment. A creature born to ride the airy vapors."

"I beg your pardon, sir?"

"You may as well know, Felix, I have surrendered to the powerful forces of raw passion."

"Raw passion? You? Chillhurst, you are talking to me, Felix Hartwell. I have been your agent here in London for nearly ten years. I know more about your business affairs and the way you manage them than anyone else on the face of the earth. I suspect I know more about you than anyone else, because we are alike in temperament."

"That is very true."

"It certainly is. And if there is one thing I know for certain about you, it is that you are not a man who is guided by passions of any sort. You are a paragon of self-control, sir."

"Not anymore." Jared thought of the kiss he had given Olympia that morning in the hall outside his bed-chamber. A hot rush of pleasure went through him. Residing under the same roof as the object of his desire was proving to be the sweet torture he had envisioned. His only consolation was knowing that Olympia was suffering, too. "I have heard the siren's call and I am lost."

"Siren?"

"Otherwise known as Miss Olympia Wingfield."

"Sir, are you amusing yourself at my expense?" Felix asked bluntly. "Because if so, I wish you would have done with the jest."

"Alas, I do not jest." Jared had given Felix a brief summary of events but he had not bothered to explain the matter of the Lightbourne diary and how it had led him to Olympia. The diary, after all, had ceased to matter. "Do you know something, Felix? For the first time in my life, I begin to comprehend the antics of the members of my own family."

"Allow me to tell you, Chillhurst, that no one could comprehend the bizarre fits and starts of your family. No offense, but you are the only rational member of the clan and well you know it. You have told me so, often enough."

"Blood will tell, apparently." Jared smiled again. "Who could be rational and deliberate when one is swept by the flames of immoderate passions?"

Felix stiffened and inclined his head in a brusque, offended fashion. "My lord, I do not comprehend any of this. The thought of you masquerading as a tutor in order to pursue this odd Miss Wingfield is beyond belief. You are not the sort to develop immoderate passions."

Jared's humor faded. "I should make something clear, Felix. I do not want any of this to go any further. Miss Wingfield's reputation is at stake."

Felix shot Jared a quick, searching glance and then looked away. "After all these years, sir," he said very quietly, "I would hope that you could trust me not to reveal a confidence."

"Of course, I trust you," Jared said. "If I did not, we would not be having this conversation. Now, then, in addition to not revealing the fact that I am employed as a tutor to Miss Wingfield's nephews, I must ask you not to tell anyone that I am even in London."

Felix's expression sharpened with sudden comprehension. His eyes reflected a measure of what might have been acute relief. "Ah, then you are indeed involved in one of your infamously clever schemes. I knew it."

Jared saw no reason to explain himself further. Romantic passion was, after all, a private affair. "You will oblige me by keeping secret my presence here in town?"

"Of course." Felix's gaze narrowed thoughtfully. "As you almost never come to London and do not go about in Society when you do, no one is likely to ask after you."

"I assumed as much. I am also counting on the fact that very few people recognize me on sight."

"There is little risk of your being recognized by even the handful of people who do know you, sir." Felix's expression was wry. "You are obviously not planning to move in polite circles and no one would think to look for you in that small house in Ibberton Street."

"That little house is just what I wanted, Felix. It is a residence perfectly suited to the requirements of a family of modest means from the country. As long as I avoid the clubs and fashionable haunts, I should be able to move about London with complete anonymity."

Felix chuckled. "You could probably ride unnoticed in Hyde Park so long as you took your three young charges with you. People see only what they expect to see. I assure you no one will expect to see the Viscount Chillhurst acting as a tutor."

"Precisely." Jared was relieved that the intelligent, pragmatic Felix actually saw some logic to the crazed scheme. His own judgment, Jared knew, was no longer to be trusted. "We should all be quite safe."

Felix slanted him a questioning glance. "Safe from what, sir?"

"Disaster," Jared said.

"What sort of disaster?"

"Why, discovery, of course," Jared said. "There is always the threat of being found out in a situation such as this and I fear the consequences. It is much too soon."

Felix began to look concerned again. "Too soon, my lord?"

"Yes. Wooing a siren is a tricky business, Felix, and one in which I have had no experience whatsoever. I would not want the entire project to come crashing down around my ears before the proper groundwork has been laid."

Felix heaved a sigh. "If I did not know you better, sir, I would say that you have become as odd as the rest of your family."

Jared laughed and clapped him on the shoulder. "A chilling thought."

"Indeed. No offense, my lord."

"Do not concern yourself, Felix. I am hardly likely to take offense at the truth. No one can deny that my family does have a certain reputation for producing Originals."

"Yes, sir." Felix hesitated. "Perhaps I should just mention one thing that you may wish to bear in mind."

"What is that?"

"Demetria Seaton is in town. She is Lady Beaumont now, you know."

"Yes, I know." Jared kept his voice even.

"I have heard that Lord Beaumont is in London seeking yet another cure for his small, but apparently rather persistent problem."

"Still cannot beget himself an heir, I take it?"

"It never ceases to amaze me how well informed you

are, Chillhurst, considering the fact that you almost never come to town. You are quite right. The *on dit* is that Beaumont cannot even consummate his recent marriage."

"Indeed?" That fact was hardly likely to bother Demetria, Jared thought.

"Apparently even the presence of the lovely Lady Beaumont in his bed is not sufficient to help him overcome his impotence," Felix murmured.

"A pity. But I suspect that Lady Beaumont is not entirely unhappy with the situation," Jared said.

"Again, you have the right of it, according to rumor." Felix watched the kite dart about in the air overhead. "If Beaumont fails to do his duty by his title, Lady Beaumont will inherit his entire fortune."

"Yes." She would no doubt shower a good portion of the funds on her damnable brother, Gifford, Jared thought. Unlimited access to money would make him even more obnoxious.

Gifford was Demetria's only blood relative and she doted on him. As far as Jared was concerned, her overprotective attitude toward her younger brother had had the effect of turning him into a spoiled, willful, hotheaded rakehell who would likely one day get himself killed.

Jared grimaced as he recalled the evening three years ago that Gifford had issued a challenge. The demand to meet for pistols at dawn had come less than an hour after Jared had ended his engagement to Demetria.

Gifford had been beside himself with fury. He had claimed that Jared had humiliated his sister and he had demanded satisfaction.

Jared had refused, of course. After all, he had still been a logical, reasonable man in those days and he had reacted accordingly. He had seen little point in risking his neck or young Gifford's in a duel that would resolve nothing.

His refusal to meet Gifford on the field of honor had only served to further enrage the younger man. Gifford had labeled him a coward.

"As Beaumont is nearly seventy and in poor health," Felix said, "there is every likelihood that his lady will find herself a very wealthy widow at any moment."

"Especially if Beaumont hastens his own demise by too much vigorous activity spent pursuing a course of treatment for impotence."

Felix smiled coolly. "It will be interesting to see if Beaumont finds a cure for what ails him."

"I wish him the best of luck," Jared said.

"You do?" Felix glanced at him with ill-concealed surprise. "I would have thought that you might be interested to hear that Lady Beaumont may soon be a free woman."

Jared shrugged. "Her freedom, or lack of it, is no longer a matter of concern to me."

"No? She is more beautiful than ever, I am told. And the rumors of a lover died down long before Beaumont married her."

"Did they?" Jared asked without much interest. The subject of Demetria's lover was one of the few topics he had never discussed with Felix. Jared had, in fact, not discussed it with anyone at all.

He knew there had been speculation after he had abruptly ended the engagement, but he had refused to acknowledge the gossip.

"If Lady Beaumont has a paramour these days," Felix continued, "she does an excellent job of keeping him out of sight."

"She would need to do so," Jared said coolly. "Beaumont would hardly countenance his wife having a lover when he, himself, has not yet managed to procure an heir."

"True enough." Felix paused. "Regarding the other matter."

"Nothing new has turned up, I presume?"

Felix shook his head. "I fear I have not uncovered any more information. It must have been the vessel's captain who arranged the fraud. He was the only one who could have done it."

"I would prefer to have proof before I dismiss him."

Felix shrugged. "I understand, sir, but in cases of this sort, it is almost impossible to discover proof. That is the difficult thing about matters of embezzlement. Very hard to follow the trail."

"So it would seem." Jared watched the kite soar and listened to Ethan's and Hugh's cheerful shouts of encouragement. "Let us wait a while longer, Felix. I am not prepared to take action against the captain just yet."

"As you wish, sir."

"Bloody hell," Jared said softly. "I do not like this business of being deceived. I do not care to play the fool."

"I am well aware of that, sir."

There was a moment of silence while both men watched the boys and their kite.

Jared slipped his watch out of his pocket and noted the hour. "You must excuse me, Felix. I have an appointment soon and I fear it will take some time to persuade my charges to bring their kite back to earth. I must be off."

"As you wish, Chillhurst. I am available, as always, in the event that I am needed."

"I do not know what I would do without you, Felix." Jared inclined his head in farewell and set off across the park to collect Ethan, Hugh, Robert, and the kite. It was almost four o'clock, time to fetch Olympia from the Musgrave Institution.

It took Jared nearly twenty minutes to collect the boys, the kite, and a hackney. He glanced at his watch twice as the hired carriage clattered through the crowded streets.

Robert tore his glance away from the fascinating sights outside the hackney's window. He saw Jared slip his watch back into his pocket for the second time. "Are we going to be late, sir?"

"I trust not. With any luck the lecture will carry on longer than anticipated."

Ethan kicked his heels against the bottom of the seat. "May we have another ice after we fetch Aunt Olympia?"

"You've already had one ice this afternoon," Jared said.

"Yes, I know, but that was hours ago and I am quite warm again."

"I'll wager Aunt Olympia would fancy an ice, sir," Hugh said with an altruistic expression that did not fool Jared for a moment.

"Do you think so?" Jared pretended to ponder the issue.

"Oh, yes, sir." Keen anticipation filled Hugh's innocent gaze. "I am certain of it."

"We shall see what she has to say about it." Jared glanced out the window. "We have arrived. Do you see your aunt?"

Ethan leaned out the window. "There she is over there. She is surrounded by several people. I'll wave to her."

"No, you will not," Jared said. "One does not hail a lady in that fashion. Robert will find her and escort her back to the carriage."

"Right you are, sir." Robert opened the cab door

and jumped down onto the pavement. "I'll be back in a moment."

"Do not forget to take her arm," Jared said.

"Yes, sir." Robert hurried across the street.

Jared closed the door and sat back against the cushions. He watched Robert's progress through the small crowd in front of the Musgrave Institution's lecture rooms.

Felix was right, Jared thought. People saw what they expected to see and no one in the Society for Travel and Exploration was likely to recognize the Viscount Chillhurst. As far as Jared knew, he was not personally acquainted with any members of the society. Nevertheless, it never hurt to be cautious.

"I did not know that Aunt Olympia had so many friends in London," Ethan said.

"Neither did I," Jared muttered. He studied the two men standing closest to Olympia. One was so heavy that he was nearly bursting his stays. The other was just the opposite; so thin that he appeared to have been fasting for the past several months.

Both were hanging on to Olympia's every word, Jared noticed.

"Is something wrong, sir?" Hugh asked anxiously.

"No, Hugh, nothing is wrong." Jared kept his voice calm and reassuring. He was aware, as always, that Hugh was easily overset by the possibility that his fragile new life with Olympia might be shattered again.

But there was no getting around the fact that Olympia was thoroughly enjoying her conversation with her new cronies.

Jared watched as Olympia spotted Robert and turned toward the carriage. He saw the glowing enthusiasm on her expressive face and felt a stab of annoyance. That look had been inspired by the conversation with the two men at her side.

So this was jealousy, he thought with a jolt of surprise.

It was a most unpleasant sensation.

Jared tried to be philosophical about the matter. After all, a man who sailed the senses on the vapors of passion was no doubt doomed to learn the dark side of such a reckless voyage.

"Here she comes." Ethan bounced up and down on the seat. "Do you think she will want an ice?"

"I have no notion. Ask her and see." Jared leaned forward and pushed open the cab door. He watched approvingly as Robert practiced his manners by handing Olympia gallantly up into the carriage.

"Thank you, Robert." Olympia sat down next to Jared. Beneath the brim of her chip straw bonnet her eyes were sparkling with excitement. "I hope you have all had a lovely afternoon."

"We flew a kite in the park," Ethan said. "It was great fun."

"Do you want a nice, cold ice, Aunt Olympia?" Hugh asked ingenuously. "I expect that it would taste ever so good on such a warm day."

"An ice?" Olympia smiled at Hugh, momentarily distracted. "Yes, that sounds delightful. It was quite warm in the lecture rooms."

Everyone looked at Jared.

"I can see that there is a consensus here," Jared said. He raised the trap in the carriage roof and gave the coachman orders to take them to the nearest respectable shop that sold ices.

"I am so excited by what I have learned today," Olympia said to him as he reseated himself. "I cannot wait to get on with my study of the diary."

"Indeed," Jared muttered with a carefully cultivated air of polite boredom.

The bloody diary could rot, he thought. What he

really wanted to know was how much Olympia liked her newfound friends.

Jared did not get the full tale until much later that evening, primarily because Ethan, Hugh, and Robert could not stop talking about their adventures in London.

That did not bother Jared. There would be time enough to hear all the particulars after Mrs. Bird had retired to her quarters and the boys were in bed.

The fierce torment of these late evenings spent closeted alone with Olympia was equalled only by the anticipation of how they would ultimately conclude. He did not think that Olympia could resist the glittering sensual tension that crackled between them for much longer. He knew that he certainly could not.

When the household had quieted down for the night, Jared shut Minotaur in the kitchen and went in search of Olympia. He knew precisely where to find her in the small house.

She looked up from the Lightbourne diary when he walked into the study. Her eyes were very bright and her smile was filled with a warmth that made Jared's blood run hot. The thought that he could have gone his whole life without ever experiencing this powerful emotion was enough to send a chill down his spine.

"There you are, Mr. Chillhurst." Olympia marked her place in the diary with a small strip of decorated leather. "I see we have peace and quiet at last. I honestly do not know how we got along without you."

"The problem was that your household lacked an orderly routine, Miss Wingfield." Jared walked over to the table that held the brandy decanter. He picked up the bottle and poured two glasses. "Now that such a routine has been established, everything is under control."

"Do not underestimate your contribution, sir," she said as he carried the brandy glasses to her desk. "You have done much more than merely establish a routine." She looked up at him with glowing admiration as she accepted one of the glasses.

"I try to earn my salary." Jared took a sip of the brandy and wondered if he would drown in her lagoon-colored eyes. "What did you learn today that got you so enthused?"

Olympia looked briefly disconcerted, as if her thoughts had gone in another direction entirely for a moment. She recovered immediately. "I know that you are not particularly interested in my study of the Lightbourne diary, sir."

"Mmm." Jared kept his voice noncommittal.

"I told you that I needed to consult some new maps."

"So you said."

"Well, I now have access to such sources." Excitement lit Olympia's eyes. "Not only does the society maintain an excellent library with a very large collection of maps, but certain members of the society have offered to let me view their personal collections."

Just what he had feared. Jared recalled the two men who had been hovering over Olympia outside the Musgrave Institution. "Which members?"

"Mr. Torbert and Lord Aldridge. Apparently their personal libraries contain many charts that deal with the West Indies."

"Have you told them about your quest?" Jared asked warily.

"No, of course not. I merely told them that I was very interested in the geography of the islands."

Jared frowned. "I suppose they know that you are a student of legends."

"Yes, but there is no reason why they should think I was searching for the treasure mentioned in the Lightbourne diary," Olympia assured him. "I have told no one about my interest in that particular legend."

"I see."

"Mr. Chillhurst, I know that this topic bores you and as it happens, I wish to discuss something else tonight."

"What is that, Miss Wingfield?"

"It is difficult to put into words." Olympia got to her feet and walked around the edge of her desk. She went to stand near the globe. "I fear you will think me overbold. And, indeed, you will be correct in that assumption."

Jared felt his lower body tighten in anticipation. "I could never think you overbold, Miss Wingfield."

Olympia put her fingertips on the globe and slowly began to rotate it. "First, I wish to thank you for making it possible for me to pursue my studies of the Lightbourne diary."

"I had little to do with that."

"That is not true. If you had not seen to the disposal of that last shipment of goods from my uncle, I would never have been able to afford this visit to London. And if you had not dealt with Squire Pettigrew, I would have been forced to abandon my studies in favor of whisking my nephews out of his reach. Regardless of how you look at it, we are here in town and I am free to do my research because of you."

"I trust you will find what you are searching for here in London."

Olympia spun the globe a little faster. "Even if I do not find the treasure mentioned in the diary, I shall not complain, sir. I have already found more than I had ever dreamed of finding because of you."

Jared went very still. "Have you?"

"Yes." She did not look at him. Her attention remained fixed on the spinning globe. "Sir, you are a man of the world. You have traveled widely and viewed strange customs firsthand."

"I have some experience of the world, yes."

Olympia cleared her throat with a small, discreet cough. "As I have often explained, I, too, am a woman of the world, sir."

Jared slowly set down the brandy glass. "Miss Wingfield, what are you trying to say?"

She looked up from the rotating globe. Her eyes were brilliant with desire. "As a woman of the world, sir, I would like to ask you a question which I wish you would answer as a man of the world."

"I will make every attempt to do so," Jared said.

"Mr. Chillhurst." Olympia's voice cracked slightly. She broke off and tried again. "You have given me some reason to believe that you might consider involving yourself in a romantic liaison with me while you are engaged as a tutor in this household. Am I mistaken?"

Jared felt the last, ragged remnants of his self-control turn to ash in the roaring flames of passion. His hands trembled as he gripped the edge of the desk on either side of himself.

"No, Olympia, you are not mistaken. I would be quite willing to consider such a liaison provided that you cease addressing me as Mr. Chillhurst."

"*Jared.*" She whirled away from the madly spinning globe and flew across the room, straight into his arms.

Chapter 8

"I was so afraid you would think me overbold," Olympia confided into Jared's shirtfront. She was dazed with a combination of joyous relief and the glorious excitement that always consumed her when she was in Jared's arms. "I know you are a perfect gentleman and I feared my question might offend you."

Jared kissed the top of her head. "My sweet siren. I am not a perfect gentleman."

"Yes, you are." She lifted her head and gave him a tremulous smile. "At least you make every effort. It's not your fault that there is a vein of excessive passion within you. I realize that I am quite delib-

erately provoking that element in your nature. It is no doubt very wrong of me to do so."

"No, Olympia." Jared framed her face with his hands. His gaze glittered with fierce certainty. "I do not think there is anything wrong with this emotion and even if there is, I do not particularly care."

"I am so glad you feel that way. I was almost certain you did." Olympia was aware of the hard, strong muscles of his thighs as she leaned against him. "You and I are very much alike, are we not? Our experience and study of other lands and peoples has given us a broad view of human nature."

"Do you think so?"

"Oh, yes. Men and women of the world such as ourselves need not be bound by Society's conventions."

Jared cupped her face and looked down into her eyes. "You cannot know the effect you have on me."

"I hope it is similar to the effect you have on me," she whispered.

"I suspect it is a thousand times greater." Jared's mouth hovered barely an inch above hers. "If you were feeling what I am feeling, you would be consumed by flames."

"I am consumed by flames."

Jared muttered something soft, hoarse, and rough with emotion. Olympia could not make out the words but there was no need. His mouth was suddenly on hers and she knew precisely what he was trying to say. Jared desired her tonight with a passion that seared her soul, a passion that equalled her own.

With a tumultuous sense of happiness Olympia gave herself up to Jared's kiss. She pressed herself closer, seeking the heat and the strength in him. She was dimly aware of him leaning back against the edge of the desk and widening his stance so that she was gently trapped between his muscled thighs.

"So soft." Jared laced his hands through Olympia's hair, tearing it free of its precarious moorings. He took great fistfuls of the stuff and clenched and unclenched his fingers in it. "So exquisitely soft."

Out of the corner of her half-closed eyes Olympia saw her little white lace cap float softly to the carpet. The sight of it filled her with an extraordinary sense of abandon.

"Oh, Jared, this is beyond anything," she exclaimed, enthralled with the emotions that were cascading through her.

"Yes, my sweet siren." Jared's voice had darkened and roughened with passion. "Beyond anything."

He launched a trail of scorching kisses down her throat, forcing Olympia's head back over his arm. When he found his path blocked by the prim, pleated frill of her chemisette, he swore impatiently.

"I cannot bear this torture much longer." Jared tugged quickly at the tapes of her gown. "If I do not have you very soon, my lovely Olympia, I shall no doubt wind up in Bedlam, a broken man."

"I understand." Olympia began to unfasten his shirt. "I, too, feel as if I shall be driven mad by this powerful emotion."

Jared gave her an odd smile as he lowered the bodice of her gown to her waist. "Then we have no choice, do we? We must save each other from insanity tonight."

Olympia got his shirt open and gazed, entranced, at the sight of his bare chest. She shook her head slightly. "I am not certain that we can save ourselves. Perhaps we are already lost, Jared."

"Then so be it." Jared untied the strings of the cambric chemisette and let the garment fall to the carpet alongside the white lace cap. He went very still as he looked down at her breasts.

Olympia blushed under his heated gaze but she

made no attempt to cover herself. Indeed, the knowledge that he wanted her so intensely only served to make her bolder. She splayed her fingers against his hard chest and then lifted her hands to his shoulders.

Jared inhaled deeply and let out his breath in a low groan. He lowered his head to kiss the high, taut crowns of her breasts as she traced the contours of his back.

"I like that very much." Jared closed his good eye and drew her closer until her breasts were crushed against him.

"Do you?" Olympia stroked him. "I like it, too. You feel so wonderful, Jared."

"My God, Olympia."

As if driven by some force he could no longer defend against, Jared moved. His hands wrapped around Olympia's waist. He lifted her, turned, and seated her on the edge of the desk. Olympia's skirts fluttered delicately.

"Jared?" Surprised to find herself sitting on the desk, Olympia raised questioning eyes to Jared's face.

"Sing your sweet song to me, my lovely siren." Jared pushed Olympia's gown up above her knees. He parted her legs with his hands and stepped between her thighs. "I want to be lured to my doom."

"*Jared.*"

Olympia was still adjusting to the very strange sensation of having him standing between her legs when Jared put his hands on the sensitive skin of her inner thighs. She clutched his arms and stared at him, not certain how to react.

"Never fear, my beautiful siren." Jared kissed the curve of her shoulder. "You will tell me when you are ready."

Before Olympia could ask him what he meant by that, his hands skimmed along the inside of her leg all the way to the soft, hot vulnerable part of her that had suddenly been opened to him.

Olympia stopped breathing when she felt him touch the unguarded core of her body. An excruciating sense of urgency radiated outward from the place where his fingers connected with her womanly flesh.

"You are already wet," Jared said. "As warm and soft as southern seas." He withdrew his fingers and touched them to his lips. His smile was slow and deeply sensual. "You even taste of the sea."

"Do I?" Olympia gripped his upper arms and held on for dear life. She wished very badly that she knew what to do next but she was lost.

"Yes. Exciting. A little salty. Incredible."

Jared put his hand back between her legs and carefully eased one finger into her.

Olympia shuddered. "Jared. I do not know what to say."

"You need say nothing at all, my sweet siren, until you are ready to sing for me."

She did not know what he meant but she did not have the strength or presence of mind to ask for clarification. The feel of his finger inside her was so wondrous and strange that Olympia could not stop trembling in reaction. Her legs tightened instinctively around him.

"Come. Sing for me, my beautiful siren." Jared drew his finger slowly back out of her, watching her face as she moaned softly. "Yes, just like that. Again, my lovely one."

He touched her with the tip of his thumb and Olympia shivered and gave a soft, whimpered moan.

"Bloody hell, but I love your song." Jared removed his hand reluctantly from between her legs.

Olympia opened her eyes slightly, wondering why he was no longer touching her so intimately. She needed the feel of his hand there in that secret place. She was certain that nothing else could ease the great, aching restlessness she was experiencing.

"Jared?" She looked down and saw that he was fumbling with the opening of his trousers. "Please, I want you to touch me again."

Jared gave a choked laugh that ended in a groan. "I could not stop touching you now if all the fiends in hell were at my heels."

Olympia saw him ease aside the front of his breeches. She stared in shock at the sight of his heavy, erect manhood as it came free of the confining fabric. *"Mr. Chillhurst."*

Jared rested his forehead on hers. His mouth curved with wicked sensuality. "Could you possibly think of it as a variation on that peculiar island wedding custom you once mentioned to me, Miss Wingfield? I realize that this particular phallus is not made of gold, but it is the only one I've got."

With a shock Olympia recalled her naive discussion of golden phalluses. She did not know whether to laugh or collapse in mortification.

"Perhaps it is just as well it is not made of solid gold, sir," she managed to say. "It is very large, after all, and would no doubt be worth a bloody fortune. Someone might attempt to steal it."

Jared's answering chuckle became a hoarse exclamation. "You mock me at your peril, siren."

She moistened her parted lips and looked up at him from beneath heavy lashes. "Do I?"

"Yes." Jared pulled her legs wider apart and wrapped them around his waist. He stepped close and fitted himself to the opening of her soft, wet passage.

If Olympia had been shocked at the sight of his male member, she was truly stunned at the feel of it pushing against the unguarded gates of her body. At the same time, the sensation seemed to be precisely what she had been craving.

"Yes, please." She clutched at his shoulders.

"My God." Jared cupped Olympia's buttocks in his hands, held her steady, and started to ease himself slowly into the portals of her womanly passage.

Olympia closed her eyes and concentrated intently on the strange feel of him as he entered her.

Excitement mingled with a delicious trepidation as Jared began to fill her. She could not believe that her body could adjust itself to his but that was exactly what seemed to be happening.

The fit was extremely snug, however, and not altogether comfortable, even if it was causing ripples of pleasure to course through her.

"Damnation." Jared suddenly stopped.

"What is wrong?" Olympia opened her eyes. Jared's face was as hard and unyielding as stone. But she had never before seen a stone that was beaded with perspiration, she thought. Beneath her fingers his muscles were like bands of steel. "Are you all right?"

He searched her face with an almost desperate expression. "Olympia, you said you were a woman of the world."

She smiled dreamily. "I am, sir."

"I thought you meant that you had some experience of this sort of thing."

"Not personal experience." She touched his cheek gently with her fingertips. "I believe I have been waiting for you to teach me, sir. You are, after all, a skilled tutor, are you not?"

"I am a madman." Jared's single-eyed gaze was fierce. "Olympia, are you very certain you want me?"

"More than anything," she whispered.

"Then I wish you would hold on to me with all of

your strength while I find my way through the storm to the safe harbor inside you."

Olympia nearly melted beneath the heated words. She could find no verbal response so she tightened her arms and legs around him and urged him closer.

Jared's palms were strong and firm around the soft curves of her bottom. He used his grip to hold her carefully still while he thrust himself swiftly and relentlessly into her softness.

Olympia stiffened and opened her mouth to cry out in astonished surprise. Jared covered her lips with his own, stifling her startled protest.

When he was lodged to the hilt, he went rigid. He did not move except to lift his mouth cautiously from hers.

"Are you all right?" he got out in a husky whisper.

"Yes." Olympia swallowed and gingerly unclenched her nails from his back. "Yes, I believe so."

"Show me. Sing for me, siren."

Jared began to move very slowly and very gently within her, never quite leaving her body before returning to sheath himself once more.

Whatever pain had been caused by his entry was soon extinguished as the flowing heat returned. Olympia clung to Jared as he drew her deeper and deeper into the sultry waters of passion.

The aching need inside her was overwhelming. She felt full to the bursting point. She heard herself pleading with Jared for a release she could not name.

"Soon, my siren, soon," he promised as he drove slowly back into her depths.

"Now, Jared. You must do something."

"You are a demanding little thing, are you not?"

But Jared sounded very pleased with her demands. In fact, to Olympia's growing frustration, he encouraged them. He seemed to know just how to drive himself into her; how far to withdraw. He stoked the fiery tension until she felt like a clockwork toy that has had its spring wound much too tight.

And then Jared put his hand down between their bodies and did something with his fingers at the same time that he surged into her.

It was too much. The spring inside Olympia shattered.

She had never dreamed she could feel such sensations. Wave after wave of pleasure raced through her, leaving her shivering in the aftermath. She wanted to scream with joy but Jared sealed her mouth with his own.

She felt him drive into her one last time. He shuddered heavily and opened his mouth against hers. Olympia found herself swallowing his fierce shout of satisfaction, just as he had swallowed her softer cries.

When it was over, Jared scooped Olympia off the desk, staggered to the sofa, and collapsed with her onto the cushions.

It was a long while before Jared recovered to the point where he could raise his head and look down at Olympia. She stretched languidly beneath him. Her smile was laced with a delightfully smug feminine satisfaction. *The smile of a siren who has finally learned her own power,* he thought.

And he was the one who had taught her the extent of that power.

"You are a man of excessive passions, Mr. Chillhurst," Olympia said.

Jared chuckled ruefully. He was exhausted. Exhausted and exhilarated. "It would appear so, Miss Wingfield. Allow me to tell you that your passions are every bit as excessive as my own."

She wriggled delightfully against him as she twined her arms around his neck. "I must tell you that it was all extremely exciting. I have never experienced anything quite like those sensations."

"I am aware of that, Olympia." He bent his head and tenderly kissed the curve of her breast. A deep sense of possessiveness flowed through him.

In spite of Olympia's opinion of his passionate nature, Jared was only too well aware that until now he had always conducted his few liaisons with the same orderly, disciplined approach he applied to his business affairs. He had certainly never involved himself with a virgin.

There had been no denying the tight, untried status of Olympia's body. He had been vividly conscious of the small amount of blood that had mingled with the sultry moisture that had coated his shaft.

He should probably be ashamed of himself, he thought. But the only emotion he could manage in that moment was one of deep, contented satisfaction. And, as Olympia herself had said, it was not as if she were a young girl straight out of the schoolroom. She was five-and-twenty. *A woman of the world.*

Jared groaned silently. She was not a woman of the world at all. She was an innocent who had been cloistered in the country all of her life and he had taken advantage of her.

It had been the most glorious experience of his life.

Jared thought of the lecherous Draycott who had attempted to seduce Olympia in her library. He wondered how many other men in Upper Tudway had seen her as legitimate prey; how many others had made dishonorable advances.

But Olympia had waited to sing her siren's song just for him.

Jared was awed by the knowledge that he had been

the one she had chosen; the one to whom she had given herself. His throat tightened and he had to swallow hard before he could speak.

"Olympia," he said very steadily, "I want you to know that I value the treasure you have bestowed upon me. I will take excellent care of you."

She drew her fingertip along the line of his jaw. "You already take very good care of me." She smiled. "I only hope that you will remain in this household for a very long time."

"As tutor and lover?"

She blushed. "Well, yes, of course. What else?"

"What else, indeed?" Jared put his arm over his eyes. He ought to tell her the entire tale now, he thought, but if he did, everything would change. She would doubtless be angry and offended by his deception.

If he were in her place Jared knew that he would be coldly furious when he learned that he had been deceived, just as he had been when he had discovered Demetria with her lover.

He recalled his own words to Felix that afternoon. *I do not care to play the fool.*

When Olympia learned the truth she would think that he had played her for the fool; that he had amused himself at her expense.

It was certainly the conclusion that he would reach were their positions reversed.

The realization made him set his back teeth. What if Olympia reacted to the knowledge that she had been deceived in the same way he had reacted to Demetria's deception three years ago, he asked himself. What if she threw him out of her life as he had thrown Demetria out of his?

What if Olympia turned and walked away from him?

He went cold inside.

Jared was unsure of what to do next. He could not seem to think logically about the situation.

The only thing of which he was absolutely certain was that he was too enthralled by the passionate beginning of his affair with Olympia to risk everything yet.

There would be the devil to pay once he told her the truth, he thought glumly. She would probably not be able to tolerate such deception in the man to whom she had given herself.

He had to face the possibility that once Olympia learned all, she would likely never again believe in him and trust in him as completely as she did tonight.

He could not bear to have her turn away from him. Not now, when he had only just found her.

It was all so bloody complicated, Jared thought, not for the first time.

Such were the wages of passion.

He had never before found himself in such a position but he sensed he needed time. *Just a little more time in which to teach her to care for him enough so that he could risk telling her the truth.*

Yes, time was the answer, he decided, grateful at having discovered a practical, eminently logical reason to stave off the inevitable.

His wild thoughts were shattered by a muffled bark from below stairs.

He raised his arm from his eyes. "What the devil?"

"It's Minotaur," Olympia said, sounding surprised.

"That bloody dog will awaken the entire household." Jared rolled off the sofa and got to his feet. He swiftly set his clothing to rights.

The thought of Mrs. Bird and the three boys bursting into the study and finding Olympia in her present state was more than a little alarming.

"Get dressed," he ordered. "Quickly. I'll see to the dog." He picked up a candle and started for the door.

"Do you know, that is just the way Minotaur barked the night that he heard someone in my library in Upper Tudway." Olympia's brows drew thoughtfully together as she pushed herself to a sitting position. "Perhaps he has heard another intruder." She hastily reassembled the bodice of her gown.

"I seriously doubt it. More likely the beast has heard someone or something out in the street. He is not accustomed to the sounds and smells of the city." Jared paused briefly at the door and turned back to watch Olympia adjust her clothing. It was an entrancing sight.

Olympia's chemisette was still lying on the carpet beside her dainty lace cap. Without the small cambric garment to fill in the area above the low neckline, her gown was miraculously transformed. It went from being modest in the extreme to a daring and provocative frame for her delicately curved breasts.

He saw her wince as she took an unsteady step forward. He realized that she was very likely experiencing some soreness. But Olympia did not complain and he did not know how to apologize.

Before he could decide what to do, Olympia recovered. She smiled at him and hurried toward the door.

Jared was bemused and rather astonished at the immediate response of his body. With an effort of will, he forced himself to pay attention to the matter at hand.

"Wait here. I shall go and see what is disturbing Minotaur," he muttered. With one last, regretful glance at the sight of Olympia's sweetly rounded bosom, flushed cheeks, and tousled hair, he went out into the hall.

Olympia hurried after him. "Hold a moment, Mr. Chillhurst. I shall accompany you."

Jared mocked her with one raised brow as he went toward the back stairs. "Mr. Chillhurst?"

"Best not to get out of the habit of formality," she said very seriously. "We must maintain appearances in front of the boys and Mrs. Bird."

"As you wish, Miss Wingfield." Jared lowered his voice as he started down the stairs. "But I warn you that I reserve the right to call you Olympia on any occasion when I happen to have my hand up under your skirts."

"*Mr. Chillhurst.*"

"That is the way such matters are handled among men and women of the world," Jared informed her with lofty certainty. He put the guilt behind him and allowed himself to feel the pleasure that was threatening to overpower him.

A grand satisfaction, more potent than brandy, flowed in his veins. He was Icarus flying too close to the sun, but it was worth the risks. The rewards of a passionate nature were very fine, he thought with a fleeting grin. Tonight he was a new man.

"You are teasing me in a most ungentlemanly fashion, sir." Olympia's breathless accusation was interrupted by another whining bark from below. "Minotaur is definitely alarmed by something."

"A nightman has probably arrived next door to empty the neighbor's cesspool."

"Perhaps."

Jared opened the kitchen door and nearly got run down by Minotaur who had been waiting impatiently on the other side. The dog dashed straight past him and skidded to a halt in front of Olympia.

"What's the matter, Minotaur?" Olympia patted him warily but gently on the head. "There is no one in the house except us."

Minotaur whined loudly and then darted around her and went up the stairs.

"Perhaps he wants to go into the garden," Olympia said. "I will let him outside for a few minutes."

"I will see to it." Jared took a quick look around the kitchen before following the dog up the stairs. There was no sign that anything had been disturbed near the large iron stove or in the vicinity of the sink. The window that opened onto the enclosed front area below the street level was securely latched.

Jared led the way back up the stairs. Olympia stayed close.

Together they went down the hall to the back door. Minotaur was already there. He scratched enthusiastically at the threshold.

"Something is wrong," Olympia said. "This is not his customary behavior at all."

"I believe you are right." Jared unbolted the door.

Minotaur squeezed through the opening as soon as possible and ran out into the small, walled garden.

"The neighbors are going to be very annoyed if he starts barking again," Olympia said uneasily.

"Just as well, then, that we have not met any of them." Jared handed the candle to her. "Remain here in the house. I shall see what it is that is troubling Minotaur."

Jared slipped quietly outside into the night. He assumed his orders to Olympia would be obeyed simply because his orders were always obeyed when he gave them in that particular tone.

Minotaur stopped when he reached the far end of the garden. He jumped up on his hind legs and sniffed industriously at the top of the wall.

Jared walked past the privy and made his way through the overgrown shrubbery to where Minotaur was looking out into the alley. There was just enough light to see that the small, cobbled lane was empty.

Jared glanced into the neighbors' gardens on either side. Both were dark and silent. There was no sign of any of the nightmen whose business flourished during the late hours. Few people wished to be bothered with having a privy emptied during the day. In most houses the contents of the cesspool had to be carried out of the garden through the main hall and deposited into a cart on the street. It was standard practice to conduct the necessary business at night when fewer people were around to be offended by the odors.

"There is no one about," Jared said softly. "But I suspect you already know that, do you not, Minotaur?"

Minotaur glanced at him and then resumed sniffing the bricks.

"Do you see anything?" Olympia asked.

Jared glanced over his shoulder and saw that she had ignored his instructions. She had left the candle behind in the house and followed him outside. Her eyes were huge in the moonlight and there were deep, fascinating shadows between her breasts.

Jared was torn between irritation at having been disobeyed and an extremely keen recollection of how soft Olympia's breasts were.

"No," he said. "There is no sign of anyone in the alley. Perhaps someone went past a few minutes ago and alarmed Minotaur."

Olympia peered over the top of the wall. "We have been staying in this house for several nights now and he has never before reacted to anyone passing by in the alley."

"I am aware of that." Jared took her arm. "Let's return to the house. There is no point hanging about out here."

She glanced at him, obviously surprised by the inflection of his voice. "Has something annoyed you?"

He wondered how a tutor went about informing his employer that when he gave logical, reasonable commands, he expected to have those commands followed to the letter. But before he could find a means of getting his point across without telling her the truth about his identity, she drew him to a halt with a sharp exclamation.

"Good heavens, what is that?" Olympia stared at a small patch of white on the grass. "Did you drop your handkerchief, Mr. Chillhurst?"

"No." Jared bent down and picked up the square of crumpled white linen. He frowned as he caught a whiff of perfume.

Olympia wrinkled her nose at the strong scent. She looked at Jared, her gaze clear and solemn. "There *was* someone here in the garden tonight."

Jared watched Minotaur trot over to sniff at the handkerchief. "It appears that way," he said quietly.

"I was afraid of this, Mr. Chillhurst. There can no longer be any doubt about it. We have an extremely urgent situation here."

"Urgent?"

Olympia narrowed her gaze as she studied the perfumed linen. "The warning I discovered in the diary about the Guardian must be taken seriously. Someone is determined to get his hands on the secret of the buried treasure. But how did the villain learn our address here in town?"

"Damn it, Olympia." Jared broke off abruptly as an unpleasant thought struck him. His mouth tightened. "Have you been indiscreet about our presence in town?"

"No, of course not. I have been most careful in that regard. Your reputation is very important to me."

"I suppose one of your acquaintances in the Society for Travel and Exploration could have followed us home or hired someone to do so."

"Yes, that is definitely a possibility," Olympia said quickly. "Perhaps one of them is connected to the Guardian in some way."

Or perhaps one of Olympia's new friends was drawn by the lure of treasure as were so many, Jared thought grimly. He knew the lengths certain members of his own family had gone to in the past when they had been on the trail of a missing fortune. It was entirely possible that there were others who would go to similar lengths.

All of the members of the Society for Travel and Exploration were no doubt well aware that Miss Olympia Wingfield's speciality was researching buried treasures and lost gold.

Chapter 9

Jared remembered the prim little cambric chemisette and the white lace cap the moment he awakened the following morning. He realized that they were both undoubtedly still right where they had been left on the floor of Olympia's study last night.

"Damnation." Jared sat up and reached for the black velvet eye patch on the bedside table.

This business of conducting a passionate affair was going to be even more difficult than he had first envisioned. He wondered how the notorious rakes of the *ton* managed to slip in and out of various and assorted boudoirs with such reputed

ease. He was rapidly discovering that conducting a simple, single affair with one woman was fraught with risks.

Perhaps he simply was not cut out for this sort of thing, Jared thought as he tossed aside the quilt and got out of bed. On the other hand, last night's tryst had to rank as one of the most incredibly spectacular events in his entire life. Perhaps *the* most spectacular event.

But now the dawn had come and with it had arrived all the pesky, annoying details that were bound to beset such extraordinary ventures. *First things first,* Jared told himself. He had to rescue the chemisette and the cap before they were discovered by Mrs. Bird or one of the boys.

He quickly located a white cotton shirt and a pair of breeches in his well-organized wardrobe. Rather than take the time to pull on a pair of boots, he chose to go barefoot.

Jared yanked on his clothes and went to the door. He opened it cautiously and warily surveyed the hall. A glance at his watch told him that it was not quite five-thirty.

With any luck, if Mrs. Bird were up and about, she was either still in her room or busy in the kitchen.

Jared went silently down the stairs, his thoughts shifting from the immediate problem of the discarded clothing to the more ominous discovery of the linen handkerchief.

There was no doubt but that someone had been in the garden last night. A thief or a housebreaker looking for a convenient opportunity, most likely. But Olympia did not want to hear such a mundane explanation.

Jared swore softly, aware that Olympia's growing concern about the legendary Guardian was going to make his already chaotic life even more difficult.

He breathed a small sigh of relief when he opened

the study door and saw the chemisette and lace cap on the floor in front of the desk. They lay where they had fallen, dainty evidence of a night of glorious, wild abandon. Jared felt the aching heat rise once more in his lower body. He would not forget last night as long as he lived.

He smiled slightly as he reached down to pluck the garments off the carpet. While he was at it he scooped up the three hairpins he had dislodged from Olympia's hair.

"Forgot something, did ye?" Mrs. Bird rumbled from the doorway. "I thought as much."

"Bloody hell." Jared straightened, the cap and chemisette in hand, and turned around with a sense of grim resignation. He smiled coldly. "You're up rather early this morning, are you not, Mrs. Bird?"

Mrs. Bird was clearly not about to be intimidated. She glowered ferociously at him and planted her hands on her hips. "There's some what calls themselves gentlemen who'd be on their way once they'd gotten what they came for. Are ye one of that sort?"

"I do not have any plans to leave, Mrs. Bird, if that is what you are asking."

Mrs. Bird narrowed her eyes in speculation. "Might be better if ye did. The longer ye hang about the more attached to ye Miss Olympia's likely to get."

Jared looked at her with mild interest. "Do you think so?"

Mrs. Bird's face turned a furious shade of red. "Now see here, ye bloody pirate, I'll not have ye breakin' her heart. Miss Olympia's a decent woman in spite o' what ye done to her last night. It's not right for ye to take advantage of her innocent, trusting nature."

Jared recalled the mysterious handkerchief and was struck by a possibility he had not considered until now. "Tell me, Mrs. Bird, how do you come to know so much about what happened in here last night? Were you by any chance spying on us from the garden?"

"Spying? *Spying?*" Mrs. Bird looked heartily offended. "No such thing. I ain't no spy, sir."

Jared belatedly remembered the scent of perfume that had been attached to the handkerchief. He could not associate it with Mrs. Bird who generally smelled of linseed oil, cleaning polish, and the occasional hint of gin.

"My apologies," he said wryly.

Mrs. Bird was not mollified. "I got eyes and I got ears. I heard all that commotion out in the garden last night. When I opened my window to see what was going on, I noticed the two of ye together talkin' real quiet-like down there. And I saw ye kiss Miss Olympia afore ye went back into the house."

"Did you, indeed?" That last kiss had been primarily designed to take her mind off the Guardian, Jared reflected. He was not certain the ploy had worked.

"That I did. What's more there was enough light to see that poor Miss Olympia weren't wearin' her chemisette under her gown. Which meant someone, more'n likely yerself, had removed it for her."

"You are very observant, Mrs. Bird."

"I knew ye were bent on seducin' her, and I was right. After what I saw in the garden last night, I decided to have a look around in here this mornin' afore anyone else was up. When I seen them things o' hers on the floor I knew for certain what had happened."

"Very clever, Mrs. Bird."

She angled her broad chin accusingly. "I was about to pick 'em up when I heard yer door open upstairs. Now I know for certain yer guilty as sin, don't I?"

"I congratulate you on your brilliant investigations and logical deductions, Mrs. Bird." Jared paused just long enough to be certain he had her full attention.

"With such talents at your disposal, perhaps you'll be able to obtain a position as a Bow Street runner after you've been dismissed from this household."

Mrs. Bird's eyes widened briefly in alarm. Then she glowered at him. "Bah. Don't ye dare threaten me, sir. Miss Olympia ain't about to dismiss me and we both know it."

"Do we? In case you have not noticed, Miss Wingfield has come to rely heavily upon my advice in matters pertaining to the organization of this household."

"She won't turn me off," Mrs. Bird declared. "She's too kindhearted. Yer the one who'll likely get dismissed if she finds out that yer threatenin' me."

"I would not want to put her loyalty to the test, if I were you, Mrs. Bird. Not once she discovers that you've been spying upon her."

"Damn yer bloody soul, I ain't been spyin'."

"Ah, but will she believe that if you tell her that you know all about what happened in here last night? Take my advice, Mrs. Bird. Mind your tongue and your own business."

Mrs. Bird's mouth thinned with outrage. "Yer a devil, ain't ye? Ye come into this household like some sorcerer from hell and ye turn everything upside down and sideways. Ye put a spell on them young hellions upstairs to make 'em behave. Ye produce three thousand bloody pounds with a snap o' yer fingers and now ye've ravished Miss Olympia."

"You have got that last bit wrong, Mrs. Bird." Jared walked purposefully toward the door.

"Ye did so ravish Miss Olympia." Mrs. Bird eyed his expression and wisely took one step back so that she no longer filled the doorway. "I know ye did."

"That only goes to show that you do not fully comprehend the situation at all." Jared strode past her and headed toward the stairs.

"What do y'mean, blast ye?" Mrs. Bird called after him.

"I was the one who was ravished," Jared said politely.

He did not look back as he took the stairs two at a time but he could feel Mrs. Bird's seething disapproval all the way to the landing.

The old harridan was an irritating problem but not an insurmountable one, he thought as he went down the hall. He could deal with her.

Jared stopped in front of Olympia's bedchamber and knocked softly. There was a soft scurrying sound from inside and a moment later Olympia opened the door.

"Good morning, Miss Wingfield." He smiled at the sight of her in her white lawn nightrail and hastily donned chintz wrapper.

Olympia's dark red hair was a magnificent cloud of fire around her piquant face. She blushed a delightful shade of pink when she saw him. In the pale light of dawn she was irresistible. Jared glanced at the invitingly rumpled bed behind her.

"Mr. Chillhurst, what are you doing here at this hour?" Olympia peered around around him to check the corridor. "Someone might see you."

"I am here to return a few personal items that you apparently forgot about last night." Jared held up the chemisette and cap.

"Good grief." Olympia glanced at the garments. Her eyes widened in shock. She snatched them from his hand. "I am so glad you remembered to collect them."

"Unfortunately Mrs. Bird discovered them before I got downstairs."

"Oh, dear." Olympia sighed. "Was she terribly overset? She has been extremely concerned about your presence in this household and now she is likely to think the worst."

"She does think the worst, but I believe she has enough sense to keep her thoughts to herself." Jared bent his head and kissed Olympia warmly. "I shall look forward to seeing you at breakfast, Miss Wingfield."

Jared stepped back and closed the door on Olympia's flushed features. He whistled softly as he went down the hall to his own bedchamber.

"Good morning, Aunt Olympia."

"You are looking very nice today, Aunt Olympia."

"Good morning, Aunt Olympia. A beautiful day, is it not?"

Olympia smiled at Hugh, Ethan, and Robert who had promptly leaped to their feet as she walked into the breakfast room.

"Good morning, everyone." She waited as Ethan hastened forward to hold her chair for her. She was still not fully accustomed to the boys' new manners. "Thank you, Ethan."

Ethan looked at Jared for approval. Jared nodded slightly. Ethan grinned and took his seat again.

Olympia glanced down the length of the table and caught Jared's knowing eye. The warm, shimmering happiness that had blossomed inside her last night welled up once more. Her fingers trembled a little as she picked up her spoon.

This was what it felt like to be in love, she thought. She had realized the truth last night. There had been no question but that what she felt for Jared was far beyond passion.

Love. She had come to believe that she would never experience the emotion. At five-and-twenty a woman of the world had to be realistic, after all.

Love.

The sensation was infinitely more exciting than discovering the secrets of a lost legend or exploring the strange customs of other lands.

Love.

Her life was a cup that was filled to overflowing this morning. The loneliness she had known since the deaths of Aunt Sophy and Aunt Ida was gone. She had found a man whose soul seemed perfectly tuned to her own.

She would not have him with her long, she reminded herself; weeks, months, perhaps a year or two at best if she was extraordinarily fortunate. There was no denying that one day Jared would leave to take up another position in another household. That was the way with tutors. Young boys grew up and their tutors moved on.

But in the meantime, Olympia vowed, she would indulge herself in this great, passionate love that had come upon her in the guise of a man with the face of a pirate.

"Well, then, where are you all off to today?" Olympia hoped her voice was steady and calm. Her insides certainly were not. Joy was a difficult emotion to conceal, she discovered. She knew from the glint in Jared's gaze that he was well aware of her euphoric mood.

"We are going to visit Mr. Winslow's Mechanical Museum," Robert volunteered.

"They say there is a giant clockwork spider there that moves just like a real spider," Hugh said excitedly. "It frightens the ladies but it won't frighten me."

"I have heard that there is also a mechanical bear and some birds, too," Ethan added.

Olympia looked at Jared, her curiosity piqued. "It sounds very interesting."

"So they say." Jared spread jam on his toast.

Olympia pondered briefly. She was suddenly torn between her own plans for the day and the novelty of touring a mechanical museum. "I believe I should like to go to the museum with you."

"You are quite welcome to come along." Jared bit into the toast.

"Yes, Aunt Olympia, do come with us," Robert said. "It will be great fun."

"And very educational," Ethan said wisely.

"I'm sure it will be." Going to the museum would not only be educational, Olympia thought, it would give her an opportunity to spend the afternoon with Jared. "Very well, then, I shall make arrangements. What time will you be leaving for the museum?"

"Three o'clock," Jared said.

"Excellent. I have an appointment to view some maps in the Musgrave Institution, but I shall be finished in plenty of time."

"I doubt that you will find anything useful in the society's collection, Miss Wingfield." Roland Torbert clasped his hands behind his back as he hovered over Olympia. "Very poor assortment of maps of the West Indies here. Now in my own, personal library, I have an excellent collection."

"I am quite looking forward to viewing them, Mr. Torbert." Olympia edged slightly away from him. Torbert smelled of a combination of musty clothing, sweat, and the perfume he used in a vain attempt to conceal the other odors. "But I wish to do my research in an orderly fashion."

"Naturally." Torbert closed the distance between them. He peered over her shoulder as she unrolled another map alongside the first that was already spread out on the desk. "Do you mind telling me what it is, precisely, that you are seeking on these maps?"

"I am trying to ascertain the correct geography of

the area." Olympia deliberately kept her answer vague. She had no intention of confiding in anyone except Jared at this stage of her research. "There appear to be some discrepancies in the records of the area."

"I see." Torbert assumed a learned air. "Difficult to chart all those islands, y'know."

"Yes, indeed." Olympia bent over the two maps comparing them with great care.

There was no sign on either chart of a mysterious, unnamed island to the north of Jamaica. There were one or two small indications of land on the newer map that were not recorded on the older one, but they were not located in the right vicinity of the West Indies.

"Perhaps later today would be suitable," Torbert said. "I shall be happy to have you call upon me this afternoon, Miss Wingfield." He watched her roll up one of the maps and set it aside. "I can arrange to have my maps ready for viewing at that time."

"Thank you, but I shall be busy this afternoon." Olympia unrolled another map. "Perhaps later this week, if it's convenient?"

"Of course, of course." Torbert clasped his hands behind his broad back and rocked on his heels. "Miss Wingfield, I understand that you will also be perusing Aldridge's collection."

"He was kind enough to offer me the opportunity." Olympia frowned intently as she examined the new map.

"I feel I should take this opportunity to give you a bit of advice."

"Yes?" Olympia did not look up from the maps.

Torbert coughed discreetly. "It's my duty to tell you that you should be extremely cautious about revealing any aspect of your studies to Aldridge."

"Really?" Olympia glanced at him in surprise. "Whatever do you mean, sir?"

Torbert cast a swift look around the library, making certain that no one else, including the elderly librarian, was within listening distance. He leaned very close. "Aldridge ain't above takin' advantage of a young woman, Miss Wingfield."

"Advantage?" Olympia wrinkled her nose as the scent of Torbert's heavy perfume assailed her. "Of me?"

Torbert looked flustered and immediately straightened. "Not of your person, Miss Wingfield," he muttered. "Of your work."

"I see." There was something oddly familiar about that perfume, Olympia thought.

"My dear, it's well known that you specialize in studying old legends as well as the customs of other lands." Torbert chuckled conspiratorially. "It's also a fact that there's often a hint or two of treasure involved in some of those old tales you publish in the society's journal."

"True." Olympia lifted one shoulder in a tiny shrug and bent over the maps. "But I have never heard of anyone actually locating a real treasure, sir. It is the task of exploration itself that is the reward."

"Only for those of us who have an intellectual appreciation for such things," Torbert said smoothly. "For others, I fear, the base lure of gold and jewels is far stronger than the more refined appeal of study and exploration."

"You are probably quite right, Mr. Torbert, but I doubt if such people would be members of a learned group such as the Society for Travel and Exploration."

"Sadly, my dear, that is where you are wrong." Torbert smiled bleakly. "Human nature being what it is, a certain number of rude, uncouth treasure seekers are in our midst." He drew himself up. "And I regret to say that Aldridge is one of them."

"I shall bear your warning in mind." Olympia

frowned as she caught another hint of his perfume. She almost recognized it, she thought. She knew she had smelled it recently. Very recently.

Last night, in fact.

"I say, it's rather warm in here, is it not?" Torbert pulled his handkerchief from his pocket and mopped his perspiring brow.

Olympia stared at the linen handkerchief. It was an exact duplicate of the one she and Jared had found in the garden.

The large clockwork spider crawled relentlessly across the bottom of the glass case. It moved with a jerky, unnatural stride that was nonetheless fascinating. It pursued a mechanical mouse that moved with a similarly uneven gait.

Olympia crowded close to the glass along with Ethan, Hugh, and Robert. They all peered into the case with rapt attention. Jared stood on the other side and watched the spider's progress with an indulgent expression.

"I say, it's awfully huge, isn't it?" Ethan glanced hopefully at Olympia. "Are you frightened, Aunt Olympia?"

"Of course not." Olympia looked up and saw the disappointment in his eyes. "Why would I be frightened when I have you three to protect me from the beast?"

Ethan grinned, satisfied. "Do not forget Mr. Chillhurst. He'll protect you, too. Won't you, Mr. Chillhurst?"

"I shall do my best," Jared vowed softly.

"It's just a mechanical spider," Robert said with the scorn only a ten-year old boy can affect. "It cannot hurt anyone, can it, Mr. Chillhurst?"

"Probably not," Jared said. "But one never knows."

"That's right," Ethan said with relish. "One never knows. If it got loose in here, for instance, I'll wager it could cause all sorts of trouble."

Robert glanced across the room to where visitors were observing the actions of a mechanical bear. "Just imagine what that lady over there would do if she suddenly felt the nasty limbs of a spider on her ankle."

"I'll wager she would scream," Hugh said. He gave the latch on top of the glass case a speculative look.

Jared's brows rose. "Do not even consider the notion."

All three boys groaned with regret and went back to studying the spider.

Olympia glanced quickly around and then moved to Jared's side. This was the first opportunity she had had to talk to him in private. She was anxious to tell him about her discoveries regarding Torbert's handkerchief.

"Mr. Chillhurst, I must speak with you."

He smiled. "I am at your service, Miss Wingfield."

"Privately." Olympia moved into another room full of clockwork oddities.

Jared leisurely followed her to a case that contained a mechanical soldier. "Yes, Miss Wingfield?" He twisted the knob on the base of the case. The soldier started to stiffen and stand tall. "What was it you wished to discuss?"

She shot him a triumphant, sidelong glance and pretended to study the clockwork figure. "I believe I have discovered the identity of the intruder. Perhaps of the Guardian himself."

Jared's hand froze on the knob. "Have you, indeed?" he asked without any inflection.

"Yes, I have." Olympia leaned closer on the pretext of getting a better view of the mechanical soldier. "You will never credit this, but it is none other than Mr. Torbert."

"Torbert?" Jared stared at her. "What the devil are you talking about?"

"I am virtually certain that the handkerchief that we found last night belongs to Mr. Torbert." Olympia watched as the mechanical soldier began to raise his small rifle. "He used one this morning in the society's library and it looked just like the one we discovered."

"Most handkerchiefs look very similar," Jared said dryly.

"Yes, but this one carried the same scent as the one we found."

Jared frowned slightly. "Are you certain?"

"Quite certain." Olympia saw that the mechanical soldier was taking aim with the rifle. "But there is one other possible explanation."

"What is that?"

"Torbert and Aldridge are apparently fierce rivals. Torbert, in fact, took great pains to warn me about Aldridge this morning. It's possible that Lord Aldridge deliberately planted that handkerchief in the garden last night."

"Why in blazes would he do that?"

Olympia slanted him an impatient look. "In hopes that it would make me think the worst of Mr. Torbert, of course."

"That assumption presupposes that you would be able to identify the handkerchief," Jared pointed out.

"Yes, I know, but that is precisely what I did."

"Aldridge could not have guessed it would be so easy for you to recognize it. No, I seriously doubt that he had anything to do with it." Jared turned toward her with a thoughtful expression. "Olympia, I do not want you getting involved in this matter."

"But, Mr. Chillhurst—"

"Leave it to me."

"I cannot do that." Olympia lifted her chin. "This

affects my studies, sir. I have every right to protect the diary from the Guardian or anyone else who happens to be after the treasure." She nibbled on her lower lip reflectively. "Although, I must admit, I cannot see Mr. Torbert as part of a legend. I do not think he can possibly be connected to the Guardian."

"Damnation, woman," Jared said between his teeth, "I will protect you from Torbert, the Guardian, and anyone else who comes along. If you require protection, that is."

Olympia stared at him in astonishment. "Whatever do you mean by that, sir? Of course precautions must be taken."

"Miss Wingfield, you will leave this matter of the handkerchief in my hands. I will see that Torbert is made to understand that there are to be no more incidents such as the one that occurred in the garden last night."

"You will speak to him?"

"Rest assured he will get the point."

Olympia subsided, satisfied. "Very well, sir, I leave everything to you."

"Thank you, Miss Wingfield. Now, then—"

Before Jared could finish, a woman's voice cut through the background murmur of conversation and the tick and clink of clockwork mechanisms.

"*Chillhurst.* What on earth are you doing here?"

Jared's gaze flashed past Olympia to someone else who was approaching from behind her. "Bloody hell."

Olympia barely had time to register the chillingly enigmatic expression he wore before the woman spoke again.

"Chillhurst, it is you, is it not?"

Olympia turned to see a strikingly beautiful woman gliding across the room toward them. The lady came to a halt and smiled coolly at Jared. Her light blue eyes were filled with amused recognition.

For a moment, Olympia could only stare at the lovely stranger. The woman's pale blond hair was elegantly pinned beneath an extremely clever and no doubt exceedingly expensive, little blue hat. She wore a dark blue spencer over her sky blue afternoon gown. The matching kid gloves, Olympia knew, had probably cost more than her own gown, shoes, bonnet, and reticule combined.

The woman was not alone. She was accompanied by an equally fashionable lady garbed in yellow. The second woman was not beautiful in the same sense as the blonde, but there was an unmistakable air of exotic attractiveness about her. She was a brilliant contrast to her friend. Her hair was a deep, rich brown beneath her feather-trimmed hat. Her eyes were dark. Her figure was fuller and more rounded than her sleek companion.

"I could not credit it when I noticed you a moment ago, Chillhurst," the blond woman said. "I had heard that you were in town but I doubted the truth. You never come to London."

"Good afternoon, Demetria. Or should I say, Lady Beaumont?" Jared inclined his head with cold civility.

"Demetria will do." Demetria glanced at her companion. "You remember Constance, do you not?"

"Only too well." Jared smiled coldly. "Lady Kirkdale."

"Chillhurst." Constance, Lady Kirkdale, smiled politely. Her eyes went to Olympia.

Demetria's gaze followed that of her companion. "And who is your little friend, Chillhurst? The *on dit* is that you are living with her in a house in Ibberton Street. But I refused to credit that tale, too. So unlike you to become involved in a liaison of that sort."

"Lady Beaumont, Lady Kirkdale, allow me to present my wife," Jared's voice was as unruffled as ever but there was a clear warning in the otherwise unread-able glance he gave Olympia.

My wife.

Olympia became aware of the fact that her mouth had fallen open. She promptly closed it and pulled her-self together to face the crisis. It had been her idea, after all, to claim that she and Jared were married in the event that they were questioned by anyone who knew him. Jared's reputation was at stake.

The poor man was only following her instructions. She had no choice but to support him.

"How do you do?" Olympia said briskly.

"How absolutely fascinating." Demetria surveyed Olympia as if she were one of the exhibits on display in the museum. "What a stunning surprise. So Chill-hurst has at long last done his duty by his title and found himself a viscountess."

Chapter 10

"Viscount?" Olympia stalked into her study a half hour later. She whisked off her bonnet and whirled around to confront Jared. It was the first time she had been alone with him since the scene in the mechanical museum. She was simmering with outrage. "You're a *viscount*?"

"I regret that you had to learn the truth under such circumstances, Olympia." Jared closed the door and locked it. He stood with his back to it and faced her with the same grim, enigmatic expression he had been wearing since he had introduced her as his wife. "I'm well aware that you are entitled to an explanation."

"I should think so. I am your em-

ployer, Mr. Chillhurst." Olympia scowled. "I mean, my lord. Whatever. Damnation. It would appear that I should have insisted upon references, after all. I suppose you did not produce any for my uncle, did you?"

"Ah, not as such," Jared murmured. "No. I'm afraid not. He did not request any, you see."

"He hired you as a tutor for my household and he did not ask to see your references?" Olympia demanded in disbelief.

"He did not actually hire me as a tutor," Jared said evenly.

"This grows worse by the moment. What, precisely, did he hire you to do, my lord?"

"He did not hire me to do anything. He asked me to do him the favor of escorting his shipment of goods to Upper Tudway." Jared looked at her. "A task I carried out very well, if I may say so."

"Rubbish." Olympia tossed the bonnet onto the sofa and went around behind her desk. She always felt strong and secure when she was sitting behind her desk, she reflected. She dropped down onto her chair and glowered at Jared. "Let me have the rest of the story, if you please, sir. I grow tired of playing the unwitting fool in this scene."

Something flickered briefly in Jared's single-eyed gaze. It might have been pain or it might have been anger. Olympia could not be certain. Whatever it was it sent a chill down her spine.

Jared sat down slowly, stretched out his booted feet and rested his elbows on the arms of the mahogany chair. He touched the tips of his fingers together and regarded her with his brooding gaze. "It's a somewhat complicated matter."

"Do not concern yourself with the complexity of the business." Olympia smiled, telling herself she could be calm and cool, too. "I feel certain I am intelligent enough to grasp the essentials."

Jared's mouth hardened. "No doubt. Very well, where shall I begin?"

"At the beginning, of course. Tell me why you are masquerading as a tutor in my household."

Jared hesitated, apparently searching for words. "Everything I told you about meeting your uncle was true, Olympia. We encountered each other in France and I agreed to escort the shipment of goods to you."

"Why did you bother with the task if you were not seeking a position as a tutor?"

"The Lightbourne diary," Jared said simply.

For the second time that day Olympia's mouth fell open in shock. "The diary? You knew about it?"

"Yes. I, too, have been pursuing it."

"Good grief." Olympia felt as if the very breath had been knocked out of her. She sat back in her chair and tried to think quickly. "Of course. That explains everything."

"Not quite."

"You were on the trail of the diary but Uncle Artemis got to it first so you arranged to meet him. Am I correct thus far?"

"Yes." Jared began to drum his fingers together. "However—"

"You soon realized the diary was stowed in the shipment of goods that was on its way to me. So you found a way to accompany the shipment."

Jared inclined his head. "Your cleverness never ceases to amaze me, Olympia."

She tried to ignore the compliment. This was no time to be swept off her feet by honeyed words from the man she loved. She had to remember that Jared had deliberately deceived her. "Once you arrived in this household, you found a way to stay. You apparently realized at once that I needed a tutor."

"Your uncle put the notion into my head," Jared admitted. "He said you had already been through three tutors in six months."

"So you took advantage of the opportunity to stay close to the Lightbourne diary."

Jared studied the wall above her head. "I realize that appears to be the reason I deceived you."

"I suppose you feared you could not decipher it, yourself, so you wanted to see if I could untangle the secrets of the legend for you."

"I know it looks that way."

Olympia frowned in thought. "What drew you to the diary, Mr. Chillhurst? I mean, your lordship."

"Jared will do," he said quietly. "The reason I was searching for the diary when I met your uncle is that it belongs in my family." He shrugged slightly. "So does the treasure, if, indeed, it actually exists."

Olympia froze. "What do you mean, it belongs in your family?"

"Claire Lightbourne was my great-grandmother."

"Never say so." Olympia nearly fell off her chair. "Your great-grandmother? A countess? But there is no reference to a title in the diary."

"She married Jack Ryder when he was still plain Captain Jack. He did not become the Earl of Flamecrest until several years after he returned to England from the West Indies. The family does not like to discuss the matter, but the truth is, he more or less bought the title."

"Good heavens."

"It was not all that difficult to buy a title in those days," Jared said mildly. "It only required a great deal of money and influence. Jack Ryder had both."

"Yes, of course." Olympia remembered some of the

entries she had skimmed over in the diary. Jack Ryder had come back from the West Indies a rich man. He had amassed even greater wealth after he had settled down in England.

"After securing the Flamecrest title," Jared continued, "my great-grandfather acquired a second title, that of the Viscount Chillhurst, which is used by the Flamecrest heir. In this instance, myself."

Olympia was reeling from the unrelenting series of shocks. "You're heir to an earldom. Your great-grandfather was Claire Lightbourne's Mr. Ryder." *Claire's beloved Mr. Ryder,* Olympia thought.

"Yes."

My beloved Mr. Chillhurst.

Olympia's spirits were plunging deeper into despair with every passing revelation. She reminded herself that she had known from the beginning that she would not be able to have her Mr. Chillhurst around for very long. Still, there was no denying that deep inside she had hoped to have him with her for longer than a few short weeks.

Her dream was ending much too soon. Too soon. She had to find a way to save it even if she could only have it for a little while longer.

And what about Jared, she thought with a growing sense of desperation. She could not bring herself to believe that their shared passion meant nothing to him, that he had deceived her even as he took her into his arms. Perhaps he did not love her, but he wanted her. She was almost certain of it.

She forced herself to think logically. "Well, no wonder you wanted to find the diary, Mr. Chillhurst. You clearly have a claim on it. You have no doubt been pursuing it for years. You must have been exceedingly annoyed when you discovered that I had located it first."

"Chillhurst will do, if you cannot bring yourself to call me Jared."

"Whatever." Olympia struggled to produce a brisk, cheerful smile. "I must say, this opens up a whole new avenue of inquiry for us."

Jared gave her a blank look. "It does?"

"Certainly." Olympia jumped to her feet and went to stand at the window. She clasped her hands behind her back and gazed out into the tiny walled garden. She was about to take a calculated risk and she knew she had to be very cautious.

"I do not comprehend your meaning, Olympia."

Olympia took a deep breath. "Your knowledge of family history may well give me some very useful clues, sir. It could assist me in deciphering the diary."

"I doubt it. My knowledge of family history is limited to a series of Banbury tales concerning Captain Jack and his ridiculous exploits."

Olympia's nails dug into her palms. She must convince Jared to let her continue with her work on the diary. It was the only excuse she had for maintaining a connection with him.

"One never knows, sir," she said. "I might be able to use some of the information in those tales to make sense out of various odd phrases in the diary."

"Do you think so?" Jared sounded dubious.

"Yes, I am certain of it." Olympia swung around to face him. "I am quite willing to continue my work on the diary, sir. I will be more than happy to share my conclusions with you. I understand that the secret of the hidden treasure belongs to your family."

Jared's expression hardened. "Olympia, I don't give a damn about the secret of the Lightbourne diary. I have tried to make that clear."

"Of course you care about it," she insisted. "You went to a great deal of trouble to find the diary and to insinuate yourself into this household so that you could learn the secret. I want you to know that I comprehend precisely why you deceived me."

"You do?"

"Yes, and I must tell you that I think your scheme was a very clever one, sir. It would have worked brilliantly if you had not encountered Lady Beaumont this afternoon."

"Only you could make excuses for my behavior, Olympia."

"Hardly excuses, sir. Now that I consider the matter, your actions make excellent sense to me."

"You must be wondering why I did not content myself with remaining a tutor," Jared said quietly. "You are no doubt asking yourself why I seduced you."

Olympia laced her fingers together and lifted her chin. "No, Mr. Chillhurst. I am not asking myself that particular question."

"Why not?" Jared got up from the chair. "Most women in your position would."

"I already know the answer." Olympia was intensely aware of him.

"Do you? And what is the answer, Olympia? How do you explain my conduct? We both know very well that I have not behaved as a gentleman should behave. Most would say that I have taken advantage of you."

"That is entirely untrue." Olympia glowered at him. "We took advantage of each other, sir."

Jared's mouth curved ruefully. "Did we?"

"Yes. We are both of the world, sir. We knew what we were about. Indeed, if anyone is to blame for what transpired between us, it is I."

"You?" He stared, astounded.

She blushed but met his gaze steadily. "You are a gentleman, sir, but I sensed at once that you were also a man of excessive passions. I fear I took advantage of that fact."

Jared cleared his throat. "Excessive passions?"

"It is no doubt a family trait," Olympia said kindly. "After all, you are a descendant of Mr. Ryder and from everything I have read about him, he was, indeed, a man of fierce emotions."

"Allow me to tell you that you are very likely the only person on the face of the earth who sees me as a man of excessive passions, Olympia." Jared's mouth twisted in rueful amusement. "In point of fact, I am considered a rather dull sort."

"Nonsense. Anyone who says that does not know you very well, sir."

"My entire family holds precisely that opinion. And they are not the only ones. Lady Beaumont does, also."

Olympia was momentarily distracted. "That brings up another matter I wish to discuss. Who is Lady Beaumont? An old friend of yours?"

Jared turned and walked back to Olympia's desk without a word. He propped himself against it and folded his arms across his chest.

"Lady Beaumont was, until recently, Miss Demetria Seaton," he said without any sign of emotion. "Three years ago she and I were engaged for a short while."

"Engaged." For some reason that news shook Olympia more than anything else that had happened thus far. "I see."

"Do you?"

"She is very beautiful." Olympia tried to force back a rising tide of panic.

The knowledge that Jared had once loved the lovely Demetria was difficult to handle. Until now, Olympia realized, she had not really considered the fact that there had been other women in his life. She had known that he was not entirely without experience in such matters, but she had not allowed herself to contemplate the notion that he might have actually loved another woman. *Loved her enough to become engaged to her.*

"For various reasons which I will not bore you with today, Demetria and I decided we did not suit," Jared said.

"Oh." Olympia could not think of anything else to say.

"The engagement was ended shortly after it was announced. There was very little gossip about it because the whole event took place at my family seat on the Isle of Flame, not in London. A year ago, she married Beaumont and that is all there is to it."

"Oh." Olympia could not think of anything to say to that, either. She knew instinctively that there was much more to the story but she also knew she had no right to pry. "Well, I suppose that is neither here nor there."

"Precisely."

"However," Olympia plowed on, determined to stick to important matters, "we are left with an unfortunate situation because of the fact that Lady Beaumont recognized you this afternoon."

"I would not call it unfortunate," Jared said. "Perhaps awkward would be a better term."

"Yes, well, whatever. The point is, we must deal with the matter."

"I have a suggestion." Jared watched her intently.

"So do I." Olympia began to pace the small study. "The answer is obvious."

"It is?"

"Of course. We must pack and leave for Upper Tudway immediately."

"If that is your wish, we can certainly do so. However, leaving town will not solve the problem."

"Yes, it will." Olympia shot him a quelling glare.

"If we are quick about it, we can be gone before we are obliged to confront any more of your friends or associates. Back in Upper Tudway you may continue to pass yourself off as a tutor."

"I do not think—"

"I can continue to work on the diary," she said enthusiastically. "Everything will be as it was before we came to London."

"May I remind you that it was your plan to pass ourselves off as a married couple in the event we were discovered?"

Olympia reddened. "I am well aware that this is all my fault, sir. But in fairness, I must point out that my plan would have worked very well had you been what you appeared, a gentleman of modest means and birth. It is the fact that you are a viscount and heir to an earldom that muddles the thing."

"I know," Jared said apologetically.

"No one would have cared a jot about our relationship before this. Now, however, your title and position makes our situation gossip fodder for the polite world."

"I am well aware of that. I am responsible for all that has transpired."

Olympia sighed. "Do not blame yourself, sir. What happened was probably unavoidable, given your nature and temperament. A man of strong passions is always at risk of causing talk. However, I believe that if we depart for Upper Tudway at once, the gossip will soon cease."

"The damage is done," Jared said. "We have introduced ourselves as Lord and Lady Chillhurst. One can hardly expect that sort of gossip to simply evaporate."

"It will if the next time you happen to be in London, you put out the word that it was all a jest," Olympia said quickly.

Jared stared at her. "You want me to pass this whole thing off as a jest?"

"It could be done," Olympia said earnestly. "You can explain that I was just a friend."

"A friend?"

Olympia frowned. "Well, perhaps you could say that I was your mistress, or paramour, or something. I know very well that gentlemen frequently keep their convenients tucked away in houses here in town. It's done all the time."

"Bloody hell." Jared's jaw went rigid. "What about your reputation, Olympia?"

"No one knows me here in London and it is highly unlikely that anyone in Upper Tudway will ever hear about this nonsense." Olympia stopped her pacing and began to tap one toe. "Furthermore, I do not particularly care if anyone does hear about it. I have told you before that I am not concerned with my reputation."

"What about me?" Jared asked quietly. "I have a reputation to consider also."

Olympia eyed him uncertainly. "I believe you will be able to brush through this without too much damage to your reputation."

"Is that a fact?"

"It is not as though you will actually be seeking work as a tutor in the future," she pointed out. "And no one will take any notice of the lady you seduced. After all, I do not have any position in Society. You apparently rarely even appear in London, yourself. All you need do is simply keep out of sight for a few months."

"I have another solution, Olympia."

"Yes? What is it?"

"I suggest we make the thing a fact. We can be married quietly by special license. No one need know precisely when the marriage took place."

"Married." Olympia's mouth went dry. "To you?"

"Why not? It seems a very logical answer to our predicament."

"Impossible." Olympia recovered herself and hurried around the corner of her desk. She collapsed into her chair and took a deep, steadying breath. "Absolutely impossible, Mr. Chillhurst. I mean, my lord."

Jared straightened and turned to face her. He planted both hands on top of the desk and leaned forward. The expression on his face appeared to have been carved in stone.

"Why not?" Jared asked through set teeth.

Olympia gave a start. Then she narrowed her eyes, refusing to give way beneath the blatant intimidation. "For one thing, you are a viscount."

"So?"

Olympia was flustered by that response. "I am hardly a suitable wife for a viscount."

"I'll be the judge of that."

She blinked. "You are asking me to marry you only because of the awkward situation in which we find ourselves."

"I would have gotten around to asking you eventually, Olympia."

"That is very kind of you to say so, my lord, but you will forgive me when I tell you that I do not entirely believe you."

"Are you calling me a liar, Miss Wingfield?"

She braced herself. "Not precisely. You are merely behaving like the noble gentleman that you are."

"Bloody hell."

"It is only to be expected," she assured him. "However, I am not going to allow you to trap yourself in an unwanted marriage when there is absolutely no need for such a sacrifice."

"I assure you, Miss Wingfield, I want the damn marriage. Having you in my bed will more than compensate me for any sacrifice on my part."

Olympia felt herself turn scarlet. "Sir, that is your passionate nature speaking. Passion is all very well and good in its place, but it hardly constitutes a sound reason for marriage."

"I disagree, Miss Wingfield." Jared lifted his hands without any warning and caught her face between his palms. He bent his head and kissed her fiercely.

Olympia was so startled that she could not even muster a token resistance. Her mouth opened beneath his and she trembled as she always did when Jared kissed her. The familiar warmth gathered in her lower body. She moaned softly.

Jared released her and stepped back with a look of fierce satisfaction. "Between my passionate nature and your own, Miss Wingfield, I am certain that we shall deal very well together."

He started toward the door.

Olympia swallowed and found her voice. "Hold one minute, sir. Where do you think you are going?"

"I am going to obtain a special license and to make arrangements for an extremely discreet marriage. You had best prepare yourself for your wedding night, Miss Wingfield."

"Now, see here, Mr. Chillhurst, I mean, Lord Chillhurst. You are, strictly speaking, still in my employ. You cannot issue orders of that sort without my permission."

Jared unlocked the door and opened it. He glanced back briefly. "In case you have failed to notice, Miss Wingfield, I have been running your household since the day I arrived. What is more, I have a talent for it."

"I am well aware of that, sir, however—"

"There is no reason for you to concern yourself with the pesky little details of day-to-day life at this juncture,

Miss Wingfield. Such matters are not your forte. Just leave everything to me."

Jared went out the door and closed it with enough force to make it shudder on its hinges.

Olympia started to rise and then fell back into her chair with a groan. Although she had never had occasion to witness Jared's streak of hot-blooded arrogance until now, she knew she should not be surprised to discover it. It went right along with his excessively passionate nature.

Nevertheless, she could not allow him to get carried away with his outrageous scheme to marry her. The man was, after all, driven by passion and honor, not true love.

He would only live to regret his impulsive decision, she told herself sadly. He would come to resent her and she would end up with a broken heart.

She had to save him from his own passions, Olympia thought. She loved him too much to allow him to go through with the marriage.

Besides, when one got right down to it, this entire mess was her fault. She was the only one who could put it right.

The knock on the door of Jared's bedchamber came shortly before the evening meal. He had just sat down at the small writing table to compose a letter to his father.

"Enter."

He glanced up as the door opened to reveal Robert, Ethan, and Hugh. Minotaur brought up the rear of the small column that filed into the room.

Jared took one look at the determined expressions on the three young faces and put aside his quill. He turned slightly in the chair, and rested one arm on the back of it.

Robert squared his shoulders. "Good evening, sir."

"Good evening. Was there something you wished to say?"

"Yes, sir." Robert took a deep breath. "We came here to find out if what Mrs. Bird says is true."

Jared stifled an oath. "What was it, precisely, that she said?"

Ethan's eyes lit with excitement. "She says you're a viscount, sir. Not a tutor at all."

Jared looked at him. "She is half right and half wrong. I am a viscount, but I believe I have also done a creditable job in my position as a tutor in this household."

Ethan glanced at his brothers in confusion. "Well, yes, sir. You are a very good tutor, sir."

Jared inclined his head. "Thank you."

Hugh frowned anxiously. "The thing is, sir, will you continue to be our tutor now that you've turned into a viscount?"

"I fully intend to continue to supervise your studies," Jared said.

Hugh relaxed slightly. "Very good, sir."

"I say." Ethan grinned. "That's good news, sir. We would hate to get another tutor."

Robert scowled at the younger boys. "That is not what we came here to talk to him about."

"What did you come here to talk about, Robert?" Jared asked quietly.

Robert's hand was clenched in a tight fist at his side. The words came out in a headlong rush. "Mrs. Bird says you've had your way with Aunt Olympia and that you've got what you wanted and everyone in town knows who you really are now and you'll disappear soon because of the scandal which will occur when everyone finds out you are not actually married to Aunt Olympia."

"Excuse me, sir," Ethan said before Jared could respond. "But what does it mean, you've had your way with Aunt Olympia?"

Robert glared at him. "Be quiet, you idiot."

"I was just asking," Ethan muttered.

"Mrs. Bird says you've ruined her," Hugh said to Jared. "But a short time ago I asked Aunt Olympia if she was ruined and she said she was feeling quite fit."

"I am pleased to hear that," Jared said.

"It appears there's more to it than that, sir." Robert shifted uneasily. "Mrs. Bird says that the only way to set things to rights is for you to marry Aunt Olympia and that you are hardly likely to do that."

"I fear that Mrs. Bird is wrong on that last account," Jared said. "I have already asked your aunt to marry me."

"You have?" Robert looked startled and then hope dawned in his eyes. "Sir, we are not precisely certain what is going on but we do not want anything bad to happen to Aunt Olympia. She has been very kind to us, you see."

Jared smiled. "She has been very kind to me, too. And I intend to see that nothing bad happens to her."

"I say." Robert grinned with relief. "If you're going to look after her, then there's no problem, is there?"

"Well," Jared said slowly, "there is one slight difficulty remaining to be resolved before matters are settled to my satisfaction, but I am certain I can deal with the issue."

Robert's face crumpled with renewed concern. "What is the difficulty, sir? Perhaps we could help."

"Yes, we'll help," Hugh said eagerly.

"Just tell us what needs doing," Ethan added swiftly.

Jared stretched out his legs, leaned back, and braced his elbows on the arms of the chair. He touched his fingers together. "I have asked your aunt to marry me, but she has not yet consented to do so. Until she agrees, matters will remain a trifle unsettled, I fear."

Ethan, Hugh, and Robert exchanged uneasy glances.

"There is," Jared continued smoothly, "some urgency about the situation. Your aunt really ought to make up her mind to marry me as quickly as possible."

"We shall speak to her," Hugh said at once.

"Yes," Ethan agreed. "I'm certain we can convince her to marry you, sir. Mrs. Bird says only a madwoman would refuse to marry under these circumstances."

"Aunt Olympia is not really a madwoman," Robert assured Jared. "Just a bit preoccupied at times. She is actually quite intelligent, you know. I'm sure we can convince her to marry you."

"Excellent." Jared sat forward and picked up his pen. "Go to work on the task, then. I shall see you at dinner."

"Yes, sir." Robert made his bow and led the way back to the door.

"We'll handle this for you, sir," Ethan told Jared. He sketched a quick, polite bow and dashed after Robert.

"Do not concern yourself, sir," Hugh said confidently. "Aunt Olympia is very reasonable about most things. I'm certain we can get her to marry you."

"Thank you, Hugh. I appreciate your assistance," Jared said gravely.

Minotaur rose from the floor, wagged his tail enthusiastically, and trotted after the boys.

Jared waited until the door had closed behind his small band of trusty supporters before going back to his letter.

Dear Sir:

By the time you receive this letter I intend to be married to Miss Olympia Wingfield of Upper Tudway. I hesitate to describe her other than to assure you that she will make me a suitable wife.

I regret that the wedding cannot be delayed until such time as you might be able to conveniently attend. I shall look forward to introducing my bride to you at the earliest opportunity.

Yrs ever,
Jared

Another knock sounded on the door just as Jared was in the process of sealing his letter.

"Enter."

The door opened and Mrs. Bird took one step into the room. She stopped and regarded Jared with wary belligerence. "I come to see what was going on here for meself."

"Did you, Mrs. Bird?"

"Is it true what ye told the boys? Did ye ask Miss Olympia to marry you?"

"Yes, Mrs. Bird, I did. Not that it's any of your business."

Mrs. Bird appeared momentarily stunned. Then her expression turned to one of deep suspicion. "If ye asked Miss Olympia to marry ye, why ain't she actin' like a woman who's about to be wed?"

"Probably because she rejected my offer."

Mrs. Bird stared at him in horror. "She turned ye down?"

"I'm afraid so."

"We'll see about that." Mrs. Bird shook her head. "That young lady ain't never had a proper attitude toward some things. Not her fault. Miss Sophy and Miss

Ida raised her up with some strange notions. Still and all, she's got to be made to see reason on this."

"I shall trust you to guide her in the matter, Mrs. Bird." Jared held out the letter. "By the by, would you kindly see that this gets posted?"

Mrs. Bird slowly took the letter from his hand. "Are ye a real viscount?"

"Yes, Mrs. Bird. I am."

"In that case, we'd best get Miss Olympia married off to ye afore ye change yer mind. She ain't likely to do any better than a viscount."

"I'm glad you feel that way, Mrs. Bird."

Chapter 11

Olympia put down her pen and gazed thoughtfully at the mysterious phrase she had just unraveled.

*Seek the secret beneath the
Siryn's surging sea.*

It made no sense, just as the warning about the Guardian made no sense. But Olympia was virtually certain it was another piece of the puzzle.

Before she could consider the problem further, a knock sounded on the study door.

"Enter," she called absently, her attention still on the new clue.

The door opened. Mrs. Bird, Robert, Ethan, and Hugh filed into the study and arranged themselves in a line in front of her desk. Minotaur ambled in behind Hugh and took up a position at the end of the column.

Olympia reluctantly looked up from the Lightbourne diary and found herself faced by a row of determined faces. She gazed back in bemusement.

"Good afternoon," Olympia said. "Is there a problem?"

"Aye," Mrs. Bird said. "There be a problem all right."

Robert, Ethan, and Hugh nodded in agreement.

"Perhaps you'd better see Mr. Chillhurst about it then," Olympia said, her attention still on the phrase that she had just finished transcribing. "He's very good at sorting out problems."

"Yer forgettin' that he be the Viscount Chillhurst now," Mrs. Bird said brusquely.

"Yes, Aunt Olympia," Ethan said helpfully, "You must address him as his lordship now."

"Oh, yes. You're quite right. It slipped my mind again. Very well, take the problem to his lordship." Olympia smiled distractedly. "I'm sure he'll deal with it. He always does."

Robert drew himself up stiffly. "Begging your pardon, Aunt Olympia, but you're the problem."

"I am?" Olympia looked to Mrs. Bird for explanations. "What is this all about?"

Mrs. Bird made fists of her hands on her broad hips and set her mouth in an inflexible line. "That bloody pirate says he's asked you to marry him."

Olympia was suddenly wary. "What of it?"

"He also says ye haven't accepted his proposal yet," Mrs. Bird continued.

Olympia gave her a determinedly reasonable smile. "I can hardly marry a viscount, can I?"

"Why not?" Robert demanded.

"Yes, why not?" Ethan chorused.

Olympia frowned. "Well, he's a *viscount*. Some day he'll be an earl. He needs a proper wife, not someone like me."

"What's wrong with you?" Hugh asked. "I like you just the way you are."

"Yes, you are a very nice sort of female," Robert said loyally.

"What's more, ye be the one his lordship ruined, Miss Olympia," Mrs. Bird muttered. "And ye be the one he wants to marry."

"I explained to Mr. Chillhurst, I mean, I explained to Lord Chillhurst, that you were not ruined after all," Ethan said. "I told him that you were really quite fit, but he still thinks you should marry him."

"That's right," Hugh added. "And we think you should marry him, too, Aunt Olympia. If you do not, he might decide to leave and we'll probably have to get a new tutor. We shall very likely not be able to find one who knows all about Captain Jack and how to measure the distance across a stream without crossing it and why a kite can fly."

"It's a matter of honor," Robert said darkly.

Olympia was stricken with yet another of the uneasy chills that she had been experiencing all day.

While it was very true that, as a woman of the world, she was not particularly concerned about her own reputation, there was no denying that Jared was a proud man. His honor would matter a great deal to him. If he truly felt that he had to marry her in order to satisfy his own sense of honor, she did not know what she could do about it.

"Who said that it was a matter of honor?" Olympia asked carefully. "Did Chillhurst tell you that, Robert?"

"I'm the one what told Master Robert that it was a

matter of honor," Mrs. Bird said. "It's a fact and ye know it, Miss Olympia."

Olympia glanced at the expectant faces of her nephews. "Perhaps we should continue this conversation in private, Mrs. Bird."

"No," Robert said quickly, "we told his lordship that we would all speak to you about this."

Olympia eyed Robert closely. "Did you, indeed?"

"Yes and he seemed quite happy to have our assistance," Robert assured her.

"I see." Olympia straightened in her chair. For Jared to stoop to such tactics could only mean that he was quite determined to secure her compliance.

Mrs. Bird appeared to realize that things had taken a new turn. After a sharp glance at Olympia's face, she shooed the boys toward the door. "Right, then. Ye three have had yer say. Run along upstairs. I'll finish talkin' to Miss Olympia."

Robert looked skeptical. "You will call us if you need us, Mrs. Bird?"

"Aye, I'll do that. Be off with ye now."

The three boys made their bows and marched back out of the room. Minotaur followed. As soon as the door of the study closed behind the little group, there was a rush of feet and the sound of dog claws on the floor.

Olympia listened to the pounding on the stairs and the thundering footsteps that followed in the upstairs hall. No one pounded and thundered that way when Jared was about, she thought.

"I take it his lordship is not at home?" Olympia said.

"No, Miss Olympia, his lordship has gone out for the afternoon." Mrs. Bird angled her chin. "Said he had important business. I wouldn't be surprised if he's out obtainin' a special license."

"Oh, dear." Olympia closed the diary and leaned back in her chair. "Whatever am I going to do, Mrs. Bird?"

"Marry the man."

"I cannot do that."

"Because ye don't think ye'll make him a suitable viscountess?"

"No, I expect I could learn whatever it is I need to know about being a viscountess. It cannot be all that difficult."

"Then what's the real reason ye won't marry him?"

Olympia glanced toward the window. "The real reason I cannot marry him is because he does not love me."

"Bah. I was afeared it were somethin' like that. Now ye listen to me, Miss Olympia, love ain't no reason fer marrying in the first place."

"I disagree, Mrs. Bird," Olympia said distantly. "I cannot imagine marrying a man who does not love me."

"Apparently ye don't mind havin' an affair with him," Mrs. Bird shot back.

Olympia winced at the arrow of truth. "You do not understand," she mumbled.

"I most certainly do understand. When are ye gonna learn to be practical? Ye want to know what yer real problem is?" Mrs. Bird leaned forward aggressively. "Ye've spent so many years with them books of yers, trackin' down strange legends and learnin' strange, foreign ways, that ye ain't learned to be logical about the important things."

Olympia rubbed her forehead. She had developed a headache this afternoon. She almost never had the headache. "He has only asked me to marry him because his fiancée saw us together yesterday in Winslow's Mechanical Museum."

"*Fiancée.*" Mrs. Bird gave her a scandalized look. "That wicked pirate's got himself a fiancée? He's been livin' under yer roof, plotting to ruin you while he's got himself a fiancée stashed away someplace?"

"No, no, she's Lady Beaumont now." Olympia sighed. "The engagement was ended some three years ago, I believe."

"Why?" Mrs. Bird asked bluntly.

"They did not suit."

"Hah. There's more to the tale than that, I'll wager." Mrs. Bird got a strange look in her eye. "Might not hurt to find out what happened between his lordship and his fiancée three years ago."

"Why?" Olympia gave her a quick, searching glance. "It is certainly none of my affair."

"I ain't so sure about that. His lordship is a very unusual man, if you ask me. 'Course, the fancy often is a bit odd. All the same, I ain't never known one as strange as Lord Chillhurst."

"You have not known any members of the fancy, as you call them, at all, Mrs. Bird. What would you know about their normal behavior?"

"I know it ain't proper for one of 'em to pretend he's a tutor when he ain't," Mrs. Bird retorted.

"Chillhurst had his reasons."

"Did he now?" Mrs. Bird frowned as Olympia rubbed her forehead again. "What's wrong with yer head? Got the headache?"

"Yes. Perhaps I shall go upstairs and rest for a while."

"I'll get ye some of me camphor and ammoniac tonic. Works wonders."

"Thank you." Anything to get away from Mrs. Bird's arguments in favor of marriage to Jared, Olympia thought. She did not want to hear any more such logic. She was already fighting hard enough as it was to resist her heart's desire. She got to her feet.

The brass door knocker clanged sharply just as she

started around her desk. Minotaur's muffled bark sounded from the floor above.

"I'll wager that's his lordship. Probably cannot open the door for himself now that he's a viscount." Mrs. Bird bustled out into the hall. "The fancy's an arrogant lot."

Olympia calculated the distance to the stairs. If she moved quickly she could seclude herself in her bedchamber before Jared tried to corner her in the study.

She was tiptoeing toward the door when she heard the sound of voices in the hall. She froze when she recognized two of the three.

"I'll see if her ladyship is at home," Mrs. Bird said in a tone Olympia had never heard her use before. It had an entirely new element of lofty disdain in it.

A moment later Mrs. Bird appeared in the doorway of the study. Her face was flushed red with excitement. "Two ladies and a gentleman have come to call," she hissed. "They asked for the Viscountess Chillhurst. They think yer already married to his lordship."

"I know. Damnation. This would have to happen."

"I put 'em in the front parlor."

"Tell them I am ill, Mrs. Bird."

Mrs. Bird drew herself up with the air of a general going into battle. "Ye'll have to see 'em or they'll wonder what's goin' on. We can handle this."

"Not without Chillhurst."

"Yes we can," Mrs. Bird nodded resolutely. "We'll pretend yer the viscountess. They'll never know the difference."

"Good grief, what a tangle. I am not up to dealing with this disaster, Mrs. Bird."

"Don't ye worry none. I'll take care of everything. Oh, here, the gentleman gave me their cards."

"Let me see them." Olympia took the cards, glanced

at them, and groaned. "Lady Beaumont, Lady Kirkdale, and someone named Gifford Seaton."

"I'll fetch tea," Mrs. Bird said. "Don't fret. I'll re-member to address ye as yer ladyship in front of yer guests."

She rushed from the room before Olympia could find a way to stop her.

With a sense of impending doom, Olympia went slowly down the hall to the front parlor. She wished Jared would miraculously arrive and deal with the sit-uation. He was always so good at dealing with situa-tions.

It occurred to her that if she did not convince him to carry on with their romantic liaison, he would prob-ably leave and she would be obliged to handle these annoying interruptions on her own.

Of course, dealing with the details of daily life would constitute the least of her problems, she thought gloomily. When Jared left, her heart was going to break. She would not have the least notion of how to repair it.

Demetria and Constance were seated on opposite ends of the sofa. Dressed in blue and primrose, respec-tively, they formed an elegant tableau that was singu-larly out of place in the modest parlor.

A handsome man who appeared to be a couple of years younger than Olympia stood near the window. His hair was the same shade of blond as Demetria's. He was dressed in the first stare of fashion with an in-tricately tied cravat, pleated trousers, and a well-cut coat that was cropped at the waist.

"Lady Chillhurst." Demetria smiled serenely from the sofa but her cool eyes were bright with speculation. "You made the acquaintance of my very good friend, Lady Kirkdale, yesterday, I believe. Allow me to present my brother, Gifford Seaton."

"Mr. Seaton." Olympia inclined her head the way she had seen Jared do so often.

"Lady Chillhurst." Gifford smiled as he walked toward her with languid grace. He took Olympia's hand, bent over it, and brushed his lips lightly across her skin. "It is a great pleasure to make your acquaintance."

"Gifford insisted on paying this call," Demetria said blandly. "Constance and I decided to come with him."

Gifford was gazing raptly at Olympia. "You are not at all what I expected from my sister's description, madam."

"What on earth is that supposed to mean?" Olympia retrieved her hand. Her headache was making her irritable, she thought. She wished all of these beautifully dressed people would depart and leave her alone.

"I did not mean to offend you, madam," Gifford said quickly. "It is just that Demetria said you were obviously from the country and I thought perhaps you would be rather countrified in appearance. I had not expected you to be so charming."

"Thank you." Olympia was not certain how to respond to the compliment. "I suppose you had best sit down, Mr. Seaton. My housekeeper is preparing tea."

"We shall not be staying long," Constance said calmly. "We are only here out of curiosity, you understand."

Olympia eyed her uneasily. "Curiosity?"

Demetria gave a soft trill of laughter. "You must know, my dear, that Chillhurst and I were once engaged to be married. When my brother discovered yesterday that his lordship had finally wed, he could not resist learning a bit more about you."

Gifford's smile turned icy. "His lordship had very particular requirements in a wife. I was curious to see the lady who had met his very exacting specifications."

"I have not the least notion of what you are talking about," Olympia said.

Gifford sat down near the window. He seemed fascinated by Olympia. "You may as well know the facts before you go into Society, madam. 'Tis no secret that Chillhurst ended the engagement with my sister when he discovered the true state of her financial affairs. He had wrongly assumed that she was an heiress, you see."

"No, I do not see." Olympia felt like a mouse surrounded by three sleek cats who were bent on toying with her before they moved in for the kill.

Gifford's gaze narrowed. "Chillhurst made it clear three years ago that his only requirement in a wife was that she bring him a fortune."

"Gifford, please." Demetria gave her brother a repressive glance and then smiled wryly at Olympia. "Chillhurst bears a noble title, but even his own family admits that he has the heart of a merchant."

"With Chillhurst everything must come down to business," Gifford said sullenly.

"Now, Gifford, I am certain Lady Chillhurst suits him very well," Constance said, not unkindly. "She appears to be a very practical creature, herself."

"What makes you say that?" Olympia asked, startled. No one had ever called her practical.

Gifford frowned. "Well, it's obvious, is it not? You must have a fortune, else Chillhurst would never have married you. And lord knows he controls a bloody fortune. Yet he's got you tucked away here in an extremely unfashionable part of town." His gaze dismissed her plain muslin gown. "Furthermore, it's clear you do not spend much money on your clothes. One can only assume you have a fine sense of economy, madam."

"Chillhurst would appreciate that." Demetria's

smile did not reach her eyes and her voice had a brittle quality. "I do believe he feared that I would spend his fortune into the ground. And he was very probably right. I must admit I do like pretty things."

Constance gave her an amused little smile. "Yes, you do, Demetria. And pretty things tend to be expensive."

"But they are worth every penny," Demetria said.

Gifford's eyes flickered unpleasantly. "Chillhurst has plenty of money. The man's rich as Croesus. He did not need to marry a fortune."

Olympia opened her mouth on an angry protest, but stopped when she caught the uneasy look Demetria exchanged with Constance.

With a flash of intuition Olympia suddenly comprehended the reason for the tension in the air. Demetria and her friend had not wanted to come here today. They were present in a vain effort to control Gifford. The man seethed with anger and pent-up frustration and all of the intense emotion appeared to be directed at Jared.

Olympia grew thoughtful.

Demetria rushed to distract attention from Gifford's rudeness. "You must forgive my brother. He is still smarting a bit even after all these years because Chillhurst very sensibly refused his challenge."

Olympia nearly stopped breathing. She stared at Demetria for an instant and then turned to Gifford. "Never tell me that you challenged Chillhurst to a duel?"

"No offense, madam, but I had no choice." Gifford got up restlessly and strode to the window. "He treated my sister in a most shabby fashion. I was forced to issue a challenge."

"Now, Gifford." Demetria shot her brother another uneasy glance. "There is no need to go into that old subject. It has been three years, after all, and I am happily married to another."

Olympia eyed Gifford's stiff shoulders. "I am certain there must be more to the story than you are telling me, Mr. Seaton."

Gifford shrugged. "I assure you, there is not. After Chillhurst ended the engagement, I called him out. Told him that as far as I was concerned, he had grossly insulted Demetria."

Demetria sighed softly. Constance touched her arm in a silent, comforting gesture.

"What did Chillhurst say when you accused him of insulting your sister?" Olympia asked curiously.

"He very properly offered his apologies," Demetria said smoothly. "Is that not right, Gifford?"

"Yes, damn him. That is exactly what he did. Offered his apologies and said he would not meet me on the field of honor. Bloody coward, that's what he is."

"Gifford, you should not say such things in front of Lady Chillhurst," Demetria said with a touch of desperation.

"Pay attention to your sister," Constance murmured.

"I'm only telling Lady Chillhurst the facts," Gifford stormed. "She ought to know the sort of man she married."

Olympia stared at Gifford. "Have you gone mad? My husband is no coward."

"Of course he's not," Demetria said quickly. "No one would dream of accusing Chillhurst of cowardice."

"Bah." Gifford's mouth tightened. "He's a coward, right enough."

Constance groaned. "I told you that it was not wise to accompany your brother on this call, Demetria."

"What was I supposed to do?" Demetria asked half

under her breath. "He was bound and determined to come here today."

Olympia's headache was getting worse. "I believe I have had quite enough of entertaining callers this afternoon. I wish all of you would leave."

Demetria made soothing noises. "Please forgive my brother, Lady Chillhurst. He is of a hot-blooded temperament and quite protective of me. Gifford, you promised you would not cause a scene. Please apologize to Lady Chillhurst."

Gifford narrowed his eyes. "I will not apologize for the truth, Demetria."

"Apologize for your sister's sake, if nothing else," Constance said coolly. "I'm certain that none of us wants that old gossip resurrected. It will only cause a great deal of grief for all concerned." She paused delicately. "Beaumont would not be at all pleased to hear it."

Olympia noticed that the last comment appeared to have some effect. Gifford gave his sister and Constance a look of simmering frustration. Then he reluctantly turned to Olympia and inclined his head in a small bow.

"My apologies, madam."

Olympia had had enough. "I am not concerned with your apologies. As it happens, I am quite busy today. If you do not mind—"

"Do not think ill of us, Lady Chillhurst." Demetria adjusted her gloves. "It was all rather unpleasant at the time, but I have told Gifford often enough that what happened three years ago was for the best. Is that not correct, Constance?"

"Quite correct," Constance said. "If Chillhurst had not cried off the engagement, Demetria would never have married Beaumont. And I am convinced that she is far happier with him than she would ever have been with Chillhurst."

"There is no question about it." Demetria looked at Olympia. "Beaumont has been very good to me, madam. I am quite satisfied with my choice of husbands. I would not have you believing that I am pining after Chillhurst. Nothing could be further from the truth."

Gifford swore softly.

Olympia's head was throbbing very badly now. She wondered how a proper viscountess went about getting rid of unwanted guests in the parlor. She wished Chillhurst would return. He would know what to do.

"Tea, madam," Mrs. Bird announced from the doorway in her new, stentorian accents. "Shall I pour?"

Olympia looked up, grateful for the interruption. "Thank you, Mrs. Bird."

Mrs. Bird beamed as she lumbered triumphantly into the parlor. She clutched a massive tray ladened with what appeared to be every single piece of the ancient tea service that had come with the house. A smaller woman would have collapsed beneath the weight of the heavy, chipped crockery.

She set the tray down on a small table and went to work with a great deal of energy. Cups and saucers clattered. Spoons clashed.

Demetria and Constance eyed the tea tray and Mrs. Bird with some trepidation. Gifford's smile was derisive.

Olympia decided to make another attempt to clear the parlor of intruders.

"Do you know," she announced with grim determination, "I have not been feeling at all well this afternoon. I do not particularly care what the rest of you do, but I am going upstairs to my bedchamber immediately."

Everyone turned to gaze at her in astonishment.

"Here now, I just brung the tea," Mrs. Bird complained in an aggrieved tone. She hefted the heavy pot. "Ain't no one leavin' here until they've had a proper cup."

"I do not believe we have time for tea," Demetria said quickly. She rose from the sofa.

"No, indeed." Constance got to her feet. "We must be on our way."

"Don't ye fret, I'll pour it real quick-like." Mrs. Bird filled one of the cups and shoved it at Demetria. "Here ye go."

Demetria automatically reached for the cup and saucer. She failed to get a grip on it before Mrs. Bird let go of it.

The cup teetered and toppled. Tea splashed on Demetria's lovely blue gown. She gave a soft cry and stepped back hurriedly.

"Oh, dear," Olympia said in resignation.

"This gown was delivered only yesterday." Demetria brushed angrily at the damp spots. "It cost a fortune."

Constance produced a lacy white handkerchief and started to dab at the stains on Demetria's gown. "It's all right, Demetria. Beaumont will buy you a dozen new gowns."

"That is hardly the point, Constance." Demetria gave Mrs. Bird a disgusted glance. "The woman is incompetent, Lady Chillhurst. Why on earth do you tolerate her on your staff?"

"Mrs. Bird is an excellent housekeeper," Olympia said loyally.

" 'Course I am." Mrs. Bird waved the teapot in a threatening manner. "I work for a genuine viscount, don't I?" Tea splashed onto the carpet.

"Good lord," Constance said with awed amusement. "This is really quite extraordinary. Wait until we see our friends at the Newburys' card party this evening. They will not believe the tale."

"You have no right to gossip about us," Olympia snapped. She got to her feet and gathered herself for another eviction attempt.

A series of loud yelps sounded out in the hall.

Hugh's voice called from the top of the stairs. "Come back up here, Minotaur. Here, boy. Come back."

A loud, piercing whistle followed. Dog claws scrabbled on the wooden floor.

An instant later Minotaur bounded into the parlor. The dog lurched forward to greet Olympia's guests. En route, his massive tail swiped the tea tray and sent two more cups crashing to the floor.

"Bloody hell," Mrs. Bird grumbled. "Now I'll have to fetch some more."

"Do not bother on our account," Demetria said hastily.

Constance reeled back in alarm as Minotaur charged the sofa. "Get that creature away from us."

Minotaur turned his huge head at the sound of her voice and, tongue lolling, veered toward her.

"I say." Gifford looked confused. He started across the room with the obvious intention of grabbing the dog's collar.

Minotaur barked in delight, apparently having concluded that the stranger wanted to play a game.

Olympia heard the front door open and close. She whirled around and saw Jared step into the hall. She went to the parlor entrance and confronted him with her hands on her hips.

"There you are, sir. It's about time you got here."

"Something wrong?" Jared asked politely.

Olympia waved a hand to encompass the noisy, chaotic scene behind her. "I wish you would do something about all these people in my parlor."

Jared walked forward and surveyed the room with calm interest.

"Minotaur," he said quietly.

Minotaur stopped trying to dodge Gifford's grasp and dashed across the room. He skidded to a halt in front of Jared, sat back on his haunches, and looked up for approval.

Jared rested his hand on the top of Minotaur's head and the dog grinned.

"Go," Jared ordered quietly. "Upstairs, Minotaur."

Minotaur rose obediently and trotted quickly out of the parlor.

Jared glanced at Mrs. Bird. "Never mind the tea, Mrs. Bird."

"But they ain't had any yet," Mrs. Bird protested.

Jared looked at Gifford with chilling politeness. "I'm quite certain that our guests do not have time for tea. You and your companions were just about to leave, were you not, Mr. Seaton?"

Gifford gave Jared a look of smoldering dislike as he brushed dog hair off the sleeve of his coat. "Yes, as a matter of fact, we were. I'm certain we've all had enough of this bedlam."

"Good day, Lady Chillhurst," Demetria said.

She and Constance walked quickly toward the door. Gifford stalked after them.

Jared stepped aside to allow everyone out of the parlor.

Olympia saw Demetria slant a mocking glance at Jared as she went through the door.

"You were always a rather strange sort, Chillhurst, but this household is quite remarkable, even for a member of your odd family. What on earth are you about, my lord?"

"My domestic arrangements need not concern you, madam," Jared said. "Do not return to this house without an invitation."

"Bastard," Gifford muttered on his way out the door. "I only hope your poor wife knows what she's gotten herself into by marrying you."

"Hush, Gifford," Demetria said. "Come along. We have other calls to make this afternoon."

"I doubt they will be as amusing as this one," Constance murmured.

The visitors made their way out onto the front steps. Jared closed the door behind them without bothering to see them into their waiting carriage. He turned to Olympia.

"You will not receive any of those three again," he said. "Is that clear?"

It was the last straw as far as Olympia was concerned. She stalked toward the stairs. "Do not give me orders, Chillhurst. Lest you forget, I am still the one in charge of this household and you are a member of my staff. You will kindly remember your place and behave accordingly."

Jared ignored her outburst. "Olympia, I wish to speak with you."

"Not now, sir. This has been a most unpleasant day. I am going to my bedchamber to rest before dinner." Halfway up the stairs, she paused and glared back at him. "By the by, sir, did you truly sink so low as to press my nephews and Mrs. Bird to speak to me on the subject of marriage?"

Jared walked to the foot of the stairs and gripped the newel post. "Yes, Olympia, I did."

"You should be ashamed of yourself, sir."

"I am quite desperate, Olympia." Jared smiled a strange, wistful smile. "I will do anything, say anything, sink to any depths, resort to any tactic in order to make you my wife."

He meant it, Olympia thought. In spite of her foul mood and aching head, a thrill of excitement went through her. The last of her resistance melted like wax in a fire.

"There is no need for any more such maneuvers, sir," she said, still annoyed with him and vividly aware of the risk she was taking. "I have decided to marry you."

Jared's hand tightened fiercely around the carved top of the newel post. "You have?"

"Yes."

"Thank you, Olympia. I shall endeavor to see that you do not regret your decision."

"I very probably shall regret it," she said waspishly, "but I cannot see any help for it. Please leave me alone for a while."

"Olympia, wait one moment." Jared searched her face. "May I ask why you changed your mind since I last saw you, my dear?"

"No." Olympia continued on up the steps.

"Olympia, please, I must know the answer. My curiosity will eat me alive. Did the boys convince you to change your mind?"

"No."

"Mrs. Bird, perhaps? I know she is very concerned about your reputation, even if you are not."

"Mrs. Bird had nothing to do with my decision." Olympia was nearly to the top of the stairs.

"Then why have you agreed to marry me?" Jared called.

Olympia paused on the landing and looked down at him with cool hauteur. "I changed my mind, sir, because I have come to realize that you excel at the task of superintending a household."

"What of it?" Jared asked warily.

"Why, it's quite simple, sir. I dare not lose you. Good staff is so very hard to get, you know."

Jared gazed at her in amazement. "Olympia, surely you are not marrying me simply because I can provide you with an orderly household."

"Personally, I think that is an excellent reason for marriage. Oh, there is one more thing, sir."

Jared's gaze narrowed. "Yes?"

"Do you happen to know what the word *Siryn* might refer to?"

He blinked. "A siren is a mythical creature who lured unwary sailors to their doom."

"Not that sort of siren," she said impatiently. "I mean Siryn spelled with a *y*."

"Siryn was the name of the ship that Captain Jack sailed while he pursued his career as a buccaneer in the West Indies," Jared said. "Why do you ask?"

She gripped the railing. "Are you certain?"

Jared shrugged. "That is what my father claims."

"The drawings on the endpapers," Olympia whispered.

Jared frowned. "What about it?"

"The drawings on the endpapers of the diary are pictures of old-fashioned vessels sailing on storm-tossed seas, *surging* seas, if you will recall. One ship bears the figure of a woman on the prow. A siren, perhaps."

"I am told Captain Jack's ship had such a prow figure."

Olympia forgot about her headache. She picked up her skirts and flew back down the stairs.

"Olympia, wait. Where are you going?" Jared demanded as she rushed past him.

"I'll be in my study." She turned in the doorway. "I am going to be very busy for a while, Mr. Chillhurst. See to it that I am not disturbed."

Jared's brows rose. "Of course, Miss Wingfield. As a member of your household staff, it is my pleasure to carry out your instructions."

Olympia slammed the study door in his face. She went over to her desk and opened Claire Lightbourne's diary.

She stood gazing down at the design which decorated the endpapers at the front of the diary for a long time and then, very slowly, she picked up a penknife.

Five minutes later she tugged back the picture of the *Siryn* sailing the surging sea and discovered the map that had been tucked beneath it.

It was a map of an island. An uncharted island in the West Indies. But it was not a complete map, Olympia saw. It had been torn in half.

The other half was missing.

There was a sentence written on the bottom of the map fragment.

The Siryn and the Serpent must be joined, two halves of a whole, a lock that awaits a key.

Olympia quickly turned to the back of the diary and looked at the picture of the ship that sailed a tumultuous sea. Sure enough, the figure on the prow was that of a serpent.

Eagerly Olympia pried up the back endpaper.

There was no sign of the other half of the map.

Chapter 12

Jared placed his appointment journal to the left of his breakfast plate. Appointment journals were very reassuring things, he thought. They gave a man a sense of control over his own destiny. It was no doubt a thoroughgoing illusion, but a man who was prey to excessive passions treasured certain illusions.

"Lessons shall be conducted from eight until ten this morning, as usual," Jared said. "Today we shall be studying geography and mathematics."

"Will you tell us another story about Captain Jack in the geography lesson, sir?" Hugh asked around a mouthful of eggs.

Jared glanced at Hugh. "There is no need to talk while you are eating."

"Beg pardon, sir." Hugh swallowed the eggs in one gulp and grinned. "There. I'm finished. What about a Captain Jack tale?"

"Yes, Mr. Chillhurst, I mean, my lord," Robert said. "Will there be another story about Captain Jack?"

"I want to hear about how Captain Jack developed a special clock to help find longitude at sea," Ethan said eagerly.

"We already heard that tale," Robert said.

"I want to hear it again."

Jared covertly studied Olympia who was absently munching toast spread with gooseberry jam. The look in her eyes made him uneasy. She had had that same remote, preoccupied expression since she had come downstairs to breakfast.

There had been no well-planned accidental collisions in the hall outside his room today, no yearning glances, no stolen kisses, and no blushes. *An inauspicious way in which to begin such an important day*, he thought.

"I believe there is a rather educational tale involving longitude calculations on one of Captain Jack's voyages to Boston," Jared said. He consulted his appointment journal again. "After the lessons have been completed, I shall escort your aunt to the library of the Society for Travel and Exploration."

Olympia perked up a bit at that. "Excellent, there are one or two more things I wish to check in the society's map collection."

One would never guess that this was her wedding day, Jared thought grimly. Evidently she was far more excited about the prospect of going to the library to prowl through old maps than she was about the notion of marrying him.

"While you are working in the society's library," Jared said, "I shall keep an appointment with Felix Hartwell. We have business matters to discuss. Robert, Ethan, and Hugh shall fly their kite in the park. When I am through, it will be time for the midday meal."

Ethan kicked his heels against the bottom rung of his chair. "What are we going to do this afternoon, sir?"

"Kindly refrain from kicking the chair," Jared said absently.

"Yes, sir."

Jared gazed at the next item on the schedule and felt every muscle in his lower body grow rigid with anticipation and apprehension. *What would he do if Olympia had changed her mind?*

She must not change her mind.

Not now when he was so close to possessing his own personal siren.

Not now when the only woman he had ever wanted with such passionate intensity was almost within his grasp. *Not now.*

"After we have eaten," he said, exerting every ounce of his self-control to keep his voice even, "your aunt and I will see to the formalities of our marriage. The arrangements have all been made. The matter should not take very long. When we return—"

Silver crashed against china at the opposite end of the table.

"Oh, dear," Olympia murmured.

Jared glanced up in time to see a pot of gooseberry jam fly off the edge of the table. The spoon that had been sticking out of the pot went over with it.

Ethan smothered a giggle. Olympia jumped to her feet and bent down to dab ineffectually at the carpet with her napkin.

"Leave it," Jared said. "Mrs. Bird will see to it."

Olympia sent him an uncertain look, lowered her eyes, and quickly sat down again.

So she was not nearly as disinterested in the matter of her marriage as she had appeared. Something inside him relaxed slightly. He propped his elbows on the table, steepled his fingers, and concentrated again on his appointment journal.

"Dinner will be served earlier than usual tonight," he continued, "as we shall be going to Vauxhall Gardens afterward to view the fireworks this evening."

Predictably enough, a cheer went up from Ethan, Hugh, and Robert.

"I say, that is an excellent plan, sir." Robert's face was alight with anticipation.

"We have never seen fireworks," Ethan confided gleefully.

"Will there be a band playing music?" Hugh asked.

"I expect so," Jared said.

"And may we have ices?"

"Very likely." Jared watched Olympia's face to see how she was taking the prospect of celebrating their wedding at Vauxhall Gardens. It occurred to him rather belatedly that some women might be heartily offended.

But Olympia's eyes were suddenly glowing. "A wonderful notion. I should love to see the fireworks."

Jared breathed a silent sigh of relief. Who said he did not have a romantic bone in his body, he thought.

"May we go for a stroll on the Dark Walk at Vauxhall?" Robert asked with a suspicious innocence.

Jared scowled briefly. "What do you know of the Dark Walk?"

"One of the boys that we met in the park yesterday told us all about it," Ethan explained. "He said it was quite dangerous to go down the Dark Walk."

"That's right, sir," Robert said. "We were told that sometimes people who go along the Dark Walk at

Vauxhall are never seen again." He shuddered. "Do you think that is true, sir?"

"No, I do not," Jared said.

"Another boy that we met said he knew of a certain maid who had worked in his house for years who had disappeared on the Dark Walk," Robert informed him. "She was never seen again."

"Ran off with a footman most likely." Jared closed his appointment journal.

"I should very much like to go for a stroll on the Dark Walk," Robert said persistently.

Hugh made a face at him across the table. "You only want to go on the Dark Walk because that boy in the park dared you to do it. But it wouldn't count if all of us went for a stroll on it together. Lord Chillhurst would be there to scare off the villains."

"That's right," Ethan added triumphantly. "The villains would not come around if his lordship and the rest of us were there with you. You'd have to go along the Dark Walk all by yourself in order to win the dare. You'd be too frightened to do it, I'll wager."

"Yes," Hugh taunted. "You'd be frightened to take a walk on the Dark Walk all by yourself."

Robert glared at his brothers. "I'm not afraid to go down the Dark Walk."

"Yes, you are," Hugh said.

Jared arched one brow at the twins. "That is quite enough. An intelligent man does not respond to the dares and taunts of others. He rises above such foolishness and makes his own decisions based on reason and logic. Now, if you have finished your breakfast, you may go prepare for today's lessons."

"Yes, sir." Hugh gave Robert one last sly look as he jumped out of his seat.

Ethan snickered and got to his feet.

Robert manfully ignored his brothers as he rose and made his bow to Olympia.

Jared waited until he and Olympia were alone in the room. Then he gazed down the length of the table. "I trust today's schedule meets with your approval, my dear?"

Olympia gave a small start. "Yes. Yes, of course." She waved her spoon in a vague fashion. "You're very good at schedules and such. I vow I have come to rely upon you in matters of that sort."

"Thank you. I do my best."

Olympia scowled briefly. "Are you laughing at me, Chillhurst?"

"No, my dear. It is myself I find rather amusing more and more often of late."

Olympia's eyes brimmed with disconcerting perception. "Jared, why do you mock yourself and your own passions? Is it because you do not like to admit that you are capable of strong emotions?"

"It has been my experience that forceful passions have a generally negative effect on a man's life. They lead to foolish excesses, dangerous adventures, and reckless behavior of all sorts."

"Only uncontrolled passions lead to such bad endings," Olympia said gently. "Your passions are always under control, sir." She blushed furiously. "Except, perhaps, when you are in the throes of romantic passion."

"Yes," Jared said, "except when I am making love to you." He met her eyes. *You are my great weakness, my most vulnerable point, my Achilles heel. My siren.* Jared finished his coffee and set the cup down with due deliberation. "You must excuse me, Olympia. My students await me."

"Jared, wait, there is something important that I wish to tell you." Olympia put out her hand as he went past. "It is about my latest discovery in the Lightbourne diary."

"My dear, the one thing that I will not discuss on my wedding day is that confounded diary. You know how much the damn topic annoys me. Once and for all, I do not want to hear another word about it." Jared lowered his head and brushed his mouth across hers.

"But, Jared—"

"Try to spare some thought for the wedding night which awaits us, siren," he ordered softly. "Perhaps you will find it almost as interesting as the Lightbourne diary."

He walked out of the breakfast room.

"You wish me to open up your townhouse?" Felix leaned across his desk to pour himself a glass of claret. "Certainly. I shall be happy to see to the matter for you. You'll be requiring staff, of course?"

"Yes." Jared tapped his fingertips together, thinking swiftly. "But you need not bother with a housekeeper. We already have one."

Felix gave him a skeptical glance. "The one you brought with you from Upper Tudway? Doubt she'll know how to run a gentleman's house here in town. She won't have had the experience."

"We shall manage."

Felix shrugged. "Your decision, of course. Claret?"

"No, thank you."

"Very well, then, allow me to toast your impending nuptials." Felix took a long swallow of claret and put down the glass. "I must say, you've gone about this matter in a most unusual fashion. Perhaps you've inherited some of your family's tendency toward eccentricity after all."

"Perhaps."

Felix chuckled. "You can hardly announce the glad tidings to the polite world in the papers because the *ton* already believes you to be married. May I inquire how you intend to celebrate this momentous occasion?"

"We are taking my fiancée's nephews to Vauxhall tonight to see the fireworks."

"*Vauxhall.* Good lord." Felix grimaced. "What does your bride think of this plan?"

"She is content to leave that sort of thing to me. On another subject, Felix."

"Yes?"

Jared reached into his pocket and brought out Torbert's handkerchief. "I want you to see that this gets returned to Mr. Roland Torbert. Along with it, you will convey a message."

Felix eyed the handkerchief curiously. "What is the message?"

"You will inform Torbert that if there are any more incidents such as the one which caused this handerkerchief to be abandoned in Lady Chillhurst's garden, he will find himself dealing personally with her lord."

Felix took the handkerchief. "Very well, but I doubt that you face much of a threat from that quarter, Chillhurst. Torbert is not the sort to be slipping in and out of ladies' gardens."

"No, I do not think I need worry about him overmuch." Jared stretched out his booted feet and regarded his old friend. "There is one more thing that I wish to discuss. Have you had an opportunity to speak with the insurers?"

"Yes, and the results were no more useful than the results of my other inquiries." Felix got to his feet with a troubled expression and began to pace the room. "You will have to accept that the person behind the embezzlement scheme was Captain Richards. There simply is no other explanation."

"Richards has been with me for a long time. Almost as long as you have, Felix."

"I'm aware of that, sir." Felix shook his head. "I regret to be the bearer of such ill tidings. I know how important loyalty and honesty are to you. I understand how you must feel about being deceived by someone you have trusted for years."

"I told you the other day that I do not care to play the fool."

Half an hour later the hired hackney rattled to a halt in front of the fashionable Beaumont townhouse.

Jared got out. "Wait for me," he called up to the coachman. "I shall not be long."

"Aye, m'lord."

Jared pulled his gold watch out of his pocket and glanced at the face as he went up the steps. He had left the boys at home with Mrs. Bird while he paid this call on Demetria.

He did not have much time to waste before he was due to fetch Olympia from the library, but he told himself that would not be a problem. He did not have a great deal to say to Demetria.

The door was opened by a butler whose disapproving look extended not only to Jared's unfashionable attire but to his equally unfashionable mode of arrival. It was obvious that most callers at the townhouse traveled by private carriage, not hackney coach.

"You will inform Lady Beaumont that Chillhurst wishes to speak with her," Jared said without preamble.

The butler looked down the long length of his nose. "Your card, sir?"

"I do not have a card."

"Lady Beaumont does not receive visitors before three in the afternoon, sir."

"If you do not let her know that I am here," Jared said very politely, "I shall see to the matter, myself."

The butler glowered but wisely withdrew into the hall to carry out the instructions. Jared waited on the steps until the door opened a second time.

"Lady Beaumont will see you in the drawing room."

Jared did not bother to respond. He walked into the hall and allowed himself to be shown into Demetria's presence. She was waiting for him at the far end of the room, her pale blue and white silk skirts artfully arranged on a blue and gilt sofa. She smiled her distant smile at him as he approached. Her eyes were cool and wary.

It occurred to Jared that she had always watched him with that same remote expression. Three years ago he had mistaken the look for an indication of self-control and self-restraint. He had thought at the time that such qualities were precisely what he wanted in a wife.

Later he had learned that what Demetria was controlling and restraining was her distaste of him.

"Good morning, Chillhurst. This is a surprise."

"Is it?" Jared took in the expensively decorated room with a casual glance. The walls were hung with blue silk. The fireplace was trimmed with carved white marble. Heavy, blue velvet draperies framed classically proportioned windows that overlooked a large garden. There was a cool opulence about the whole that underlined Beaumont's great wealth.

"You've done very well for yourself, Demetria."

Demetria inclined her head. "Did you seriously doubt that I would?"

"No. Not for a moment." Jared came to a halt and studied her, aware that she was very much at home in the richly furnished room. No one looking at Demetria now would ever guess that she had once been nearly penniless. "You were always a very determined woman."

"Those of us who were not born into wealth must either learn determination or consign ourselves to a very insecure life. But you would not understand that sort of problem, Jared, would you?"

"Very likely not." There was no point telling her that he had learned that lesson long ago. He did not think Demetria would care to hear of how his own childhood had been fraught with both financial insecurity and the emotional chaos created by his eccentric, passionate family.

It occurred to Jared that he had never gotten around to talking to Demetria about his past. Not that she would have been particularly interested. She was concerned only with her own future and that of her brother.

Demetria rested one arm languidly along the back of the sofa. "I assume you have a particular reason for calling upon me at such an early hour?"

"Of course."

"Of course." Demetria's voice held a bitter edge. "You never do anything without a particular reason, do you, Jared? Your whole life is controlled by reason, your watch, and your damnable appointment journal. Very well, then, tell me why you are here."

"I wish to know why you and your brother and your very good friend, Lady Kirkdale, paid a visit to my wife yesterday."

Demetria's eyes widened guilelessly. "Why, Jared, what a strange question. We merely wished to welcome her to town."

"Save your lies for your husband. At his age he is no doubt content to believe them."

Demetria's mouth tightened. "You are in no position to pass judgment on my marriage, Chillhurst. You know nothing about it."

"I know that it was very probably inspired by greed on your part and desperation for an heir on Beaumont's part."

"Come now, Chillhurst. We both know that greed and the desire for an heir are the two factors which characterize the vast majority of all marriages in the polite world." Demetria's eyes narrowed in speculation. "Surely you do not expect me to believe that your own alliance with that rather odd female you've got hidden away in Ibberton Street is based on more noble sentiments?"

"I did not come here to discuss my marriage with you."

"Then why did you come here?"

"To warn you and that extremely annoying brother of yours to stay away from my wife. I will not allow either of you to play your cat-and-mouse games with her. Is that very clear?"

"What makes you think we were playing a game with her? Perhaps we were merely curious to see what sort of female had met your requirements?"

"You must be very bored, indeed, these days to bother with Olympia."

"Is she so very dull, then?" Demetria gave him a look of mocking innocence. "What a pity. How long will she retain your interest, do you think? Or do you find a boring little bluestocking perfectly suited to your taste?"

"Enough, Demetria."

"Have you gotten what you wanted, Chillhurst?" Demetria's eyes glinted with cold anger. "A woman who will conform to your bloody schedule? A woman who knows nothing of passion, herself, and therefore will not notice that you are sorely lacking in such matters?"

"You need not concern yourself with my private affairs." Jared turned to leave and then paused. "You got what you wanted, Demetria. Be content."

"Is that a threat, Jared?"

"I believe it is."

"You cold-blooded, arrogant bastard." Demetria's hand curved into a small fist on the back of the sofa. "It is so easy for you to make threats. Just because you were born with everything, a fortune and a title to go with it, you believe yourself to be far above the rest of us. But do you know something, Jared? I do not envy you."

Jared smiled. "I am relieved to hear that."

"No, I do not envy you in the least, my lord." Demetria's eyes blazed. "You are doomed to live your whole life never knowing the kind of passion that sets fire to your blood. You will never know what it is to surrender to a river of violent emotions capable of sweeping you away."

"Demetria—"

"You will never learn the sweet joy of being with another whose soul touches your own. You, with your merchant's heart, will never know what it is to have the power to make a lover respond, will you, Jared?"

Jared met her eyes and knew that she was recalling the same afternoon that he was. It was the day he had kissed her in the stables at the Isle of Flame.

That kiss had not been a polite, chaste caress as the others had been. It had been a desperate effort on his part to incite a response in her. He had surprised them both with that kiss, but not with the answer it had given him.

He knew that both of them had realized the truth that day. There could be no passion between them. It was the first time Jared had even acknowledged that he had wanted passion in his marriage. He supposed he owed Demetria for having opened his eyes to his weakness.

"I shall just have to manage as best I can," Jared said. "Good day to you, Demetria. Do not let me find you pestering my wife again. And I advise you to keep your damned brother out of my sight."

"Why?" Alarm flared in Demetria's eyes. "You cannot hurt him. My husband is a rich and powerful man. He will protect Gifford from you if necessary."

Jared's brows rose. "Your husband is far more concerned with finding a cure for his unfortunate affliction than he is with protecting that fool brother of yours. Furthermore, if you want to do Seaton a favor, you will cease trying to protect him. He is three-and-twenty years old. 'Tis past time he became a man."

"He is a man, damn you."

"He is a boy, with a boy's wild, uncontrolled emotions. He is spoiled, sullen, and temperamental. You have kept him confined to leading strings by shielding him at every turn. If you would have him grow up, you must let him learn to accept responsibility for his own actions."

"I have taken care of my brother all of my life," Demetria said fiercely, "I do not want or need your advice."

Jared shrugged. "As you wish. But if either you or Seaton crosses my path, you had best not depend upon me to play the gentleman a second time. I did that once, if you will recall. Once was enough."

"You do not understand," Demetria hissed. "But, then, you never understood. Get out of here, Chillhurst, or I vow I will have you thrown out."

"Do not trouble yourself. I am only too happy to take my leave."

Jared strode out into the hall without a backward glance. The butler had disappeared but Gifford was standing just outside the drawing-room door. He was pale with fury.

"What are you doing here, Chillhurst?"

"Visiting your charming sister, not that it is any concern of yours." Jared stepped around Gifford and went toward the front door.

"What did you say to her, damn you?"

Jared hesitated, his hand on the doorknob. "I will tell you precisely what I told her. Do not come near my wife again, Seaton."

Gifford's handsome face twisted into an angry sneer. "We both know your threat is an empty one. You cannot harm me. Beaumont is too powerful, even for you."

"I would not count on Beaumont's protection, if I were you." Jared opened the door. "Or your sister's."

Gifford took a step forward. "Devil take you, Chillhurst, what are you saying?"

"I am saying that if you offend me by coming near my wife, I will see to it that you pay for it."

"I say, Chillhurst," Gifford taunted softly, "surely you are not threatening to call me out? We both know you are far too reasonable, far too sensible, *far too much of a coward* to risk meeting me on the field of honor."

"I can see that there is no point discussing the matter with you. You have been warned." Jared went out onto the front steps and closed the door very quietly behind himself.

The hackney was still waiting in the street.

"The Musgrave Institution library," Jared called to the coachman. "And be quick about it. I have an appointment." He opened the door and got into the cab.

"Aye, sir." The coachman gave a long-suffering sigh and loosened the reins.

Jared sat back against the cushions as the hackney pulled away from the Beaumont townhouse. Demetria was wrong about him being consigned to an emotionless existence, he reflected. At the moment he was wracked with an inner turmoil that exceeded anything he had ever experienced.

This was his wedding day, he should have felt calm and controlled now that his plans had come to fruition. Olympia would soon be his by all the laws of God and man. Yet he had awakened that morning with a disturbing sense of unease that was still with him.

He did not understand the feeling that gripped his insides like a vise. After all, he was on the verge of claiming the woman he wanted.

But he could not be entirely certain of precisely why she was accepting his claim.

Olympia had initially refused to marry him, yet after that scene with Demetria yesterday, she had announced that she had changed her mind.

Jared gazed out at the busy streets. Surely Olympia had not agreed to wed him simply because he could keep her household in order. He knew there was more to it than that. There had to be more to it.

She wanted him, he reminded himself. The memory of her passionate response should have reassured him, but for some reason it did not. Olympia had made it clear she would not marry him for the sake of desire alone or to salvage her reputation. She was a woman of the world, he thought wryly, such things were not reasons for marriage in her view.

So why had she finally agreed to wed him, he wondered for the thousandth time. The question had plagued him since yesterday. He was convinced that something Demetria had said or done during the visit yesterday afternoon had pushed Olympia into accepting his proposal. But that made no sense.

Unless the confrontation in the parlor had finally made Olympia realize that she was obliged to marry for the sake of propriety.

After all, Jared thought, it was one thing to talk of deceiving the world by claiming to be married; quite another to actually carry out such a breathtaking deception. In spite of her talk of worldliness, Olympia was an innocent from a tiny village in the country. She'd had no notion of what she had been about when she had blithely assumed she could falsely claim marriage and get away with it.

Of course, when she'd made her plans, she'd had no notion that she might be thrust into the position of claiming marriage to a viscount, Jared reminded himself. She had believed him to be a tutor. He was forced to admit that her plan might have worked very well had he not deceived her at the beginning of their relationship.

Jared knew that it was his own fault that he was in this outrageous situation. No doubt he deserved to be consumed with uncertainty, tormented with questions that he did not know how to ask, precariously balanced on a knife-edge of hope and despair.

Such were the consequences of reckless passion.

So be it. He smiled grimly. It was clear that nothing was for certain once a man surrendered to the raging torrent of desire. All he could do was strive to stay afloat in the swirling waters.

Tonight was his wedding night. He would let nothing stand in the way of what he craved most. Tonight when he took her to bed, Olympia would be his wife. He would revel in their lovemaking, secure in the knowledge that he at last had some tangible claim on her.

He might not be certain of her reasons for agreeing to the marriage, but he could be gloriously certain that she wanted him with the same degree of passion that he felt for her.

It was not enough to satisfy him, he realized, but it was a great deal more than what he'd had with Demetria.

The fireworks that lit the skies over Vauxhall Gardens were so spectacular that they almost succeeded in distracting Olympia from the turmoil of her thoughts.

She was married.

She still could not quite bring herself to accept the shattering reality of her new state.

Married to Jared.

It did not seem possible. The small businesslike ceremony conducted by a parson on the outskirts of the city earlier that afternoon had had an element of unreality about it.

They were bound together forever.

What if she had made a terrible mistake, Olympia thought, suddenly frantic. What if Jared never learned to love her as she loved him?

There could be no doubt that he desired her, she reminded herself. Surely she could build upon that foundation of passion.

She must build upon it.

But passion was not love. She was a woman of the world. Aunt Sophy and Aunt Ida had taught her the importance of love, they had taught her what love was and what it was not. Olympia knew very well that there was a great difference between physical desire and a deeper, more binding commitment.

She loved Jared with all her heart but she was not certain if he could allow himself to love her. Jared did not trust strong passions. He mocked his own and kept them under a tight rein.

Except when it came to making love to her, Olympia thought.

She gripped her reticule very tightly as she watched another explosion of lights in the dark sky.

Except when it came to making love to her.

Tonight she felt as bold and daring as any adventurer setting out to seek a legendary treasure. She was risking all on a wild quest to turn Jared's passion into love.

"Ooh, look at that," Ethan breathed in awe as a burst of colored fire cascaded down from the sky. He glanced at Jared who was standing beside him. "Have you ever seen anything so beautiful, sir?"

"No," Jared said, but he was watching Olympia's face, not the fireworks. "I do not believe I have."

Out of the corner of her eye, Olympia caught a glimpse of the controlled fire of Jared's gaze. He had never looked more dangerous.

Jared's gaze ignited brilliant, flashing sparks inside Olympia that were more dazzling than the display overhead. When he looked at her in that fashion she felt truly beautiful, a legend in her own right.

"I like the music very much." Hugh exclaimed. "Don't you think it is ever so exciting, Aunt Olympia?"

"Oh, yes." Olympia heard the breathlessness in her own voice and saw Jared's mouth curving in a knowing way. He knew full well that she was thinking of how he would touch her later tonight, not the music. "Very thrilling, indeed."

"A siren's song," Jared murmured for her ears alone. "And I cannot resist it."

Olympia risked another glance at his hard, unyielding profile and nearly melted beneath the masculine expectation she saw in his face.

Jared took her arm in his as the rousing strains of

the music soared over the grounds of Vauxhall, delighting the crowds.

"There must be thousands of people here tonight," Robert observed.

"Two or three thousand at least," Jared said. "And that means it would be easy for any one of you to get lost." He surveyed the boys' excited faces. "I want each of you to give me your word that you will not stray out of my sight."

"Yes, sir," Robert said dutifully. He broke off to cheer as another shower of fireworks exploded in the skies.

"Yes, sir." Ethan clapped enthusiastically, his attention on the colorful display.

Hugh stared at the orchestra, his expression rapt. "Yes, sir. Is it very difficult to play a musical instrument, sir?"

Jared met Olympia's eyes. "It requires a great deal of time and effort," he said softly, "but then, most worthwhile things do. If one truly wishes to succeed in a quest, one must be willing to dedicate oneself to the task."

Olympia knew he was not talking about the task of learning to play a musical instrument. Jared was speaking directly to her. She was not quite certain what he meant, but she sensed that he was making a commitment of some kind. She smiled tremulously, aware of the heavy weight of the gold ring he had placed on her hand earlier that day.

"What about the drums?" Hugh persisted. "Perhaps they would not be so very difficult to master."

"The piano would doubtless prove more satisfactory."

"Do you think so?" Hugh looked up at him with a serious expression.

"Yes." Jared smiled slightly. "If you are interested

in learning how to play a musical instrument I shall see about hiring an instructor for you."

Hugh glowed. "I should like that very much, sir."

Olympia touched Jared's arm. "You are very good to us, my lord."

Jared kissed the back of her gloved hand. "It is my pleasure."

"Where's Robert?" Ethan asked abruptly.

"He was here a minute ago," Hugh said. "Perhaps he went to get an ice. I would like one, too."

Olympia came back to her senses with a start of concern. She glanced hurriedly about. There was no sign of Robert in the crowd of excited people watching the fireworks. "He is gone, my lord. He promised he would stay close, but I do not see him."

Jared released her hand with a soft oath. "The Dark Walk."

Olympia glanced at him. "I beg your pardon?"

"I suspect Robert could not resist the temptation of a stroll along the Dark Walk."

"Oh, yes. He spoke of a dare this morning." Olympia was alarmed by Jared's grim expression. "Is the Dark Walk really so very dangerous?"

"No," Jared said. "But that is not the point. Robert gave me his word that he would stay within my sight. And now he has vanished."

"Are you going to beat him, sir?" Ethan asked uneasily.

Hugh frowned. "It was because of the dare, sir. That is why he went off."

"His reason is not important," Jared said with an ominous calm. "What matters is that he has broken his vow. But that is between Robert and me. Now then, I am going to leave your aunt in your care while I go to look for him. I shall expect to find the three of you waiting right here when I return."

"Yes, sir," Ethan whispered.

"We shall take care of Aunt Olympia," Hugh promised.

Jared looked at Olympia. "Do not concern yourself, Olympia. Robert is fine. I shall return with him in a short while."

"Yes, of course." Olympia took Hugh's hand and reached out for Ethan's. "We shall wait right here for you."

Jared turned and walked away. Within seconds he had disappeared into the crowd.

Hugh clutched Olympia's hand very tightly. His lower lip trembled. "I think Mr. Chillhurst, I mean, his lordship, is very, very angry with Robert."

"Nonsense," Olympia said reassuringly. "He is merely annoyed."

"Perhaps he will be annoyed with all of us because of Robert," Hugh said worriedly. "He may decide that we are too much trouble to bother with after all."

Olympia bent down toward Hugh. "Calm yourself. Chillhurst is not going to toss us out on our ear because of Robert or anything else."

"He can hardly do that now, can he?" Ethan said, brightening. "After all, he has married you, Aunt Olympia. He is stuck with us, is he not?"

Olympia looked at Ethan. "Quite right. He is stuck with us."

It was a sobering thought. Olympia's mood of anticipation and excitement evaporated. When one got down to the heart of the matter, one had to acknowledge that Chillhurst had married her for reasons of honor and passion.

And now he was stuck with her.

Chapter 13

He should have guessed that Robert would be unable to resist the dare of the Dark Walk Jared thought. It was his own fault that the boy had slipped away. He had been thinking of his wedding night, not his responsibilities. Passion had ruled his brain all day and now, as always when passion was involved, there were consequences.

The myriad colored lanterns that lit Vauxhall's grounds became increasingly sparse as Jared made his way toward the Dark Walk. The weak moonlight provided little illumination. The music and the noise of the crowd faded behind him as he moved deeper into the vast gardens.

The trees grew close and thick along the darkest of the long paths that had been laid out on the extensive grounds. Here and there Jared saw couples that had sought out the shadows for obviously amorous purposes. When he passed a particularly dense area of foliage he heard a woman's soft, sensual laughter followed by a man's low, eager murmur.

But there was no sign of Robert.

Jared studied the shadows intently, wondering if he might have miscalculated. Perhaps Robert had not come this way, after all. In which case, Jared thought, he had a much larger problem on his hands than he had anticipated.

Visions of his wedding night receded into the distance. At this rate he would be lucky to get everyone home and in bed by one in the morning.

His entire schedule for the evening was rapidly being thrown into serious disarray.

Leaves shivered at the side of the path. A man coughed softly.

"Ahem. Ye wouldn't happen to be a rich cove named Chillhurst, would ye?"

Jared came to a halt as the rough whisper cut into his thoughts. He turned toward the thick stand of trees that stood on the left of the walk.

"I'm Chillhurst."

"Thought so. He said ye'd be wearing a patch over one eye. 'Looks like a bloody pirate,' he said."

"Who said that?"

"Me employer." A thin, short, wiry man dressed in a dirty brown cap, a badly stained shirt, and a pair of loose-fitting trousers emerged from the trees. He sauntered out onto the path and gave Jared a gap-toothed smile. "Evenin' yer lordship. Nice night for doin' business, ain't it?"

"That depends. Who are you?" Jared asked.

"Let's see now." The wiry little man rubbed his jaw reflectively. "Got friends what calls me Travelin' Tom." He grinned cheerfully. "Ye can call me that, if ye care to."

"Thank you. Now as you already appear to know who I am, perhaps we could dispense with the introductions and get directly to the subject at hand. I have a rather important appointment to keep tonight."

Traveling Tom nodded, pleased. "The little blighter said ye was keen on keepin' to yer schedule. Suits me. I'm a man o' business meself, same as you and the cove what employed me this evenin'. A man o' business is obliged to pay prodigious attention to his appointments, ain't he?"

"Quite correct."

"We men o' business know how to deal with each other." Traveling Tom shook his head sadly. "Not like the other sort."

"What other sort?" Jared asked patiently.

"The sort what's all flash and show and no brains. Ye know what I'm talkin' about, I'm certain. There's the type what always seems to get emotional about a simple matter of business. They start wavin' pistols about and makin' ridiculous threats."

"Yes, I know the sort."

"But then there's rational men such as ourselves, m'lord." Traveling Tom nodded sagely. "Men what keeps cool heads and uses logic instead of passion to make business decisions. We don't let the blood get hot over a triflin' financial matter, do we?"

"No point in it," Jared agreed. "Ah, just where is the little blighter, if I might ask?"

"Safe enough. Got him stashed just outside the grounds. Now, then, if ye want him back in a timely fashion, which I'm assumin' ye do, I suggest we get the business done."

"I am at your service." Jared held on to his temper

and refused to let his concern for Robert show in his face. Nothing good would come of displaying any sign of emotion. Traveling Tom was right. For Robert's sake, the matter must be treated as nothing more than a business transaction.

Jared had been through a similar scene a few months ago in Spain. On that occasion he had found himself negotiating with hill bandits for the release of his two cousins.

It seemed to be his fate to be relegated to the task of rescuing others from the consequences of their reckless ways.

Who would rescue me? he wondered.

He pushed the fleeting thought aside to concentrate on the matter at hand.

The weight of the dagger inside his coat was reassuring but he was loathe to produce it. In his experience violence was frequently an unnecessary last resort, the mark of failed negotiations. There were usually better methods of dealing with problems. Calmer, saner, more reasonable methods.

"Glad to hear it." Traveling Tom gave him a wink that implied they were both men of the world. "Now then, it's very simple, m'lord. Me client wants something from ye. In exchange, he'll give ye back the little blighter."

"What does your client want from me?"

"Now that he didn't say. Between ourselves, m'lord, I expect it'll be a prodigious amount of money. Ye know how this sort o' thing works, I'm certain. All I was told is that I'm supposed to spirit the little blighter away tonight and deliver a message to ye. The rest is none o' my concern."

"What is the message?" Jared asked.

Traveling Tom hitched up his belt and assumed an air of grave importance. "Ye'll be receivin' a letter tomorrow tellin' ye to come to a certain place at a certain time. The letter will tell ye what it is yer to bring with ye."

"That's all?"

"Afraid so, sir." Traveling Tom shrugged. "As I said, my part in the matter is of a somewhat limited nature."

"May I inquire how much your client is paying you for your efforts this evening?" Jared asked softly.

Traveling Tom gazed at him with deep interest. "A very pertinent question, if I may say so, m'lord. Very pertinent, indeed. As it happens, I do believe I'm not bein' paid quite enough for all my time and trouble."

"That does not surprise me. You said your employer was a man of business and such men always seek a bargain, do they not?"

"It's as natural to 'em as breathin' air, m'lord."

"I am well aware that a man of your talents must place a high value on his time." Jared eased his watch out of his pocket and frowned thoughtfully at the face. It was so dark he could not read the hour, but there was just enough moonlight to reveal the glint of gold.

"Aye, sir, I do." Traveling Tom's eyes gleamed as he eyed the handsome watch. "Time is money to a man of a business-minded nature."

Jared allowed the timepiece to dangle tantalizingly from his fingers. "To busy men such as ourselves, there is no substitute for efficiency. Transactions that are dealt with satisfactorily in a few minutes rather than over a period of several hours allow one to engage in several profitable enterprises in an evening rather than just one."

"Ye are, if I may say so, a man of prodigious understandin', sir."

"Thank you." Jared swung the watch gently so that it glimmered with every movement. "I suggest, sir, that we could both save ourselves a great deal of bother by striking a bargain here and now."

Traveling Tom eyed the watch the way a trout eyed a lure. "Perhaps we could, sir. Perhaps we could."

"What has your current client offered for your services?"

Traveling Tom's gaze narrowed in a sly manner. "Forty pounds. Twenty to start and the rest to follow when I deliver the goods."

He was lying, Jared thought. Traveling Tom had probably been paid no more than twenty pounds in all, if that. The gold watch was worth far more.

"Very well, then, let us be done with it." Jared closed his fingers around the watch. "As I said, I have an important appointment tonight. I am offering this watch upon delivery of the little blighter. If you accept, it will mean that you can have your profit immediately rather than postponing it until tomorrow."

"The watch, eh?" Traveling Tom considered the matter. "Well, now, I got no guarantee I'll be able to collect the second half o' me payment from me client, do I?"

"No." Jared paused. "Unless you know his true identity and can pursue your claims."

"Don't know his name and he don't know mine. I prefer to work through an arranger, y'see. Safer for all concerned."

"Very wise." Jared concealed his irritation. It would have made matters simpler if he had been able to learn the client's identity tonight. Now he would be obliged to waste time locating him.

"Yes, sir, I exercise great caution in me work. Now, then, about the watch."

"The case of this watch is of solid gold, as I'm certain you can tell. Very nicely worked gold, I might add. The fob is set with a rather valuable plaque. It's worth a hundred and fifty pounds but you may wish to keep it as a souvenir of this night's work rather than sell it to a fence."

"A souvenir, eh? Me friends would be mightily impressed, wouldn't they?" Traveling Tom licked his lips and hitched up his belt again. "In exchange ye'll be wantin' the little blighter back, I take it?"

"Indeed. I shall want him tonight." Jared looked at Traveling Tom. "I have more important things to do on the morrow than waste my time paying ransoms."

"I can understand that, sir." Traveling Tom grinned his black and white grin. "Follow me, yer lordship, and we'll have done with this matter in a few short minutes."

Traveling Tom turned and sauntered off the path, into the thick foliage.

Jared put the watch back into his pocket and eased one hand inside his coat. He gripped the hilt of the dagger but did not remove it from its hidden sheath.

It took several minutes to wend their way through the grounds and out onto the street. Once outside the gardens, Traveling Tom cut through rows of waiting coaches and hurried toward a narrow lane. A small, darkened hackney waited in the shadows.

A coachman, shrouded in a filthy cape, huddled on the seat. He gave a start when he caught sight of Jared. He slowly lowered his gin flask and tucked it under his perch.

" 'Ere now, what's goin' on?" The coachman scowled at Traveling Tom. "Weren't nothin' said about this cove comin' along."

"He ain't comin' with us," Traveling Tom said soothingly. "He and I have come to terms on a business matter. We're turnin' the little blighter over to him."

"In exchange for what?" the coachman demanded sourly.

"A watch that'll fetch us three times what we got paid for this job."

The coachman looked sharply at Jared. He thrust his hand inside his many-layered cape. "Well, then, why don't we take his watch and the little blighter, too?"

Jared took one step toward Traveling Tom and

wrapped an arm around the little man's neck. He slipped the dagger out of its sheath and held the point to Traveling Tom's throat. "I would prefer to keep this a matter of business," he said softly. "But we can make it more complicated, if you wish."

"Calm yerself, m'lord," Traveling Tom said quickly. "Me friend is a mite hasty. Not coolheaded like you and me. But he works for me and he'll do as I say."

"Then tell him to remove the pistol from his pocket and toss it to the ground."

Traveling Tom glowered at the coachman. "Do as he says, Davy. We're goin' to see a fine bit o' blunt out of this night's work. Stop makin' things difficult."

"Ye sure ye can trust him?" Davy looked skeptical.

"'Od's blood, man," Traveling Tom muttered. "Even me client said he was a man what always honored a bargain."

"All right, then. If yer certain."

"I'm certain I don't want to get me throat slit," Traveling Tom snapped. "Now get the little blighter out o' the coach and let's be off."

The coachman hesitated briefly and then jumped down from the seat. He opened the door of the coach, reached inside, and hauled Robert, arms bound, mouth gagged, out onto the cobbles.

"Here ye go, then," the coachman growled. "Now hand over this watch Tom says ye got for us." He gave Robert a push toward Jared.

Robert's eyes were huge with fear as he stumbled blindly forward. Jared lowered the point of the dagger before the boy caught sight of it. He shifted the blade around behind Traveling Tom and held the concealed tip against the little man's back.

"Over here, Robert."

Robert's head jerked around at the sound of Jared's quiet command. He gave a muffled exclamation. The fear in his eyes vanished. It was replaced by a look of desperate relief.

Jared slipped the dagger into its hidden sheath. He stepped back and withdrew the watch from his pocket. Then he gave Traveling Tom a purposeful push toward the coach.

"Be off with you," Jared said. "Our business is finished."

"What about me watch?" Traveling Tom whined.

Jared tossed the watch toward him in a high, wide arc. The golden case flashed in the moonlight. Traveling Tom snatched it out of the air with a chortle of satisfaction.

"Pleasure doin' business with ye, sir," Traveling Tom said. The watch vanished into his pocket.

Jared did not bother to reply. He caught hold of Robert and yanked him swiftly out of the lane and into the relative safety of the busy street. He removed the boy's gag.

"Are you all right, Robert?"

"Yes, sir." Robert's voice shook slightly.

Jared undid the ties that bound Robert's wrists. "There, you're free. Let's be off. Your aunt and brothers are waiting. They will be worried."

"You gave him your watch." Robert gazed up at Jared with a stricken expression.

"And you gave me your word of honor that you would not stray from my sight." Jared led Robert through the milling carriages, back toward the pleasure gardens.

"I am very sorry, sir," Robert said in a hushed tone. "I just wanted to go along the Dark Walk by myself. It was the dare, you see."

"The dare was more important than your word of honor?" Jared strode swiftly through the crowds to the well-lit area where he had left Olympia and the twins.

"I thought I'd be back before you missed me," Robert said miserably.

"Enough. We will discuss this in the morning."

Robert slid another glance toward Jared's face. "I expect you're very angry."

"I'm very disappointed, Robert. There is a difference."

"Yes, sir." Robert lapsed into silence.

The display of fireworks had concluded but the band was still performing enthusiastically in the pavilion. Olympia was waiting with the restless and bored looking twins. The anxiety in her eyes disappeared when she caught sight of Jared and Robert.

"There you are," she said with obvious relief. "We were just about to go in search of you on the Dark Walk ourselves."

"That's right," Ethan volunteered. "Aunt Olympia said we would be safe enough if we all stayed together and went to search for you."

Jared thought of what could have happened had Olympia and the twins appeared at an inopportune moment during the negotiations with Traveling Tom. The anger and concern he had been holding back for the past half hour slipped free of his self-control.

"I told you that you were to stay here with the twins," he said very softly. "When I give an order I expect it to be obeyed, madam."

Olympia stared at him as if he had struck her. Then swift understanding flashed in her eyes. "Yes, my lord," she said gently.

She looked quickly at Robert. "What happened, Robert? Where have you been?"

"A villain kidnapped me right off the Dark Walk," Robert said, not without a touch of pride. He glanced at Jared and the excitement died in his eyes. "He spirited me straight out of the gardens. He told me he was going to keep me with him until tomorrow."

"You're bamming us, ain't you?" Ethan demanded.

Hugh's expression hovered between disbelief and awe. He turned to Jared for confirmation. "It's all a tale, is it not, sir? No one kidnapped Robert. He's having us on."

"I'm afraid Robert is telling the truth." Jared took Olympia's arm and started toward the gates.

"What are you saying?" Olympia wriggled free of Jared's grasp and caught Robert by the shoulders. She pulled him toward her. "Robert, is it true? Someone took you away tonight?"

Robert nodded and hung his head. "I should not have gone down the Dark Walk by myself."

"My God." Olympia hugged him fiercely. "Are you all right?"

"Yes, of course." Robert struggled free of Olympia's arms and straightened his shoulders. "I knew that Mr. Chillhurst, I mean, his lordship, would come after me. I just didn't know if he would come tonight. I thought I might have to wait until tomorrow, you see."

"But why did someone try to kidnap you?" Olympia demanded. She looked at Jared. "I do not understand. What did the villain want?"

"I do not know." Jared said. He took her arm again and led the small group out through the gates and onto the streets. "I confess I did not hang about long enough to discover the motives behind the matter."

"Good heavens," Olympia whispered. "There is only one reason why someone might have wanted to kidnap Robert."

"What is that?" Hugh asked eagerly.

"He must have been after the Lightbourne diary," Olympia said with grim certainty.

"Bloody hell," Jared muttered.

"Whoever it was must have intended to hold Robert for ransom," Olympia explained. "He would very likely have demanded the diary in exchange for returning

Robert. Such villainy could have been perpetrated by only one individual."

Jared realized belatedly where her inventive brain was leading her. "Now, Olympia . . . "

"It was the Guardian," Olympia said very gravely. "Don't you see? It must have been him. We have got to stop him before something terrible happens. Perhaps we should hire a Bow Street runner to track him down. Do you think that would work, my lord?"

Jared had had enough. "Damnation, Olympia, will you cease prattling on about that wretched Guardian? There is no such person. If he ever existed, he is long since dead. Furthermore, this is neither the time nor the place to indulge your silly imaginings."

Olympia stiffened in his grasp. All three of the boys looked at Jared in silent reproach. Jared cursed himself under his breath.

He knew that the simmering rage he was experiencing was aimed largely at himself. He had failed in his responsibilities. He should have kept a closer eye on Robert. Instead, he had been contemplating his wedding night.

That knowledge only served to stoke the fires of Jared's foul mood. All he could think about was how close they had all come to disaster tonight and of how Olympia had nearly compounded that disaster with her plans to go in search of him.

And now she was attributing the entire matter to the Guardian.

A man should not have to suffer such nonsense on his wedding night, Jared thought as he hailed a hackney. Even if he had been personally responsible for the entire affair.

"How did you get Robert back, my lord?" Ethan asked with his usual unquenchable curiosity.

"Yes, sir," Hugh echoed as he bounced up into the carriage. "How did you rescue Robert?"

It was Robert who answered. He slid a sober glance at Jared and then quickly looked away. "His lordship gave the villain his watch in exchange for me."

"His watch?" Ethan's eyes grew very round.

A hushed silence fell on the darkened carriage. As the vehicle clattered off down the street everyone gazed at Jared in stunned amazement.

"Oh, dear," Olympia murmured.

"Bloody hell," Ethan whispered.

"I don't believe it," Hugh said. "Your beautiful watch, sir? You paid for Robert with it?"

Robert sat up very straight. "It's true, is it not, my lord? You gave the villain your watch in exchange for me."

Jared looked at each of them in turn and finally settled on Robert. "We will discuss this matter tomorrow morning at nine o'clock, Robert. Until then, no one is to say another word on the subject."

Silence descended again on the carriage.

Satisfied that he had managed the last word for the moment, Jared lounged back against the cushions and gazed broodingly out the window. It was, he reflected, a damnable prelude to a wedding night.

He wondered why it was that nothing went according to plan in his life these days.

Olympia paced her small bedchamber an hour and a half later. She glanced at the clock on the bureau for the fourth time since she had dressed in her nightgown and chintz wrapper. There was still no sound from Jared's bedchamber.

The house had been quiet for nearly an hour. Everyone but Jared was in his or her bed. Even Minotaur had disappeared into the kitchen.

Jared had ensconced himself in the study with a bottle of brandy immediately after ordering everyone else upstairs. He was still down there.

This was her wedding night, but Olympia was no longer looking forward to it with longing and anticipation. Indeed, she was not at all certain she was even going to have a wedding night. The pall of Jared's grim mood hung over the entire house.

Olympia felt it but she did not entirely understand it. She had told herself that Jared had been overset by the extraordinary events of the evening. It was a reasonable enough explanation for his short temper. After all, he had been obliged to go very much out of his way to rescue Robert, who should have known better than to go haring off on his own.

She was also aware that there must have been a few very nasty moments for Jared in the course of dealing with the villains who had kidnapped Robert. And it was perfectly dreadful that he had been obliged to give up his treasured watch in exchange for Robert.

All in all, Olympia thought, she could see how the happenings of the evening could ruffle even Jared's normally unflappable composure.

Nevertheless, she thought, there was no call for him to behave in such an unpleasant fashion on their wedding night.

She reached the far end of the tiny bedchamber, turned around, and paced back toward the opposite wall. A growing sense of unease was beginning to unfurl deep inside.

She prayed that Jared was not nursing a newly discovered sense of regret downstairs in the study.

What if tonight's happenings had caused him to have serious doubts about the wisdom of marrying her, Olympia thought suddenly.

What if he had concluded that she and her nephews were too much bother after all?

What if Jared was downstairs drinking brandy to forget that he was stuck with the lot upstairs?

Olympia paused in front of the glass on her dressing table and scowled at her image. It was not entirely her fault that she and Jared had been obliged to marry, she thought. Jared had set the entire disaster in motion when he had insinuated himself into her household as the children's tutor.

He had deceived her right from the start. And while she could certainly sympathize with his reasons for doing so, the fact nevertheless removed some of her own guilt in the matter.

Furthermore, she had employed Jared at the start of this business and he had never actually resigned.

Olympia's chin lifted. Jared had no right treating his innocent employer to such surly behavior on her wedding night.

Inspired with righteous resolve, Olympia straightened her cap on her hair, retied her wrapper, and went to the door. She opened it and stepped out into the silent hall.

From the top of the stairs she could make out the glow of candlelight under the study door. She squared her shoulders, stalked down the stairs, and crossed the small downstairs hall.

She raised her hand to knock on the door, changed her mind, and turned the knob, instead. Head high, she sailed into the study and closed the door behind her.

She halted abruptly when she saw Jared. The sight of him unsettled her far more than she had expected.

Jared sprawled in her chair with the relaxed grace of a carnivorous beast. His boots were arrogantly propped on her desk, as if he owned the study and everything in it.

He had long since discarded his coat. The single candle that burned in the room revealed that Jared's shirt was undone halfway down his chest. He had a half-finished glass of brandy in one hand.

The black velvet patch over his left eye only served to make the hooded gleam in his good eye all the more intimidating.

"Good evening, Olympia. I assumed you would be sound asleep by now."

Olympia fortified herself against the decidedly unpleasant tone of his voice. "I came downstairs to speak to you, Mr. Chillhurst."

Jared's brow rose. "*Mr.* Chillhurst?"

"Your lordship," she corrected herself impatiently. "I wish to discuss a certain matter with you."

"Do you, indeed? I would not advise it, madam. Not tonight." He saluted her with the brandy glass. "I am not in the best of moods, you see."

"I understand," Olympia gave him a small, tremulous smile. "You have been through a great deal this evening. A man of your refined sensibilities is bound to be affected by such an unfortunate experience. No doubt you need time to recover."

"No doubt." Jared's mouth twisted. Harsh amusement gleamed in his gaze as he took a swallow of the brandy. "We men who are cursed with refined sensibilities and passionate natures have somewhat emotional reactions to kidnappings and such."

"There is no need to mock me or your own nature, Chillhurst," Olympia said quietly. "We are what we are and we must make the best of it." She took a deep breath and gathered her courage. "And I feel the same applies to our marriage, my lord."

Jared regarded her with a look of disgust. "Does it, indeed?"

Olympia took a step forward and clutched her wrapper very tightly together just below her throat.

"The thing is, sir, we are stuck with each other, if you see what I mean."

"Stuck with each other. A charming notion."

"I realize you are having second thoughts about the wisdom of our marriage and I am truly sorry about that. I did try to dissuade you, if you will recall."

"Only too well, madam."

"Yes, well, unfortunately, there is nothing to be done about it now. We must try to make the best of it."

Jared put down his brandy glass and rested his elbows on the arms of the chair. He placed his fingertips together and regarded her with an enigmatic expression.

"Are you having second thoughts about our marriage, Olympia?"

She hesitated. "I regret that you felt compelled to marry me, my lord. I would not have had it thus."

"I was not compelled to marry you."

"Yes, you were."

"Must you argue with me at every turn?" Jared's mouth thinned. "I married you because I wished to do so."

"Oh." Olympia was taken aback by that statement. Her spirits lifted. "That is very reassuring, my lord. I had been a trifle anxious, you see. One does not like to feel that one has been married simply because there was no honorable alternative."

"I dissolved one engagement, if you will recall. Rest assured, had I wished to do so, I would have found a way out of this alliance, too."

"I see."

"Like you, I am not overly concerned with appearances or the potential of a scandal."

Olympia took another step toward the desk. "I am very pleased to hear that, my lord."

He tilted his head slightly, his expression mockingly quizzical. "Do you think you might manage to call me

Jared? We are quite alone here tonight. And as you have just pointed out, we are married now."

Olympia blushed. "Yes, of course. Jared."

"Why did you marry me, Olympia?"

"I beg your pardon?"

He watched her face in the candlelight. "I asked why you married me. Was it solely because you have found me somewhat useful about the place?"

"*Jared.*"

"I believe that was what you implied when you accepted my offer yesterday. You made it clear that you valued me primarily because I could keep your household in order."

Olympia was horrified. "I only said that because I had the headache and I was very overset by that scene in the parlor with Lady Beaumont and Lady Kirkdale and Mr. Seaton. There are many other reasons why I was pleased to accept your offer."

"Are you quite certain?" Jared tapped his fingertips together. "I should point out that I am not quite so useful as you might have once believed me to be. I almost lost Robert for you tonight."

"You did not lose Robert, he got himself lost." Olympia was growing desperate. "You rescued him, Jared. And I shall never forget it."

"Is that the reason you have come down here tonight? Did you wish to thank me for rescuing Robert after I lost him?"

"That is quite enough." Olympia stormed the rest of the way across the room to stand directly in front of the desk. "I believe you are being deliberately difficult, sir."

"Quite possibly. I am in a difficult mood."

Olympia narrowed her eyes. "What's more, I begin to believe that you have instigated this quarrel merely to cause me distress."

"I did not start this quarrel." Jared abruptly took

his boots down off her desk and got to his feet. He towered over her. "You did."

"I did not." Olympia refused to draw back.

"Yes, you did. I was sitting alone down here, minding my own affairs, when you came traipsing through that door a moment ago."

"This is our wedding night," Olympia said through her teeth. "You should have been upstairs with me. I should not have had to come down here to look for you."

Jared flattened his hands on the desk and leaned closer. "Tell me why you agreed to marry me, Olympia."

"You know the answer to that." Passionate outrage swept through Olympia. "I married you because you are the only man I have ever wanted. The only man whose touch fills me with desire. The only man who understands me. The only man who does not think me odd. Jared, you have given life to my very dreams. How could I not want to marry you, you bloody pirate?"

A thundering hush settled on the room. Olympia felt as though she had just stepped off a very high bridge above a roaring, fathomless torrent.

"Ah," Jared said softly. "Well, there is that, I suppose." He reached for her.

And caught her just as she plummeted into the sea of passion that cascaded over them both.

Chapter 14

The instant he touched her, Jared felt the fine rage within Olympia transform itself into an even grander passion.

You have brought my very dreams to life.

No woman had ever said such things to him, Jared thought. No woman had ever wanted him like this.

Nothing seemed to shake Olympia's desire for him. She had wanted him when she thought him a lowly tutor. She had wanted him after she had discovered his true identity. She had continued to want him even though she had every reason to believe that he was after the same thing

she sought, the secret of the Lightbourne diary. She was not interested in his titles or his fortune.

She wanted him.

It was more than he had ever thought to have, Jared realized. But it was not quite enough. It would never be enough. The real treasure still eluded him, although he could not name it.

Still, he had never been so close or had so much. A wise man took what he could get and counted himself fortunate.

A pirate held on to what he had seized and let the future take care of itself.

Jared hauled Olympia across the desk. He gathered her into his arms and sank back down onto the chair. She tumbled against him, warm and fragrant and vibrant with flowering desire.

"Jared." Olympia wound her arms around his neck and crushed her mouth softly against his. A low, sensual moan escaped her lips.

Jared touched her gently rounded calf where it was exposed by the hiked-up skirts of her nightgown and wrapper. For some reason the memory of the first time he had seen her in her library, struggling to free herself from Draycott's unwanted touch flashed into his mind.

Olympia did not want any other man's touch, Jared thought. Only his.

Only his.

He felt her mouth opening for him, inviting him inside where it was moist and close and dark. Jared pierced the depths, reveling in the intimacy of the drugging kiss. Olympia trembled. Her tongue touched his with the eagerness of a small, curious cat.

He tightened his fingers around her leg and then slid his hand up along her thigh. Her skin made him think of rose petals. She was so soft.

He, on the other hand, was hard and taut and

straining toward the ultimate possession. His hands trembled with the force of his need.

Jared eased his fingers between Olympia's thighs. She gasped, tore her mouth free from his, and buried her face against his shoulder.

And then she parted her legs a little for him.

"Yes," Jared muttered. He cupped the wet heat of her and thought he would shatter. She moved restlessly against his hand and he groaned against her mouth.

The heady scent of her desire enticed him, lured him, bound him to her with the power of a magical spell.

"*Siren.*"

Olympia cried out softly when he found the small pearl between her legs. Her nails became delicate claws as she clung to his shoulders. His fingers grew damp.

Jared parted the chintz wrapper and untied the collar of the prim lawn nightgown. He freed the sweet fruit of Olympia's breasts and took a small, careful bite.

Olympia convulsed with longing. "Jared, I cannot bear it."

She seized his face between her soft palms and kissed him with a wild, sweet passion that seemed as uncontrollable as the wind. Jared inhaled sharply when he felt the firm, lush curve of her buttocks pressing against his erect shaft.

One of Olympia's hands was inside his shirt now, stroking him, tugging gently at the curling hair on his chest. She wriggled lower, tasting him with her tongue as she worked her way down his body.

Jared felt her start to slide out of his lap. He held her more tightly so that she would not slip to the floor. And then he realized she was trying to unfasten his breeches.

He sucked in his breath and swiftly performed the task for her. And then he was free. He heard Olympia's soft exclamation as he thrust himself into her fingers. She touched him with feminine awe.

"I love the feel of you," Olympia whispered. Her fingers tightened softly around him. "So fierce and proud and powerful."

Her words and her touch nearly sent Jared over an invisible edge. It was as if all the breath had suddenly been squeezed out of him. He closed his eyes and waged a violent battle to avoid spilling his seed into her gentle hands.

It was the first time she had touched him so intimately and he was not certain he would ever recover from the experience.

He was not certain that he even wished to recover.

Jared felt Olympia slide all the way down onto the floor. And then she was kneeling in front of him, cradled between his thighs. He lifted his lashes and looked down at her.

She was gazing intently at his throbbing manhood.

"Olympia?"

She did not seem to hear him. Her fingers touched him with increasing wonder. "You are so magnificent, Jared. So exciting. Like a mighty hero from an ancient legend."

"Bloody hell," Jared whispered. "You make me feel like one." His hands clenched very tightly in her hair. He was barely aware of her lace cap falling to the floor.

Olympia threaded her fingers through the dark, curling hair of his groin. She turned her head and kissed the inside of his thigh.

"*Enough.*" Jared knew he could not stand any more of the sensual torment.

He got out of the chair and sprawled on the carpet. With a low, hoarse exclamation he pulled Olympia down on top of him.

"Jared? I do not understand." Olympia braced herself against his bare chest. She looked down at him with earnest confusion mingled with shimmering excitement.

Jared tugged her legs alongside his hips so that she straddled him. " 'Tis a common custom among the inhabitants of several—" Jared broke off and ground his teeth together to keep from exploding. The moist, warm opening of her body was lodged against the broad tip of his shaft. "Among the, ah, inhabitants of certain foreign lands."

Olympia blinked and then her slow smile filled with a wise, womanly comprehension. She lowered herself cautiously until he was firmly lodged at the very entrance of her feminine passage. "Which lands would those be, Mr. Chillhurst? You know I am ever eager to learn new facts."

Jared looked up at her, saw the delightfully wicked, thoroughly sensual laughter in her eyes and grinned. "Remind me to make a list for you later, Miss Wingfield."

"If it would not be too much trouble."

"Not at all. I'm a tutor, if you recall. And I am very good at making lists."

He locked his hands around her hips and thrust himself upward with a swift, sure movement that took Olympia by surprise.

"Jared." Her eyes widened with amazement and then narrowed again with heightened desire. "A most interesting custom."

"I thought you would find it quite fascinating." Jared traced the curve of her thighs with his hands. "I certainly do."

He could barely get the words out. His entire body was responding to the siren's song. He was rigid with desire, desperate with it. Olympia was snug and hot and wet. She wrapped herself around him, enveloped him, made him a part of her.

For these few minutes while he was lodged deep within her, Jared knew he was not alone. He was with the one other person in the world who could touch his very soul. The one who could rescue him from his lonely island.

"My lovely siren. My wife."

Olympia cried out. She shivered and her body tightened unbearably around Jared.

Then she was singing her high, sweet, siren's song, the song she sang only for him. He thrust himself into her one last time and abandoned himself to the wild, uncharted seas.

"Fireworks," Jared mumbled.

Olympia stirred. She was lying on top of Jared's hard, damp body, her legs tangled with his, her hair flowing across his chest in a red wave.

"What did you say?" Olympia asked politely.

"Making love to you tonight was like being in the middle of a display of fireworks." Jared gathered a fistful of her hair in his powerful hand and studied it in the candlelight. He smiled slowly. "You are a siren of many talents. You can seduce me even as you argue with me."

Olympia chuckled. "No offense, my lord, but you are remarkably easy to seduce."

His smile vanished. "Only by you."

She was vaguely startled by his sudden mood shift this time. Probably because she herself was feeling so relaxed and content. She met his single-eyed gaze and once again she had the sensation that some inner veil had been momentarily pulled aside. She found herself peering past the calm facade he presented to the world into the tempestuous depths of his passionate soul.

"I am pleased to hear that, Jared, because it is the

same with me," she said gently. "You are the only man I have ever wanted in this fashion."

"We are well and truly wed now," he said very quietly, as though sealing an invisible pact. "There is no going back for either of us."

"I understand. That is what I was trying to tell you earlier."

"Ah, yes. Your little lecture on how we are stuck with each other and must make the best of the situation."

She flushed beneath his mockery. "I was only trying to put a practical face on the matter."

"Leave the practical and the mundane to me," he said. "I am very good at handling that sort of thing."

Olympia frowned. "It is very odd, is it not?"

"What?"

"That you are so very clever with practical matters when it is obvious that you are a man of strong emotions. Your powers of self-restraint are most impressive, my lord."

"Thank you," he said. "I do try to control myself for the most part."

She smiled approvingly. "Yes, you do. And you are successful a great deal of the time. Jared?"

"Hmm?"

She touched the black band that secured his velvet eye patch. "You have never told me how you lost the sight in your eye."

"It is not a very edifying tale."

"Nevertheless, I would like to hear it. I want to know everything about you."

Jared laced his fingers through her hair. "I have two cousins, Charles and William, who have spent a great portion of their lives living up to the family reputation."

"What do you mean?"

"They are likable enough, but they are reckless,

rash, and a damn nuisance for the most part. When they were fourteen and sixteen, respectively, they decided to engage in the free-trade. They fell in with a smuggler who was doing business with the French."

"What happened?"

"I learned of their plans on the very night they were to begin plying their new trade. My father and uncle were in Italy on some hare-brained venture. My aunt came to me. She begged me to see to it that Charles and William did not get hurt."

"How old were you?"

"Nineteen."

"So you . . . Did something go wrong that night?" Olympia asked uneasily.

Jared's mouth curved in disgust. "Of course something went wrong. Things usually go wrong when any of my family hatch one of their idiotic plans. In this particular instance the problem was the captain of the vessel which had brought the smuggled goods across the channel."

"What did he do?"

"After my cousins had unloaded the ship and gotten the goods safely stowed ashore, the captain decided he no longer required their assistance. Nor did he wish to split the profits with two young boys. He decided to take possession of the goods and leave no witnesses."

Olympia stared in horror at Jared's sightless eye. "He tried to kill them?"

"I arrived just as he was about to shoot Charles. My cousins had no weapons. I had brought along my father's dagger." Jared paused. "Fortunately, he had taught me how to use it. Unfortunately, the ship's captain had had more experience than I in knife fighting. He took my eye with his first lunge."

"Good lord," Olympia whispered. "It must have been a very near thing. You could have been killed."

Jared lifted his gaze from her hair to her face. He gave her a strange smile. "But, as you see, I was not. And neither were my cousins. All's well that ends well, siren."

Olympia hugged him fiercely. "You must not take such chances ever again, Jared."

"I assure you, I have no particular liking for such situations," Jared muttered. "I certainly do not seek them out."

Olympia held him closely. "Jared, whenever I think of what that night cost you—"

"Do not think of it." Jared framed her face with his hands. "Do you comprehend me? Do not think of it and do not raise the subject again."

"But, Jared—"

"Olympia, it is finished. It was finished fifteen years ago. This is the first time I have spoken of the matter to anyone since the night it happened. I do not wish to speak of it again."

She touched his hard jaw with gentle understanding. "He died, didn't he? You were forced to kill that man who tried to murder you and your cousins. That is why you do not wish to speak of what happened that night."

He silenced her by putting his fingers against her mouth. "Not another word, siren. No good can come of it. Nothing can change what happened. It is best left in the past where it belongs."

"Yes, Jared." Olympia fell silent. She rested her head against his shoulder. Her mind swirled with visions of how terrible that night had been for Jared.

He was an intelligent man, she thought, a man of strong emotions and refined sensibilities. Such a man could not escape unscathed from an act of violence. The worst scars would always lie beneath the surface.

Jared stirred. "About Robert."

Olympia frowned as her thoughts immediately

shifted back to the present. "Yes, poor Robert. Perhaps it is time we discussed what happened at Vauxhall Gardens tonight."

"There is actually not much to discuss, Olympia."

"On the contrary. We must reason out who kidnapped him and why. I know you do not think much of my theory about the Guardian being after the Lightbourne diary, but I really do feel you should consider the possibility."

"Damnation." Jared sat up reluctantly, adjusted the opening of his breeches and rested his arm on one upraised knee. He pondered Olympia's concerned face for a long moment. "Just what do you think is going on here? Do you actually believe that some ghost from the time of Captain Jack is hanging about, searching for the treasure?"

"Do not be ridiculous." Olympia pushed her hair out of her eyes and fumbled with her wrapper. "Of course I do not believe in ghosts. But it has been my experience that there is usually a grain of truth behind even the most bizarre legend."

"No one is after the secret of the Lightbourne diary except yourself, madam."

"What about Mr. Torbert?" she demanded.

"Torbert undoubtedly knows that you are investigating an old legend, but he cannot know which one. Furthermore, I do not believe that he would resort to kidnapping. He is not short of funds. *And he is certainly not the Guardian.*"

Olympia thought about that. "Well, I grant you that he does not appear to be the sort who would be involved in a legend."

"An astute observation," Jared said dryly.

"But whoever took Robert tonight must have had a reason for doing so."

"Of course he had a reason and it was no doubt a very simple one. Money."

"Money?" Olympia gazed at him in dismay. "You mean someone knows about the three thousand pounds I received from Uncle Artemis's shipment of goods?"

"No," Jared said quite forcefully, "I do not." He got to his feet and drew Olympia up to stand in front of him. "Olympia, I do not believe that whoever kidnapped Robert was after your three thousand pounds any more than he was after the diary."

She searched his face anxiously. "Then why would anyone bother to kidnap Robert? He is not connected to a wealthy family."

"He is now," Jared said simply.

Olympia was stunned into momentary silence. She swallowed quickly. "Your family?"

"The Flamecrest fortune is doing quite nicely, thank you, even without the addition of Captain Jack's lost treasure. It is more than likely that Robert was spirited off tonight in hopes of forcing me to pay a considerable ransom."

"Good heavens." Olympia groped for the chair and sat down very suddenly. "I had not thought about that. I had not realized that someone might assume you would feel responsible for Robert now that you have been obliged to marry me."

"Olympia, I give you fair warning. If you ever again imply that I was forced to marry you against my will, I shall very likely lose my temper. I married you because it suited me to do so. Is that quite clear?"

She glanced up at his unyielding expression. "Yes, my lord."

"Very well, then." Jared reached for his watch and swore softly when he found the pocket empty. He glanced at the tall clock. "I suggest we go upstairs to bed. It has been a very long night and I find that I am more than ready for bed."

"Yes, of course." Olympia rose. She felt oddly deflated. The exuberant happiness she had known a short while ago when she and Jared had made love had dissolved.

Jared watched closely as he picked up the candle. "Olympia, you are my wife but that changes nothing in our relationship. Do you comprehend? I will continue to manage the household affairs and see to Robert, Ethan, and Hugh. You need not concern yourself with the bothersome details of such matters. I will take care of all of you."

Olympia smiled wistfully. "Yes, Jared." She stood on tiptoe and kissed his taut jaw. "But there is one detail that will not be as it was before."

He arched one brow. "And what is that?"

Olympia blushed but she did not look away from his challenging gaze. "I was referring to the matter of our sleeping arrangement, sir. It has occurred to me that there is no longer any need for us to, ah, use the study for the sort of thing we used it for just now."

Jared smiled his buccaneer's smile. "No, madam, there is no longer any reason for us to skulk about in your study. It is high time we experimented with the traditional English custom of making love in a bed."

He gave her the candle to hold and swept her up into his arms. Then he carried her out the door and up the stairs.

The Master of the Siryn must make his peace with the Master of the Serpent before two halves may be joined to make a whole.

Olympia frowned intently over the most recent clue she had uncovered in the Lightbourne diary. The master of the *Siryn* could only refer to Captain Jack, she knew. The master of the *Serpent* would no doubt be his erstwhile friend and partner, Edward Yorke.

Claire Lightbourne had not known much about the quarrel that had taken place between the two men. It had occurred in the West Indies, long before she had met her Mr. Ryder in England. She had, however, recorded the fact that her new husband had vowed never to have dealings with Yorke or any of his clan.

But both men had long since passed on to whatever heavenly rewards awaited a pair of buccaneers. There was no way for the two to meet and make their peace.

No way for the two halves of the map to be joined together.

"Damnation," Olympia whispered under her breath. She had the feeling she was very close to the answer she sought. But she had to find the missing half of the map. She wondered if it had descended down through the Yorke family, just as the Flamecrest half had come down through the Ryders.

How did one go about finding a descendent of a long-dead buccaneer?

Olympia tapped her pen thoughtfully on the polished surface of her desk. She wished that Jared would show more interest in the search for the lost treasure. She badly wanted to talk to someone intelligent about the matter. But on that point, he remained adamant. He would not become involved in the search.

She sensed that Jared's refusal to discuss the diary was his way of showing her that he had not married her in order to learn the secret. Nevertheless, it was making her study difficult.

A knock on the door interrupted her thoughts.

"Enter," she called impatiently.

The small parade that marched into her study consisted of Ethan, Hugh, Mrs. Bird, and Minotaur. Olympia could not help but note that even the dog appeared morose.

"Is there something wrong?" she inquired uneasily.

Hugh stepped forward. "Robert cost too much."

Olympia put down her pen. "I beg your pardon?"

"We fear that Robert cost too much," Ethan explained soberly. "Lord Chillhurst had to pay for him with his beautiful gold watch. Now Robert is receiving a terrible thrashing in the dining room and very soon we shall all likely be asked to leave."

"Oh, I really do not think that Chillhurst will thrash Robert because of what happened last night," Olympia said. "And we certainly will not be leaving."

"Some of us will be leaving right enough." Mrs. Bird looked defeated but defiant. "His lordship told me so himself."

Olympia was shocked. "He did?"

"Aye, that he did. Says we'll all be movin' into a big townhouse tomorrow. Says we'll be takin' on staff." Mrs. Bird's defiant expression crumpled without warning and her voice cracked with anguish. "He's going to hire a *butler*, Miss Olympia. A real butler. What'll become of me, I ask ye? His lordship won't be needin' an ordinary housekeeper like me once he hires himself town staff."

"And his lordship will not be wanting us around, either," Hugh muttered. "Especially not after he had to give up his watch on account of Robert. He's going to ship us all off to our relatives in Yorkshire."

Ethan stepped forward. "Do you think we could afford to buy his lordship a new watch, Aunt Olympia? I've got sixpence."

Hugh glared at him. "Don't be a fool, Ethan. Sixpence ain't near enough blunt to buy a watch like the one his lordship had to trade for Robert."

Mrs. Bird burst into noisy tears. "He won't be wanting any of us, least of all me."

Olympia jumped to her feet, thoroughly exasperated. "That is quite enough. I do not want to hear any more of this nonsense. I do not know about this business of moving into a large townhouse, but it does not matter a jot if we do. Nothing is going to change around here. Chillhurst told me so himself last night."

Mrs. Bird gave her a morbid look. "Then he deceived ye again, Miss Olympia. Everything's changed now that yer married to him."

"That is not true." Olympia faced her small family with stout conviction. "He said everything will continue to function just as it has functioned since he came to us. Chillhurst will not thrash Robert. He will not replace you, Mrs. Bird. And he will not be shipping anyone off to Yorkshire."

"How do ye know that, Miss Olympia?" Mrs. Bird demanded. She still sounded like a doomed soul, but there was a small spark of hope in her eyes.

"Because I trust him to keep his word," Olympia said calmly. "Furthermore, you are all part of my family and Chillhurst knows that. He would never try to separate us. He knows very well that I would not permit it."

The flicker of hope died in Mrs. Bird's eyes. "Yer talkin' as if ye was still his employer, Miss Olympia. Truth is, ye ain't the one givin' the orders around here any longer. Ye be Chillhurst's wife and that changes everything. He's the master of the house now. He can do as he likes."

Minotaur whined softly and thrust his big head under Olympia's hand.

———

"I am very sorry for what happened last night, sir." Robert stood very stiffly in front of Jared. He gazed straight ahead at the wall behind Jared's left shoulder.

Jared rested his elbows on the dining room table and tapped his fingertips together. He studied Robert's face, well aware that the boy was struggling valiantly to keep his lower lip from trembling. "Do you understand precisely why I am disappointed in you, Robert?"

"Yes, sir." Robert blinked several times.

"It is not because you got yourself into trouble. And it is not because you cost me a fine watch."

Robert glanced quickly at him and then went back to staring straight ahead. "I am sorry about your watch, sir."

"Forget the watch. It is cheap compared to a man's honor. Nothing is as important to a man as his honor."

"Yes, my lord."

"When you give someone your word, Robert, you must do all in your power to live up to that vow. Nothing less is acceptable. Nothing less is honorable."

Robert sniffed loudly. "Yes, sir. I promise I will be very careful about my honor in the future."

"I am pleased to hear that."

Robert glanced at him anxiously. "Sir, I wish to ask you for a very great favor. I know I do not deserve it, but I promise I will do anything in exchange."

"What is the favor?"

Robert swallowed. "I wish to ask that you do not punish the others for what I did. Ethan and Hugh are very young, sir. They are terrified they will be sent off to Yorkshire. And I know Aunt Olympia would be very sad if they were sent away from her. She is quite fond of all of us, you see. She will be lonely without us."

Jared sighed. "No one is going to be sent away, Robert. You and your brothers and your aunt are in my care now. You may rest assured that I will fulfill all of my responsibilities toward you." His mouth curved wryly. "With any luck, I shall do a better job of it in the future than I did last night."

Robert frowned. "What happened last night was my fault, sir."

"I fear that we both must assume a share of the blame. I ought to have kept an eye on you. I should have guessed that you would be lured to the Dark Walk by that young man's dare."

Robert looked confused. "Why would you guess that, sir?"

"Because I was your age once, myself."

Robert stared at him in astonishment.

"Yes, I know. It is difficult to believe." Jared lowered his hands and sat back in the chair. "Now, then, that is quite enough on that subject. Let us move on to another."

Robert hesitated. "Sir, if you do not mind, I would like to know exactly how I will be punished for what I did last night."

"I said the matter is over, Robert. I can see that you have already chastised yourself for what happened and that is sufficient."

"It is?"

"Of course. It is a sign that you are very swiftly becoming a man." Jared smiled with satisfaction. "I am quite pleased with you, Robert. Seeing one's charges turn into honorable young men whose word may be relied upon is one of a tutor's primary goals."

He spoke no less than the truth, Jared realized with some surprise. There was, indeed, something very satisfying about this business of being a tutor. A man could do a lot worse for himself than to engage in such a career, he thought. One literally shaped the future when one instructed young people.

Robert stood very tall. "Yes, sir. I shall try very hard

not to fail again, sir. Does that mean you will continue to be our tutor, even though you are now married to Aunt Olympia?"

"Yes, indeed. I rather enjoy the task. But there is something else which requires my immediate attention. Robert, I want you to think back very carefully and tell me exactly what happened last night. I want to know everything those villains said while you were with them."

"Yes, sir. But I thought you just said the matter was finished."

"It is as far as you are concerned," Jared said. "But there are still one or two small details that I must deal with."

"What sort of details, sir?"

"I must find out who employed those villains to kidnap you."

Robert's eyes widened. "You are going to find him, sir?"

"With your help, Robert."

"I shall do my best." Robert scowled in thought. "But I do not know if I can help you. The only thing I remember them saying about their employer was that he was a man of business rather like yourself, sir."

"I suppose you have heard that there were rumors of a lover." Lady Aldridge gave Olympia a very knowing look as she handed her a cup of tea. "It is said that Lord Chillhurst discovered his fiancée in a most compromising position with her paramour and ended the engagement on the spot. The tale was never confirmed, of course. No one involved would discuss it."

Olympia beetled her brows in annoyance. "I seriously doubt that there is anything to the rumors and I certainly do not wish to discuss them, madam."

She was not enjoying herself at all, Olympia reflected. She had accepted the offer of tea from Lady Aldridge because there had been no polite way to avoid it. After having spent the past two hours in Lord Aldridge's library, she felt more or less obliged to be civil even though she had discovered nothing useful in Aldridge's map collection. Unfortunately, she had learned the hard way that Lady Aldridge was an inveterate gossip.

"You are quite correct, Lady Chillhurst. I, too, doubt that there is anything to the gossip." Lady Aldridge's smug expression stated far more clearly than words that she believed every word of the tale.

"Excellent. Perhaps we could change the subject." Olympia tried to sound bored.

Lady Aldridge gave her a chagrined look. "But, of course, madam. I did not mean to offend. You do comprehend that I was not remarking upon your husband's family so much as I was commenting on Lady Beaumont."

"I would rather not discuss her, either."

"What's this about Lady Beaumont?" Lord Aldridge scowled as he walked into the drawing room. He had stayed behind in his library for a few minutes after Olympia had finished in order to replace all of his precious maps in their proper drawers. "What's she got to do with this map of the West Indies that Lady Chillhurst is attempting to locate?"

"Nothing, my dear." Lady Aldridge smiled benignly. "I was merely relating the old tale of how and why the engagement between Chillhurst and Lady Beaumont came to an end three years ago."

"Lot of rum nonsense." Aldridge stalked to the brandy table and poured himself a glass. "Chillhurst was quite right to end the thing. A man in his position cannot marry a female who starts carrying on with another man even before the wedding."

"Of course not," Lady Aldridge murmured. She gave Olympia a speculative glance.

"Got his honor to think of," Aldridge said. "That Flamecrest bunch is a devilish lot of Originals, but they've always been quite keen on matters of honor."

Lady Aldridge smiled coolly. "If Chillhurst was so very keen on his honor, sir, why did he not call out his fiancée's lover after he discovered them together? I also heard that Lady Beaumont's brother issued a challenge which Chillhurst ignored."

"Probably because he's too bloody intelligent to risk getting himself killed over a female." Lord Aldridge downed another swallow of brandy. "In any event, everyone knows Chillhurst ain't got an ounce of hot blood in him. Rest of the clan's damned volatile, but not him. Ask anyone who's done business with him. Cold and levelheaded as they come."

"You've done business with my husband?" Olympia asked in another desperate attempt to change the subject.

"Certainly. Made a packet in the process." Lord Aldridge nodded with brusque satisfaction.

"I was not aware that you were acquainted with my husband," Olympia said.

"Well, I ain't. Never dealt directly with him, naturally. Man never comes to town. Does all his business through that agent of his."

"Mr. Hartwell?"

"Precisely. Felix Hartwell has handled your husband's affairs for years. But everyone knows that Chillhurst gives the orders. Singlehandedly rebuilt the Flamecrest fortune after his grandfather and father ran through the last of it. Family's always had its ups and downs when it comes to financial matters. Leastways they did until Chillhurst took charge."

"My husband is very skilled at taking charge of such things," Olympia said with quiet pride.

"It is obvious that you are very fond of your husband, Lady Chillhurst." Lady Aldridge picked up her teacup. "I find that very touching, if rather odd under the circumstances."

"What circumstances?" Olympia demanded, thoroughly irritated with her hostess. If being polite to such people was a requirement of being a viscountess, Olympia thought, she was going to have a very difficult time fulfilling her new duties.

"As my husband says, Chillhurst has a reputation for being quite lacking in the stronger emotions. He is said to be altogether without feeling. One wonders if that is not why Lady Beaumont sought solace from another during her engagement to him."

Olympia crashed her cup down on its saucer. "My husband is an admirable man in every respect, Lady Aldridge. Nor is he lacking in the stronger emotions."

"Really?" Lady Aldridge's eyes gleamed with malicious intent. "Then I wonder why he did not feel compelled to call out his fiancée's lover or respond to her brother's challenge?"

Olympia got to her feet. "My husband's decisions are none of your affair, Lady Aldridge. Now, if you will excuse me, the clock has just struck four and I really must be going. My husband said he would fetch me at four and he is very precise in such matters."

Aldridge hurriedly put down his brandy glass. "I shall see you to the door, Lady Chillhurst."

"Thank you." Olympia did not wait. She stalked out of the drawing room.

Aldridge caught up with her in the hall. "I regret I

was unable to assist you this morning, Lady Chillhurst."

"Do not concern yourself."

The truth was Olympia had almost abandoned hope of discovering a map that would give her a clue as to the location of the uncharted island referred to in Claire Lightbourne's diary. She had half of a map of the island itself but no notion of where the blasted chunk of land was located.

"Lady Chillhurst, you will not forget my warning about Torbert, will you?" Aldridge eyed her nervously. "The man is not to be trusted. Promise me you will be extremely cautious in your dealings with him."

"I assure you I shall be careful." Olympia tied the strings of her bonnet as the Aldridge butler opened the door.

Jared was waiting in a hackney at the foot of the steps. Ethan, Hugh, and Robert were with him.

Olympia smiled in relief and ran down the steps to join her family.

Chapter 15

"I say," Hugh whispered when Jared unlocked the door at the top of the stairs in the Flamecrest mansion. "Will you look at that?"

"This is the best room of all. There are all sorts of interesting things in here," Ethan said. He crowded into the chamber behind his twin and surveyed the array of trunks and shrouded furniture that filled the room. "I'll wager there's a fortune in fabulous jewels hidden in one of those old trunks."

"I would not be at all surprised." Olympia held the candle higher and peered over the boys' heads to survey the vast, shadowed room. Huge, delicate cob-

webs vibrated like tattered veils in the dim glow of the taper.

Ethan was right, she thought. This chamber, which appeared to be a storage room, was the most intriguing of the many rooms Jared had shown them on the tour through the old mansion.

It was not the most unusual chamber. That honor had to go to the gallery on the floor below which contained a staircase that led nowhere. It simply stopped midway up a stone wall. The room they were exploring now, however, contained the most interesting collection of bits and pieces, Olympia decided.

"There is no telling what one might discover in here," Olympia said.

"We'll likely uncover a ghost or two," Robert predicted with ghoulish delight. "This is a very eerie place, is it not? It looks just like one of the chambers in a haunted castle that is described in a book that I am reading."

"Ghosts," Hugh repeated in a voice that crackled with excitement and dread. "Do you really think there might be ghosts in here?"

"Perhaps the ghost of Captain Jack, himself," Ethan suggested in a voice laced with sepulchral horror. "Perhaps he walks through the walls and goes down that flight of stairs in the gallery."

Jared glanced at Ethan with slightly raised brows.

Olympia frowned in thought. "Now there's an interesting notion. The ghost of Captain Jack."

"Captain Jack died peacefully in his bed," Jared announced in a thoroughly dampening tone. "He was eighty-two at the time and he was laid to rest in the family plot on the Isle of Flame. This house had not even been built at the time of his death."

"Then who built this wonderful house, sir?" Hugh asked.

"Captain Jack's son, Captain Harry."

Hugh's eyes widened. "Your grandfather built it? I say, he must have been a very clever man."

"He was clever, all right," Jared said. "Clever at spending money. This house represents one of the more interesting methods he concocted to demolish a considerable portion of the family fortunes."

"What happened to the rest of your family fortunes?" Ethan asked.

"My father and uncle took care of most of the remainder. If it had not been for my mother, we would all have been sunk in poverty by now," Jared explained.

"What did your mother do to save you from poverty?" Robert asked.

"She gave me one of her necklaces." Jared met Olympia's eyes. "It had been given to her by my grandmother, who had received it from my great-grandmother."

"Claire Lightbourne?" Olympia asked, her eyes widening.

"Yes. It was fashioned of diamonds and rubies and was quite valuable. My mother gave it to me when I turned seventeen and told me to give it to the woman I eventually married. She meant for it to descend down through the family in an unbroken line of Flamecrest viscountesses. Mother was something of a romantic, you see."

"Aunt Olympia is the woman you eventually married," Robert pointed out. "Did you give the necklace to her?"

"Yes, did you give it to Aunt Olympia?" Hugh asked, obviously enthralled by the tale.

"No," Jared said without any sign of emotion. "I sold it on my nineteenth birthday."

"*Sold* it." Ethan grimaced with disappointment.

"You didn't, sir." Robert looked crestfallen.

Hugh stared at Jared. "You sold your great-grandmother's beautiful necklace? How could you when you knew it was supposed to go to your wife?"

"I used the money to help refit the one ship my family still owned at the time." Jared did not take his gaze off Olympia. "That ship became the foundation for all of my present business enterprises."

Olympia saw the bleak determination in him and knew beyond a shadow of a doubt how much it had cost him to sell his mother's necklace. "That was very practical of you, my lord," she said bracingly. "I am certain that your mother was proud that you used her necklace to rebuild the Flamecrest family fortunes."

"Not particularly," Jared said coolly. "My mother was as melodramatic as everyone else in my family. She wept when she learned how I had financed that first ship. That did not stop her from enjoying the results, however."

"What do you mean?" Hugh asked.

Jared made a motion with his hand that took in the vast mansion. "Mother gave many a fine party here in town. She loved to entertain and she spent a considerable amount on the balls and soirées she gave in this house. I remember one in particular where she arranged for a waterfall and a small lagoon of champagne to be created in one room."

"I say," Hugh whispered. "A whole waterfall of champagne."

Robert tilted his head inquiringly. "I'll wager you bought her necklace back after you got rich."

Jared's jaw tightened. "I attempted to do so but I was too late. The necklace had long since been destroyed by the jeweler who bought it. The stones had been removed and reset in various bracelets, rings, and brooches. The whole lot had been sold off into a variety of hands. It was impossible to find all the gems and put them back together."

"So it was lost forever," Hugh said with a dramatic sigh.

Jared inclined his head. "I'm afraid so."

Olympia lifted her chin. "It sounds to me as though you did the right thing, my lord. You are to be commended for taking the logical, practical approach under the circumstances and I suspect every member of your family is secretly glad that you did."

Jared lifted one shoulder in a seemingly negligent shrug and glanced around the dark chamber. The heavy key he had used to unlock the door dangled from the iron ring in his hand. "It makes no matter now, does it? The thing is done. As for ghosts and such, I doubt that you will discover anything of interest in here except some dusty furniture and a few moldering family portraits."

"*Portraits.*" A surge of excitement swept through Olympia. "Of course. Mayhap there is a picture of Claire Lightbourne stored up here. Or even of Captain Jack, himself."

Jared swept the room with one last, dismissive glance. "Mayhap. You can search for them later, if you like. It is getting rather late and I suspect it is almost time for dinner." His hand went automatically to his empty watch pocket.

Olympia winced. Ethan, Hugh, and Robert stared at Jared's hand and held their breath.

Jared's mouth curved ruefully as his fingers brushed the empty pocket. He turned without comment and started toward the door. "Let us be off. We have wasted enough time on this tour."

The boys trailed reluctantly after him. Olympia took one last, wistful look around the chamber before following everyone else out the door. She consoled herself with the knowledge that she would be able to explore the room more thoroughly at another time.

Jared steepled his fingers and regarded his new butler with an assessing gaze. He had hired the man, himself, after telling Felix not to bother filling that particular post.

Felix had been surprised by the announcement that Jared planned to interview his own candidates for the position. "Never tell me you want to be bothered with the task of selecting a butler, Chillhurst."

"I fear I must handle the matter personally," Jared had said. "The position requires a unique set of qualities, you see."

Felix had stared at him uncomprehendingly. "Why is that?"

Jared had smiled slightly at his friend's bewilderment. "Because this person will be obliged to work with my present housekeeper who is a most unusual female."

"I told you to let me replace her with a trained and experienced housekeeper," Felix had muttered.

"I cannot do that. My wife would not hear of replacing Mrs. Bird. She is quite attached to her."

Felix had given Jared a strange look. "You are letting your wife dictate to you in such matters?"

Jared had opened his hand in a mocking gesture of resigned submission to the lot of a husband. "Let us say that I am happy to indulge my new bride."

Felix had snorted loudly. "I begin to believe you are telling me the truth when you say that you are a man caught up in the web of passion, Chillhurst. This is not like you, my friend. Perhaps you should consult a physician."

"Do you think so?"

Felix chuckled. "Yes, but I would not advise consulting the same one Beaumont is seeing. From all accounts the quack has had no luck in curing Beaumont of his unfortunate affliction."

The memory of Felix's advice on physicians made Jared smile faintly as he surveyed Mr. Graves of Bow Street.

Graves was suitably named, Jared thought. The man was tall, stoop-shouldered, and cadaverously thin. He wore the perpetually doleful expression of an undertaker. Jared had chosen him after interviewing several candidates from Bow Street because of the gleam of canny intelligence in the man's eyes.

"Now, then, do you understand your duties in this household?" Jared asked.

"Aye, m'lord, I believe I do." Graves tugged uncomfortably at his new black jacket. He was clearly not accustomed to such finery. "I'm to keep an eye on the inhabitants of this house and see to it that no one is admitted to the premises who is not known and approved of by yerself."

"Correct. You will also watch for any unusual or suspicious occurrences. I want a daily report of all events, no matter how mundane, that transpire while I am not in residence. Is that clear?"

"Aye, m'lord." Graves made a valiant effort to straighten his stooped shoulders. "Ye may depend upon me, sir. I done well by ye on the other matter, did I not?"

"Yes, Graves you did." Jared tapped his fingertips together. "You and your friend Fox did an excellent job collecting the evidence I needed to prove my theory."

"Fox and I are proud to give satisfaction, sir."

"As I told you, I have reason to believe that someone attempted to kidnap my wife's nephew on one occasion. In addition it is possible that someone made an effort to break into our former residence in Ibberton

Street. I want you to keep an eye on things. I am not concerned so much with the possibility of theft as I am with the safety of my family."

"Understood, yer lordship."

"Very well, you will take up your tasks immediately." Jared frowned. "One more thing, Graves."

"Aye, m'lord?"

"You will make every effort to get along with our housekeeper, Mrs. Bird. I do not wish to be bothered with squabbles among the staff. Is that clear?"

Graves's eyes gleamed. "Aye, sir. Mrs. Bird and I have already made our acquaintance. A fine figure of a female, if ye don't mind me sayin' so, sir. Got plenty of spirit. Always did like a female with spirit."

Jared concealed a smile. "I see that I need not concern myself with the matter, then. You may go, Graves."

"Aye, yer lordship."

Jared waited until his new butler had left the library. Then he got to his feet and walked around his desk to stand at the window. The gardens were still in a sorry state but the big house, which had been closed up for years, had been completely transformed inside. Everything had been dusted off and polished to a rich gloss. The woodwork gleamed and the windows sparkled. The old monstrosity of a mansion had been miraculously turned into a home for his lively young charges and his wife, Jared reflected.

No, it was the other way around, he thought suddenly. The three boys and Olympia had transformed the house into a home.

After a few minutes of quiet reflection Jared went back to his desk and sat down behind it. He unlocked a drawer and removed his appointment journal. Opening it, he contemplated the series of notes he had made over the past few months.

There was no longer any way he could avoid the obvious conclusion. The evidence had grown too strong to be ignored. Jared wondered why he had put off the inevitable for so long. It was not like him to hesitate over such matters.

He had suspected the culprit from the beginning but he had been hoping that another explanation could be found for the embezzlement.

It was time to take practical action. He had played the fool long enough.

Word that Olympia was married to the Viscount Chillhurst spread like wildfire. She rather wished it had not.

Being a viscountess was turning out to be a great nuisance, she thought two days later as she was handed down from the ancient Flamecrest town coach. It seemed that one could not even go about on one's own when one had a title.

Jared had ordered the old coach to be taken out of storage, polished up, and horsed with a team of sturdy grays. He had then stipulated that Olympia be accompanied by one of the new footmen and a maid whenever she left the mansion.

The new maid, an anxious-to-please young woman of seventeen, dutifully followed Olympia out of the heavy coach and up the steps of the Musgrave Institution.

"You may wait on one of those benches, Lucy." Olympia waved toward the wooden benches in the hall outside the library. "I shall be back in an hour or so."

"Yes, ma'am." Lucy curtsied politely.

Olympia hurried into the vast library. The elderly librarian nodded in greeting.

"Good day to you, Lady Chillhurst. Regret any discourtesy I may have given in the past."

"Good morning, Boggs." Olympia stripped off her gloves and smiled at the man. "What is this business of some discourtesy? You have always been most gracious."

"Regret to say I was unaware that you were the Viscountess Chillhurst, madam." Boggs gave her an injured look.

"Oh that." Olympia waved the matter aside. She and Jared had discussed how to handle this sort of situation. "Of course you were unaware of the facts. My husband prefers his privacy and therefore we attempted to go about anonymously while here in town. But we have been discovered so his lordship has decided there is no longer any point trying to avoid the nonsense of having our identity known to all and sundry."

Boggs was clearly confused about why anyone with an illustrious title would wish to be anonymous but he was much too polite to comment. "Yes, madam."

"Will you mind very much if I go through the charts and maps in the West Indies cabinet one more time?"

"Not at all." Boggs bowed her into the map room. "Help yourself, madam. Already unlocked it for another member of the society. He's in there now, nosing about."

"Oh?" Olympia frowned slightly. "Mr. Torbert or Lord Aldridge?"

"No, Mr. Gifford Seaton," Boggs said.

"Mr. Seaton?" Olympia was so startled she nearly dropped her reticule. "I did not know he was a member of the society."

"Yes, indeed. Joined right after his sister married Lord Beaumont. That would have been about two years ago, I believe. Spends a great deal of time in the West Indies cabinet."

"I see." Olympia went to the door and looked into the musty room.

Gifford was standing in front of a large mahogany table, poring over a map he had unrolled. He glanced up and saw Olympia. His smile was calculating.

"Lady Chillhurst." Gifford kept one hand on the edge of the unfurled map as he gave Olympia a small, elegant little bow. "How nice to see you. I had heard that you were in the habit of using the society's library."

"Good morning, Mr. Seaton. I did not realize until this moment that you are active in the Society for Travel and Exploration."

"I have read all of your papers that were published in the society's journal," Gifford murmured. "Extremely informative, if I may say so."

"How kind of you." Olympia was ridiculously pleased. The wariness she had experienced on seeing Gifford in the library subsided. She stepped closer to the table and glanced at the map. "I see you are studying the West Indies. Are you writing a paper or planning to travel there?"

"Either is a possibility." Gifford watched her closely. "I understand that you are also interested in the region, Lady Chillhurst. Boggs tells me you have been studying the charts and maps of the area."

"He is correct." She surveyed the map that Gifford had unrolled. "I have not had an opportunity to view this particular chart, however. It appears to be quite old."

"It is. I found it last month and had it put aside in a special drawer so that I could get to it readily."

"Really?" Olympia studied the map eagerly. "That is no doubt why I did not come across it in my earlier investigations."

"No doubt." Gifford hesitated and then gestured toward the map. "You are welcome to inspect it now, if you wish. I find it interesting because it depicts several small islands that I have never been able to locate on any other map in the society's collection."

"How very exciting." Olympia tossed aside her reticule and bent over the old sheet of parchment.

"I collect you are interested in uncharted islands in the West Indies, madam?"

"Yes, indeed." Olympia bent closer to the map, seeking familiar reference points that she had located on other charts of the area. The plain, undecorated chart was disappointing at first glance. "This is a very unusual depiction of the geography of the area. It is not nearly as elaborate as most."

"I am told it was drawn personally by a buccaneer who sailed the West Indies over a hundred years ago."

"A buccaneer's map?" Olympia looked up quickly and found Gifford staring at her intently. "Truly?"

He shrugged. "That's what Boggs told me. But who can be certain about such things? The map is not signed so there is no way to verify the name of the man who drew it."

"Fascinating." Olympia went back to perusing the map. "It certainly appears to be old."

"Yes." Gifford shifted slightly, moving to stand close beside her so that he could continue to study the map. "Lady Chillhurst, I would like to apologize for my behavior the other afternoon. I regret any offense."

"Do not concern yourself, sir." Olympia peered more closely at a small dot of land that she had not noticed on other maps. "I understand that there is a great deal of emotion involved in the matter."

"My sister and I have long been alone in the world," Gifford said. "Until she married Beaumont, our financial situation was extremely precarious. There were times when I feared we would both end our days in a workhouse or debtor's prison."

Sympathy welled up in Olympia. At least she had been spared such fears, thanks to the small inheritance she had received from Aunt Sophy and Aunt Ida.

"How very dreadful for both of you," Olympia said gently. "Did you have no relatives to whom you could turn?"

"None." Gifford's smile was rueful. "We lived on our wits, madam. And most of the time I regret to say that my sister carried the greater portion of the burden. For many years I was too young to be of much help. She took care of both of us until she could secure a good marriage."

"I see."

Gifford's mouth hardened. "My family was not always impoverished. Demetria and I were reduced to embarrassing circumstances because my father had no talent for financial matters. To make matters worse, he had a taste for the gaming hells. He shot himself the morning after he gambled away the last of his inheritance."

Olympia forgot all about the map on the table in front of her. The pain in Gifford's eyes could not be ignored. "I am extremely sorry to hear that."

"My grandmother was a great heiress, you know."

"She was?"

"Yes." Gifford assumed a far-away expression, as though he were looking into the past and seeing it clearly. "She had inherited a shipping empire from my great-grandfather and she managed it as well as any man."

"She must have been a very clever woman," Olympia said.

"They say she was extremely shrewd. There was a time when her ships sailed from America to the farthest corners of the globe, bringing back silk and spices and tea."

"America?"

"Yes. My great-grandfather established his shipping business in Boston. My grandmother was raised there. She eventually married one of her captains. His name was Peter Seaton."

"Your grandfather?"

Gifford nodded. "I never knew him or my grandmother. My father was their only child. He inherited the business when his parents died. He sold the ships and then moved to England." Gifford's hand closed into a fist. "He married and then he proceeded to destroy the entire fortune."

"What happened to your mother?"

Gifford looked down at his tightly knotted hand. "She died when I was born."

"And now you have no one but your sister."

Gifford's eyes narrowed. "And she has no one but me. I trust you can understand why I was consumed with rage when Chillhurst ended the engagement. She had worked so hard to secure his interest. She had pawned the last of my mother's jewelry to buy the gowns she needed to impress him that summer."

Olympia touched his sleeve. "Mr. Seaton, I am very saddened to learn of your unfortunate family situation. But please do not blame my husband for what happened. I know him well enough to be quite certain that he did not end the engagement because he learned of your sister's financial circumstances."

"Demetria told me the truth and I prefer to believe her, not Chillhurst." Gifford turned abruptly away from the table. "It is all so damnably unfair."

"But your sister has made a financially secure marriage and seems content. You have the advantages of a connection with Lord Beaumont. Why are you not content, also?"

Gifford swung around to face her, his face tight with

anger and despair. "Because it is not right. Don't you understand? It is not fair that Chillhurst has it all and we have nothing. *Nothing*."

"Mr. Seaton, I do not understand. It seems to me that you have everything you wanted."

Gifford made an obvious effort to regain control of himself. He closed his eyes briefly and drew a deep breath. "I beg your pardon, Lady Chillhurst. I do not know what came over me."

Olympia smiled uncertainly. "Perhaps we should change the subject. Shall we study this chart together?"

"Some other time, perhaps." Gifford drew his watch out of its pocket and glanced at the face. "I have another appointment."

"Yes, of course." Olympia looked at his watch, thinking of the one Jared had used to ransom Robert. "That is a very handsome watch. Can you tell me where I might buy one like it?"

Gifford frowned briefly. "I purchased it at a small shop in Bond Street. I had it and the fobs specially designed for me."

"I see." Intrigued, Olympia took a step closer. "That is a most unusual motif on the plaques and on the case. Is it some sort of serpent?"

"A sea serpent." Gifford slipped the watch back into his pocket. "A creature of myth and legend, you understand." His smile was not reflected in his eyes. "It is a symbol of a time when my family held its rightful place in the world. Now, if you will excuse me, I must be off."

"Good day to you, Mr. Seaton."

Olympia watched thoughtfully as Gifford strode from the room. When she was alone she turned back to the old chart on the table. But her mind was no longer on the poorly drawn map.

She was preoccupied with the elaborate design that decorated Gifford's watch and the attached fobs.

It was a strangely familiar motif.

"Welcome home, madam." Graves held the door of the Flamecrest mansion open as Olympia hurried up the steps. "We have guests."

"We do?" Olympia came to a halt in the hall and turned to look at the new butler. "Does Mrs. Bird know?"

"Yes, madam, she does." Graves chuckled. "And she's in a fine taking on account of it."

Mrs. Bird hove into view. "Is that you, Miss Olympia? About time you got home. His lordship tells me there's going to be two extra for dinner this evening. And on top of that, I'm expected to get two of the bedchambers ready. I'd like to know if this sort of thing is going to become a regular occurrence around here."

"Well, I really cannot answer that," Olympia said. "I have no notion of how many friends his lordship will be entertaining."

"These ain't friends," Mrs. Bird said ominously. "They're relations. His lordship's papa and his uncle." She lowered her voice and glanced around to ensure that the hall was empty. "His lordship's papa is an *earl*."

"Yes, I know." Olympia untied her bonnet strings. "I'm certain you can handle the problem of guests in the household, Mrs. Bird."

Graves smiled at Mrs. Bird with an infatuated expression. "Of course she can, madam. In the short time I have worked in this household, it has become clear to me that Mrs. Bird is a woman of great ability."

Mrs. Bird blushed a fiery shade of red. "I was just wantin' to know how often I'm going to be expected to handle this sort of thing, is all. Got to make plans, you know."

"Feel free to call upon me for assistance, Mrs. Bird," Graves intoned. "I stand ready to aid you in any way I can. Together, I feel sure we shall manage."

Mrs. Bird fluttered her lashes. "I suppose we'll get by somehow, then."

"Never doubt it," Graves said.

Olympia looked from one to the other. "Where is his lordship and our guests?"

"His lordship is in the library, madam," Graves said. "His guests are upstairs with the young gentlemen. I believe the Earl and his brother are telling stories to Masters Robert, Ethan, and Hugh."

Olympia paused in the act of turning toward the library. "Stories?"

"About an individual known as Captain Jack, I believe, madam."

"Oh, well, I'm sure my nephews will be vastly entertained by those tales." Olympia reached for the knob of the library door.

"Allow me, madam." Graves sprang forward to open the door.

"Thank you," Olympia said politely, a little taken back by the unfamiliar service. "Do you do that all the time?"

"Yes, madam, I do. Part of my duties." Graves inclined his head and ushered her into the library.

Jared was sitting at his desk. He glanced up as Olympia entered the room. "Good day, my dear." He got to his feet. "I am glad to see you are home. We have visitors. My father and uncle have arrived."

"So I understand."

Jared waited until the door had closed behind her. Then he smiled invitingly.

Olympia hurled herself across the room and straight into his arms. She lifted her face for his kiss.

"I believe I rather like this business of being married," Jared mused when he finally raised his head.

"So do I." Olympia took a reluctant step back. "Jared, I have just had the most unusual conversation with Gifford Seaton. There are one or two points that I . . ."

Jared's sensual smile vanished in a flash of anger. "What did you say?"

Olympia frowned. "There is no need to raise your voice, my lord. I can hear very well. I was just saying that I have come from a rather strange conversation with Mr. Seaton."

"Seaton talked to you?"

"Yes, that is what I am trying to tell you. We met in the society's library at the Musgrave Institution. It is the most amazing thing, sir, but it transpires that Mr. Seaton and I are both interested in the West Indies."

"That bastard," Jared said in a dangerously soft voice. "I told him to stay away from you."

Olympia glowered. "I do not think that you should call him such unpleasant names. Mr. Seaton is a troubled man. He has had a very difficult life."

"Seaton is a conniving, bloody-minded young scoundrel who is bent on mischief. I gave him strict orders to keep away from you."

"For heavens sake, Jared, it is not Mr. Seaton's fault that we encountered each other in the society's library."

"Do not be so certain of that. Seaton probably learned that you are in the habit of spending a great deal of time there and deliberately planned his own visit to coincide with yours."

"Really, Jared, you go too far. Mr. Seaton appeared to have a genuine scholarly interest in the West Indies.

Indeed, he even allowed me to view a map that he has discovered in the library."

"I'll wager he had an ulterior motive for doing so." Jared sat down behind his desk, his expression grim. "Be that as it may, I shall handle the matter. In the meantime, you are to avoid any further contact with Seaton. Is that clear, madam?"

Olympia stared at him in shock. "That is quite enough, sir."

"Enough? I have not even begun. I will teach young Seaton a lesson he will not soon forget."

"Jared, I will not permit this sort of talk. Surely you do not think you can start issuing irrational orders and making wild statements like that simply because you are now my husband."

Jared eyed her coldly. "I am well aware that you prefer not to concern yourself with the pesky little details of day-to-day life, madam. For the most part that is neither here nor there. However, in regard to our marriage, there is one small detail which I fear you will have to note well."

Olympia narrowed her eyes. "And what is that small detail?"

Jared leaned back in his chair, rested his elbows on the arms and placed his fingertips together. "I am the master of this household. I will do what I think best and I will make decisions accordingly. You will obey those decisions, madam."

Olympia's mouth fell open. "I will do no such thing. Not unless I happen to agree with those decisions and I do not happen to agree with your edict regarding Mr. Seaton."

"Damnation, Olympia, I am your husband. You will do as I tell you."

"I will do as I bloody well please, just as I have always done," Olympia stormed. She heard the library door open behind her but she paid no attention. "You will listen to me, Mr. Chillhurst, and you will pay close attention. Do not forget that I took you on as a tutor in this household. When all is said and done, it seems obvious to me that you are still in my employ."

"That's a nonsensical thing to say," Jared shot back. "You are my wife, not my employer."

"That, sir, is a matter of opinion. As far as I am concerned, nothing has changed regarding our original arrangement."

"Everything has changed," Jared said between set teeth. "And that, madam, is not a matter of opinion. It is a matter of legal record."

"What, ho." An unfamiliar voice broke into the argument before Olympia could respond.

"I say, what is going on around here?" another voice said from the door. "Are we interfering in a domestic quarrel, do y' think, Thaddeus?"

"It certainly appears that way," the first speaker said cheerfully. "Never saw your son in a temper, Magnus. Mayhap marriage is good for him."

"Bloody hell," Jared muttered. He glanced toward the door. "Madam, allow me to present my father, the Earl of Flamecrest and my uncle, Thaddeus Ryder. Gentlemen, my wife."

Olympia turned around and found herself confronting two extremely dashing men of mature years. Handsome, silver-haired, and dressed to the nines, they smiled at her with a wicked charm that had no doubt captivated many a female heart.

"Flamecrest, at your service," the taller of the two men said as he made an elegant bow. "It is a pleasure to meet you, madam."

"Thaddeus Ryder." The second man grinned cheerfully. "Glad to see Jared's finally done his duty by the family. Don't suppose you've had time to find the key to Captain Jack's treasure yet, have ye?"

Jared gave an exclamation of sheer disgust. "Damnation, Uncle. Have you no sense of discretion?"

Thaddeus looked at him in surprise. "No need to be discreet now, lad. She's one of the family."

"Best of all possible situations, if ye ask me," Magnus said with a gleaming smile for Olympia. "No need to sneak about like a thief in the night trying to worm the secret out of her. She'll be glad to tell us everything she learns about the treasure, won't ye, m'dear?"

Olympia studied both men with great interest. "I will be happy to share whatever I can with all of you, but I think you should both know that someone else is after the treasure."

"God's teeth." Magnus's grin became a snarl of outrage. "I was afraid of that." He looked at his brother. "Did I not say that I had a chill in me bones, Thaddeus?"

Thaddeus looked grave. "Aye, so ye did, Magnus. So ye did. And premonitions are always to be respected in our clan. We all know that." He studied Olympia. "Any notion of who might be after the family treasure, m'dear?"

Olympia realized with a great sense of relief that she was at last in the company of people who understood her concerns and who would not mock her fears. "Well, my idea of who is behind the threats may strike you as unlikely, sir. Chillhurst has certainly refused to give it any credence."

Magnus wrinkled his nose. "My son is smart enough about some things, but he's got no imagination. Do not pay him any heed. Tell us your thoughts, girl."

Out of the corner of her eye, Olympia saw Jared's mouth tighten. She ignored it. "I believe that something or someone known as the Guardian is after Captain Jack's treasure."

"The *Guardian*." Magnus stared at her in amazement.

Thaddeus appeared equally dumbfounded as well as slightly confused. "Guardian, eh?"

Olympia nodded quickly. "The diary contains a clear warning about a Guardian of some sort."

Magnus and Thaddeus looked at each other and then they both looked at Olympia.

"Well, if that's the case, ye got nothing to worry about, do ye, m'dear?" Magnus explained with an air of great patience.

Thaddeus beamed. "Precisely."

Jared spoke up in an ominous tone. "I would prefer that this subject be abandoned at once."

"Why? What do you know of this Guardian?" Olympia asked Magnus.

Magnus arched one bushy brow in a hauntingly familiar gesture. "The Guardian is your husband, m'dear. Has my son failed to tell ye that he has borne the great honor and responsibility of that title since he was nineteen?"

"Family's called him the Guardian since the night he rescued my two lads from a bit of a scrape with a smuggler," Thaddeus said.

Olympia could not believe her ears. For a moment she was speechless. She recovered and whirled around to confront Jared. "No, he did not bother to mention that small fact."

Jared put his hands on the arms of the chair and started to rise. "Now, Olympia, I can explain . . . "

Olympia was furious. "Mr. Chillhurst, you have deceived me from the very beginning of our association. If it wasn't one thing, it was another. I have made allowances for your fierce passions and emotions all along, but in this, sir, you go too far. How could you not tell me that you were the Guardian?"

"Damn it, Olympia, it is nonsense. You have been concerned about some legendary ghost who is after the secret of the diary. I am neither a legend nor a ghost and I could not care less about the damned treasure."

"Mr. Chillhurst, I must tell you that you have not been of any assistance at all in this matter. Indeed, you have made my task more difficult at every turn by refusing to take an interest in the search for the diary's secret. I am very annoyed with you, sir."

"So I see," Jared muttered. "But what good does it do to know that my father saddled me with the idiotic title of the Guardian when I was nineteen years old? The information cannot possibly assist you in your search."

Olympia drew herself up. "That remains to be seen, Mr. Chillhurst."

"Olympia, wait . . . "

But Olympia was not in a mood to wait. Another piece of the puzzle had been discovered. She needed to think about it. She rushed out of the library without a backward glance.

Chapter 16

Magnus grinned at Jared. "*Mr.* Chill-hurst?"

"Occasionally my wife forgets that I am no longer in her employ," Jared said coldly.

"Her employ?" Thaddeus chuckled. "I say, where did she come by that notion?"

"It's a long story, sir." Jared walked around the desk. "And I do not have time to tell it at the moment. Now, if you will excuse me, I must speak with my wife. As you can see, she is a woman of somewhat volatile temperament."

Magnus slapped his leg and roared with laughter. "Glad to see ye've found

yourself an interesting female, my boy. Don't mind telling ye I was more than a little concerned that ye'd end up with some dull, prosing little wren who'd bring out the worst in ye."

Thaddeus chuckled. "She seems to think you're a man of strong passions, lad. Where the devil did she get that notion?"

"It defeats me." Jared's hand closed tightly around the doorknob. "I shall return shortly. There is something that I must make clear to Lady Chillhurst before the day gets any older."

"Go right ahead, son," Magnus said cheerfully. "We'll help ourselves to your brandy while you're gone. Some of Captain Harry's good French stuff from the cellars, I trust?"

"Yes," Jared said. "It is. Try not to consume all of it before I get back."

"Take your time, lad, take your time." Thaddeus waved him out of the room.

Jared stalked from the library, crossed the marble tiled hall, and went up the stairs.

The door to Olympia's bedchamber was closed. Jared's mouth thinned. He raised his hand and knocked loudly.

"Go away," Olympia called in a muffled, distracted tone. "I am very busy."

"Olympia, I wish to speak with you."

"I really do not have time to chitchat about who is in charge around this house, Mr. Chillhurst. I have work to do."

"Hellfire and damnation, woman, you will cease ordering me about as though I were a member of your staff."

Jared dropped his hand to the knob. He twisted it violently, half expecting to find the door locked.

To his surprise, it was not.

The door opened with a great deal more force than Jared had intended. It slammed against the wall with a crash that made Olympia start in her chair.

She glowered at him from her writing desk. "I told you I was busy, sir."

"Too busy to speak with your husband?" Jared closed the door and strolled into the room with a nonchalance he did not feel.

Olympia's brows drew together in a repressive scowl. "I am not feeling very much in charity with you at the moment, my lord. I cannot believe that you did not tell me the truth about yourself."

"Devil take it, Olympia, I have been attempting to put that nonsense about my being the Guardian behind me for years."

Olympia's eyes went to his black velvet patch and her expression softened. "I realize that the title must bring back terrible memories. But it is an important piece of the puzzle. It may be a key to this entire project."

"It is not the key. How could it possibly be the key? I admit I am known as the Guardian within the circle of my family but I do not give a damn about the diary or the treasure. The warning about me is a lot of foolish nonsense. You must not take it seriously."

Understanding lit Olympia's gaze. "That was why you did not tell me the truth in the beginning. You were afraid of how I would interpret the warning. You thought I would assume the worst about you."

"I did not want you to fear me. Bloody hell, madam, I am not the ghost of Captain Jack."

Olympia tapped her pen against a sheet of foolscap. "I never said you were. I do not believe in ghosts, my lord."

"Then how can I possibly have anything to do with the riddle of the diary?" Jared demanded.

Olympia's gaze grew thoughtful. "That is the problem I am attempting to sort out at the moment, sir. I must discover the connection between the warning and the Master of the *Siryn* and the rest that I have learned. Kindly take yourself off. I know you are not interested in this and I cannot concentrate when you are standing about yelling at me."

"I am not yelling at you."

"Yes, you are. Honestly, Jared, your emotional nature is making this very difficult. I understand, of course, but I really must insist that you remove yourself from my bedchamber."

Outrage washed over Jared. "Do not dare to throw me out of your bedchamber, madam."

"Why not?" She eyed him warily. "It is my bedchamber and at the moment I do not want you in it."

"Is that right?" Jared swooped down on her and plucked her from the chair. "In that case, we shall adjourn to my bedchamber."

"Mr. Chillhurst, put me down this instant." Olympia grabbed her cap as it started to slide off her hair. "I have work to do."

"Indeed you do. It is high time you performed a few of your wifely duties." Jared stormed through the connecting door that linked his bedchamber with Olympia's.

He stalked to the vast bed and tossed Olympia lightly down on top of it. Her cap slipped off and her brilliant red hair spilled out across the pillows. Her gown had climbed above her knees, revealing the enticing length of her stocking-clad legs.

"Siren," Jared whispered. Desire surged through him, a powerful wave that threatened to sweep him away.

He fell on top of Olympia, pinning her to the counterpane. His body was already hard. He could feel the fire in his veins and the driving need in his loins.

Olympia's eyes widened in astonishment. "Good heavens, Mr. Chillhurst, it's the middle of the day."

"Allow me to inform you, madam, that it is the custom in certain lands to make love in the middle of the day."

"Really?" The astonishment in Olympia's eyes turned into sensual speculation. "In broad daylight?"

"The notion would no doubt shock certain dull, narrow-minded people who are not of the world. But we are different, Olympia."

"Yes." Olympia's smile was slow and infinitely tender. Her eyes filled with sensual welcome. "We are different, sir."

He kissed her throat and felt her melt. She thrust her fingers into his hair and arched against him.

A hot, pulsing joy seized Jared. Olympia's intoxicating response to him opened the floodgates of his own passion. She was his, he thought exultantly. She could not resist him even when she was annoyed with him.

She must love him. She had to love him.

With sudden, searing understanding, he realized that he had been waiting to hear the words from her. Why had she never spoken them aloud? he wondered.

Surely she loved him.

He pushed the matter aside as passion had its way. Olympia smiled her siren's smile and drew her slippered foot up along his leg.

"It is very fortunate that we found each other, is it not, my lord? I do not believe there is another man on the face of the earth who would be in tune with me as you are."

"I am pleased that you think so." Jared cupped one soft breast possessively. "Because there is certainly no other female on the face of the earth who understands my nature as you do."

———

A long while later Jared reluctantly rolled off Olympia and relaxed against the pillows. He put one arm behind his head and contemplated the ceiling with a sense of bone-deep satisfaction.

Olympia stirred and stretched beside him. "Making love in the middle of the day is a very pleasant custom, sir, is it not? We shall have to experiment with it again soon."

"We will most definitely do so." Jared cradled her close against his side. "I trust you will not attempt to throw me out of your bedchamber again in the near future."

"I shall certainly think twice about it," Olympia said very seriously.

Jared scowled. "I meant what I said earlier, little siren. You may bewitch me with a glance or a smile, but you will not order me about as though I were still in your employ. I will be master in my own home just as I am the master of my business affairs. *And I will be master of my wife.* Is that quite clear?"

"That's it." Olympia sat straight up in bed, heedless of her nudity. She looked down at Jared, her eyes alight with excitement. "Master of your wife."

"I am glad you agree, madam." Jared studied the beautiful curve of her bare breasts. "A man's got to put his foot down at some point."

"Master of your wife. Jared, you have always called me a siren."

"So I have." Jared traced the outline of her left nipple with the tip of his thumb. "That is because you are one."

"Do you not understand, sir?" Olympia knelt beside him amid the tumbled bedclothes. "You have just called yourself the master of the siren. Captain Jack was the

Master of the *Siryn* and you are his descendent. You are the new Master of the Siryn."

Jared belatedly comprehended the direction of her logic. He groaned. "Olympia, you have stretched logic too far."

"No, I have not been stretching it far enough." Olympia bounced out of bed. "I must get back to work immediately. Be off with you, Jared. You distract me."

"Madam, I happen to be in my own bedchamber."

"Oh, yes. So you are. Then you must excuse me. I must get back to my bedchamber." Olympia whirled about and rushed through the open door.

Jared contemplated the view of her sweetly curved derriere until it vanished around the edge of the door. Then he sighed and sat up slowly.

He surveyed the discarded clothes that littered the bed and the carpet. He picked up Olympia's little white cap and smiled faintly.

He glanced up and frowned when his gaze fell on the clock. It was nearly one and he had an appointment at the docks in forty-five minutes.

"Damnation."

Jared reached for his shirt. Marriage played havoc with a man's daily schedule.

Forty-five minutes later Jared alighted from a nondescript hackney and walked across a busy street to a small tavern. The man he had employed to ask questions along the docks was waiting for him.

Jared sat down in the booth and waved away the buxom tavern wench. "Well then, Fox, what have you learned?"

Fox wiped his mouth on the sleeve of his shirt and belched. "Just what you suspected, m'lord. The man was badly dipped six months ago. So far under the hatches, everyone figured he'd never climb out. Then he somehow managed to pay off all his debts. Same thing happened three months ago. Lost everything and then found a way to cover his losses."

"I see." Jared pondered that for a moment. "I knew what was happening, I just did not know the why of it. Now I do."

Gambling. Well, it seemed that everyone had his secret passion, Jared thought.

"Typical case, m'lord." Fox's world-weary sigh of understanding was somewhat marred by another belch. "Man gets sucked into the gaming hells and gets himself bled dry. Sad, but all too common. Only difference this time, is that the cove managed to come about afore it was too late. Fortunate for him, eh?"

"Yes, very fortunate, indeed." Jared got to his feet. "You will receive your payment through Graves this afternoon, as we arranged. Thank you for your services."

"Anytime, m'lord," Fox took another swallow of his ale. "As I told Graves, I'm always available."

Jared strode out of the tavern and stood for a moment on the sidewalk. He started to hail a hackney and then changed his mind. He needed to think about what he had just learned.

He walked slowly with no particular direction in mind. He was vaguely aware of the taverns and coffeehouses he passed. Even at this hour they were filled with the usual assortment of laborers, sailors, pickpockets, whores, and thieves.

A part of Jared's attention remained on his surroundings as it always did. The weight of his dagger rested comfortably against his ribs.

As he walked, he sorted through the facts that he had learned. Now he knew the motive behind the embezzlement scheme but it did not make matters easier.

The time had come to confront the person who had

betrayed his trust but Jared was in no rush to do so. He did not, after all, have very many friends.

The man with the knife emerged from the alley with virtually no sound. It was his shadow that Jared saw first. The dark shape of it flickered briefly on the brick wall as he launched himself forward.

The instant of warning was just barely enough. Jared threw himself to the side. His assailant's blade sliced through thin air instead of flesh.

The man whirled about, dancing nimbly to catch his balance and then he struck out a second time.

Jared was ready for him. He raised his arm to block the knife thrust and simultaneously slipped his dagger out of its sheath. Sunlight glinted on the good Spanish steel.

The attacker sucked air between his teeth. "No one said anythin' about you havin' a blade o' yer own."

Jared did not bother to answer. He circled his opponent, aware that the man's eyes were riveted on the dagger. When he was certain the villain's whole attention was focused on the blade, he lashed out with one booted foot.

The blow connected with the man's thigh. He howled in pain and rage and flailed wildly in an effort to catch his balance. Jared feinted with the knife and the man jerked backward, toppled, and fell to the pavement.

Jared kicked the knife out of the man's hand and leaned down to put the tip of his own blade against his victim's throat.

"Who hired you?" Jared asked.

"I don't know." The man stared at the hilt of the dagger. "It was just a business arrangement made through me usual arranger. I never saw the cove what paid me."

Jared straightened in disgust and resheathed the dagger. "Get out of here."

The man needed no second bidding. He scrambled to his feet and started to reach for his own blade which lay on the cobbles.

"Leave it," Jared ordered softly.

"Aye, sir. Whatever you say, sir. More where that one came from."

The villain ran off down the street. A moment later he disappeared into a narrow lane between two massive warehouses.

Jared looked down at the blade that his attacker had left behind.

No, he thought, there was no point in putting off the inevitable confrontation any longer.

An hour later Jared went up the steps of the premises that Felix Hartwell had occupied for nearly ten years. A sense of weary sadness pervaded him as he opened the door and walked into the small outer room. He was not altogether certain what one said at a time like this.

Finding the proper words proved unnecessary. When Jared opened the door of the inner office he discovered that he was too late.

Felix was gone.

A letter lay on top of the desk. It was addressed to Jared and had obviously been scrawled in a great rush.

Chillhurst:

I now realize that you know everything. It was only a matter of time. You were always so bloody clever. You may have a few questions. The least I can do is answer them.

I was the one who let word slip about your presence here in town and about the odd arrange-

*ment you had with Miss Wingfield. I hoped that
once you were discovered, you would make haste
back to the country. It was worrisome to have
you in the vicinity, Chillhurst.*

*But you chose to stay in London and I decided
to see if I could use one of your charges to gain
the money I needed. I would have you know that
I meant no harm to the boy. I merely intended to
hold him for ransom. But you foiled me once
again. So damn clever.*

*You will no doubt seek justice because that is
your way but I trust that you will not find me
before I leave England. I have had everything in
readiness for months because I knew this day
might come.*

*I regret everything. I never intended for matters
to go this far. My only excuse is that I had no
choice.*

*Yrs,
FH*

*P.S. I know you will not believe this, but I am
rather glad you survived this afternoon. It was the
action of a desperate man and I regretted it as
soon as I had given the order. At least I will not
have your death on my conscience.*

Jared crumpled the note in his fist. "Felix, why in
God's name did you not ask me for help? We were
friends."

He stood gazing at the surface of Felix's orderly
desk for a long while before he turned and walked back
out onto the street.

At that moment Jared wanted only to talk to Olympia. She would understand.

———

"Jared, I am so very sorry." Olympia scrambled out of bed and went to where Jared stood gazing out into the night. "I did not know of your friendship with this man, but I understand how you must feel."

"I trusted him, Olympia. Over the years I gave him increasing responsibilities. He was as familiar with my business affairs as I was. Damnation. I do not usually make mistakes of this sort."

"You must not blame yourself simply because you placed your trust in the wrong person." Olympia put her arms around him from behind and hugged him fiercely. "A man with a passionate nature such as yours often listens to his heart rather than his head."

Jared braced his hand against the window frame. "My friendship with Hartwell had been tested by time. He knew me better than anyone. He was the one who arranged for me to meet Demetria."

Olympia frowned. "Well, I do not see that he did you any great favor there."

"You do not comprehend. No one felt worse about the outcome of that meeting than Hartwell did."

"If you say so, Jared."

Olympia had known that something was seriously wrong as soon as Jared had returned to the house late in the afternoon. She had tried to talk to him earlier, but he had not wanted to speak of the matter until now when the household was finally abed.

"I have conducted some investigations and I believe I know how it must have started." Jared took a sip of brandy from the glass he was holding. "Felix developed a passion for the gaming hells. He won at first."

"But his luck changed?"

"Yes." Jared took another swallow of brandy. "His luck changed. It always does. He appears to have covered his early losses with money paid to him by some of our investors. He replenished those accounts with money received from other sources. As long as he kept shifting things about, he could conceal what was happening."

"His scheme worked for a time so he no doubt grew bolder."

"You are quite right. His play grew deeper. The losses grew larger. Six months ago I realized that something was wrong and decided to look into the matter." Jared's mouth hardened. "Naturally I asked my trusted agent to investigate."

"He must have been very clever to conceal the evidence of his thefts from you for so long."

Jared shrugged. "Hartwell was a very clever man. That was why I employed him."

"I wonder how he came to realize that you had finally tumbled to his tricks," Olympia mused.

"He obviously realized it this afternoon when the man he hired to kill me failed to carry out his task."

"What did you say?" Olympia tugged furiously at Jared's arm, obliging him to turn around so that she could see his face. "Are you telling me that someone tried to kill you, Jared?"

Jared smiled faintly as he took in the sight of her horrified expression. "Calm yourself, my dear. It was a matter of no great moment. As you can see, the man failed."

"It is a matter of very great moment to me, sir. We must do something at once."

"What do you suggest?" Jared asked politely.

"Why, summon the magistrate." Olympia started to pace furiously back and forth. "Hire a Bow Street runner. We must find this mad fiend and have him clapped up in irons immediately."

"I doubt that would be possible. It was obvious this afternoon that Hartwell had planned for the possibility that I would find him out. He left me a note informing me that he has left England."

"He did?" Olympia spun around. "Are you quite certain that he has gone?"

"Reasonably certain." Jared swallowed the last of the brandy. "It is the obvious course of action and Hartwell is nothing if not a careful, logical man." His mouth twisted again. "Rather like myself. It was one of the reasons I employed him."

Olympia scowled. "This is most annoying, Jared. I would very much like to see him pay for his attempt to have you murdered. He must be a coldblooded monster."

"No. I think he was simply a very desperate man at the end. He probably had creditors hounding him, perhaps threatening him with physical harm or exposure."

"Bah, you are too kind, my lord. He is clearly a monster. I shall not sleep a wink tonight for thinking of what might have happened to you today. Thank God you escaped."

Jared's eyes gleamed. "I appreciate your concern on my behalf."

She glared at him. "You need not make it sound as though I'm merely being polite. It's perfectly natural for me to be alarmed by this incident."

"True. I suppose a dutiful wife is expected to show some concern when her husband tells her he has narrowly escaped death."

"Jared, are you mocking me or yourself this time?"

The amusement in his eyes faded. "Neither. I am merely wondering how deep your concern goes."

She stared at him, appalled. "That is a very stupid question, Mr. Chillhurst."

"Is it? You must forgive me. I am not at my best today. The excitement, no doubt."

"How could you possibly question the depth of my

concern for even one small second?" Olympia demanded, outraged.

Jared smiled. "You are very loyal to those in your employ, are you not, madam?"

"You are something more than a mere employee, sir," Olympia snapped. "You are my husband."

"Ah, yes, there is that, is there not?" Jared put down his brandy glass and reached for her.

Chapter 17

Mrs. Bird plunked the coffeepot down onto the breakfast table and surveyed the crowd with a baleful eye. "Cook wants to know how many to expect for dinner tonight, yer lordship. Like me, she ain't too keen on havin' a bunch of visitors arrive with no notice."

Jared picked up his coffee cup. "You may tell Cook that I happen to know precisely how much each of you is being paid. In your case, Mrs. Bird, there was a considerable increase because of your new duties. I am well aware that I am paying some of the highest wages in town and I expect the best service in return. Inform Cook that all of us will be present for dinner."

"Aye, yer lordship. But she's a mite annoyed. Don't blame me if she takes a notion to burn the soup."

Jared cocked a brow. "If she serves scorched soup tonight, she will be looking for a new position in the morning. The same goes for anyone else on the staff who feels unable to accommodate the requirements of this household."

Mrs. Bird snorted and bustled on back to the kitchens.

"Kindly take the dog with you, Mrs. Bird," Jared called after her.

Mrs. Bird stopped and turned around. "What's all the fancy new staff for, if I'm still expected to see to everything around here, I ask ye?" She snapped her fingers at Minotaur. "Out from under that table, you bloody monster. You don't need another sausage."

Minotaur slunk out from beneath the table, mouth full of sausage.

Ethan gave Jared an innocent look. "I didn't feed him the sausage, sir. Word of honor."

"I know who gave Minotaur the sausage." Jared cast a quelling glance at his father. "We are attempting to break him of the habit of dining with the family, sir. I would appreciate it if you would not encourage him."

"Right you are, son. Where did you acquire your housekeeper, may I ask?" Magnus sliced into a plump sausage. "Mouthy wench. Doesn't seem to have much respect for her employers."

"She came with the rest of the lot," Jared said absently.

Robert clapped his hand over his mouth to stifle a giggle.

Olympia looked up from her eggs. "You musn't mind Mrs. Bird. She's been with the household forever. I do not know what I would do without her."

"Hire another housekeeper, more'n likely," Thaddeus said. "One that doesn't scowl at your guests first thing in the morning."

"Oh, I could never let Mrs. Bird go," Olympia said quickly.

Jared propped his elbows on the table and placed his fingertips neatly together. He regarded his father with a thoughtful expression.

"You need not concern yourself with Mrs. Bird, sir," he said coolly. "She and I arrived at an understanding some time ago. And I must admit, she brought up an interesting point. Just how long will you and Uncle Thaddeus be staying with us?"

Magnus affected a hurt expression. "Trying to boot us out already, son? We just got here."

Thaddeus grinned. "Save your breath, lad. Your father and I ain't goin' anywhere until we help your lady work out the secret of the Lightbourne diary. Best count on us being around for a while."

"I was afraid of that." Jared gazed down the length of the table at Olympia. "I trust you will uncover the mystery very shortly, my dear or we shall be saddled with our uninvited guests indefinitely."

"I shall do my best, my lord." Olympia blushed faintly. She was not certain whether to be embarrassed by his rudeness or not. As far as she could tell neither Flamecrest nor Thaddeus appeared the least offended by Jared's blunt remarks.

"Very well, then, I shall leave the matter to you." Jared reached for his missing watch and grimaced when he failed to find it. "Must make a note to purchase a new one." He glanced at the tall clock and then looked at Ethan, Hugh, and Robert. "It is time for your lessons. Geography and mathematics this morning, I believe."

Thaddeus groaned. "How very dull."

"That's my boy," Magnus growled. "Give him a perfectly fine summer morning and he wastes it on geography and mathematics."

Robert gazed ingenuously at Jared. "Sir, we were hoping that we could be excused from our lessons this morning. His lordship, the Earl, says that boys our age should go fishing every summer morning."

"That's right," Ethan piped up. "And Uncle Thaddeus told us that when he was a lad he used to sail paper boats in a stream on summer mornings."

"And practice fighting with a real sword," Hugh put in helpfully.

"You are all three dismissed from breakfast," Jared said calmly. "I shall give you five minutes to get upstairs to the schoolroom and open your books."

"Yes, my lord." Robert jumped to his feet and made his bows.

"Yes, my lord." Ethan hopped up, bowed hastily, and dashed for the door.

"Yes, my lord." Hugh scrambled to follow his brothers.

Jared waited until they were out of the room before he fixed his father and uncle with a grim expression. "This household is run on a few simple but absolutely inflexible rules. The first rule is that I make the rules. And one of my rules is that the boys receive lessons every morning unless I decide otherwise. I will thank you not to interfere."

Olympia was shocked. "Chillhurst, you are talking to your elders."

Magnus grinned widely. "Damn right, son. Show a little respect, if you please."

Thaddeus chuckled wickedly. "That's the spirit, lass. Don't let him get away with sassing his elders."

Jared looked at Olympia as he got to his feet. "You need not concern yourself with my behavior, madam. I assure you I have been dealing with my elders long enough to know that unless I make myself clear from the start, they will turn this household into a menagerie in no time."

"I hardly think so," Olympia said stiffly.

"Trust me," Jared said. "I know them far better than you do. Good day to you, my dear. I shall see you at noon. Until then I shall be in the schoolroom." He inclined his head briefly toward his father and uncle. "Sirs."

"Off you go, son," Magnus said easily. "We'll still be here when you return."

"I was afraid of that," Jared said from the door.

He walked on out into the hall, leaving Olympia alone with Magnus and Thaddeus. She slanted them another anxious sidelong glance and was relieved to see that neither appeared in the least offended.

"Chillhurst prefers an orderly household," Olympia explained.

"No need to apologize, my dear." Magnus beamed at her. "The boy always was something of a stick-in-the-mud. There were times when his mother and I almost despaired of him."

"He's a good lad," Thaddeus assured her. "But he don't take after the rest of the family."

"In what way?" Olympia asked.

"No hot blood in him," Magnus said sadly. "He lacks the Flamecrest fire, if you know what I mean. Always on about his appointments or checking the time on his watch. Buries himself in his business affairs. No violent emotions, no strong passions. In short, a very abnormal member of the clan."

Olympia frowned at both men. "I do not think you understand Chillhurst very well at all."

"Fair enough," Thaddeus said. "He don't understand us, either."

"He's a man of refined sensibilities and deep passions," Olympia said earnestly.

"Bah. You'd never know he's got the blood of buccaneers in his veins, but he's a good lad, for all that." Thaddeus frowned. "Speaking of his watch, what happened to it?"

Olympia's mouth tightened. "Chillhurst used his beautiful watch to pay the ransom for my nephew."

Magnus stared at her. "You don't say. Just like him to purchase the boy's safety rather than go in with his dagger clenched between his teeth and two pistols blazing. A tradesman at heart. Who do you think kidnapped the boy?"

"Chillhurst suspects it may have been a trusted acquaintance who has since left the country," Olympia said. "I, however, am not so certain."

Thaddeus narrowed his eyes. "Let's discuss your notions on the subject m'dear."

Olympia glanced toward the door to make certain Jared had not returned unannounced. "Well, sirs, as to that, I have a strong suspicion that whoever kidnapped Robert was after the Lightbourne diary."

"Ah-hah." Magnus slammed the flat of his hand against the table so hard that the silverware jumped. "I agree. The diary is most likely at the bottom of all this. We're getting closer to the secret, Thaddeus. I can feel it in my bones."

Thaddeus's eyes gleamed. "Tell us what ye've learned so far, lass. Mayhap Magnus and I can assist you."

Enthusiasm soared through Olympia. "That would be wonderful. I would greatly appreciate your help. I must say, Chillhurst has taken a rather dampening approach to the matter."

Magnus heaved a heavy sigh. "That's my boy for ye. Damp as a fish. Now, then, let's get on with the matter. How far have ye got in the diary?"

"Very nearly all the way through." Olympia pushed aside her plate and folded her hands on the table. She eyed her two new assistants intently. "But although I've managed to translate most of the mysterious phrases, I have not been able to completely decipher their meanings."

"Let's have at 'em," Magnus said.

"Well, there's a phrase about the Master of the *Siryn* making peace with the Master of the *Sea Serpent*. Now, on the surface, that appears to be a fairly obvious reference to Captain Jack and Captain Yorke."

"Bit too late to patch up the quarrel," Thaddeus said. "Both been in their graves for years."

"I realize that. But I have begun to believe that it's necessary for the descendents of both families to meet in order to solve the mystery," Olympia explained. "I have found half of a treasure map. I suspect someone from Yorke's family has the other half."

"If that's the case, we'll never discover the treasure," Magnus said glumly.

"Damme." Thaddeus bunched a hand into a fist and struck the table forcefully. "To be so close only to learn we stand no chance of finding it."

"Why do you say that?" Olympia looked from one disappointed face to the other.

"Won't be able to turn up a descendent of Captain Edward Yorke," Thaddeus said sadly. "He never had a son. Whole bloody clan died out, as far as I know."

Olympia started to respond and then stopped when Graves spoke from the doorway.

"Beggin' yer pardon, madam." He held up a silver salver heaped with cards and invitations. "Morning post has arrived."

Olympia waved him away. "His lordship will see to those. He handles that sort of thing."

"Aye, madam." Graves started to withdraw.

"Hold a moment." Magnus looked at Graves. "Let's see what you've got there."

"They're merely invitations to various social affairs," Olympia explained, irritated by the interruption. "They've been pouring in ever since people realized that Chillhurst was in town."

"Is that right?" Thaddeus wrinkled his brows. "Been goin' to a lot of parties and soirées and such, have ye?"

"Oh, no," Olympia said, surprised. "Chillhurst throws them all away."

Magnus groaned. "Sounds like him. That boy never did know how to have fun. Let's open a few of those invitations and see what's happening in Society. Mayhap we'll find something interesting to do while we're in town, Thaddeus."

"Right you are." Thaddeus motioned Graves to give the salver to Olympia.

"I really don't think—" Olympia broke off as Graves placed the salver full of cards and notes in front of her.

"Got to learn how to amuse yourself if you're going to spend the rest of your days with Chillhurst." Magnus regarded her with an affectionate glance. "Slit a few of those seals and let's see who's doing what this week."

"Very well, if you insist." Olympia reluctantly picked up one of the small white notes and frowned at the blob of wax that sealed it. "Do either of you have anything I can use to open this?"

Steel hissed softly against leather.

Olympia stared in amazement as daggers appeared in the hands of both of her in-laws. She gazed at the ornate hilts of the blades that Magnus and Thaddeus presented to her.

"Here you go, my girl," Magnus said.

Olympia remembered the blade that Jared had worn on his thigh the day he had arrived in Upper Tudway. "Does every man in the Flamecrest clan make a habit of carrying a dagger upon his person?"

"Family tradition." Thaddeus assured her. "Even my nephew keeps his handy."

" 'Course the dagger Chillhurst carries is special," Magnus said with a touch of pride. "Carried it myself for years until I passed it on to him. It's the one Captain Jack himself carried."

"Really?" Olympia forgot all about the pile of invitations in front of her. "I did not realize that Jared's blade once belonged to his great-grandfather."

"Damned fine piece of steel," Magnus said. "Saved Captain Jack's life more'n once. Saved my son's life, too, and that of Thaddeus's boys on one occasion. Captain Jack nicknamed it the Guardian."

"The Guardian." Olympia jumped to her feet. "You called Jared the Guardian."

"So he is." Magnus arched his brows. "Another family tradition. The man that carries the blade carries the title."

"Good grief. I hadn't realized." Olympia thought swiftly.

"What's up, lass?" Thaddeus demanded.

"Maybe nothing. Maybe everything. One of the mysterious phrases in the diary is 'Beware the Guardian's deadly kiss when you peer into its heart to find the key.' " Olympia whirled away from the table. "I must see that blade for myself."

She heard chairs scrape on the floor behind her as she dashed toward the door.

"What, ho," Thaddeus boomed. "She's off, Magnus. She's onto something."

"After her, man," Magnus roared.

Olympia did not wait for them. She ran out into the hall and took the stairs two at a time to the third floor.

When she reached the landing, she turned and raced down the corridor to the schoolroom. Breathing quickly, she reached for the knob, turned it, and threw open the door. It crashed against the wall.

Ethan, Hugh, and Robert were gathered around the globe. They turned to stare at her in astonishment.

Jared looked up and saw Olympia, noting her excited expression. "Is something wrong, my dear?"

"Yes, no, I do not know." Olympia heard Magnus and Thaddeus arrive in the doorway behind her. "Chillhurst, would you mind very much if I took a close look at your dagger?"

Jared glanced over her head to where his father and uncle stood. "What is going on here?"

"Damme if I know," Magnus said cheerfully. "The lass has got the wind in her sails. We're merely followin' in her wake."

Jared gave Olympia a repressive look. "If this has something to do with your study of the diary, my dear, it can wait until the afternoon. You know I do not like to have the lessons interrupted."

Olympia flushed. "Yes, I know, but this is extremely important, my lord. May I please examine the dagger?"

Jared hesitated and then shrugged in obvious resignation. He crossed the room to where his coat hung on a hook. He reached inside and removed the dagger from its sheath. Without a word he handed it, hilt first, to Olympia.

She took the blade cautiously and touched the lethal tip. "*Beware the Guardian's deadly kiss,*" she whispered. She studied the intricate design of the hilt. "Your father tells me this dagger belonged to your great-grandfather and that it is called the Guardian."

Jared slanted his father an ironic glance. "Another nonsensical family legend."

Olympia turned the blade over in her hand. "Is there any way to remove the hilt?"

"It can be done," Jared said slowly. "But why would you wish to do so?"

She looked up eagerly. "Because I wish to peer into the heart of the Guardian."

Jared took the blade from her, his eyes on her face. "Very well. It is obvious that there is no other way to satisfy your curiosity."

Olympia smiled. "Thank you, sir."

A short while later, Jared eased the chased hilt free of the blade shaft. He glanced into the hollow interior of the hilt. "Bloody hell."

"What is it?" Robert asked eagerly. "What do you see, sir?"

"Yes, what is it?" Ethan demanded as he and Hugh crowded close.

Jared looked at Olympia and smiled wryly. "I believe the honors belong to my lady."

Olympia whisked the hilt out of his hand and peered into it. There was an aged piece of paper neatly tucked inside. "There is something in here."

"Damme," Thaddeus muttered.

"Remove it, lass. The anticipation is going to be the death of me," Magnus said.

Fingers trembling with excitement, Olympia tugged the folded paper out of the hilt. She opened it carefully and studied what was written on it. "I believe these numbers will prove to be the longitude and latitude of the mysterious isle where the treasure is hidden."

Jared put his hand on the globe. "Read them to me."

Olympia read the numbers aloud. "They must be in the vicinity of the West Indies."

"They are." Jared gazed thoughtfully at a spot on the globe that was slightly north of Jamaica. "From all accounts Captain Jack was an excellent mathematician. He could calculate longitude and latitude with great accuracy."

"By God, son," Magnus said in ringing tones. "Your lady has done it. She's found the key to the treasure."

"So it would seem," Jared said slowly.

"Not quite," Olympia said.

Everyone turned to look at her.

"What do you mean?" Thaddeus demanded. "We have in our hands the precise information we need to sail to that damned island where Captain Jack hid the treasure."

"Yes, but we only have half of the map of the island, itself," Olympia said. "The other half is still missing. I grow more and more convinced that Captain Yorke's descendents hold the other half of the map."

"Then all is lost." Magnus slammed his fist into his palm. "There are no bloody descendents."

"Could try digging up the whole island, I suppose," Thaddeus said thoughtfully.

Jared gave him a derisive glance. "Assuming you could even find the island, it is highly doubtful that you could discover the treasure by digging at random."

"We could help you, sir," Robert volunteered.

"We are very good at digging," Hugh assured Jared.

"So is Minotaur," Ethan said.

"Enough." Jared held up a hand for silence. "Olympia is quite right. We do not have all the pieces of the puzzle yet. The search for clues must go on."

Olympia gazed at the scrap of paper that had been

hidden in the dagger hilt. "We must try to discover if any of the Yorkes are still around."

Magnus frowned. "Told you, the line died out. Captain Yorke had no son to carry on the name, as far as I know."

"What about a daughter?" Olympia asked quietly.

A stunned silence fell on the room.

"Damme," Thaddeus muttered. "Hadn't thought about that."

"A daughter can pass along a family treasure or secret just as well as any son," Olympia said. "Indeed, only yesterday Mr. Seaton was telling me the tale of how his grandmother ran a shipping empire that she had inherited from her father."

Jared's indulgent expression vanished. His gaze turned cold. "I will not have Seaton involved in this, is that clear, Olympia?"

"Yes, of course. Excuse me." Olympia turned toward the door. "I must get back to the diary. There are one or two points I wish to check."

Magnus and Thaddeus swung around to follow her.

"Allow us to assist you," Magnus called.

"No, I really do not think that would be helpful," Olympia said. "I will let you know when I have something to add to our investigations."

"Well, we'll just have to amuse ourselves in some other fashion," Thaddeus said. He glanced speculatively at Jared. "What are ye teachin' the boys, lad?"

"You will not amuse yourselves in this schoolroom," Jared said. "I will tolerate no further interruptions today."

"The lad always was a killjoy," Magnus muttered to Olympia as he held the door for her. "Call us when you are ready for us, my dear."

"Very well." Olympia looked at him. "What are you two going to do today?"

Magnus and Thaddeus exchanged speculative glances. Then Magnus smiled brilliantly at Olympia.

"I believe we'll sort through a few of those invitations you received a few minutes ago. I'll wager my son hasn't bothered to introduce you to the polite world, has he?"

Jared swore softly. "Olympia is not interested in going about in Society, sir."

"How do you know that?" Magnus demanded. "It's obvious she ain't had a chance to experience Society yet. You go on back to your bloody lessons, son. Leave your wife's social activities to us."

Olympia looked from one stubborn male face to the other. "The thing is," she said uneasily, "I really do not have a thing to wear."

Magnus patted her shoulder in an indulgent, fatherly fashion. "You leave that to Thaddeus and me, my dear. The two of us cut quite a dash in our youth. And our wives were considered diamonds of the first water, God rest their souls. We have a fine sense of style, do we not, Thaddeus?"

"Aye, Magnus, that we do." Thaddeus started to close the schoolroom door. He paused to lean back into the room. "Better hunt up a tailor this afternoon, lad. You won't want to embarrass your wife."

"Damn it, Uncle—" Jared began.

Thaddeus closed the door on the protest and grinned cheerfully at Olympia. "Run along and see what you can discover in that diary, my dear. I'll send for a fashionable modiste and some samples. Should be able to get you outfitted with a couple of decent gowns in no time."

"As you wish," Olympia said absently. She clutched the scrap of paper that she had removed from the dagger. Her mind was churning with fresh notions. "Pray excuse me. I really must get back to work."

———

Against his better judgment, Jared was waiting dutifully in the hall at nine o'clock the following evening. He was wearing a black coat, breeches, and the crisply folded cravat that had been ordained by his father. The heavy old town coach was at the bottom of the steps ready to whisk the Flamecrest clan off to a ball at the home of Lord and Lady Huntington.

Jared did not know the Huntingtons but Magnus had assured him that Lady Huntington was an old acquaintance from the days when he had courted Jared's mother.

"Couldn't ask for a better hostess to launch Olympia into the *ton*." Magnus had rubbed his hands together with glee as he explained the plan to Jared. "Knows all the right people and they'll all be there."

"I do not see any reason to launch my wife anywhere," Jared had grumbled. "She's perfectly content with her present round of activities. I do not think she will enjoy going out into Society."

"That only goes to show how much you know about women, son." Magnus had shaken his head in despair. "Don't know how you managed to land yourself a spirited female like Olympia."

Jared had slanted his father a thoughtful glance. "I collect that you approve of your new daughter-in-law?"

Magnus had practically chortled. "She'll fit right in to the family."

Jared smiled wryly at the memory of the conversation and then glanced impatiently at the hall clock. Neither Magnus nor Thaddeus had come downstairs yet. He had not seen Olympia at all since noon.

Jared was anticipating her appearance with some trepidation. He knew his father and uncle had been closeted with the modiste and her minions for several hours the previous day. A gown had been delivered at five this afternoon along with several mysterious boxes but he had no notion of what to expect.

He had seen enough of current fashion in town to know that low-cut bodices and thin, delicate fabrics were all the crack.

If Olympia's gown proved to be too outrageous, Jared decided, he would simply refuse to allow her to leave the house. A man had to stand his ground on some things.

Graves appeared from the opening behind the staircase. Jared frowned when he saw that his new butler appeared even more dour than usual.

"Beggin' yer pardon, m'lord. Message just arrived at the kitchen door for ye. Figured ye'd want it right away." He held out a sealed note.

Jared took the note from him and glanced at the poor handwriting. "What the devil is this?"

"Don't know, m'lord. The boy said it was urgent."

"Bloody hell." He ripped open the note and scanned the contents.

Sir:

Regret to inform you that the gentleman in question has not left the country after all. An associate saw him not more than an hour ago. I believe him to be headed toward his old place of business. Thought you might care to meet me there as soon as possible. I will wait for you in the alley behind the premises.

Yrs,
Fox

Jared glanced once more at the top of the stairs as he folded the note. "This has to do with our old problem, Graves. Please do not inform my wife about it. She will only worry. Tell her that I will meet up with her later at the Huntingtons'."

"Right you are, sir." Graves opened the door. "Perhaps I should accompany you?"

"No need. Fox will be there."

Jared went out the door and down the steps. He wondered what he would do if he managed to get his hands on Felix Hartwell.

Chapter 18

"I was afraid of this." Thaddeus cast a grim eye over the crowded ballroom. "Looks like that son of yours ain't going to show at all, Magnus."

"Damn and blast." Magnus swiped a glass of champagne off a passing tray and downed the contents in a single gulp. "Knew he wasn't looking forward to the thing, but I thought he'd be gentleman enough to put in an appearance if only to avoid humiliating Olympia."

"I'm not humiliated," Olympia said forcefully. "I'm certain Chillhurst had a very good reason for having to go out this evening. You heard what Graves said. He received an urgent message."

"Bah, the only sort of message Jared would consider urgent is one having to do with his business affairs," Thaddeus muttered. He swept Olympia from head to toe with an appraising glance. "He don't know what he's missin'. Young Robert was right. Ye do look like a fairy-tale princess tonight, lass. Don't she look like a princess, Magnus?"

"Aye, that she does." Magnus smiled his charming pirate's smile. "A diamond of the first water. By tomorrow morning you'll be all the rage, m'dear. Damme, but that modiste was right about puttin' you in emerald green."

Olympia smiled. "I am glad you approve of your creation, my lord. I must say, I do not feel at all like my customary self tonight."

In truth, she did feel quite unreal. The ankle-length silk skirts of her high-waisted gown seemed to float on the very air around her. The bodice was cut far lower than anything else Olympia had ever worn and fitted with tiny off-the-shoulder sleeves.

Her hair had been parted in the center and drawn up into an elegant chignon. The style was trimmed with green satin flowers and artless little curls that danced around her ears. Her satin slippers and long kid gloves were the same gem-green as her gown.

Thaddeus, Magnus, and the modiste had all agreed that the only jewelry that could possibly be allowed was a pair of emerald earrings. Olympia had explained that she did not own any emerald earrings.

"I'll take care of the matter," Thaddeus had promised.

He had produced a pair of spectacular emerald and diamond earrings the afternoon of the ball. Olympia had been horrified.

"Where on earth did you get those?" she demanded suspiciously.

Thaddeus had contrived to look hurt. "They're a gift, lass."

"I could not possibly accept such a valuable gift, sir," she had said at once.

"Ain't me who purchased 'em for ye," Thaddeus had assured her with a sly wink. "It was your husband."

"Chillhurst bought these for me?" Olympia had stared at the jewels in wonder. She had been startled and secretly thrilled at the thought that Jared had taken time from his busy schedule to select a pair of earrings for her. "He chose them, himself?"

"What I meant," Thaddeus had explained very carefully, "is that he purchased 'em for ye in a manner of speakin'. True, he didn't actually pick 'em out for ye, but rest assured it was his money that paid for 'em."

"Oh." Olympia had promptly lost interest in the earrings.

"Here now, it's very nearly the same thing as buyin' 'em for ye himself, lass," Thaddeus had insisted. "The thing is, Chillhurst is a nice enough nephew but he ain't got no notion of style."

"That's right, girl," Magnus had said solemnly. "No notion of fashion at all. But he's the only one in the family since Captain Jack himself that's had the knack of makin' money, y'see."

Thaddeus had nodded cheerfully. "No gettin' around the fact that any blunt Magnus and I and everyone else in the clan has to spend came from Chillhurst in one way or another."

Olympia had scowled in annoyance. "In that case, I would think that you and the Earl and the rest of the family would treat Chillhurst with a bit more respect, sir."

"Oh, we're quite fond of the lad," Thaddeus had

said. "Don't doubt it for a minute. But there's no denyin' he ain't out o' the same mold as the rest of us."

Robert, Hugh, and Ethan had been awestruck at the sight of Olympia as she had descended the stairs that evening.

"I say, you look beautiful, Aunt Olympia," Hugh had whispered.

"The most beautiful lady in the whole world," Ethan had added.

"Like a fairy-tale princess," Robert had concluded.

Olympia had been touched by their admiration. It had buoyed her up a bit after the letdown she had experienced upon discovering that Jared was not in the hall to witness her transformation.

The flare of disappointment had made her aware for the first time that she had been eagerly anticipating Jared's reaction to her new finery.

"Damme, here comes Parkerville," Magnus announced. "No doubt he'll be wantin' an introduction and a dance, just like the others." He glanced at Olympia. "Sure you don't want to take the floor, m'dear?"

"I told you, I do not know how to dance," Olympia said. Aunt Sophy and Aunt Ida had not considered dancing an important accomplishment for a young woman. They had favored instruction in Greek and Latin and geography.

"We'll take care of that little problem soon enough," Thaddeus whispered as an elderly, bewhiskered man drew close. "I'll engage a dancing instructor tomorrow."

"In the meantime, I'll handle old Parkerville," Magnus muttered under his breath. "Man always did have a talent for lechery." He inclined his head at the newcomer.

"Evening, Parkerville," Magnus boomed. "Been an

age since we last ran into each other. How's your lovely lady wife?"

"Dead, thank you." Parkerville turned an oily smile on Olympia. "Heard you've got a daughter-in-law at long last, Flamecrest. Word has it your boy's been keepin' her tucked away out of sight until tonight. Now that I've seen her for myself, I can see why. You'll introduce me to her, will you not?"

"Of course." Magnus went through the introduction with a bored air.

Lord Parkerville took Olympia's gloved hand in his and lingered over the back of it. "Charmed, madam. May I have this dance?"

Olympia smiled distractedly as she wriggled her hand free from his grasp. "No, thank you, sir."

Parkerville looked deeply distressed. "Perhaps later?"

"I doubt it," Magnus said, with casual satisfaction. "My daughter-in-law is extremely particular in her choice of partners."

Parkerville glared at him. "Is that a fact, sir?"

"Yes, indeed." Magnus smiled benignly. "She hasn't danced with anyone all evening, in case you've failed to notice."

"I have not failed to notice," Parkerville said. "Nor has anyone else in the room." He gave Olympia a speculative smile. "We are all waiting to see whom she will favor."

Olympia did not care for the tone of his voice. "Sir, I do not . . . "

"Lady Chillhurst." Lord Aldridge emerged from the crowd and came to a halt in front of Olympia. "Delighted to see you here this evening."

Magnus assumed a threatening expression. "Do you know this man, my dear?"

"Oh, yes." Olympia smiled at Aldridge. "How nice to see you, sir. Is your wife with you?"

"She's about somewhere." Aldridge smiled hopefully. "I say, can I convince you to dance with me, madam? It would be my great honor to be the first to lead you out onto the floor."

"No, thank you," Olympia began. "You see, I do not . . . "

"*Olympia*. I mean, Lady Chillhurst." Gifford Seaton made his way through the throng to Olympia's side. "Heard you were here this evening. Everyone's talking about it." He surveyed her with surprise and open admiration. "Allow me to tell you, madam, that you look ravishing."

Magnus scowled at him. "You're young Seaton, ain't you? I recall meeting you when your sister was engaged to my son."

"Aye, I remember him, too." Thaddeus bristled. "I doubt that Chillhurst has seen fit to introduce you to Lady Chillhurst, Seaton, and we certainly do not intend to do so. Off with you, now."

Gifford gave him an annoyed glance. "Lady Chillhurst and I have already met. We have mutual interests." He turned back to Olympia. "Is that not right, madam?"

"Yes, quite correct." Olympia could feel the palpable tension in the atmosphere. "Please, gentlemen, do not embarrass me or your son by causing a scene. Mr. Seaton and I are acquainted."

Magnus and Thaddeus gave her disgruntled looks.

"If you say so," Magnus muttered. "Surprised Chillhurst allowed the introduction, if you don't mind my sayin' so."

"Chillhurst had nothing to do with it." Gifford gave Magnus a sarcastic smile. "I told you, Lady Chillhurst and I have mutual interests. We are both members of the Society for Travel and Exploration."

Magnus grimaced. Thaddeus continued to glower.

Olympia frowned severely at her new in-laws. "That is quite enough out of both of you. Mr. Seaton has as much right to be here tonight and to speak to me as anyone else."

Gifford smiled at her. "Thank you, madam. I trust I also have as much right to request a dance as anyone else here tonight."

Olympia smiled ruefully. "Yes, of course. Unfortunately, I fear I must refuse." She paused as her eye fell on the elaborate fob of Gifford's watch. "But I would like to speak to you for a few minutes if I may, sir."

Seaton's smile assumed a hint of triumph. "My pleasure, madam. Allow me to escort you to the buffet room."

Olympia took the arm that Gifford extended. She saw Magnus's eyes narrow. Thaddeus's scowl grew more fierce. She quelled them both with a look.

"I shall be back shortly, my lord," Olympia said to the Earl. "Please excuse me. I wish to discuss something important with Mr. Seaton."

"Well, well, well," Parkerville murmured behind the pair. "Now, this is an interesting development, is it not?"

Magnus and Thaddeus turned to him with thunderous expressions.

Olympia ignored them all and urged Gifford forward. "Come, sir, I have been most anxious to speak with you. I have a few questions I must ask you."

"What sort of questions?" Gifford guided her through the crush of brilliantly dressed people.

"About your watch."

Gifford gave her a startled glance. "What in blazes does my watch have to do with anything?"

"I'm not certain yet, but I would very much like to know why you chose the motif of a sea serpent for the decoration."

"Damnation." Gifford came to an abrupt halt near the open French doors. His eyes were very intent as he searched her face. "You know, don't you?"

"I believe so," Olympia said gently. "You are Captain Edward Yorke's great-grandson."

Gifford ran a hand through his carefully tousled hair. "Hellfire and damnation. I had a feeling you would guess the truth. Something about you made me think that you would add up all the parts and get the correct sum."

"You have no cause to be alarmed, Mr. Seaton. I see no reason why we cannot work together in this matter." Olympia eyed him curiously. "May I ask why you have kept your identity a secret?"

"I never lied about my identity," Gifford said wearily. "And neither did Demetria. Our family name is Seaton. We just never told Chillhurst who our great-grandfather was."

"Why ever not?"

"Because Captain Jack Ryder was my great-grandfather's sworn enemy, that's why not," Gifford burst out in a savage snarl. "Ryder believed that Yorke betrayed him to the Spanish but it's not true. He was betrayed by someone else. In any event Ryder escaped that damned Spanish vessel. He went back to England a rich man."

"Mr. Seaton, please, you will cause a scene."

Gifford flushed a dull red and glanced quickly about to see if anyone had overheard him. "Lady Chillhurst, could we discuss this outside in the gardens? I do not want half the *ton* listening to this conversation."

"Yes, of course." Worried by the obvious volatility of his emotions, Olympia allowed Gifford to lead her out into the balmy night. "Mr. Seaton, I understand your interest in the missing treasure, but I do not comprehend why you have been so secretive. That old feud between your great-grandfather and Chillhursts was finished long ago."

"You are wrong, madam. It was never finished." Muscles bunched in Gifford's arm. His hand clenched. "The Earl of Flamecrest vowed eternal vengeance against my family. He swore that he would never allow Edward Yorke to get his half of the treasure they had buried together on that damned island. He also swore that his descendents would honor his vow in the name of family honor."

"How do you know all this?"

"My grandmother left an accounting of the entire affair together with my great-grandfather's half of the map."

"So you do have the other half of the map?" Olympia asked eagerly.

"Of course. My grandmother left it to my father." Gifford's mouth twisted. "It was the only thing my father managed to leave to Demetria and me. He probably would have pawned that along with everything else if there had been a market for partial treasure maps."

"What did you learn from your grandmother's account of the affair?"

"Not much. Apparently she made an overture to the Flamecrest clan after her father's death. It was rebuffed. She urged my father to try again some day." Gifford sneered faintly. "For the sake of the old friendship that had once existed between Yorke and Ryder."

Olympia peered at him, trying to read his face in the deep shadows. "She tried to make peace?"

"Trust a female to try something so useless. The Flamecrests have never wanted to mend the quarrel. Harry, Captain Jack's son, sent word to my grand-

mother saying he intended to honor his father's sworn
vow. He would not allow the treasure to fall into the
hands of any descendent of Edward Yorke. Claimed it
was a matter of family honor."

"That's a Flamecrest for you," Olympia mused. "An
emotional lot."

"It was not right," Gifford whispered fiercely.
"Flamecrest and his family have prospered but Demetria and I had nothing. *Nothing*."

"Neither did the present Earl of Flamecrest until he
had the wit to turn his business over to his son," Olympia retorted. "Sir, there is another thing I do not comprehend. If you hated my husband's family so much,
why on earth did your sister consent to marry Chillhurst?"

"She never intended to go through with the marriage," Gifford said. "In fact, she never intended to get
herself engaged to him in the first place."

"I do not understand."

Gifford sighed impatiently. "I convinced Demetria
to arrange an introduction. We had heard that Chillhurst was searching for a bride. Demetria found a way
to get herself introduced to him through a connection
that would intrigue him."

"Felix Hartwell."

"Yes. She learned that Hartwell was his trusted man
of affairs and she found a way to meet him. Demetria
is very beautiful." Brotherly pride shone in Gifford's
eyes. "No man can resist her."

"So Mr. Hartwell saw to it that Demetria received
an invitation to the Isle of Flame."

"Correct. Naturally, as her brother, I was invited to
go with her. I thought that if I had an opportunity to
search the Flamecrest family castle, I might be able to
turn up the missing half of the map."

"What happened?"

Gifford laughed sourly. "We were not in the house more than a few days before Chillhurst asked Demetria to marry him. Demetria accepted because we had not yet found the map. I told her that I just needed a little more time."

"Good heavens," Olympia murmured. "I'd had no notion that Chillhurst had gone about searching for a wife in such a logical, practical fashion. It is not at all like him, you understand."

"On the contrary. It is very like him from what I know of him. The man has no blood at all in his veins."

"That's not true. I believe he must have formed a tendre for your sister," Olympia said slowly. "He would never have asked her to marry him otherwise."

Gifford looked at her as if she were a simpleton but he did not argue. "Be that as it may, the fact is, he did ask her to marry him. Which gave me more time to hunt for the missing half of the map."

"Which you never found," Olympia said with cool satisfaction. "It serves you right, sir, if you do not mind my saying so. You should never have gone about it in such a sneaky manner."

"I had no choice," Gifford raged softly. "Captain Jack Ryder refused to allow my great-grandfather to hunt for his share of the treasure out of sheer spite and all of his descendents have been just as spiteful."

Olympia wrinkled her nose. "It is quite obvious that we are dealing with two passionate, highly emotional families, not just one. I think the time has come to make peace. Do you not agree, Mr. Seaton?"

"Never." Gifford's eyes flashed with fury. "Not after the way Chillhurst treated my sister. I shall never forgive or forget."

"For heavens sake, Mr. Seaton, it does not sound as though your sister particularly wanted to marry him in the first place. And as for yourself, you were just using her and her engagement as an excuse to prowl through the Flamecrest castle. You can hardly act the offended party."

"The point is Chillhurst insulted her," Gifford said with righteous indignation. "He ended the engagement in a most cruel fashion simply because he discovered she was not an heiress. I only wish he had not been too cowardly to meet me on the field of honor."

Olympia touched his arm. "I realize this is a very emotional subject for you. Please believe me when I say that I am certain Chillhurst did not end the engagement merely because he learned that your sister was not an heiress."

"Oh, I know he insists that he ended it because he and Demetria did not suit, but that was a lie. I know the truth. He was quite content with the engagement for several days. Then, one afternoon, he simply ended it without any warning."

"No warning at all?"

Gifford's eyes slitted angrily. "Demetria and I and Lady Kirkdale were ordered to pack and leave within the hour."

Olympia gazed at him in startled surprise. "Lady Kirkdale was with you at the Isle of Flame?"

"Yes, of course," Gifford said irritably. "There were a number of guests there, and she came along as Demetria's companion. She has been Demetria's very great friend for several years. It was Lady Kirkdale who later introduced Demetria to Beaumont, you know."

"I see."

Gifford's hand clenched and unclenched. "Madam, your loyalty to your husband is laudable, but I must tell you that you have a sadly misguided view of him. I regret to inform you that, based on what I know of him, it is impossible to believe that he married you because he loved you."

"I really do not wish to discuss such a personal matter, sir."

Gifford gave her a pitying look. "My poor, naive lady. What could you, an innocent who has spent all her life in the country, know of a man like Chillhurst?"

"Nonsense. I assure you I am not nearly as naive as you believe. I received an excellent and far-reaching education, thanks to my aunts and I have pursued my own studies quite diligently. I am very much a woman of the world."

"Then you must realize that he married you only because he believed you could find the secret of the Lightbourne diary."

"Rubbish. My husband would never marry for such a paltry reason. He is not at all interested in the missing treasure. He has no need of it. He is a very wealthy man in his own right."

"Do you not comprehend? Money is the only thing Chillhurst *does* care about. A man like that can never have enough to satisfy him."

"How do you know that?"

"Because I spent nearly a month in his household," Gifford's voice rose in exasperation. "I learned a great deal about Chillhurst in that time and the most important thing I learned is that he has no warmth or feeling in him for anything or anyone except his business affairs. He's a damned cold fish."

"Chillhurst is not a cold fish and I will thank you not to insult him. Furthermore, I assure you that he did not marry me to obtain the secret of the diary. I would very much appreciate it if you would refrain from spreading such a wicked rumor."

"But it must be the reason he married you. Why else would a man like that marry a woman with no fortune?"

"Mr. Seaton, please do not say anything more. I am sure you will regret it."

Gifford seized her upper arms and gazed down at her with grave concern. "Lady Chillhurst," he began and then paused. His voice thickened with emotion as he continued. "My dear Olympia, if I may be so bold. I know what you must be going through. You are an innocent pawn in this matter. I would be honored if you would allow me to aid you in any way that I can."

"Take your hands off my wife." Jared's voice was as cold as the steel blade of the Guardian. "Or I will very likely kill you here and now, Seaton, rather than at a more convenient time."

"*Chillhurst.*" Gifford released Olympia and swung around to confront Jared.

"Jared, you decided to attend the ball, after all," Olympia said. "I am so glad."

Jared ignored her. "I warned you to stay away from my wife, Seaton," he said very softly.

"You bloody bastard." Gifford's voice was laced with disgust. "So you finally decided to put in an appearance tonight. Everyone wondered if you would bother. I trust you realize that your poor wife has been thoroughly humiliated by your absence?"

"Nonsense," Olympia said briskly. "I was not in the least embarrassed."

Neither man paid any attention to her. Jared regarded Gifford with an expression of cold boredom. But Olympia saw the dangerous gleam in his eye.

"I shall deal with you later, Seaton." Jared took Olympia's arm.

"I shall look forward to it." Gifford inclined his head in a mocking little bow. "But we both know that you will never find a convenient time in your appointment journal to meet me, will you? You certainly could not find one the last time."

Olympia was well aware that Jared's temper was on a very short leash. "Mr. Seaton, hush. Pray, do not say another word, I beg you. My husband is very slow to anger, but I fear that you are pushing him to the very brink of his control."

Gifford's expression turned scornful. "You need not concern yourself on my account, Lady Chillhurst. There is no danger of a duel. Your husband does not believe in taking such risks in the name of honor, do you, Chillhurst?"

Olympia began to panic. "Mr. Seaton, you do not know what you are doing."

"I think he knows very well what he is doing," Jared said. "Come, my dear. I grow weary of the conversation." He took Olympia's arm and started walking back toward the ballroom.

"Yes, of course." Olympia was so relieved that no challenge had been issued that she picked up her emerald skirts and almost broke into a run.

Jared glanced down at her, amused. "Are you in such a hurry to dance with me, then, madam? I am honored."

"Oh, Jared, I thought for a moment there that you would allow Mr. Seaton to goad you into a stupid duel." Olympia smiled tremulously. "I was very concerned."

"You need not be concerned, my dear."

"Thank heavens. I must say, I never cease to be amazed at the degree of restraint you are able to exert over your darker passions, sir. It is most impressive."

"Thank you. I make every effort. Most of the time."

She gave him an apologetic glance. "I was afraid you would be deeply offended by some of the nonsense Mr. Seaton was spouting."

"May I inquire what you were doing out in the gardens with him?"

"Heavens, I almost forgot." The excitement Olympia had experienced earlier returned. "I went out there because Mr. Seaton wished to speak privately with me."

"So I concluded." Jared drew her to a halt just outside the glittering ballroom. "A great many other people here tonight apparently came to the same conclusion. There was certainly no shortage of whispers as I walked into the room."

"Oh, dear."

"Perhaps you will enlighten me as to the nature of this very private conversation?"

"Yes, of course." Olympia was almost bubbling now. "Jared, you will never credit what I have discovered. Gifford Seaton and his sister are the direct descendents of Captain Edward Yorke. They have possession of the other half of the treasure map."

"Good lord." Whatever Jared had been expecting to hear, that was obviously not it. He stared at her, astounded. "Are you certain?"

"Absolutely certain." Olympia smiled proudly. "I began to suspect the truth after I heard a brief history of his family and after I learned that Mr. Seaton was as interested in maps of the West Indies as I was. Then I chanced to see his watch and recognized the motif of the design on it."

"What motif is that?"

"It is a picture of a sea serpent." Olympia could not keep the triumph from her voice. "The same sort of sea serpent that is pictured on the prow of the ship on one of the endpapers of the Lightbourne diary."

"The emblem of Yorke's ship?"

"Precisely. Tonight I confronted him with my information and he admitted that he was, indeed, Yorke's great-grandson. That is what we were discussing out in the gardens."

"Bloody hell."

"He and Demetria are descendents of Yorke's daughter and that is why they do not bear Yorke's name."

Jared looked thoughtful. "So someone really was after the map all along."

"Yes." Olympia touched his arm. "Please do not be offended, Jared, but I must tell you that the reason Demetria arranged to meet you three years ago was so that her brother could search for the missing portion of the map."

"She persuaded Hartwell to introduce her to me solely so that idiot brother of hers could look for a legendary treasure map?" Jared sounded thoroughly disgusted.

"I'm certain Mr. Hartwell did not know her true intentions," Olympia said quickly.

"Then again, perhaps he did and thought to use the knowledge in some manner in the future," Jared said. "Perhaps he was as taken with her beauty as every other man generally is. But that is neither here nor there now."

"Quite right," Olympia agreed quickly. She did not want Jared to dwell too long on thoughts of Demetria's beauty. "It is all in the past, my lord."

Jared surveyed her from head to toe. "I regret I was not able to escort you here tonight, my dear."

Olympia warmed beneath the admiration she saw in his gaze. "Do not concern yourself, Jared. I know you received an urgent message. Graves told me about it."

"The message was that Hartwell was still in London."

Olympia was shocked. "You went out to find him tonight?"

"Yes. I went to his former premises because I had been told he might be there. But he was not around and there was no sign that he had returned. I am convinced that the information that I received in the note was incorrect."

"Thank goodness." Olympia relaxed. "I am very glad to hear that. I hope that wretched man will stay out of England forever."

"So do I." Jared took her hand and led her toward the French doors. "Now that I am here at long last, I trust you will favor me with a waltz, my dear?"

Olympia heaved a sigh of regret. "I only wish that I could. I am very sorry, Jared, but I do not know how to dance the waltz."

"Ah, but I do."

"You do?"

"I took the trouble to learn three years ago when I realized that I was going to have to court a wife. I have never made use of the skill, but I do not believe that I have completely forgotten it."

"I see." He had learned the skill in order to court Demetria, Olympia thought dourly. "I wish that I could partner you. The waltz appears to be a very exciting dance."

"We shall find out together just how exciting it is." Jared drew her through the curious crowd and led her out onto the dance floor.

Olympia was nearly overcome with anxiety. "Jared, please, I do not wish to embarrass you."

"You could never embarrass me, Olympia." He fitted his hand to the small of her back. "Now, pay attention and follow my instructions. I am a tutor, after all."

"Quite true." Olympia smiled slowly as the music swirled around her. "You do have a rare talent for instruction, Mr. Chillhurst."

The message from Demetria reached Olympia the following morning just as she was preparing to go back to work on the Lightbourne diary.

> *Madam:*
>
> *I must speak with you at once about a matter of grave urgency. Please do not tell anyone about this note and above all do not inform your husband that you are to meet with me. A life is at stake.*
>
> *Yrs,*
> *Lady B.*

A cold chill swept through Olympia. She leaped to her feet and ran to the door.

Chapter 19

"Are you certain of this information?" Olympia asked. She sat tensely on the blue and gilt sofa, shocked by what Demetria had just told her. Shocked, but not terribly surprised.

"I have many sources of rumors. I have checked and double-checked all of them." Anguish and fear haunted Demetria's beautiful eyes. "There can be no doubt. Chillhurst has engaged to meet my brother in a duel."

"Dear heaven," Olympia whispered. "I was afraid of this."

"You have no cause to be afraid, damn you." Demetria whirled away from the window where she had been gazing

out into the garden. "I am the one who is terrified. Your husband means to kill my brother."

"Demetria, calm yourself." Constance poured tea from a silver pot and helped herself to sugar. It was obvious she was as much at home in Demetria's drawing room as she would have been in her own. "There is nothing to be gained from panic."

"That is easy for you to say, Constance. It is not your brother who is about to die."

"I am aware of that." Constance glanced meaningfully at Olympia. "But all is not yet lost. I believe Lady Chillhurst is as alarmed by the situation as you are. She will want to help us."

"If what you say is true, then we must find a way to stop the duel," Olympia said. She rallied herself and tried to think in a logical fashion.

"How can we stop it?" Demetria fluttered restlessly from one window to another, a wild, exotic bird trapped in a luxurious cage. "I was not able to establish the day or the place or even the time of the affair. Such things are kept closely guarded secrets by those involved."

"I may be able to discover those particulars." Olympia got to her feet and began to pace the other side of the room. Her brain was reeling with the implications of what she had just heard.

Jared was about to risk his life in a duel. *And it was all her fault.*

"You think you can discover the date, time, and place of the duel when I, with all my sources, have failed?" Demetria demanded.

"It should not be difficult," Olympia said soothingly. "My husband is a man of very precise habits."

"Yes, he is, is he not?" Demetria snapped. "Rather like one of those clockwork toys in Winslow's Mechanical Museum."

"That is not true," Olympia said coldly. "But he believes in the value of a well-planned day. If he has made a dawn appointment I suspect it will be noted in his appointment journal along with all the rest of his engagements."

"Good God." Constance's eyes widened. "She's quite right, Demetria. We all know that Chillhurst is a great believer in habit and routine. It would be just like him to write down the particulars of the duel."

Demetria looked at Olympia. "Can you find a way to inspect his appointment journal?"

"Very likely. But that is not the chief obstacle we face." Olympia concentrated fiercely. "The real problem is finding a way to halt the duel."

"I suppose that we could notify the authorities," Constance said slowly. "Dueling is illegal, after all. But such an action might result in the arrest of Gifford and Chillhurst. At the very least it would cause an enormous scandal."

"Dear God," Demetria breathed. "Beaumont would be furious if there is a scandal of that proportion in the family. He would very likely cut Gifford off without a penny."

Olympia drummed her fingers on the arm of the sofa. "And Chillhurst will certainly not thank me if I get him arrested. We must think of another way to stop this nonsense. Have you tried to talk Gifford out of the affair?"

"Of course I have tried." The skirts of Demetria's blue and white morning gown swished furiously as she strode to another window. "He will not even admit that he has planned a duel, let alone listen to me when I tell him that Chillhurst will very likely put a bullet in his heart."

"My husband will certainly not deliberately attempt to kill your brother," Olympia said brusquely. "He will only try to defend himself. I am far more concerned that your brother will kill Chillhurst."

"My brother is no match for your husband," Demetria whispered. "I am told that victory on the duelling field generally goes to the man who possesses the coolest head and the steadiest hand. It is cold blood, not hot, that wins out. And Chillhurst is nothing if not coldblooded."

"That is untrue," Olympia said tightly.

"I know Chillhurst well and I assure you he would not break into a sweat were he to dine in hell with the devil himself," Demetria flung back. "But Gifford will not see that. He is actually looking forward to the event." She closed her eyes briefly. "He says he wants a chance to avenge my honor. He has never forgiven Chillhurst for what happened three years ago."

Olympia exhaled deeply. "Your brother is a very emotional man. As is everyone else involved in this blasted affair."

"In addition to avenging my honor," Demetria went on grimly, "I believe he feels he will be doing you a very great favor if he lodges a bullet in your husband, madam."

"Your brother's emotions tend to rule his head, do they not?" Olympia shot Demetria a considering look. "A family trait, no doubt."

Demetria gave her a sharp glance. "Gifford told me that you know that he and I are Edward Yorke's great-grandchildren."

"Yes."

Constance arched her finely plucked brows. "It was very clever of you to reason that out, Lady Chillhurst."

"Thank you," Olympia muttered. "But to return to our problem, I would suggest that I first ascertain the particulars of the duel. Once I have done that, I must determine a way to keep Chillhurst from attending the affair."

"Even if you can manage such a feat, what good will it do?" Constance asked quietly. "Chillhurst and Gifford will merely schedule another dawn meeting."

"If we can prevent the first meeting, which has clearly been arranged in the heat of anger," Olympia said slowly, "it will purchase us some time in which Gifford and Chillhurst can calm themselves. We must take advantage of that time."

Demetria wrung her hands. "What do you mean?"

"You must talk to Gifford and I shall undertake to reason with Chillhurst."

"It will not work." Demetria bit her lip in despair. "Gifford believes Chillhurst to be a coward because he would not accept the challenge that my brother issued three years ago. But I know the true reason why Chillhurst would not meet him and it had nothing at all to do with cowardice."

Olympia smiled wistfully. "I am well aware of that."

Constance and Demetria looked at each other and then they gazed thoughtfully at Olympia.

"You are?" Demetria asked delicately.

"Of course." Olympia looked down at her untouched tea. "It is quite obvious that the reason Chillhurst refused to meet your brother was because of his concern for you."

"For me?" Demetria was nonplussed.

Constance gave Olympia a strange smile over the rim of her teacup. "Are you quite certain of that, Lady Chillhurst?"

"Yes," Olympia said. "It's clear that Chillhurst refused to meet with Gifford because he knew how much Demetria cared for her brother. My husband had no wish to cause her the anguish that a duel would create."

"Bah. He cared nothing for me," Demetria muttered. "Chillhurst approached marriage with me as he would any other business arrangement. You obviously know nothing of the truth."

"I disagree," Olympia said. "I have thought about the matter a great deal and have come to some conclusions."

Demetria swung around again. "Let me explain something to you, madam. The reason Chillhurst did not accept Gifford's challenge three years ago was because he was afraid that the true facts of the scandal might emerge and he would be humiliated."

"I assume that you are referring to the rumor that he found you with your lover?" Olympia asked.

A small, brittle hush descended on the drawing room.

Constance finally set down her teacup. "I see you have heard the old tale that circulated for a while after the engagement was broken."

"Yes, I have heard it." Olympia said. "It was not merely a rumor, was it? It was the truth."

"Yes," Demetria admitted softly. "But I told everyone, including Gifford, that the reason Chillhurst called off the engagement was because he discovered that I had no inheritance. We have all, Chillhurst included, stuck by that story."

"It was in everyone's best interests to do so," Constance murmured. "The truth would have done a great deal of damage to all concerned."

Demetria slanted Olympia a sidelong glance. "Gifford considers Chillhurst a coward not only because he refused his challenge but also because Chillhurst never called out my lover."

"Well, he could hardly do that, could he?" Olympia said calmly. "A gentleman cannot challenge a lady to a duel at dawn."

Constance and Demetria gazed at her wordlessly. It was Constance who recovered first.

"So you know that, too, do you?" Her eyes gleamed with wry amusement. "Did Chillhurst tell you? I must admit I am surprised that he would confide the truth to you. It is difficult enough for a man to discover his intended with another man. It is even more awkward for him to discover her with another woman."

"Chillhurst told me nothing about it," Olympia said. "He is a gentleman. He would never gossip about a woman to whom he had once been engaged."

Constance frowned. "I did not think he would tell anyone the truth. But how, then, did you learn that I was the woman he found with Demetria that day?"

"It was not all that difficult to deduce." Olympia lifted one shoulder in a small shrug. "I was told that you had accompanied Demetria to the Isle of Flame three years ago. It has been obvious to me from the first that you and Demetria enjoy a special friendship, just as my aunts did. I merely added the two facts together."

"Your *aunts*." Demetria's mouth fell open in astonishment.

"Aunt Sophy was the one who was actually related to me by blood," Olympia explained. "Her very good friend and companion was named Ida. I always thought of her as Aunt Ida because that is what I called her."

"You knew these aunts well?" Constance asked with great interest.

"Very well. Aunt Sophy and Aunt Ida raised me from the age of ten when I was left, penniless, on their doorstep," Olympia said. "They took me in when no one else in the family could be bothered. They were very good to me."

"I see." Constance glanced at Demetria. "Her ladyship is not quite the naive little country-bred girl that you had believed her to be, my dear."

"So I see," Demetria's smile was rueful. "My apologies, madam. I comprehend that you are much more a woman of the world than I had at first believed."

"That is precisely what I keep telling Chillhurst," Olympia said.

The entry in Jared's appointment book was stark and chilling. Olympia shielded the candle flame with one hand while she read the grave words.

Thurs. Morn. Five o'clock. Chalk Farm.

Olympia knew at once that Chalk Farm was to be the site of the duel. She closed the appointment book with a sense of dread and blew out the candle.

Thursday morning. Five o'clock.

She had one day in which to come up with a way to keep Jared from meeting Gifford. It was clear she would need help.

"Olympia?" Jared stirred as Olympia slipped back into bed. "Something wrong?"

"No. I just got up for a drink of water."

"You're very cold." He gathered her close.

"There is a chill in the air tonight," Olympia whispered.

"I'm certain that we shall find a way to keep each other warm."

Jared's mouth came down on hers, hot, fierce, and demanding. His hand flattened on her stomach. Olympia wrapped her arms very tightly around his hard, muscled body. She clung to him as if she could keep him safe by simply hanging on to him for dear life.

He called her his siren, she thought, but she would not allow him to dash himself against the rocks. She would find a way to rescue him.

―――――

"You want us to help you save my son?" Magnus gazed at Olympia in amazed confusion. Then he looked at the others who were gathered in the study in front of Olympia's desk.

"I need your help, sir." Olympia turned away from the Earl and fixed Thaddeus, Robert, Hugh, and Ethan with a determined expression. "You must all help me. My plan cannot succeed without your cooperation."

"I'll help you, Aunt Olympia," Hugh said quickly.

"So will I," Ethan echoed.

Robert straightened in his chair. "I say, you can certainly count on me, Aunt Olympia."

"Excellent," Olympia said.

"Hold on a moment." Thaddeus wriggled his brows. "Who says the lad needs saving?"

"Thaddeus is right. My son can take care of himself." Magnus grinned proudly. "Taught him how to use a pistol myself. Don't agitate yourself over this little matter of a duel, my dear. Jared will come out the winner."

"Aye, that he will." Thaddeus laced his fingers across his belly. "Got a keen eye and a steady hand. Never seen a cooler head in a crisis. He'll do just fine."

Olympia was furious. "You do not seem to understand, sir. I do not want my husband to risk his neck in a stupid duel over my honor."

Magnus scowled. "Nothing stupid about it. A lady's honor is damned important, my dear. I, myself, had fought two or three duels over my wife's honor by the time I was Jared's age."

"I will not allow it," Olympia said, outraged at Magnus's lack of concern.

"Doubt you can stop it." Magnus stroked his jaw.

"I must say, I'm surprised my son is showing such spirit. Looks like he's got the Flamecrest fire, after all."

"The lad is turning out to be a credit to the family," Thaddeus said warmly. "You can be proud of him, Magnus."

"Enough of this nonsense." Olympia jumped to her feet and flattened her hands on top of her desk. "You, sir," she said to Magnus, "have never understood your own son." She turned to Thaddeus. "And you do not know him very well, either. You have both been content to take him for granted."

Thaddeus's whiskers twitched. "Now, see here . . ."

"I do not want to hear any more talk about how you feared he lacked the family fire. The truth is, Chillhurst has more fire in him than you will ever know. But he has conquered that fire and kept it under control all of his life because he had so much responsibility to bear."

"What are you talking about?" Magnus demanded.

"Chillhurst could not afford to indulge his wild passions and emotions like the rest of you because he got stuck with the task of taking care of everyone else. He was forever having to rescue the lot of you."

"I say, that's going a bit too far," Magnus grumbled.

"Is it?" Olympia narrowed her eyes. "Do you deny that he had a tremendous responsibility thrust upon him at a very tender age, my lord?"

"Well, only in a manner of speaking," Magnus said grudgingly. "It was not as if I wasn't around to see to the important things. Isn't that right, Thaddeus?"

"Quite right. You were around and so was I," Thaddeus said. " 'Course neither of us had much of a head for business, Magnus. Got to admit it. Your son was the only one who understood finance and economy."

"And you were both quite happy to take advantage

of his talents, were you not?" Olympia fixed each of the men in turn with a challenging look.

"Well, now," Magnus began.

"Hah," Olympia interrupted. "You and the rest of the family are content to spend the money he makes but you condemn him for the very temperament it takes to make that money."

"It ain't that, exactly." Magnus shifted unhappily in his chair. "Making money is all well and good, but the Flamecrest blood is supposed to burn hot, not run cold."

Thaddeus sighed. "Jared ain't like the rest of us, Olympia. Leastways, he didn't show any signs of it until lately. Last thing we want to do is put the damper on him now that he's displaying the Flamecrest fire."

"We are going to save him, not put the damper on him," Olympia said tightly. "And you are all going to help me."

"We are?" Magnus looked skeptical.

"Let me put it this way," Olympia said in a voice that dripped ice, "If you do not assist me in this matter, I will make certain that neither of you ever learns the location of the missing Flamecrest treasure. I will personally destroy the Lightbourne diary and all its secrets."

"Good God," Thaddeus whispered.

Magnus and Thaddeus exchanged horrified looks.

Magnus turned to Olympia with a charming smile. "Since you put it that way, m'dear, I suppose we can give you a hand."

"Glad to do our bit," Thaddeus said cheerfully.

Robert spoke up. "What do you want us to do, Aunt Olympia?"

Olympia sank slowly back down into her chair and folded her hands in front of her. "I have come up with a plan that I believe will work very well. Chillhurst will not be pleased, but I am certain that once he has calmed down, he will listen to reason."

"No doubt," Magnus said sadly. "My son always did listen to reason. One of his chief failings."

Jared held the candle higher and surveyed the crowded storage room at the top of the stairs. "What was it that you wanted me to see up here, Olympia?"

"One of the portraits." Olympia, wearing an apron over her morning gown, struggled with a large, heavy trunk. "It is lodged directly behind this."

"Could the matter not wait until tomorrow? It is nearly nine o'clock."

"I am very anxious to see this particular painting, Jared." She heaved unsuccessfully on the brass handle of the trunk. "I am hoping that it is a picture of your great-grandfather."

"Very well, stand aside. I shall move the trunk for you, my dear." Jared smiled at the sight of the tendrils of hair that were floating free of Olympia's dainty muslin cap. "What makes you think it's a portrait of Captain Jack?"

Olympia straightened, breathing quickly, and dusted her hands off on her apron. "Because I caught a brief glimpse of it and from what little I could see, the man in the picture looked just like you, patch and all."

"I doubt that very much. But I shall be glad to get the painting for you. Here, hold the candle."

"Yes, of course." Olympia took the candle from his hand and gave him a very brilliant smile. "I appreciate your assistance."

Jared contemplated her smile. "Is anything wrong, Olympia?"

"No, no, of course not." The candle trembled slightly in her hand. "I want to see the painting because if it is of Captain Jack, it may contain some clue to the missing treasure."

"Ah, yes. The bloody treasure." Jared went over to the heavy trunk and shoved it aside. The pale glow of the candle grew more faint as he picked up the next object in his path, a chair draped in heavy muslin. "Olympia, come closer with that taper."

"I am very sorry," Olympia said from the door. Her voice was strangely thin, almost a squeak. "But I fear I cannot do that."

Jared set the chair down and swung around just in time to see Olympia slam the door shut. It closed with a reverberating thud that shook the whole room. The draft blew out the candle that she had set on the floor.

Jared was instantly plunged into a stygian night. He heard the heavy iron key turn in the lock on the other side of the door.

"I know you are probably going to be very angry for a while, Jared." Olympia's voice was barely audible through the thick wooden door. "And I am really very sorry. But this is for your own good."

Jared took a step forward. The toe of his boot collided with a trunk. He winced and cautiously put out a hand to feel his way. "Open the door, Olympia."

"I will open it in the morning, I give you my word of honor, sir."

"What time tomorrow morning?" Jared asked.

"Around six or seven o'clock, I should imagine."

"Hellfire and damnation." A clever wife could be something of a nuisance on occasion, Jared thought. "I collect that you have learned of my dawn appointment, madam."

"Yes, Jared, I have." Olympia sounded more sure of herself now. "And since I know that there is very likely no way that I can talk you out of it while you are in the grip of such powerful passions, I concluded I must take drastic action."

"Olympia, I assure you, this is entirely unnecessary." Jared took another step forward and drove his shin into the seat of a draped chair. "Damnation."

"Are you all right, Jared?" Olympia asked anxiously.

"It's as black as midnight in here, Olympia."

"But I left the candle for you."

"It was blown out when you slammed the door."

"Oh." Olympia hesitated. "Well, there are more candles and a tinderbox near the door, Jared. I put them there earlier. Light one of them. I also arranged a cold collation for you. It's on a covered tray near the large box in the corner."

"Thank you." Jared rubbed his shin.

"Mrs. Bird prepared the lamb and veal pie herself. And the bread was baked fresh this morning. There is also some cheese."

"I can see you've thought of everything, my dear." Jared inched his way toward the door.

"I hope so," Olympia said. "There is a chamber pot under one of the chairs. I must admit it was Robert who suggested that item."

"Robert is an intelligent lad." Jared found the door with his hand. He leaned down and groped for a second candle.

"Jared, there is something else I must tell you. The staff has been given the night off. They were told not to come back until after dawn, so there is no use yelling for a footman or a maid."

"I had no intention of yelling for anyone." Jared got the candle lit after the third attempt. "I doubt I would be heard from this chamber."

"Quite right." Olympia sounded relieved. "Also, your father and uncle have taken the boys off to Astley's theater. They will not be back until very late. They have all sworn not to open this door."

"I understand." Jared hoisted the candle and surveyed the walls of the chamber.

"Jared?"

"Yes, Olympia?"

"I hope you will be able to forgive me. I realize that at the moment you are probably quite furious. But you must see that I could not allow you to risk your life at dawn."

"Go to bed, Olympia. We will discuss this business in the morning."

"I can tell that you are very angry, my lord." Olympia's tone was resigned but resolute. "However, there really is no alternative. You need time to calm yourself. Time to reconsider your actions. Right now you are no doubt consumed by passion and emotion."

"No doubt."

"Good night, Jared."

"Good night, my dear."

He listened to her footsteps as they receded in the distance. He had been a boy of ten the last time he had explored this room. It would not be easy to relocate the secret entrance that opened onto the flight of stairs in the gallery below.

He would have to move a great many boxes and trunks just to get to the wall. And when he did reach it, he would have a devil of a time finding the hidden spring that operated the concealed door. A layer of dust obscured the old landmarks.

Jared smiled to himself as he contemplated the considerable effort and planning Olympia had done in order to save him from risking his neck in a duel.

All his life he had wondered who would rescue him. Now he knew the answer.

———

It took Jared over an hour to find the hidden door. When his fingers touched the fine line in the paneling, he swore with soft satisfaction. Then he slipped the Guardian from its sheath and slid the tip into the tiny crevice.

The old mechanism gave a rusty hiss inside the wall but the panel opened. Jared sheathed the dagger, picked up the candle, and started down the flight of stairs that Captain Harry had built.

It was true the Earls of Flamecrest were a flamboyant lot, but no one had ever called them stupid, Jared reflected. They always had reasons for what they did, even if those reasons were not always fully comprehended by others.

If visitors to the house had chosen to believe that the staircase that went nowhere in the upper gallery was merely more evidence of Flamecrest eccentricity, that was their concern. Grandfather Harry had believed in having escape routes in every room.

Jared frowned when he saw that the third floor of the house was completely dark. He descended to the second floor and found it, too, was wrapped in shadows. Perhaps Olympia had decided to work in the library until the Earl and the others returned home.

He had made love to Olympia often enough in a library, Jared reflected as he started down the last flight of stairs. He had no objection to doing so again tonight.

Jared reached the bottom of the stairs and discovered that the hall was as dark as every other room in the house. But he smiled when he saw a faint trace of light under the library door.

He took one long stride forward and nearly stumbled over a large, soft, very heavy object. Visions of

Olympia tumbling down the darkened stairs made his whole body go stone cold.

When he looked down, however, he saw at once that it was not Olympia who lay there. It was Graves.

Jared dropped to one knee and touched the side of the man's throat. The pulse was strong. Graves had not broken his neck in the fall. Then Jared spotted the small pool of blood on the marble floor and the silver candlestick lying beside the prone form.

Graves had not fallen. He had been struck on the head.

Jared glanced at the closed door of the library. The chill inside him grew stronger. He stood and walked silently across the hall. His hand closed around the knob.

He slipped the dagger back out of its sheath, inserted it inside the sleeve of his shirt, and palmed the hilt.

Then he blew out the flame of his candle and opened the door.

The glow of a single candle on the desk revealed Olympia. She was standing near the window. Her eyes were wide with silent apprehension.

Felix Hartwell had his arm wrapped around her throat. In his other hand he held a pistol.

"Good evening, Felix," Jared said calmly. "I was afraid that you had not had the good sense to leave town."

"Do not come any closer, Chillhurst, or I swear, I'll kill her." Felix's voice was hoarse. There was a fine, dangerous tremor in it.

Olympia's eyes were brilliant as she looked at Jared. "He told me that he has been watching the house, waiting for an opportunity to gain entrance when it was empty," she said very steadily. "I fear that my scheme to lock you in the storage room and send everyone away for the evening gave him his chance. He believed no one to be home."

"Had you asked my advice, my dear, I could have told you that there were one or two flaws in your plan," Jared said gently. He did not take his eyes off Felix.

"Be quiet," Felix ordered. "Chillhurst, I must have ten thousand pounds and I must have it at once."

"He is quite desperate," Olympia whispered. "I have already told him that I do not think there is anything worth that much money in the house."

"You are right," Jared said. "There is not. At least, there is nothing small and portable about that is worth that kind of money. You could take some of the furniture, I suppose, Felix."

"Do not mock me, Chillhurst, I'm warning you. I am as eager to leave England as you are to have me go. But I am very deep in dun territory and my creditors are a rather nasty lot. They got word I was about to leave London and they threatened to kill me. I must repay them before I can be free."

"Well, there's some silver," Jared said thoughtfully. "But you will need a large cart to carry ten thousand pounds worth away with you. Somewhat awkward, I should think, when one is in a hurry to flee the country."

"There must be some jewelry about." Felix looked desperate. "You have a wife now. You must have given her some valuable jewelry. A man in your position always buys baubles for a new bride."

"Jewelry?" Jared took a step closer. He would only get one chance, he thought. "I doubt it."

Olympia cleared her throat. "Well, there are the emerald and diamond earrings, my lord. The ones that I wore to the Huntingtons' ball."

"Ah, yes," Jared said. "There are the earrings. Of course."

"I *knew* it." Felix's eyes narrowed with a combination of triumph and relief. "Where are they, Lady Chillhurst?"

"Upstairs in a box on my dressing table," Olympia whispered.

"Very well." Felix released her and gave her a push. He kept the pistol trained on Jared. "You will go upstairs and fetch them, madam. You have no more than five minutes. If you delay any longer, I swear I shall kill your husband. Do you understand me?"

"Yes." Olympia rushed forward. "Do not worry, sir. I shall be right back with the earrings."

"Do not hurry on my account," Jared said as she flew toward the door. "You will need a candle, my dear. Best go back to the desk and light one to take with you."

"Oh, my God, yes, of course. I'll need a candle." Olympia whirled about and hurried over to the desk.

"Be quick about it," Felix ordered.

"I am trying to hurry, sir." She picked up an unlit taper and reached for the one that was already lit. Her eyes met Jared's.

He smiled slightly.

Olympia snuffed the candle with her fingertips and plunged the room into darkness.

"Damn you," Felix shouted. His pistol roared. Light flashed from the small explosion.

The Guardian fell neatly into Jared's hand. He hurled it toward the spot where Felix had been standing.

There was a high, terrified cry of pain and rage and then a thud.

"Jared?" There was a scratching sound in the darkness. The candle in Olympia's hand flared into life. "Jared, are you all right?"

"Quite all right, my dear. Next time I trust you will

consider my potential usefulness before you lock me away in a storage room for the night."

On the floor, Felix groaned. He opened his eyes and looked up at Jared. "You always were so bloody clever."

"I thought you were clever, too, Felix."

"I know you will never believe me, but I am truly sorry that it came to this."

"So am I." Jared crossed the room and knelt beside Felix. He examined the hilt of the dagger as it protruded from Felix's shoulder. "You will live, Hartwell."

"Not much point in that," Felix whispered. "I do not care to hang, sir. I wish you had killed me while you were about it."

"You will not go to prison," Jared said. "I will see to it that your creditors are repaid. In exchange you will leave England for good."

"You actually mean that, do you not?" Felix searched his face. "I do not understand you, Chillhurst. But, then, I have never really understood you."

"I realize that." Jared glanced up at Olympia who was hovering nearby. "There is only one person on the face of the earth who understands me."

Graves stumbled into the doorway. He had his hand pressed gingerly to the back of his head, but he looked reasonably alert. "M'lord. I see I'm a bit too late."

"All is well, Graves. How are you feeling?"

"I'll live, thank you, sir."

Olympia whirled around in concern. "Graves. You've been hurt."

"Nothing to worry about, madam. Been hit on the head more'n once in the course of me career. Never does much damage, I'm proud to say." Graves grinned his skeletal grin. "Trust ye won't go tellin' Mrs. Bird how hardy I am. I'm plannin' to play on her sympathies a bit, y'see."

"She'll be horrified," Olympia assured him.

Graves's smile disappeared as he looked at Jared. "Sorry about what happened, sir. I snuck back to the house after madam sent me and the rest of the staff off for the evening, but I got here too late. He was already inside. Never saw him come up behind me."

"It's all right, Graves. We have survived the evening."

A loud knock on the front door interrupted Jared.

"Perhaps you had better answer that, Graves."

"I'll get it," Olympia said quickly. "Graves is obviously not up to performing his duties tonight." She lit a second candle and went out into the hall.

Protesting vehemently, Graves followed her to the door.

Jared touched Felix's wounded shoulder.

"Damn." Felix sucked in his breath and passed out.

"Demetria. Constance," Olympia exclaimed out in the hall. "What are you two doing here? And why have you come at this hour, Mr. Seaton? Now see here, if it is to discuss the duel, I may as well tell you that it is not going to take place. Is that quite clear?"

"You may set Chillhurst free," Constance said dryly. "Demetria has told her brother everything. Gifford wishes to make his apologies and call off the duel. Is that not correct, Gifford?"

"Yes." Gifford's voice was very subdued. "Please tell your husband that I wish to speak with him."

Jared glanced toward the door. "I'm in here, Seaton. Before you make your apologies, would you mind very much summoning a doctor?"

Gifford came to stand in the doorway. "Why in God's name do you want a doctor?" Then his eyes went to Felix. "Damnation. Who is he? Why is there so much blood about?"

Olympia stood on tiptoe to peer over Gifford's

shoulder. "That is Mr. Hartwell. He tried to rob me of my emerald earrings just now. That's his pistol over there on the floor. He threatened to shoot Jared with it."

"But what happened to him?" Gifford stared at the fallen man with sick fascination.

"Chillhurst used his dagger to save us." Olympia's eyes glowed with wifely pride. "He threw it at Mr. Hartwell just as Mr. Hartwell fired his pistol."

"Chillhurst downed him with a dagger?" Gifford asked weakly.

"Oh, yes. Chillhurst always carries it with him, you see. It was the most amazing thing because it all took place in the dark. I had just snuffed the candle and—"

Gifford made an odd sound as Jared took hold of the dagger and pulled it quickly out of Felix's arm. Blood flowed in the few seconds that it took Jared to bind Felix's cravat snugly around the wound.

"My God," Gifford looked distinctly ill now. "Never saw a man with a dagger stuck in him."

"If you think this is unpleasant," Jared said easily, "You should see a man with a bullet in his chest. That's why I sent you a note reminding you to make certain there would be a doctor present at our meeting."

"You're a bloody pirate after all, aren't you?" Gifford's face turned an ashen color. He sank gracefully to the floor in a dead faint.

Chapter 20

"I must say, it was very clever of you to escape from the storage room." Olympia snuggled into Jared's warmth. "But, then, you never cease to amaze me, my lord."

"I'm glad you continue to be impressed with my humble skills." Jared threaded his fingers through her hair.

It was nearly three in the morning. The household was quiet once more and everyone was abed at long last. But although she was exhausted, Olympia was finding it impossible to sleep. The events of the evening were still too fresh.

"I have always been impressed by your many abilities, sir." Olympia pressed her lips to his shoulder. "I am very glad

that you are not angry with me for locking you in the storage room."

"My lovely siren," Jared whispered. "I could not possibly be angry with you. When you turned the key in the lock, I realized that you loved me."

Olympia went very still. "How on earth did you reason that out?"

"No one else has ever tried to rescue me." He searched her face in the shadows. "I'm not wrong, am I? You do love me?"

"Jared, I have loved you since the day you walked into my library and rescued me from Mr. Draycott."

"Why didn't you tell me?"

"Because I did not want you to feel obliged to have to love me in return," Olympia said. "You had already given me so much. I hoped you loved me, but I did not want to press you. In truth, it was difficult not to long for more. I wanted your love more than anything else in the world."

"You have had it since the day I met you." Jared brushed his mouth lightly, reverently, across hers. "I will admit that I did not realize at first that I was in love. I was too occupied with trying to deal with the strong passion that you aroused in me."

"Ah, yes, the passion." Olympia smiled. "There is that, is there not, sir?"

"There is definitely that." He kissed the tip of her nose. "But the love was there, too. I have never felt like this about anyone else, Olympia."

"I am glad, sir."

"I sought you out in order to find a missing fortune," Jared said against her lips. "But I realized soon enough that you were the only treasure I wanted."

"My lord, you take my breath away." She twined her arms around his neck and drew him toward her. "Come close and tell me more traveler's tales. I would hear of strange, far-off islands where lovers meet to make love on beaches scattered with priceless pearls."

Jared needed no further urging. He came down on top of her, his mouth seeking hers.

Olympia shivered beneath his exciting, demanding weight. Jared was already hard and heavy with his arousal. The passion in him drew the familiar, answering response from her. She sank her nails into his shoulders.

And when the time was right and she was ready and the world outside the bedroom door no longer mattered, Jared sheathed himself in her warmth and whispered thickly in her ear.

"Sing for me, my sweet siren."

"Only for you," Olympia vowed.

"I wasn't planning to kill Seaton, you know," Jared said a long while later.

"Of course not. You would never intentionally kill anyone. But in the heat of a duel, anything can happen." Olympia's hand tightened around Jared's arm. "You could have been killed."

"I do not believe it would have come to that." Jared smiled into the shadows. "I had decided that it was time someone taught Seaton a lesson. He was becoming something of a nuisance."

"What did you plan to do?"

"I knew Seaton was so convinced of my cowardice that he thought I would not show for the dawn appointment. I also suspected that when I did turn up at Chalk Farm, he was going to be very worried."

"What did you think would happen?" Olympia asked.

"It was to be his first duel," Jared said. "His first experience with real violence. It was almost a certainty that his hand would have been shaking so badly, his shot would have gone wide. I planned to let him fire first. Then I intended to give him a minute or two to contemplate the situation before I fired my pistol into the air."

"Honor would have been satisfied and Gifford would have been taught a lesson," Olympia said slowly.

"Precisely. So you see, my dear, there was no need to go to all the trouble of locking me away in the storage chamber." Jared gathered her close to his heart. "But I am rather pleased that you did."

"How was I to know of your scheme?" Olympia's voice was muffled against Jared's throat. "And what if something had gone wrong? You really must consult with me in the future on such matters, Mr. Chillhurst."

Jared's laughter filled the bedchamber.

The scene in the library two days later was one of noisy chaos. Everyone was present except Jared, who was interviewing his new man of affairs behind the closed doors of Olympia's study.

The dull roar of conversation in the library was the result of a number of people attempting to speak at the same time. In one corner of the room Magnus and Thaddeus exclaimed over Gifford's half of the map. Gifford was full of questions about the half that had been in the possession of the Flamecrest family.

Robert, Hugh, and Ethan were caught up in the excitement. They hovered over the maps and made endless suggestions about how to go about digging up the treasure.

Minotaur bounded from one person to the next, wagging his tail and sniffing inquiringly at everyone's boots and shoes.

At the other end of the room Demetria explained to

Olympia how she had come to the realization that it was time to tell her brother the full truth about what had happened three years ago.

"I have spent my whole life protecting him since Mother died. I could not allow him to get himself killed because of me," she said.

"I understand," Olympia said. "He is fortunate to have you as his sister."

"Chillhurst was right, however," Constance said. "It was time for Demetria to stop trying to protect her brother. She has done far too much for him already."

"Gifford nursed his ill-will toward your husband's family all these years because it was all he had to cling to," Demetria said. "And I allowed the rage in him to fester and grow because it seemed to give him a purpose, a sense of pride. I did not know what would become of him if he ceased to be obsessed with finding the treasure. I feared he would wind up in the gaming hells."

"We never expected him to locate the missing half of the map, of course," Constance said. "But three years ago when he told Demetria that he had a plan to search for it, she did not know what else to do but go along with his scheme."

"One thing led to another," Demetria confided. "The next thing I knew Chillhurst had actually asked me to marry him. It came as a shock, but it occurred to me that marrying him was not such a bad notion, after all."

"She thought that he could provide the financial security and position that Gifford desperately wanted," Constance said.

Demetria smiled wryly. "And Chillhurst did not seem the type to demand too much of a wife. I did not think him possessed of a passionate nature, you see. There was only one occasion when he startled me with his advances. When I could not respond, he did not appear to take offense. I thought him completely unmoved by the entire affair."

"It was I who realized the marriage would never do," Constance murmured. "It was clear that Chillhurst did not intend to spend much time in London. He had no interest in town life. I dreaded being separated from my dear friend for months at a time."

"And then he found us together one afternoon and that was the end of the matter," Demetria said quietly.

A pleasant, sensual tingle of awareness made Olympia realize that Jared was nearby. She turned around and saw him standing in the doorway of the library. Her heart soared, as it always did at the sight of him.

He looked exactly as he had that first time she had seen him in her library, she thought, dangerous and exciting, a man who had walked straight out of a legend.

Jared's gaze met hers and his mouth curved knowingly. Then he spoke to the room at large.

"Good day to you all." He did not raise his voice but the small crowd in the library instantly fell silent. Expectant faces glanced toward him.

When he had everyone's attention, Jared strode across the room and took up a position behind his desk. He opened his engagement journal and consulted it. The excitement in the room was palpable.

"Well, son?" Magnus demanded eagerly. "Did ye make the arrangements?"

"I have made a decision which I believe will be of interest to all of you." Jared turned a page in the journal. "I have arranged to have one of the Flamecrest ships sail to the West Indies in a fortnight."

"I say." Thaddeus grinned in anticipation.

"The vessel will be under the command of one of my most trusted and experienced men, Captain Richards. All those who wish to search for the treasure may sail on board," Jared said. "I assume that will include Seaton, my cousins, and very likely my father and uncle."

"It will, indeed." Magnus chortled with satisfaction.

"I shall certainly be on board," Thaddeus assured him. "What, ho, for the sight of the open sea, eh, Magnus?"

Gifford grinned broadly. Olympia noticed that the simmering resentment had vanished from his eyes sometime during the past two days.

"Thank you, Chillhurst," Gifford said sincerely. "This is really very good of you."

"There is no need to thank me," Jared said. "I am only too happy to send the lot of you off to the West Indies. I look forward to restoring some semblance of order and routine to my life."

"Does that mean that you will not be sailing off to the islands to search for the lost treasure, yourself, sir?" Robert asked quickly.

"It means precisely that, Robert. I'm going to stay home and attend to my business affairs and see to my duties as a husband and tutor."

Robert looked relieved.

Hugh and Ethan exchanged grins.

"Now, then." Jared closed his appointment journal. "I believe that concludes my announcements for this morning. My new man of affairs is waiting out in the hall. He will provide the details of the sailing arrangements."

Magnus, Thaddeus, and Gifford rushed toward the door.

When they were out of the room, Demetria looked at Jared. "Thank you, Chillhurst."

"You're welcome." Jared glanced at the tall clock. "Now, if you do not mind, I have several appointments which must be kept this morning."

"Of course." Demetria smiled wryly and rose to her feet. "We would not wish to impose further on your busy schedule, my lord."

"No, indeed." Constance looked amused. She inclined her head gracefully at Olympia. "Good day to you, madam."

"Good day," Olympia said. She waited until Demetria and Constance had taken their leave and then she nodded to Robert.

Robert flushed and looked at Jared. "Sir, if you do not mind, my brothers and I have a gift we would like to present to you."

"A gift?" Jared's brows rose in surprise. "What is it?"

Robert removed a small box from his pocket, took two steps toward the desk, and handed it to Jared. "It is not nearly as beautiful as the one you used to ransom me, sir, but we hope you will like it."

"There's an inscription on the inside," Hugh volunteered eagerly. "Aunt Olympia had the jeweler put it there."

Ethan elbowed him in the ribs. "Shut your mouth, you bloody idiot. He ain't even opened the box yet."

Jared slowly opened the box and studied the contents. A suspenseful silence filled the room.

Jared stood gazing down at the new watch for a long time.

Then, very carefully, he removed it from the box and examined the inscription. " 'To a most excellent tutor.' " When he looked up there was an odd brilliance in his gaze. "You are wrong, Robert. It is far more beautiful than the one I gave to the villain who kidnapped you. I thank all of you very much."

"Do you really like it?" Ethan asked.

"It is the nicest gift anyone has given me since I was

a boy," Jared said quietly. "In fact, I believe it is the only gift anyone has given me since I was seventeen."

Robert, Ethan, and Hugh grinned at each other. It was all Olympia could do to keep from bursting into tears.

Jared broke the mood by slipping his new watch into his pocket. He looked at the boys. "Now, then," he said crisply, "I do believe it is time for your next scheduled activity."

"What is that, sir?" Robert asked with a doubtful expression. "I do hope it is not Latin."

"No, it is not Latin." Jared smiled. "Mrs. Bird is expecting you in the kitchen for tea and cakes."

"Very good, sir," Robert exclaimed.

Hugh laughed with glee. He bobbed a quick bow. "I say, I'm rather hungry. I hope there are gingerbread cakes."

"I hope there are currant cakes," Ethan said as he made his bow.

"I would rather have plum cakes," Robert said thoughtfully. He swept Olympia a graceful bow and followed his brothers from the room.

Jared looked at Olympia. "I had begun to fear that we would never find ourselves alone this morning."

"It has been a trifle hectic around here, has it not, my lord?" Olympia searched his face. "Are you quite certain you do not wish to go with the others to search for the lost treasure?"

"Absolutely certain, madam." Jared removed his coat and dropped it on the back of a chair. Then he went to the door. "I have better things to do than go haring off after a treasure that I do not need."

"What sort of things, my lord?" Olympia watched him turn the key in the lock.

He walked deliberately back toward her, his gaze

gleaming with a smoldering desire. "Making love to my wife is at the top of my list."

He swept Olympia into his arms and started toward the sofa.

Olympia wrapped her arms around his neck and looked up at him from beneath her lashes. "But, Mr. Chillhurst, what about your appointments for the day? This sort of thing will make a hash of your schedule."

"Hang my appointments, madam. A man of my nature cannot be a slave to routine."

Olympia's soft laughter was swallowed up by her pirate's plundering kiss.

Look for Amanda Quick's
historical romance

With This Ring

available now in paperback
from Bantam Books

*A writer of shocking "horrid novels," Beatrice Poole is no stranger to
gothic terrors. Yet she declares it's all poppycock when Leo Drake, the
enigmatic Earl of Monkcrest and England's foremost expert on
arcane matters, warns her about the Forbidden Rings of Aphrodite.
Nothing can stop her from investigating the disappearance of the
Rings from her uncle's home, and her uncle's death. Beatrice is
clearly on a collision course with danger, and Leo insists on being her
protector. All the while, a whisper of evil swirls through London and
a sinister villain plots to test the power of the Rings, with Leo and
Beatrice as the victims.*

"I believe that you may be the only person in all of England who
can assist me, sir," Beatrice said. "Your extensive study of old legends is unequaled. If there is anyone who can supply me with the
facts concerning the Forbidden Rings, it is yourself."

"So you have come all this way to interview me." He shook his
head. "I do not know if I should be flattered or appalled. You certainly did not need to trouble yourself with a difficult journey,
madam. You could have written to me."

"The matter is an urgent one, my lord. And to be perfectly truthful, your reputation is such that I feared you might not see fit to reply to a letter in, shall we say, a timely manner."

He smiled slightly. "In other words, you have heard that I am inclined to ignore inquiries that do not greatly interest me."

"Or which you deem to be unscholarly or based on idle curiosity."

He shrugged. "I do not deny it. I regularly receive letters from people who apparently waste a great deal of their time reading novels."

"You do not approve of novels, my lord?" Beatrice's voice was curiously neutral in tone.

"I do not disapprove of all novels, merely the horrid ones. You know the ones I mean. The sort that feature supernatural horror and strange mysteries."

"Oh, yes. The horrid ones."

"All that nonsense with specters and glimmering lights in the distance is bad enough. But how the authors can see fit to insert romance into the narrative in addition is beyond me."

"You are familiar with such novels, then, sir?"

"I read one," he admitted. "I never form an opinion without first doing a bit of research."

"Which horrid novel did you read?"

"One of Mrs. York's, I believe. I was told that she is among the more popular authors." He grimaced. "Perhaps I should say authoresses, since most of the horrid novels seem to be written by women."

"Indeed." Beatrice gave him an enigmatic smile. "Many feel that women writers are more adept at depicting imaginative landscapes and scenes that involve the darker passions."

"I would certainly not argue with that."

"Do you disapprove of women who write, my lord?"

"Not at all." He was startled by the question. "I have read many books that have been authored by ladies. It is only the horrid novels which I do not enjoy."

"And in particular, Mrs. York's horrid novels."

"Quite right. What an overwrought imagination that woman possesses. All that wandering about through decayed castles, stumbling into ghosts and skeletons and the like. It is too much." He shook his head. "I could not believe that she actually had her heroine marry the mysterious master of the haunted castle."

"That sort of hero is something of a trademark for Mrs. York, I believe," Beatrice said smoothly. "It is one of the things that makes her stories unique."

"I beg your pardon?"

"In most horrid novels the mysterious lord of the haunted abbey or castle turns out to be the villain," Beatrice explained patiently. "But in Mrs. York's books, he generally proves to be the hero."

Leo stared at her. "The one in the novel I read lived in a subterranean crypt, for God's sake."

"*The Curse.*"

"I beg your pardon?"

Beatrice cleared her throat discreetly. "I believe the title of that particular horrid novel is *The Curse*. At the end of the story the hero moves upstairs into the sunlit rooms of the great house. The curse had been lifted, you see."

"You have read the novel?"

"Of course." Beatrice smiled coolly. "Many people in town read Mrs. York's books. Do you know, I would have thought that a gentleman who has made a career out of researching genuine legends would have no great objection to reading a novel that takes an ancient legend as its theme."

"Bloody hell. Mrs. York invented the legend she used in her novel."

"Yes, well, it was a novel, sir, not a scholarly article for the Society of Antiquarians."

"Just because I study arcane lore, Mrs. Poole, it does not follow that I relish outlandish tales of the supernatural."

Beatrice glanced at the greathound Elf, who was sprawled in front of the fire. "Perhaps your intolerance for horrid novels stems from the fact that you have been the subject of some rather unfortunate legends yourself, my lord."

He followed her gaze to Elf. "You have a point, Mrs. Poole. When one finds oneself featured in a few tales of supernatural mystery, one tends to take a negative view of them."

Beatrice turned back to him and leaned forward intently. "Sir, I want to assure you that my interest in the Forbidden Rings of Aphrodite is not in the least frivolous."

"Indeed?" He was fascinated by the way the firelight turned her hair to dark gold. He had a sudden vision of how it would look falling loose around her shoulders. He shook off the image with an effort of will. "May I ask how you came to learn of the Rings and why you are so determined to discover them?"

"I am in the process of making inquiries into a private matter that appears to touch upon the legend."

"That is a bit vague, Mrs. Poole."

"I doubt that you would wish to hear all of the particulars."

"You are wrong. I must insist on hearing all of the

details before I decide how much time to waste on the subject."

"Forgive me, my lord, but one could mistake that statement for a veiled form of blackmail."

He pretended to give that some thought. "I suppose my demand to hear the full story could be viewed in that way."

"Are you telling me that you will not help me unless I confide certain matters that are very personal in nature and involve only my family?" Beatrice raised her brows. "I cannot believe that you would be so rude, sir."

"Believe it. I certainly do not intend to gratify what may be only idle curiosity."

Beatrice rose and walked to the nearest window. She clasped her hands behind her back and gave every appearance of gazing thoughtfully out into the night. But Leo knew she was watching his reflection in the glass. He could almost feel her debating her course of action. He waited with interest to see what she would do next.

"I was warned that you might be difficult." She sounded wryly resigned.

"Obviously the warning did not dampen your enthusiasm for a journey to the wilds of Devon."

"No, it did not." She studied him in the dark glass. "I am not easily discouraged, my lord."

"And I am not easily cajoled."

"Very well, since you insist, I shall be blunt. I believe that my uncle may have been murdered because of the Forbidden Rings."

Whatever it was he had expected to hear, this was not it. A chill stole through him. He fought it with logic. "If you have concocted a tale of murder in order to convince me to help you find the Rings, Mrs. Poole, I must warn you that I do not deal politely with those who seek to deceive me."

"You asked for the truth, sir. I am attempting to give it to you."

He did not take his eyes off her. "Perhaps you had better tell me the rest of the story."

"Yes." Beatrice turned away from the window and began to pace. "Three weeks ago Uncle Reggie collapsed and died in somewhat awkward circumstances."

"Death is always awkward." Leo inclined his head. "My condolences, Mrs. Poole."

"Thank you."

"Who was Uncle Reggie?"

"Lord Glassonby." She paused, a wistful expression on her face. "He was a somewhat distant relation on my father's side. The rest of the family considered him quite eccentric, but I was very fond of him. He was kind and enthusiastic and, after he came into a small, unexpected inheritance last year, quite generous."

"I see. Why do you say that the circumstances of his death were awkward?"

She resumed her pacing, hands clasped once more behind her back. "Uncle Reggie was not at home when he died."

This was getting more interesting by the minute. "Where was he?"

Beatrice delicately cleared her throat. "In an establishment that I understand is frequented by gentlemen who have rather unusual tastes."

"You may as well spell it out, Mrs. Poole. I am certainly not going to let you get away with that meager explanation."

She sighed. "Uncle Reggie died in a brothel."

Leo was amused by the color that tinted her cheeks.

Perhaps she was not quite so much the woman of the world after all. "A brothel."

"Yes."

"Which one?"

She stopped long enough to glare at him. "I beg your pardon?"

"Which brothel? There are any number of them in London."

"Oh." She concentrated very intently on the pattern in the Oriental carpet beneath her feet. "I believe the establishment is known as the—" She broke off on a small cough. "The House of the Rod."

"I have heard of it."

Beatrice raised her head very swiftly and gave him a quelling glance. "I would not boast of that if I were you, sir. It does you no credit."

"I assure you, I have never been a client of the House of the Rod. My own tastes in such matters do not run in that direction."

"I see," Beatrice muttered.

"It is, I believe, a brothel that caters to men whose sensual appetites are sharpened by sundry forms of discipline."

"My lord, please." Beatrice sounded as if she were on the verge of strangling. "I assure you, it is not necessary to go into great detail."

Leo smiled to himself. "Carry on with your story, Mrs. Poole."

"Very well." She whirled around to stalk toward the far end of the library. "In the days following Uncle Reggie's death, we discovered to our great shock that sometime during the last weeks of his life he had gone through a great sum of money. Indeed, his estate was on the very brink of bankruptcy."

"You had counted on inheriting a fortune?" Leo asked.

"No, it is vastly more complicated than that."

"I am prepared to listen."

"I told you that Uncle Reggie could be very generous." Beatrice turned and started back in the opposite direction. "A few months before he died, he announced his intention to finance a Season for my cousin, Arabella. Her family has very little money." She broke off. "Actually, no one in my family has a great deal of money."

"Except Uncle Reggie?"

"He was the exception, and the inheritance he came into last year could be called only modest at best. Nevertheless, it amounted to considerably more than any of my other relatives could claim."

"I see."

"In any event, Arabella is quite lovely and perfectly charming."

"And her parents have hopes of marrying her off to a wealthy young gentleman of the ton?"

"Well, yes, to be frank." She scowled at him. "It is not exactly an unusual sort of hope, my lord. It is the fondest dream of many families who are somewhat short of funds."

"Indeed."

"Uncle Reggie graciously offered to pay for the costs of a Season and to provide a small but respectable dowry for Arabella. Her family arranged for her and Aunt Winifred—"

"Aunt Winifred?"

"Lady Ruston," Beatrice explained. "Aunt Winifred has been widowed for several years, but at one time she moved in the lower circles of the ton. She is the only one in the family who has any claim to social connections."

"So Arabella's parents asked Lady Ruston to take your cousin into Society this Season."

"Precisely." Beatrice gave him an approving glance. "My aunt and my cousin are staying with me. I have a small town house in London. In truth, everything was going rather well. Arabella managed to catch the attention of Lord Hazelthorpe's heir. Aunt Winifred was in expectation of an offer."

"Until Uncle Reggie collapsed in a brothel and you discovered that there was no money to pay for the remainder of the Season or to fund Arabella's dowry."

"That sums it up rather neatly. Thus far we have managed to conceal the true facts of Uncle Reggie's estate from the gossips."

"I believe I am beginning to perceive the outline of the problem," Leo said quietly.

"Obviously we cannot hide the situation indefinitely. Eventually my uncle's creditors will come knocking at our door. When they do, everyone will discover that Arabella no longer has an inheritance."

"And you can all wave farewell to Hazelthorpe's heir," Leo concluded.

Beatrice grimaced. "Aunt Winifred is beside herself with worry. Thus far we have managed to keep up appearances, but our time is running out."

"Disaster looms," Leo murmured darkly.

Beatrice stopped pacing. "It is not amusing, sir. My aunt may view the alliance in financial terms, but I fear that Arabella has lost her heart to the young man. She will be devastated if his parents force him to withdraw his attentions."

Leo exhaled slowly. "Forgive me if I do not seem overly concerned about your cousin's heart, Mrs. Poole. In my experience, the passions of the young are not necessarily strong foundations on which to build the house of marriage."

To his surprise, she inclined her head. "You are quite right. I am in complete agreement. As mature adults who have been out in the world for a number of years, we naturally have a more informed perspective on the romantical sensibilities than does a young lady of nineteen."

They were in full accord on the subject, but for some reason Beatrice's ready willingness to dismiss the power of passion irritated Leo.

"Naturally," he muttered.

"Nevertheless, from a practical point of view, one cannot deny that an alliance between Arabella and Hazelthorpe's heir would be an excellent match. And he really is a rather nice young man."

"I will take your word for it," Leo said. "Did your uncle lose his money at the gaming tables?"

"No. Uncle Reggie was considered an eccentric, but he was definitely no gamester." Beatrice went to stand behind a chair. She gripped the back with both hands and gazed at Leo down the length of the room. "Shortly before he died, Uncle Reggie made a single very expensive purchase. There is a record of it among his personal papers."

Leo watched her closely. "And that one purchase destroyed his finances?"

"From what I have been able to determine, yes."

"If you are about to tell me that your uncle purchased the Forbidden Rings of Aphrodite, save your breath. I would not believe you."

"That is precisely what I am telling you, sir."

She was deadly serious. Leo studied every nuance of her expression. Her clear, direct gaze did not waver. He thought about the rumors he had heard.

"What led you to believe that your uncle acquired the Rings?"

"Some notes that he left. The only reason I have them is because Uncle Reggie kept a detailed appointment book. He also kept a journal, but it is missing."

"Missing?"

"Thieves broke into his house the night he died. I believe the journal was taken by them."

Leo frowned. "Why would common housebreakers steal a gentleman's personal journal? They could not hope to fence it."

"Perhaps these housebreakers were not so common."

"Was anything else of value removed?" Leo asked sharply.

"Some silver and such." Beatrice shrugged. "But I think that was done only to make it appear that the housebreaking was the work of ordinary thieves."

He eyed her thoughtfully. "But you don't believe that."

"Not for a moment."

"Impossible." Leo drummed his fingers on the mantel. "It defies credibility." But he could not forget the tales of the Rings that had come to his attention. "Did your uncle have an interest in collecting antiquities?"

"He was always interested but he could not afford to collect them until he came into his inheritance. After that he did not purchase many, however. He claimed that most of the items that were for sale in the antiquities shops were fakes and frauds."

Leo was impressed in spite of himself. "He was right. It sounds as if your uncle had good instincts for artifacts."

"A certain sensibility for that sort of thing runs in the family," she said vaguely. "In any event, Uncle Reggie apparently believed that the Forbidden Rings were the key to a fabulous treasure. That is what compelled him to pursue them."

"Ah, yes. The lure of fabled treasure. It has drawn more than one man to his doom." Leo frowned. "Did he go to the House of the Rod often?"

Beatrice turned pink. "Apparently he was a regular client of the proprietress, Madame Virtue."

"How do you know that?"

Beatrice studied her fingers. "Uncle Reggie made a note of the visits in his appointment book. He, uh, treated them rather as if they were visits to a doctor. I believe he suffered from a certain type of, uh, masculine malady."

"A masculine malady?"

She cleared her throat again. "A sort of weakness in a certain extremity that is unique to gentlemen."

"He was impotent."

"Yes, well, in addition to his appointments at the House of the Rod, he was apparently a regular patron of a certain Dr. Cox, who sold him a concoction called the Elixir of Manly Vigor."

"I see." Leo released his grip on the mantel and crossed the room to his desk.

For the first time, he considered seriously the possibility that there had been some truth to the rumors that he had heard. The notion was absurd on the face of it. The tales stretched logic and credibility to the limit. *But what if the Forbidden Rings had been found?*

Beatrice watched him intently. "I have told you the particulars of my situation, sir. It is time for you to keep your end of the bargain."

"Very well." Leo recalled what he had read in the old volume he had consulted after the antiquities dealer had contacted him. "According to the legend, a certain alchemist crafted a statue of Aphrodite some two hundred years ago. He fashioned it out of a unique material that he had created in his workshop. Supposedly the stuff is extremely strong. It is said to be impervious to hammer or chisel."

Beatrice's brows drew together in a small frown of concentration. "I see."

"It is also said that the alchemist hid a fabulous treasure inside the statue and sealed the Aphrodite with a lock fashioned from a pair of Rings. The statue and the Rings disappeared shortly thereafter." Leo spread his hands. "Treasure seekers have searched for them from time to time down through the years, but neither the Rings nor the statue has ever been found."

"Is that all there is to the tale?"

"That is the essence of the matter, yes. There have been a number of fakes produced over the years. It is quite conceivable that in spite of his instincts for antiquities, your uncle fell victim to a scheme designed to make him believe that he had purchased the actual Forbidden Rings."

"Yes, I know that it is possible he purchased some fraudulent artifacts. But I have no choice. I must pursue the matter."

"Assuming that he somehow managed to obtain a pair of Rings, genuine or otherwise, what makes you believe that he was murdered because of them?"

Beatrice released the back of the chair and went to stand at the window again. "In addition to the fact that his house was torn apart the very night he died, Uncle Reggie left some notes in his appointment book. They indicate that he was becoming quite anxious about something. He wrote that he thought someone was following him around London."

"You said he was a noted eccentric."

"Yes, but his was not a fearful or overanxious temperament. I also find it rather suspicious that he died shortly after purchasing the Forbidden Rings."

A chill of dread stirred the hair on the back of Leo's arms. *Control yourself, man. You study legends, you do not believe in them.* "Mrs. Poole, if, for the sake of argument, you were to find the Rings, what would you do with them?"

"Sell them, of course." She sounded surprised by the question. "It is the only way we can hope to recover at least some of my uncle's money."

"I see."

She turned away from the window. "My lord, is there anything else you can tell me about this matter?"

He hesitated. "Only that it can be dangerous to get involved in an affair that lures treasure hunters. They are not a stable lot. The prospect of discovering a great treasure, especially an ancient, legendary one, has unpredictable effects on some people."

"Yes, yes, I can well understand that." She brushed his warning aside with a graceful flick of her wrist. "But can you tell me anything more about the Rings?"

"I heard an unsubstantiated rumor that a while back they turned up in a rather poor antiquities shop operated by a man named Ashwater," he said slowly.

"Forgive me, my lord, but I already know that much about the business. I went to see Mr. Ashwater. His establishment is closed. His neighbors informed me that he had left on an extended tour of Italy."

It occurred to him that she was losing her patience. He did not know whether to be annoyed or amused. She was the uninvited guest here. This was his house. She was the one who had descended on him without a by-your-leave and demanded answers to questions.

"You have already begun to make inquiries?" he asked.

"Of course. How do you think I came to learn of your expertise in legendary antiquities, my lord? Your articles, after all, are published in somewhat obscure journals. I had never even heard your name before I began my investigations."

He wondered if he should be insulted. "It's quite true that I am not an author of popular novels such as Mrs. York."

She gave him a smile that bordered on the condescending. "Do not feel too bad about it. We cannot all write well enough to make a living, sir."

"I write," he said through his teeth, "for a different audience than does Mrs. York."

"Fortunately, in your case, there is no need to convince people to actually purchase your work, is there? The Monkcrest fortune is the stuff of legend, according to my aunt. You can afford to write for journals that do not pay for your articles."

"We seem to be straying from the subject, Mrs. Poole."

"Indeed, we are." Her smile was very cool. There were dangerous sparks in her eyes. "My lord, I am extremely grateful for the information, limited as it is, that you have given me. I shall not impose on your hospitality any longer than necessary. My maid and I will leave first thing in the morning."

Leo ignored that. "Hold one moment here, Mrs. Poole. Precisely how do you intend to pursue your inquiries into the matter of the Rings?"

"My next step will be to interview the person who was with my uncle when he died."

"Who is that?"

"A woman who calls herself Madame Virtue."

Shock held him transfixed for the space of several heartbeats. When the paralysis finally wore off, Leo sucked in a deep breath. "You intend to speak to the proprietress of the House of the Rod? Impossible. Absolutely impossible."

Beatrice tipped her head slightly to the side, frowning. "Why on earth do you say that, my lord?"

"For God's sake, she is a brothel keeper. You would be ruined if it got out that you had associated with her."

Amusement lit Beatrice's eyes. "One of the advantages of being a widow of a certain age, as I'm sure you're aware, my lord, is that I have a great deal more freedom than I did as a younger woman."

"No respectable lady possesses the degree of freedom required to consort with brothel keepers."

"I shall exercise discretion," she said with an aplomb that was no doubt meant to reassure him. "Good night, my lord."

"Damnation, Mrs. Poole."

She was already at the door. "You have been somewhat helpful. Thank you for your hospitality."

"And they call me mad," Leo whispered.